SOUND TRACK

SOUND TRACK

John Timpson

HUTCHINSON
London Sydney Auckland Johannesburg

This edition first published in 1991 by
Hutchinson

Random Century Group Ltd
20 Vauxhall Bridge Road, London SW1V 2SA

Random Century Australia (Pty) Ltd
20 Alfred Street, Milsons Point, Sydney, NSW 2061, Australia

Random Century New Zealand Ltd
PO Box 40–086, Glenfield, Auckland 10, New Zealand

Random Century South Africa (Pty) Ltd
PO Box 337, Bergvlei, 2012, South Africa

British Library Cataloguing in Publication Data

Timpson, John
 Sound track.
 I. Title
 823 [F]

ISBN 0–09–174158–0

Photoset by Deltatype Ltd, Ellesmere Port, Cheshire
Printed and bound in Great Britain by
Mackays of Chatham PLC, Chatham, Kent

To my friends and former colleagues in the BBC News Division, who may recognise each other, if not themselves, in these pages –and to my wife Pat, who played the most important role in real life, but in this fictional story does not appear at all.

ONE

'Then there's Toronto . . .'

Albert Pollitt, secretary of Toftham Rotary Club, local chemist, and ardent traveller to foreign parts, turned another page of his notes. At the far end of the room somebody sighed. Or it might have been a gentle snore.

'Now thass a big place, Toronto. Bigger than Norwich, I'd say. But then, that hent got a castle the same as Norwich. There weren't much call for castles in Canada, I reckon. Not a lot o' Norfolk farmers around to cause 'em trouble.'

He chuckled appreciatively at the joke. Along the tables, nobody stirred. Charles Benson, looking around at his somnolent neighbours, might have believed they were actually dead, had he not seen the effect of Mr Pollitt's after-lunch talks before.

'Funny thing about Toronto, thass got squirrels, right in the middle of town, running about on the pavements. Not red squirrels, mind you, nor yet grey squirrels. These Toronto squirrels' – Mr Pollitt paused for effect – 'they're black!'

There was a stunned silence – but it was just a continuation of the stunned silence that had fallen over the Rotarians since the President had announced that unfortunately the scheduled speaker had been unable to attend, but Albert had kindly agreed to give a talk about his recent holiday in Canada. Albert had talked to the Rotary Club about every holiday he had ever taken, each one more staggeringly uneventful than the last. Canada, 1959, was no exception.

So Charles was the only one of his listeners to react. On the blank page of his notebook he dutifully wrote: 'Toronto. Black squirrels.' Then he added hopefully, 'Vote of thanks by . . .' and settled back, like his neighbours, into a state of suspended animation.

As he did so, a disturbing thought crossed his mind. Would he emerge from this stupor to find that thirty years had passed, and he was still sitting at a Toftham Rotary Club meeting, and Albert Pollitt was still talking? He tried to concentrate on Toronto, but the thought stayed with him . . .

Generally it was Mr Juby, as editor of the *Toftham and Wettleford*

1

Journal, who attended the Rotary Club luncheons. It was a useful opportunity to hear the latest gossip from the town's bank managers and shopkeepers, and even the Town Council: George Flatt, Clerk to Toftham Urban District Council, was one of its members. But Mr Juby had decided to make one of his rare excursions to Wettleford, and Charles had been entrusted with representing the Journal in his place. He had worked his way manfully through the flavourless consommé, followed by the undistinguished cottage pie and the alcohol-free sherry trifle, in the hope that he would glean a few paragraphs from the visiting speaker. Instead he found himself stuck with Albert Pollitt and his black squirrels.

Toftham Church clock struck twice. It was as if a spell had been lifted. Rotarians stirred, and blinked, and murmured. Watches were consulted, feet began to shuffle.

'Then there was Quebec,' Mr Pollitt persevered. 'Big place, Quebec. Sort of French . . .'

He got no further. Major Clarence Burney, District Coroner, Clerk to the Toftham Bench and president of the Rotary Club, was on his feet.

'Thank you, Albert,' he announced firmly. 'Most interesting.'

Mr Pollitt reluctantly subsided into his chair while Major Burney peered round the room. 'Mr Juby was due to give the vote of thanks this week, but I'll ask his able deputy to oblige. Mr Benson?'

Charles gulped, and rose. Now he knew why Mr Juby had decided to visit Wettleford; he hated giving votes of thanks. Indeed Mr Juby hated any form of public utterance – he preferred to pull the strings behind the scene. The crafty monk Rasputin had once tried to visit the Royal Family at Sandringham. He only got as far as Wolferton station, but Charles sometimes wondered if he had stayed long enough in the vicinity to impart his devious skills to the youthful Juby . . .

'Yes, of course, Mr President.' He groped desperately for something civil to say about Mr Pollitt's talk which would sound convincing, and failed. 'I'm sure we've all listened with great interest to Mr Pollitt's excellent address.' The Rotarians stared at him blankly, and he hastily consulted his notes. 'I mean, after all, well, black squirrels. Quite amazing. Not too many of them about in Toftham. Black sheep, perhaps, but not black squirrels . . .' He tried to chuckle, but it came out as a titter. He suddenly felt a great sympathy for Mr Pollitt.

'We're very grateful to you for stepping into the breach at such short notice.' The faces around him remained stony, but he continued defiantly. 'We hope you'll have many more holidays and come back to give us many more talks. And I'm sure we'd like to express our appreciation in the usual way.'

As he sat down the applause was barely detectable, which was what he might have expected. The Rotarians were in fact expressing their appreciation in their usual way.

'Thank you, gentlemen,' said Major Burney briskly. 'I declare the meeting closed.' But the Rotarians were already on their feet and heading for the door; it was time to get the wheels of Toftham commerce moving again. Charles found himself alone in what the Dog and Partridge liked to call its conference room, an unwanted sitting-room on the first floor permanently impregnated with the stale smell of cigarette smoke and last week's cottage pie.

But at least the Rotary Club could always be relied on to finish sharp at two o'clock. That left him time for a quick beer before going back to the Journal office. He hastened down the stairs as the last Rotarian went out into the market-place and opened the door of the farmers' bar. Inside, Mr Juby was perched on his usual stool, enjoying one of his specials, old ale laced with Navy rum. It was primarily a winter drink to keep out the chill Norfolk wind, but Mr Juby drank it all the year round, and the Dog and Partridge maintained a supply almost entirely for his consumption.

As Charles stared at him coldly Mr Juby nodded at the pint of bitter on the bar beside him. 'There you are. I thought I'd timed it right. They don't linger upstairs after two o'clock – they might miss making the odd bob or two.' He lifted his own tankard and buried his bushy grey moustache in it. The ruddiness of his cheeks indicated that other specials had already passed that way.

'What happened to Wettleford, then?' asked Charles a little sourly as he picked up his pint.

'Got back quicker'n I thought,' said Mr Juby calmly. 'Did you get anything interesting out of Rotary?'

'Anything interesting out of Rotary?' Charles gave a laugh that was more like a bark. 'You must be joking.'

'Well, you never know.' Mr Juby beamed at him cheerfully. 'Albert Pollitt might have revealed that he had another wife in Montreal, or he'd come across George Flatt's illegitimate daughter in a house of ill repute in Vancouver . . .'

'So you knew it was going to be Mr Pollitt.' As he said it he realised that of course Mr Juby knew. If anything happened in Toftham unknown to Mr Juby, it was not worth knowing.

'Talking of George Flatt,' continued Mr Juby, unperturbed, 'did he tell you anything about tonight's council meeting?'

3

'Why should he? You look after Toftham Council. I'm quite happy with the Rural District Council.' He ordered another pint and a special. There was obviously no hurry to get back to the office.

'Course you are,' Mr Juby agreed. 'Quite right too. Very civilised council, the R.D.C. Not like all our budding Trotskis in Toftham. But you've got to face the hard facts of life some time, Charlie, and Toftham Council is a hard fact of life.'

Charles realised that the day had started badly and was falling away. He sipped his fresh pint. 'So where have you got to go tonight? A return visit to Wettleford, perhaps, to fit in one or two things you missed this morning? Or a lightning trip to your brokers in the City?'

'Now thass enough o'that,' said Mr Juby sharply, and Charles realised he had gone too far. After seven years as Mr Juby's second-in-command at the Journal office he was allowed to take one or two liberties, but no more. 'I've got other things to do tonight, and you'll be doing the Council meeting. It'll be straightforward enough, just the usual snapping at each other's ankles – you don't want to take any note o' that. You just keep your ears open for one p'tickler word, boy.' Mr Juby's Norfolk accent thickened, as it always did when he became conspiratorial, or angry, or both. He leaned forward and said it syllable by syllable into Charles's ear. 'O-ver-spill, Charlie boy. Thass the word. O-ver-spill.'

Charles was impressed. 'Overspill? You mean, like Thetford? Hordes of Londoners coming up, factories all over the place, miles of council houses . . .'

'Hold you hard, boy.' Mr Juby raised a mocking finger. 'Don't forget you're a Londoner yourself, Charlie. You'd see all your old mates again.'

Charles denied it hotly. 'I haven't got any mates in London – I'm from Wembley Park. And after seven years I reckon I'm more of a Norfolkman than a Wembley man.'

He saw Mr Juby's expression of amused disbelief and tried another tack. 'Anyway, I haven't exactly changed the face of Toftham, like a few thousand Londoners would. It sounds appalling.'

'It sounds like progress to some folk. We got all sorts in Toftham.' Mr Juby sipped his special. 'But thass early days yet. Just keep your ears open tonight.'

Charles looked at him suspiciously. 'You seem to know all about it already.'

Mr Juby shook his head modestly. 'Just a whisper, boy. No more'n that. But I don't think you need worry too much about Londoners.

4

Those rail tickets George Flatt bought last week weren't for London; they were for Birmingham.'

'Birmingham?' Charles drained his glass. 'My God. Birmingham.'

Outside the sun was pouring down on Toftham market-place, glinting on the roofs of the parked cars, showing up the cracks in the greying facade of the Regal Cinema, sparkling in the puddles where George Perkins was sweeping out his butcher's shop. George was the only sign of activity in the square; the somnolence of the Rotary luncheon seemed to have pervaded the whole town during this post-prandial lull. Charles and Mr Juby strolled slowly across the cobbled parking area to the Journal office, Mr Juby apparently untroubled by the heat in his thick tweed jacket and waistcoat, Charles removing the tie he had donned in honour of the Rotary Club. They both nodded to George and George nodded back, thus preserving the niceties without disturbing the tranquility. Then the church clock struck half-past two, one or two shoppers appeared on the pavements, a few cars drove into the square, and Mr Perkins put aside his broom, straightened his striped apron and returned behind his counter. Toftham's lunch-hour was officially over.

Inside the Journal front office Anthea was tidying her piles of advertisement forms. Anthea was very tall, and very thin, and quite inordinately plain. She stuttered slightly when she was nervous, which was most of the time, and she blushed a lot. She was also passionately in love with Charles; his mere presence reduced her to simpering speechlessness.

Each time he encountered her Charles could not avoid the comparison with her predecessor, the voluptuous Big Nellie, with whom he had once had an ineffectual grapple during a Victor Mature film at the Regal. She had given up her job to marry an athletic young tractor-driver, one of the many Toftham youths who clustered round her desk in the front office, and Big Nellie was now bigger than ever, but in different places.

'Anything happening, Anthea?' asked Mr Juby as they walked through the office towards the stairs. Anthea could only produce a giggle and a shake of the head, her eyes fixed devotedly on Charles. Mr Juby followed her gaze.

'Quite right, m'dear. He looks a mess without his tie on. Glad you pointed it out.' And ignoring her stuttered cry of protest he took Charles's tie from his hand and draped it round his neck. 'Do smarten up, boy.'

5

Charles, well used to Mr Juby's baiting, gave Anthea a reassuring smile, and immediately regretted it. Her eyes filled with tears and she sank helplessly into her chair. Mr Juby beamed at them both and went upstairs, leaving Charles to escape as best he could.

'He was only pulling your leg, Anthea.' He tried not to sound too impatient. 'There's no need to get upset.' But he was only making matters worse. Any hint of kindness was liable to be interpreted as an expression of undying love, and she was already rising from her chair, showing every sign of flinging her arms around him. He side-stepped and dived for the stairs.

In his office on the first floor he stared out of the window across the market-place. Above him he could hear Mr Juby hitting the keys of the ancient office Remington, and he knew he should be writing up the tale of the Toronto black squirrels for the delectation of the Journal's readers, but he was feeling too unsettled to concentrate even on that undemanding chore. He was remembering the thought that struck him at the luncheon. He had been twenty when he first came to Toftham. He was twenty-seven now. Would he still be standing at this window in thirty years' time? Would nothing be changed, except that instead of a peaceful square with just a handful of passers-by, most of whom he knew, he would be looking out on a jostling mob in flat caps shouting at each other in Brummie accents as the lorries thundered through on their way to the industrial estates?

He had been restless before. A year after his arrival in Toftham a London editor had seen his work, he had been for an interview, and there was the offer of a researching job in Fleet Street, lowly by Fleet Street standards but worth three times his Toftham salary. He had been on the brink of accepting it; then the great floods of 1953 had intervened, and during the devastation and deaths that he reported, when he had helped with the rescue work and got to know more about the people who lived in the coastal villages, he found himself linked to Norfolk too strongly, and he chose to remain among his friends in surroundings which he now regarded as home.

Until lately he had never regretted it, but the qualm he had felt at the Rotary luncheon was not the first. It had come to him in recent months at village darts club finals, at British Legion annual dinners, at meetings of Launford Rural District Council, all the regular functions he had attended so often over the past seven years, each one so similar to the one before. It came to him most strongly on wintry Saturday afternoons, when he stood on the touchline in the recreation ground, shivering in the icy Norfolk wind, watching a game which bored him with rules he did not understand, just to phone the result to an evening paper in Norwich which he never read.

Would he still be doing all this in thirty years?

It started off as another average meeting of Toftham U.D.C.

'I move we go into committee,' announced Len Cloppett, self-styled leader of the Opposition. He had once attended a course on local government procedure and was regarded with some awe by his Labour colleagues. His Conservative opponents – who were officially Independents, but Charles had never understood the distinction – regarded Len quite differently.

'What the hell for?' demanded Harry Hurn. As secretary of the Chamber of Trade, as well as the town's most efficient hairdresser –a short back-and-sides took six minutes dead – he could have claimed the leadership of the Conservative group, but being Independents they were not supposed to have one. 'If you got something to say about me, Len, you say it in public like a man. There's too much of this going into committee, just so you can have a go at me.'

'If I want to have a go at you, I don't need to go into committee,' snapped Len Cloppett. 'This matter's confidential. Why not ask for a seconder, Mr Chairman?'

In the chair the Rev Henry Stackpole-Gubbins was about to speak, but one of the Labour councillors got in first. 'I second,' he shouted.

'What you do that for?' cried Harry Hurn. 'You don't know what the matter is yet, so why should we take it into committee?'

'Never you mind,' said the seconder. 'Len knows what he's doing. I second.'

'Well then, I move we don't,' said Mr Hurn defiantly.

Len Cloppett sneered at him. 'You can't do that. That's a direct negative.'

'I don't need you to tell me what I'm allowed to do. If you can propose what you like, so can I.'

Mrs Henrietta Bleddington, sitting next to Harry Hurn, rose majestically to her feet. 'Mr Chairman, I propose an amendment that we don't take a vote until we know what it is we're going to discuss.'

Again the chairman attempted to speak, but Len Cloppett was on his feet too. 'We can't say what it is before we go into committee, otherwise there'd be no point in going into committee.'

'Thass just gobbledegook,' growled Mr Hurn. 'I never heard such a load o' squit.'

'What about a seconder for my amendment?' asked Mrs Bleddington, still on her feet.

'You sit down,' cried Len Cloppett, too exasperated by now to follow the usual rules of procedure in which he was so well versed. The councillors beside him shouted their support, and the councillors beside Mrs Bleddington shouted back. The Great and the Good of Toftham were in full debate.

At the Press bench Charles sighed and prepared to vacate it yet again. When it came to shouting, Len Cloppett's colleagues rarely suffered defeat. He had been sent out of the chamber a number of times already, when they had decided for one reason or another that his presence was not required. Sometimes the reason was genuine, when they discussed council house applicants or the future of an employee. At least once, as Mr Hurn had indicated, it had merely been to exchange insults with greater freedom. Whatever lay behind this latest request, Charles strongly disapproved of it – not on ethical grounds, but because he found it very tedious hanging about in the corridor, and the door was too thick to let him eavesdrop.

The Rev Henry Stackpole-Gubbins sighed too. He had only become chairman because nobody else would do it. Indeed he had only agreed to stand for the Council at all because he had been persuaded that the forces of darkness, in the form of Len Cloppett and his followers, might take over the town.

The ploy had succeeded all too well. Len's group had failed to gain a majority, though only just. The Vicar now found himself in the appropriate but uncomfortable role of peacemaker. Unfortunately this required a knowledge of council procedure which, unlike Len Cloppett, he totally lacked, so he had to rely on the guidance of the Clerk, who was wont to interpret the rules to suit his own purposes. On this occasion George Flatt made his position quite clear.

'Just tell them we're going into committee, Mr Chairman. Never mind all these motions and amendments. Waste of time.'

The Vicar surveyed the scene of confusion before him. Len Cloppett and Harry Hurn were leaning across the table, shouting in each other's faces. Mrs Bleddington was making threatening gestures at the seconder of Len's motion, who seemed about to leap across and take her by the throat. Other councillors were waving their papers or banging on the table. Even old Matthew Nelson, who at eighty-five was incapable of much violent movement, was brandishing one of his sticks in quite a dangerous manner.

'You tell them,' said the Vicar.

8

'But you're the chairman, Mr Chairman,' said the Clerk, in a rare display of self-effacement.

The Vicar had a sudden inspiration. 'But it's your report we're going to talk about, Mr Clerk. I think it's up to you.' And he banged his gavel on the table. 'The Clerk wants a word,' he tried to shout above the uproar, and kept banging until it subsided. Len Cloppett and Harry Hurn sat down; the others stopped banging and waving, and old Matthew rather reluctantly put down his stick. None of them had much regard for the Vicar, but they knew where the real power lay.

'The report I shall be presenting,' said George Flatt, 'is a confidential report. The chairman has therefore decided that we shall go into committee. The Press will withdraw.'

'Now hold hard,' protested Mr Hurn. 'It's not up to the chairman to decide, it's up to us to vote on it. Hent it?' That last note of uncertainty was not lost on the Clerk.

'There's no need for that. If it comes to a vote the chairman will have the casting vote and he'll vote to go into committee.'

'How do you know that?' enquired Mr Hurn, but he did not really expect an answer. He knew, as well as George Flatt knew, that the chairman would do as he was told.

'I think that's enough, ladies and gentlemen,' said the Vicar, entering the fray at last. 'I'm certainly in favour of going into committee to discuss the Clerk's report.' He heard a slight muttering on Mr Hurn's side of the table, but he sensed that the argument was over, and in his relief he got carried away. 'I'm sure you'll all agree that a delicate matter like making an application under the Town Development Act needs to be discussed in private.'

Len Cloppett's groan echoed round the Council chamber. George Flatt raised his eyes to the ceiling. Harry Hurn leapt to his feet.

'So that's what it's all about.' He pointed accusingly at the Leader of the Opposition. 'That's why you and George went off to Birmingham together. And you must have been in on it too, Vicar. Bit of shady dealing going on here, I'd say. Why didn't we hear about this before?'

'You're hearing about it now, Harry,' snapped the Clerk, before Len could answer. 'But it would have been far better to hear about it in private. Mr Chairman, it's high time we went into committee.' He glared across at Charles, who had been taking notes frantically. Nobody had mentioned Mr Juby's vital word, but he knew what the Town Development Act of 1952 was all about. At the top of the page in his notebook he had written in big capitals: 'OVERSPILL'.

The Vicar looked across at him too, though his look was

9

unaccompanied by daggers. 'Thank you, Mr Benson. If you wouldn't mind.' Charles rose to go, but Harry Hurn had not quite finished.

'We may talk about it privately now,' he said weightily, 'but nothing stays private long in Toftham. I give it twenty-four hours.'

As Charles left the chamber for another draughty vigil in the corridor he estimated how long it would take Harry Hurn to reach the Dog and Partridge after the meeting. More like twenty-four seconds . . .

He strolled to a window and cast a yearning glance towards the hostelry. A familiar figure was just entering it. Whatever Mr Juby's secret mission had been which kept him away from the council meeting, it was obviously now completed.

He debated whether to wait in case of an early recall to the Council chamber, or go across to give Mr Juby the story so far. It was more the thought of a beer than duty to his editor which decided him. As he entered the farmers' bar he half-expected to see a newly-drawn pint awaiting him on the bar, but not even Mr Juby could forecast the precise timing of the Council's thought processes. He greeted Charles with some surprise. 'They can't be finished yet – not unless the Vicar's finally cracked. But I didn't see any men in white coats.'

Charles explained what had happened. Mr Juby nodded thought-fully and sipped his special. 'That Len wanted to get it all cut and dried with the people in Birmingham before Harry got to hear of it. Must've persuaded the Vicar to keep quiet about it too. And George Flatt wouldn't tell anyone what he was up to anyway, even if he was just going out to buy a packet of Woodbines.'

'But why is Len Cloppett so keen on this overspill business?' asked Charles. 'He's lived here all his life. Why should he want the place over-run with people from Birmingham?'

'I know what he'll tell you – same as what he must have told the Vicar, and what he's telling Harry and the rest of them now. That it'll be good for the town, he'll say. More jobs, and more money, and better amenities, and all the rest of it. But that'll bring a lot more voters too – and which way do you reckon they'll vote, all these folk from Birmingham? Not against Len Cloppett, thass for sure. He's an ambitious man, our Len. He wants this town to get much bigger, and he wants to get bigger with it.'

'But he does have a point.' Charles had not expected to find himself defending Len Cloppett, but he was trying to be fair. 'It would bring a lot of money into the town, and Harry Hurn can hardly object to that, not as secretary of the Chamber of Trade.'

'That's just what Len will be telling him, and that'll be difficult for

10

Harry to argue.' Mr Juby sipped his special for a moment. 'But he knows as well as I do – and Len knows it too – if we do get all these people then we'll get the big chain stores too, all cutting their prices and doing special offers and spending a fortune on advertising. And what chance will Harry Hurn's lot have against all that? But o' course he can't very well say so, or folk'll say they can't face the competition, and why don't they bring their prices down too?'

'Well, at least the Journal should do well,' said Charles, not too seriously. 'Our circulation should rocket. I doubt they'll print special editions of the *Birmingham Mail* in Toftham.'

Mr Juby looked at him solemnly. 'Never you mind about circulation. Thass Toftham we got to think of, not circulation. And I don't fancy living in another Thetford, any more'n you do. Harry may not be the fanciest of barbers, but I don't see myself going to one of those chrome-plated gin palaces with blow-dryin' and shampoos and all that old squit.'

Charles had a quick mental picture of Mr Juby with a skiffle-cut; it was an image to treasure. But he was curious about how he was going to circumvent Len Cloppett. He was bold enough to ask.

'Get you back to that meeting,' said Mr Juby. 'If they've started shouting again you may catch a few words through the door.'

Charles finished his pint and rose to leave. But he made one more attempt. 'What have you been up to tonight? I'd have thought you'd want to hear what was happening over the way.'

'I knew they wouldn't say anything until they'd shut the door on us – and I reckon you're more suited to standing about in corridors than I am. Thass where you should be now, boy, not standing around here having a mardle. I give 'em another ten minutes, but you never know.'

It turned out to be nearer twenty. Charles did lurk by the door in the hope of hearing something, but though voices were sometimes raised they were never raised quite enough. Then he heard the sound of chairs being pushed back and he moved swiftly away from the door before it opened and George Flatt came out with a sheet of paper. Behind him the councillors were still standing in little groups, arguing among themselves.

'Here you are.' The Clerk handed over the paper. It was headed 'Press Release', and had obviously been typed out beforehand. If you'd given this to me before you went into committee, thought Charles sourly, I could have stayed in the farmer's bar. 'There'll be no further statement,' said the Clerk. 'Thank you for waiting.' Then he sniffed ostentatiously a couple of times. 'I'm glad you managed to get some refreshment.' And he went back into the chamber.

11

Charles resisted the temptation to make a gesture as the door closed, and glanced through the press release.

'Under the terms of the Town Development Act (1952) Toftham Urban District Council has made an informal approach to the Corporation of Birmingham to discuss the possibility of attracting industry and population to the town. It is envisaged that the present population of 7000 could be expanded to 15,000 in the course of the next fifteen to twenty years. This approach was received sympathetically. The Council has tonight decided to pursue negotiations with the Corporation of Birmingham with this target in mind. The delegation will consist of the Chairman of the Council, the Clerk to the Council, and Councillors L. Cloppett and H. Hurn.'

Charles hastened across the market-place to the Journal office. Mr Juby, his timing as impeccable as ever, was just ahead of him. Up in his second-floor office he studied the press release while he got his breath back from the climb.

'Fifteen thousand, eh? Not as many as Thetford, but quite enough to turn us upside down. I see Harry's got himself into the delegation, so Len won't have it all his own way. I like this little line from George Flatt: "The approach was received sympathetically." That hent what I heard, not by a long chalk.'

'So what have you heard?' asked Charles. 'And who from?' And this time Mr Juby was more forthcoming.

'Well, I thought as the Vicar was busy this evening it might be a good time for a little mardle with his wife about this new sewing circle of hers. Very chatty lady, Mrs Stackpole-Gubbins. Once she gets started there's no stopping her.'

Charles began to understand. 'You knew the Vicar had gone to Birmingham, then?'

'Ben Kingsworthy thought I might be interested,' admitted Mr Juby. Mr Kingsworthy was the station-master. 'Anyway, she didn't think they'd got on all that well with these Birmingham folk. For a start they weren't too sure where Toftham was, some of them. When they found out we were in the middle of Norfolk, they didn't seem too excited somehow. But apparently Len and George Flatt kept on at 'em and in the end they said all right, they'd see them again when they had more detailed proposals. But it don't sound as though they were falling over themselves, like. Lukewarm, that was the Vicar's word for it, so she said. So I suppose you could say they were sympathetic, just like they'd be sympathetic watching a spider trying to climb out the bath. But that's not to say they'd give it a hand.'

12

Charles listened, fascinated. Mr Juby had been doing his Rasputin act again. 'So we're going to print all that?'

'Don't be such a duzzy fule,' said Mr Juby. 'Thass a nice story as it stands, for the moment. We hent goin' to spoil it, not just yet. You're the one that was worried about circulation, Charlie boy. I reckon this'll sell a few extra copies on Friday, just the way George has written it. Then we got next week to think about, and the following week, and the week after that . . .'

That's fine, thought Charles as he went down to his office and sat behind his typewriter. That's fine. So long as it's not thirty years.

TWO

The Journal sold several extra copies that week and in the weeks that followed, as the town split into opposing factions over the Council's proposal. Toftham had known nothing like it since the rumours that disused Army huts on the town's outskirts were to be converted into an open prison. There were those who saw a certain similarity between the two projects; there was little to choose, in their view, between old Army huts full of criminals and new housing estates full of Midlanders.

Others opposed the idea automatically, just as they had opposed the conversion of the street lamps from gas to electricity, and replacing garden wells with mains water. The town that was good enough for their grandfathers was good enough for them – and that tap water, thass full o' chemicals; it hent natural to drink chemicals, boy. There were also quite a number who objected because of a genuine fear of the effect on Toftham's way of life. They were not uninfluenced by the fact that Toftham's way of life, in their own case, was a very comfortable one.

But the trade unions, led by Len Cloppett, hailed the proposal with delight, dazzled by visions of more jobs and higher pay. So, officially, did the Chamber of Trade, bravely concealing any misgivings about cut-price chain stores. And of course so did the builders and electricians and plumbers and furnishers, anticipating a vast building programme of housing estates and factories. As for the estate agents, it looked like being Christmas all the year round.

The Journal, meanwhile, took a careful path between the opposing factions, avoiding any comment one way or the other. Mr Juby was biding his time.

Charles remained on the sidelines too, but only because he was not sure what he supported. His first instinctive reaction against the idea had faded as the arguments in favour of it were skilfully circulated by Len Cloppett and George Flatt. After all, he had been complaining of boredom and repetition and small-town limitations; he ought to welcome an influx of new ideas and experiences and people. His good sense assured him that the overspill must be A Good Thing; somehow he remained unconvinced.

When the Toftham delegation next visited Birmingham there was no private council meeting before the result was revealed. An exultant Len Cloppett burst into Mr Juby's office to report the news personally.

'You'll be glad to hear,' he announced, 'we've had a breakthrough.'

Mr Juby had been talking to Charles about the afternoon's assignments, and he did not take the interruption kindly. 'A breakthrough? Make a note of that, Charlie. Len here has had a breakthrough. Must be very painful.'

He turned back to the office diary. 'Now off you go to Remingham for that golden wedding couple. They're not holding the party till Saturday but I told 'em you'd be along today and we'll get a picture of them at the party.'

'You mean I miss all that sweet sherry?' Charles displayed deep hurt. 'No knees-up round the cake, no speeches saying we've never had a cross word in fifty years, no arguing over who's given the most expensive present, no grandchildren being sick in the kitchen. . . ?'

Len Cloppett, much put out by all this, interrupted again. 'Never mind that, Mr Juby. You're supposed to be a newspaperman, hent you? Well, here's some real news for you. We've had a breakthrough in Birmingham.'

'A breakthrough in Birmingham.' Mr Juby repeated it carefully. 'Very nasty indeed. Can you get the National Health in Birmingham, Charlie?'

'Mostly cod-liver oil and leeches, I believe,' said Charles. Len ignored him.

'I don't suppose you'll like it, Mr Juby, but you'll have to print it all the same. These officials we've been talking to in Birmingham, they say they'll support the overspill. They'll put it to the development committee.'

'Now why shouldn't I like that?' asked Mr Juby innocently. 'I'm always glad to print good news, and I know this must be good news because you never stop telling us. I'll be with you in a moment, Len. Now, Charlie, give old Herbert and Aggie my very best, and don't forget to ask Herbert about his shummicking.'

Charles paused on the way to the door. 'Shummicking? What's that supposed to mean?'

'Herbert'll soon tell you, boy,' Mr Juby reassured him. He turned to the fuming Len Cloppett. 'Now then, you tell me all this good news you're bustin' with.' And Charles left them to it.

He always enjoyed getting away to the villages. Sometimes he felt a little oppressed by the small-town gossip and wheeler-dealing which

Mr Juby indulged in with such relish and skill. He had long since discovered that wherever two or three were gathered together in Toftham, whether it be in Harry Hurn's hairdressing salon or a back room at the Council offices, or even in the alley behind the Regal where the town's younger element liked to congregate, Mr Juby either had a hand in it or an ear to it, and it all filtered back to his corner stool in the farmers' bar. His antennae reached out to the villages too, but at least when Charles escaped from Toftham itself he felt a taste of independence, more of an individual in his own right instead of just Mr Juby's assistant. To Mr Juby and most of the town he was still 'the boy Charlie'.

He drove out to Remingham in the battered old Vauxhall that had taken the place of his Triumph motorbike. Before the Triumph there had been the second-hand delivery bike which he paid far too much for at a market day auction. He had not been too astute in any of his transport dealings. The engine of the motorbike he had bought from Mr Knock, the night-soil contractor, did not actually have a knock, which might have been appropriate, but it had very little else of any merit, and although it looked a magnificent machine it required much spare-part surgery to make it move. The Vauxhall, on the other hand, seemed to run quite well when the farm foreman who was selling it gave him a trial ride on a smooth stretch of road, but once he had bought it he soon found that after years of bouncing around on farm tracks the suspension had given up the struggle. The slightest ridge in the road surface sent terrible shudders through the car, and cornering at any speed meant the risk of turning over completely.

In the heady days when he had first become a car-owner he tempted Mr Juby to come out for a spin. He managed to find a flat piece of road to work up a reasonable speed, but failed to spot the hump-backed bridge just beyond. They took off spectacularly, and seemed to hang in the air for several seconds before touching down again. Later he heard Mr Juby describing it to a crony in the farmers' bar. 'We come down,' he said succinctly, 'like a canteen o' cutlery.' He never travelled in it again.

Charles also discovered after a few days that the wings and runningboards were only held together by layers of mud, accumulated during countless excursions round the beet fields. Quite a few odd pieces dropped off at that hump-backed bridge, but he only realised the full extent of the problem when he scraped away some of the mud and found nothing but a rusty hole underneath. Now he relished driving on muddy roads to maintain the protective layer. But in spite of its failings,

Charles developed a certain affection for his rusty old banger. He even gave it a name. In view of its violent tremors every time it went over a bump he christened it the Vauxhall Vibrator – but to avoid any misunderstanding he kept the name to himself.

There was no helpful mud on the Remingham road today. Plenty of dust, to blow in through the cracks round the doors and the holes by the driving pedals, but no mud. There were also ridges and bends and even a hump-backed bridge, but Charles knew them all and treated them with respect. He had been back and forth on this road when he rented a room with the young Rector, John Cranmer, until John had departed for more sophisticated pastures, and he had to find less congenial quarters in a cramped little flat over Mr Pollitt's pharmacy in Toftham. His friend's move to a busy city parish had given him his first twinge of doubt about staying in Norfolk himself; lately each twinge was more like a nudge.

Remingham had other memories for him too: of Willum, the gentle soul whose simple mind could just cope with taking round the groceries from the village shop, and who still did his rounds on Charles's old delivery bike; of Lord Remingham at the Hall, who owned most of the village and employed most of the people in it – Charles had once sat in his pew in Remingham Church and the shock waves were felt for miles; of Dr and Mrs Bateman, who lived at the Old Rectory, a much grander building than its little red-brick successor, but who treated him kindly when he came courting their daughter; and special memories of Rebecca herself, with whom he first dallied at a Young Farmers' Club ball, who shared an idyllic picnic with him one summer's afternoon, and who went off to college, became engaged to a student, and vanished from his ken. There had been other dalliances since, but each time he came to Remingham he remembered Beccy and that first dance, and the picnic by the river, and the freckles on her bare shoulders disappearing down into the low-cut summer dress . . .

Lost among the freckles he failed to spot a new pot-hole in the road. The Vibrator bounced alarmingly, the exhaust pipe scraped along the tarmac and a piece of running-board fell off and clattered into the ditch. He did not stop to retrieve it; that piece had fallen off many times before and he was tired of trying to mud-plaster it on again. He had left some of his heart in Remingham, he mused morosely as he drove on; may as well leave some of his running-board there too.

Herbert and Aggie Eke lived in a tiny farm cottage on the edge of the village. The cottage was tied to the Remingham estate, and legally they could have been evicted when Herbert stopped work, but Lord Remingham looked after his men and the couple were allowed to stay on there, virtually rent-free. No one was quite sure how long this would continue; there was always the chance that His Lordship might need the cottage urgently for another farmworker. But in rural Norfolk in 1959 folk like Herbert and Aggie counted what blessings they had, and tried not to think about the future.

Charles had never met them while he was living in the village, but that was not surprising. He was generally in Toftham during the day, and older folk rarely stirred out after tea-time. In fact Herbert and Aggie rarely stirred out at all, as Charles realised when he arrived. Aggie was in a bed by the fire, which was well alight even on this fine summer's day, and Herbert was hobbling on two sticks. The only hint of a celebration was a cake-tin on the table, but the lid was firmly closed.

This is going to be really jolly, thought Charles as he closed the door behind him and felt the full heat of the fire. But he summoned up what he hoped was a benevolent smile. 'Good day to you,' he said brightly. 'I think Mr Juby let you know I was coming.'

Herbert exchanged a glance with his wife. They seemed unaccountably amused. 'Ah,' he said. 'We'd known you bin a gorn ta cum.' He settled himself in a chair by Aggie's bed and ushered Charles into another. 'Now, 'fore y'start, heya got inny bacci onya; inny bacci y'reckon?'

Charles gaped at him blankly. After seven years he thought he had got the hang of the Norfolk dialect, but sometimes it still baffled him. 'I'm sorry? Could you say again?'

'Bacci, boy. Heya got inny?' And Herbert produced a venerable pipe from his pocket and waved it invitingly. Charles blushed. 'No, I'm sorry. I don't smoke.'

'Thassa pity then,' grunted Herbert, and grudgingly produced a pouch from another pocket. He started to fill his pipe in silence, while Aggie stared solemnly at Charles from the bed. He decided to attempt a pleasantry.

'How are you today, Mrs Eke?'

She looked at him mournfully. 'Very sadly, sir. Very sadly indeed.'

Herbert paused in his pipe-filling. 'Ah. Tidily queer she be today.'

Charles tried to be encouraging. 'You don't look it, Mrs Eke; not at all sadly.'

Mrs Eke sat up angrily in her bed. 'Du I am, then!' she snapped, and

18

Herbert was quick to support her. 'Du she say she is, then she is, marster, and no mistearke. She fare shruck with the misery of it sometime, du she wish she die.'

Much abashed, Charles apologised again. He did not understand all the words but he got the gist of them. Mrs Eke was not feeling at her best.

'Well, congratulations anyway. Fifty years together. You must have many happy memories.'

'Ah.' Herbert seemed unconvinced. Charles produced his notebook and pressed on.

'Let's start at the beginning, Mrs Eke, let me make a note of your maiden name.'

'Agatha Eke,' said Mrs Eke.

Charles nodded gamely. 'I know that's your name now, Mrs Eke, but what was it before you were married?'

'Agatha Eke,' she repeated. Charles turned appealingly to Mr Eke, who merely nodded confirmation. 'You put that down, marster. Agatha Eke.'

Charles tried to explain about maiden names, but he'd only said a few words before Herbert interrupted him sharply. 'Stop yer slarver and yer winnicking, boy. Eke she is and Eke she were. We'm cousins, ye duzzy fule.'

Charles, already glowing from the heat of the fire, grew even hotter under Herbert's onslaught. He wrote down: 'Eke: cousins'. They were about the only words he had so far understood. But they did explain perhaps why Willum was still as simple as a six-year-old. Willum was an Eke as well.

'Is Willum a relation of yours, then?'

'Course he is,' snapped Herbert. 'Stand to reason, don't it? He's Aggie's brother's wife's nephew's boy. That makes him our great-nephew, is Willum.'

Aggie shook her head firmly. 'You got that wrong, Herbert. Willum's father is Bertha's cousin's boy, not her sister's. He hent a great-nephew, he's a sorta cousin twice-removed like.'

'You daft owld mawther, thass a load o' gammarattle you're a-talkin'.' Mr Eke rose and stood over her bed. 'Willum's mother, she were Bertha's cousin's daughter, and she married her cousin what was your sister-in-law's nephew. He were a bit neither-here-nor-there, remember? And Willum's much the same.'

'Don't you go a-mobbin' me, Herbert Eke.' Aggie was sitting up in the bed, waving her arms. 'I'll give you a good ding on the lug, du you go on like that.'

Charles wished he had never asked. Desperately he wondered how to change the subject and take their minds off their complex family tree. Then he remembered Mr Juby's parting advice.

'Would you care to tell me about your shummicking, Mr Eke? Sounds fascinating.'

Mr Eke resumed his seat and stared at Charles coldly, leaving Aggie still waving her arms threateningly from the bed. 'I'll tell you about shummicking, boy, and I tell you what, that hent "fascinating", thass bluddy hard work. Had to learn it as a lad fom the village shummicker. My father, he say to the shummicker, du you make him du as you du, don't he 'on't du as he should du. And if he don't du as he should du I should give him a duin' to if I was you, cos we du too . . .'

Charles sat, transfixed. The words flowed over him in a meaningless jumble. He looked down at his notebook. All it still said was 'Eke: cousins.' He felt he had wandered into a madhouse.

'Then the shummicker, he said, I'll du that, he say, du he don't du what I du tell him to du. Now I'm off, he say, but there's a sight o' sluss in the pightle where I come in, we'll ha' to imitate to crowd th'ole morphry tru' the drift into the loke, I reckon, and thassa fact . . .'

It dawned on Charles that Mrs Eke was no longer waving her arms, and she no longer looked like giving anyone a ding on the lug. She was not very sadly, nor even tidily queer. In fact she was chuckling, and the chuckle was developing into a full-scale laugh.

Mr Eke noticed too. 'Stop your gimbling, you great mawkin,' he roared. Then he too dissolved into laughter, and the pair of them had to take out handkerchiefs and wipe away the tears as Charles, feeling more than ever he was just the boy Charlie, gazed at them in amazement.

Herbert got up and patted him on the shoulder. 'You look all of a mish-mash, boy, all hulled into a buffle.'

'Now that's enough, Herbert. You leave the boy be. You've had your fun.'

'What on earth was all that about, then?' Charles wondered again if all the Eke family were 'neither-here-nor-there'.

'Well now, it's that Mr Juby,' Herbert explained. 'Great one for a joke, Mr Juby. He tell us you reckon you're near enough a Norfolkman now, so he thought maybe you ought to hear some real Norfolk and see how you get on.' The Norfolk accent was still there, but entirely comprehensible.

Charles remembered his unguarded comment in the farmers' bar. Mr Juby had obviously remembered it too, even though it had been weeks ago. Memories in Norfolk could be as long as accents were broad.

'I did keep up with some of it,' he said defensively. 'I know that sluss in the pightle is mud in the field, because that's what holds my car together, and I suppose a morphry is some sort of cart, but what's all this shummicking you kept on about?'

'Shummicking? That's simple enough, boy. Hent you heard of people who make shoes?' Herbert Eke poked him gently in the ribs. 'I suppose you might say . . .' – he could hardly get the words out before dissolving again – 'I suppose you might say it's a load o' cobblers, Charlie boy.'

They made him a cup of tea and offered him a slice of cake. He protested that he wasn't hungry, but they would have none of it. 'Du you eat it agin y'du,' urged Herbert in a final dose of 'dus'. Then they answered all his questions for the report – 'and don't you say we never had a cross word, that'd be a load o' squit' – and curiously, Charles felt that it had all been some kind of compliment, that he had been considered acceptable enough to have his leg pulled without taking offence. His feeling was confirmed when they invited him to their family party on the Saturday.

'We can't move too far so they're all coming here, and we'll have the place tricolated up for them,' explained Mrs Eke. 'We'll even have your friend Willum come along, and we'll ask 'em all what relation they reckon he is; that should keep us a-goin' for an hour or two.' He nudged Aggie. 'We had a bit o' fun with that, eh?' Aggie smiled back.

'And tell you what, boy,' added Herbert, 'you'll be a rare 'un, du you come that day. You'll be the only 'un here that hent an Eke!'

They chatted on for a while, and Herbert taught him some Norfolk phrases that might come in useful. When he finally bade them farewell Herbert came out with him to the Vibrator, hobbling cheerfully on his two sticks. 'Give my best to Mr Juby,' he said, and as Charles shook his hand he dropped back into his broad Norfolk. 'He know suffin, doonty, the old devil.'

'He know suffin all right,' agreed Charles ruefully. 'Full of surprises, our Mr Juby.' He started to thank him again, but his host would have none of it.

'Way you go, my man.' Herbert opened the car door for him. 'Cock yar leg inter this hare dicky-cart, and fur the Lord's sake leave orf a'crackin' a yar jaw.'

As he drove off down the lane he saw Herbert waving a stick in

21

farewell and he waved back. 'Keep you a-goin', Herbert,' he murmured to himself, smiling. And Herbert probably would, he reflected, and so would Aggie, and maybe he'd be back in ten years' time to celebrate their diamond wedding too.

The thought sobered him considerably. As he drove out of Remingham, the smile disappeared.

When he got back to Toftham he found Anthea poised for his arrival. Not for the first time he wished there was a back entrance to the stairs. She hastened across to him, and he wearily prepared to fend her off. But this time there was a reason for her approach.

'Would you take this up to Mr Juby, Charles, please?' She handed him a magazine. 'I think he wants it quite urgently.'

'If he wants it quite urgently,' said Charles a little shortly, 'why didn't you take it up yourself?' As usual he had said the wrong thing. Anthea's eyes moistened, her angular shoulders slumped, she turned and retreated to her desk. He hurried past her to the stairs, mumbling something about an urgent golden wedding report. He felt as though a puppy had just sat up and begged in front of him, and he had kicked it over backwards.

He climbed the two flights to Mr Juby's office and found him in conclave with Harry Hurn. They stopped talking abruptly as he appeared.

'Anthea said you wanted this urgently,' he said from the doorway.

'Not as urgent as all that, boy,' growled Mr Juby. 'That's just Anthea's excuse for talking to you, that's all. You wait till Harry and I have finished our little chat, eh?'

Charles retreated downstairs to his own room and glanced at the magazine. It was *World's Press News*, the trade paper for journalists and other toilers in the media. Mr Juby took it occasionally to keep an eye on the activities of his old cronies on other papers, and Charles had heard him muttering incredulously over some unlikely promotion or unexpected retirement. Charles himself had no old cronies in the media to mutter over, and he took little interest in the *W.P.N.*, even when Mr Juby allowed him to see it. There was a section on job vacancies, but he had experienced Fleet Street reporters in action on occasions like the East Coast floods, when they came down to lord it over the locals, and he had decided that wasn't for him. In his more desperate moments he had toyed with the idea of trying to join another provincial paper, but a darts club dinner was a darts club dinner, whether it was in

Remingham or Rotherham, and he was inclined to stay with the devil he knew, even if that devil was Mr Juby.

So he only cast a casual glance at the 'Sits. Vac.' column. He observed, with no great enthusiasm, that there were the usual jobs for sub-editors in Swindon, junior reporters in Jarrow, copy-takers in Crewe. He did pause over a reporting job in the Channel Islands: 'Senior reporter on *Jersey Evening Post*, responsibility for covering Guernsey, Alderney and Sark; accommodation available.' But no doubt the queue of applicants was already forming in St Hélier, and anyway he had never much liked the sea after he had seen what damage it could do.

'Public Appointments' was a column he had never bothered to look at before. It created visions of bowler hats and furled umbrellas and the Central Line in the rush-hour, but it was the initials that caught his eye. 'BBC requires two reporters, News Division. Candidates must have journalistic experience, good news sense, wide knowledge of current affairs and ability to write accurate, concise reports for bulletins and to broadcast their own reports in Sound and Television. Office car. Possibility of short-term assignments abroad . . .'

It all seemed wildly out of reach, but he read on. The age range was twenty-five to thirty-five; at least he qualified there. The salary was considerably less than he had been offered as a researcher in Fleet Street, but it was still a lot more than anything he could earn on the *Toftham and Wettleford Journal*. One did not just apply, he noted. One applied for an application form, and the application for the application form had to bear the correct reference number from the *W.P.N.*, and had to reach the Appointments Officer within five days. No wonder it was under Public Appointments instead of simple old Sits. Vac.

He looked at the date on the magazine. It had taken two days to reach the Journal office and the last post had already gone. Even if he caught the first post next morning it would be touch and go whether the letter reached London in time, such were the vagaries of the Norfolk postal service. Still . . .

He heard footsteps coming down the stairs from Mr Juby's office and hastily put aside the magazine, but Harry Hurn hurried past his door, eyes averted and looking curiously furtive. Then came the familiar bellow from upstairs: 'Chaaarlie, come you up here. And bring that pairper with you.'

Mr Juby was almost invisible behind a cloud of pipe smoke, and Charles appreciated its significance. Whenever the editor was brewing up some machiavellian scheme he took to his pipe, much as Sherlock

Holmes took to his violin, and sometimes with equally remarkable results. He took the magazine from Charles, ignored the Sits. Vac. and the Public Appointments, and turned straight to 'Moves and Promotions'.

Maybe I'll be in that section soon, thought Charles, still savouring the reference to 'journalistic experience' and blotting out the thought of 'wide knowledge of current affairs'. His wide knowledge extended about as far as Toftham Conservative Club's annual dinner for its MP and last week's fat stock prices in Toftham Market; he had a lot of swotting to do.

'Here we are.' Mr Juby pointed out a three-line paragraph. 'I thought the boy Jimma would get it all right. Always a bright lad, young Jimma.'

The boy Jimma, it seemed, was James Renshaw of the *Birmingham Post*, newly promoted from the sub-editors' desk to news editor. 'Before moving to Birmingham,' the paragraph ended, 'Mr Renshaw spent a number of years in Norfolk as a district reporter at Thetford.'

'Did well for himself, young Jimma.' Mr Juby puffed energetically at his pipe. 'Grew up in Thetford, joined the paper there, then they had all this overspill business and he reckon if his little market town was going to be an imitation industrial town he might as well try the real thing, so he went off and got a job on the Post. I heard he was due to move up a peg about now, and so he has. Thass very handy for us, Charlie boy, very handy indeed.'

'You mean he can tell us what Birmingham Corporation are up to?' Charles thought he had caught up, but Mr Juby was still a step ahead.

'Not only that, boy. We can tell him what *we're* up to. He can pass it on to the right quarter, see?'

Charles was lost again. 'What *are* we up to, Mr Juby?'

'We are up to . . .' Mr Juby paused, then announced grandly, '. . . a meeting of minds. The people of Birmingham and the people of Toftham. We want these Birmingham folk to know what we're like here in Toftham, and we want Toftham to meet these folk from Birmingham. Thass only fair, now hent it?'

'That should be quite an encounter.' Charles was getting the drift of it now, but he still couldn't see how it would happen. 'Is Mr Hurn going to arrange all this through the Council?'

'Harry don't know narthin' about it,' said Mr Juby quickly. 'You get that straight, boy. He just come here to pass the time o' day. If anybody ask, he hent even been here. Didn't old Herbert tell you? Niver know narthin about narthin, marster, then nobody can't git at you over that.'

24

'That's about the only thing he didn't tell me.' Charles remembered his uncomfortable trial by dialect. 'I did get all that stuff about "du you du as you should du, if I were you". What did *I* do to deserve all that?'

'There's always something new to learn, Charlie, specially in Norfolk. Don't you never reckon you know it all, boy.' Mr Juby leaned back in his chair and puffed his pipe vigorously for a moment, then pointed it at Charles in a familiar gesture. The talking was over; it was time for action.

'Now you get down to the Jubilee Hall and see what evenings they got free in the next week or two. I'd say a Wednesday would be a good day, that'll give us nice time to get it into the paper on Friday. Then get along to the Vicar and tell him we're planning an independent meeting to bring the people of Toftham and Birmingham together, and we assume we have his support. He won't argue, the Vicar, so long as he don't have to do anything himself. Then I'll tell George Flatt we've got his chairman's support, and after that I'll tell Len Cloppett it's all arranged.' Mr Juby chuckled. 'Good news, he reckoned that was from Birmingham. Well, now I've got some good news for him. And he can't argue, because I'm just trying to help things along.'

'Now hang on,' said Charles, trying to keep up with the pace of developments. 'When I tell the Vicar that "we" are planning this meeting, who's "we"?'

'We,' said Mr Juby, rising majestically to his feet, 'we are the *Toftham and Wettleford Journal*, in conjunction with the *Birmingham Post*.'

'And does the *Birmingham Post* know about this?'

It was a silly question. 'Not yet they don't. But they will. I'll have a word with our Jimma, and if need be I might mention a little tale or two from his young days in Thetford, and he'll recognise a good news story when he sees it, thass for sure.'

'So will you be taking the chair?' He knew that was a silly question too.

'Don't be ridiculous, boy. I hent no chairman. I had a word with Major Burney after Len came to see me today; he rather fancied being chairman, once he got the general idea.'

Charles nodded thoughtfully. Mr Juby's plan became clearer. Major Burney had indicated more than once in recent weeks that he belonged to the 'Preserve Our Way of Life' school. He had a large Georgian house on the edge of town next to some land owned by the Council, which would make an ideal site for a housing estate.

'And how do we get all these Birmingham people to Toftham? We can hardly pay their fares out of the petty cash.'

'No more we can, but the *Birmingham Post* can, and plenty to spare. A very public-spirited gesture that would be, and the boy Jimma is just the one to arrange it – and pick the right people to come, what's more.'

'You mean the sort of people who might not quite grasp our funny little ways in sleepy old Toftham?' Charles was catching on fast by now.

'That's it, boy.' Mr Juby beamed at him. 'Employers looking for a skilled work force that knows about production lines and machine tools, not just how to drive a tractor. And working men who are looking for greyhound tracks and bands playing in the pubs, and women who want to play bingo and see colour films at the cinema.' He paused for breath. 'Oh yes, our Jimma will know who to bring; he won't forget what happened to Thetford. Now get you along, boy. There's a lot for you to do, and there's only you to do it.'

In spite of himself, Charles was impressed. He hoped the boy Jimma would be too. Meanwhile he had one minor score to settle with Mr Juby. As he walked towards the door he mentally rehearsed what Herbert Eke had taught him. Then he paused in the doorway, cleared his throat, and announced to Mr Juby in his broadest imitation Norfolk:

'Thass the wust of this hare plairce. There hent nivver nobody nowhere to help nobody with narthin.'

He was so pleased with himself as he went down the stairs he quite forgot that Mr Juby still had the *World's Press News*, with the vital reference number and the address of the BBC Appointments Officer. When he remembered a little later and returned to the office, Mr Juby had disappeared on his devious mission, and the magazine had disappeared too.

THREE

Charles arrived early in the office next morning but Len Cloppett was there ahead of him, pacing up and down in the front office while Anthea crouched nervously behind her desk.

'So what's goin' on, Charlie?' he demanded. 'What are you two up to?'

Charles remembered Mr Juby's latest dictum: never know narthin. He tried a diversionary move. 'You mean Anthea and me, Mr Cloppett? What do you have in mind?' He smiled conspiratorially at Anthea and immediately, as always, regretted it. Her eyes filled with tears, either of devotion of ecstasy, or even grief; he was never quite sure.

'Don't come that, boy. You know what I mean; you and Mr Juby. What's all this about a public meeting? What's the old fule up to?'

Charles preserved his air of innocence. 'Didn't he explain it all last night? I thought he'd been to see you.'

'So he did,' snapped Len. 'I was out last evening. He just left a message, some squit about a meeting of minds, and nation shall speak unto nation. What's he on about?'

'Not exactly nations, just Toftham and Birmingham,' explained Charles. But he had recognised the words and they reminded him why he had come in early. They were the cipher on the crest of the BBC.

'Come upstairs and wait in comfort, Mr Cloppett. I'm sure he'd like to tell you all about it himself.' He risked addressing Anthea. 'When Mr Juby comes in can you warn him . . .' – he caught Len's eye and corrected himself – '. . . can you advise him that Mr Cloppett is waiting for him in his office?'

'Yes of course, Charles, of course I will.' Anthea got up and bobbed about and sat down again, beaming. Charles had entrusted her with an important duty; the day had suddenly improved.

Another thought struck him as he led Len towards the stairs. 'I suppose Mr Juby didn't leave his *World's Press News* down here? I was hoping to have a look at it.'

Anthea's beam faded. 'No, I'm terribly sorry, I haven't seen it. I wish

I had, I really do. Can I order another one for you? Or shall I ask Mr Juby when he comes in?' She was desperate to help.

'No, don't do that,' said Charles sharply. Too sharply. Her eyes filled again. 'It really doesn't matter, Anthea. Just forget all about it.' He ventured the tiniest of smiles, and headed for the stairs.

With Len safely esconced on the second floor he returned to his own office below. The sun was pouring in on his dusty desk and he opened the window and looked out at the growing activity in the square. It was Friday, market day, and the stalls were going up on the central cobbled area, as they had done every Friday for centuries, but the wares they offered had changed. There were still the vegetables from the surrounding villages, and the fishmongers were there with crabs from Cromer and Sheringham and whelks and cockles from Wells and Stiffkey, just as they had always been, but much of the fish came in a fish-and-chip van these days, and some stalls were draped with jeans and dufflecoats and pyjamas. Others had displays of stained crockery and chipped decanters and rusty fire-irons, labelled whimsically as antiques. Toftham did not get many tourists, even in high summer, but those who did come were readily welcomed by the local dealers.

On the far side of the market-place Charles could see the battered vans driving into the back yard of the Dog and Partridge with their second-hand wardrobes and lawnmowers and bicycles for the weekly auction. That was where he had bought his delivery bike soon after he arrived, allowing himself in his innocence to be carried away by the bidding, so he paid twice its real worth. He had learned his lesson over the years and picked up quite a few bargains, like the Windsor chair he had bought for his office for a shilling, which Mr Juby had generously agreed he could put on his expenses. His visitors could now sit in comfort instead of on the window-ledge, so long as they came singly. He found it gratifying that his office now had as much furniture as Mr Juby's.

At the other end of the market-place the lane leading to the cattle market was jammed with cattle trucks and Landrovers, and he could hear the shouting and the squealing as the pig pens were filled. There were sheep there too, as well as the cattle. One of his market day duties was to take down the prices from the auctioneer after the sale; even after seven years he was still baffled by this world of heavy hogs and in-calf cows, but he made it sound convincing when he phoned the figures to Norwich.

Outside the pubs in the market-place the farmers and the corn merchants were already assembled in little groups, the same groups

28

always outside the same pubs, the mock-Tudor Red Lion and the rather seedy Golden Fleece and the flint-walled, low-beamed Bull's Head. Years earlier they would have met in the Corn Exchange, but that was now the Regal cinema, so they met outside the pubs instead, and when business was done they could conveniently adjourn inside. The pubs were open all day on market day, and the farmers were unlikely to emerge again before tea-time.

Charles watched this scene every Friday, and he enjoyed comparing it with the featureless suburbs of Wembley Park and the anonymous crowds in London. In spite of all the noise and bustle people always had time to pause for a chat, and although he was still regarded as a foreigner most people in Toftham knew he was the boy Charlie from the Journal, and they accepted him as part of the town's life. As he stood by the window Harry Hurn gave him a wave from his barber's shop, then placed a finger significantly beside his nose. Mr Juby must have told his fellow conspirator that Charles was helping to set up the meeting of minds with Birmingham. He nodded back knowledgeably, feeling rather pleased that he had been allowed in on one of Mr Juby's plots.

He spotted other familiar figures among the stalls below, and when they caught his eye they shouted a greeting to him, or raised a friendly hand in his direction. Perhaps, he thought, as he waved back, it was some sort of destiny that had removed the *World's Press News* from his reach. Perhaps he was not intended to storm the battlements of Broadcasting House. Life in Toftham wasn't that bad, and Mr Juby would have to retire some day . . .

But not yet. He heard the footsteps on the stairs and he recognised the puffing and muttering which always accompanied Mr Juby's ascent. He left the window to intercept him, but Mr Juby came into his office anyway.

'I hear you were looking for this, boy,' he growled, and handed him the *World's Press News*. Charles mentally cursed the hapless Anthea.

'Just thought I'd have another look at that paragraph about Jimmy Renshaw,' he explained lamely.

'Ah,' said Mr Juby. But his mind was on other things. 'Had a busy night last night. Thass comin' together nicely. Just got to straighten out our friend Len upstairs, then we can start passing the word round about the meeting. I must make sure they have the bar open at the Jubilee Hall good and early; that'll help to get things a-goin'.' He headed for the door. 'Don't you stir far for a while, Charlie. Don't forget it's Friday; no doubt we'll get the usual callers.'

'No doubt,' agreed Charles gloomily. As well as being market day, it was also publication day for the Journal, the day when the complaints came in about items omitted, names misspelt, words misquoted. It was Charles's duty, unless the complaint was really serious, to placate the aggrieved, calm the aggressive, mollify the offended – and blame everything on the printers. 'I'll be here. I've got one or two things to do myself.'

'Ah,' said Mr Juby, and eyed the *World's Press News*. 'No doubt you have.'

He turned to resume his climb upstairs, but as he did so, above the bustle of the market place, they both heard through the open window the wail of a distant siren. Mr Juby stopped, and they listened to it silently for a couple of moments.

'Marford Heath?' Charles queried.

'Thass Marford all right. May be just a practice. Let's see what the Yanks are up to.' Mr Juby picked up the phone on Charles's desk and dialled the number of the United States Air Force base at Marford Heath.

'That must be a hell of a siren,' said Charles. 'Marford's miles away.'

'That needs to be, don't it,' snapped Mr Juby. 'If they got real trouble there, it'll spread for more miles than that siren can reach. Hallo; Marford Heath? Dooty Press Officer, please. This is Juby on the Journal.'

Charles looked out of the window. The hubbub around the stalls was quieter now, and people were standing about, listening. The wail of the siren became clearer.

'What's happening, Charlie?' George Perkins had come out of his butcher's shop and was standing on the pavement below.

'Just finding out, Mr Perkins. We're on to Marford now. Maybe it's just a practice.'

'Maybe it's not. They always used to warn us if they had a practice – and they hent had one for years.' A little crowd was gathering around Mr Perkins and there were nods of agreement. The faces looking up at Charles were grim.

'Dooty Press Officer? This is Juby. What's a-goin' on up there?'

The reply was brief. Mr Juby showed signs of exasperation. 'Evenchewality? What's that supposed to mean?'

This time the reply was longer, but apparently no more informative.

'So thass just a precaution, y'say? Then you won't mind if I send one of my reporters along, just to keep an eye on things?' Mr Juby nodded across to Charles. 'Right, he'll come straight away. Name of Charles Benson. Very good man, he is, he'll do things right. We don't want a

30

panic, do we, so the more you can tell him about these "precautions" the better for all of us. What's that?' Mr Juby spluttered slightly, then recovered. 'Yes, you have a nice day too, boy.'

He put the phone down heavily. 'These Yanks,' he growled. 'If they met you walking up the scaffold they'd say "have a nice day".' Then he noticed Charles's rather self-satisfied smirk. 'Never mind all that squit about being such an ace reporter, boy. I had to say that to get you in there.'

Charles stopped smirking. 'So what's happening, then?'

'Thass an evenchewality, he say.' Mr Juby's Norfolk accent had thickened, always a dangerous sign. 'So whass that, I say. Well, he say, he ha' to go by the book, and the book say that in certain evenchewalities they have to sound the siren. But that don't mean narthin serious, necessarily, he say, thass just procedure. Thass what they call a precautionary measure, he say, till they investigate further. I never heard such a load of old squit.'

'And that's all he said?'

'No,' snapped Mr Juby. 'He said, "Have a nice day".'

A shout came up from the market place outside. 'What's a-goin' on, Mr Juby?'

He paused to adjust his expression, then went over to the window and beamed reassuringly at the gathering crowd below. 'Thass nothing to worry about, George. Just a precaution, they say. I'm sending the boy Charlie to the base to help them sort things out.'

There were one or two guffaws and the grim faces relaxed. Charles went to the window and bowed graciously, and there was a ragged cheer and some shouts of advice. 'Mind you don't trip over none of those bombs, Charlie!' 'Don't go striking no matches, boy!' And from a younger group at the back of the crowd: 'You tell those bloody Yanks to go home.' There was not much ill-feeling these days against the Americans at Marford Heath – indeed many of the locals earned their living there – but the younger locals seeking romance on a Saturday night regarded them as unfair competition.

George Perkins returned to his shop and the others dispersed among the stalls, and Mr Juby sent Charles on his way. 'Off you go, boy. Don't forget your fancy Press card; they like to go by the book up at Marford. You give me a ring soon as you can. And let's hope no idjut has rung up the papers in London yet, or they'll have the whole of Norfolk running for their lives.'

'Still, it could be serious, couldn't it?' Charles knew, as everyone in Toftham knew, what kind of unpleasant devices were stored

31

somewhere in the bunkers and hangars of Marford Heath. It was generally better just not to think about it.

'Thass for you to find out, Charlie. Unless you'd rather stay and deal with Len Cloppett? Right, then.' He headed off up the stairs and Charles followed him to the door. Then he turned, came back to the desk and picked up the *World's Press News*. If destiny had delivered it back to him he ought not to lose it twice.

The entrance to Marford Heath air base presented an imposing vista of barbed wire, red-and-white poles, and black-and-white military policemen – the faces black, the helmets white. Charles had been to the base before, to the Christmas parties which the Americans held for local children, to receptions for local dignitaries when a new base commander arrived, and on one memorable occasion to the visit of a Hollywood starlet on a morale-boosting tour of American forces in Europe. She arrived in a clinging woollen dress several sizes too small, cut low at the top and high at the bottom; the wedding photographer from Toftham who normally took pictures for the Journal of darts winners and bowls teams could hardly believe his luck.

At his behest she happily draped herself on sofas, wrapped herself round soldiers, dangled from the wallbars in the gymnasium, waved a baseball bat over her head, and lifted what skirt she had to kick a football. He only had to name it, she did it. She would have been happy to pose on Charles's lap, but he felt Mr Juby might not find it amusing. As it was, the Journal used a comparatively modest shot of her kissing the commanding officer's cheek, under the cautious heading, 'Morale Raised at US Base'; the rest of the photographs proved a great success in the farmers' bar at the Dog and Partridge . . .

There was a very different atmosphere at the base now. Entry formalities on his previous visit had been confined to a quick glance at his Press pass and a friendly salute. This time there was a large contingent of military police at the barrier and more in the guardhouse beyond. The captain in combat gear and sunglasses was checking each new arrival.

He pulled up at the barrier and the captain eyed the Vibrator with some distaste. Charles felt inside his jacket for his Press pass and immediately the car door was flung open. 'Hold it, sir. Out of the car, please. Hands on the roof. Brojinski, check this gentleman.'

Charles did as he was told, feeling faintly ridiculous. He had seen this procedure so often in second-feature films at the Regal, but he never expected to play the main character himself. Brojinski, an enormous sergeant with assorted weapons dangling from his belt, thrust a hand under his jacket, extracted his wallet and handed it to the captain. Then he turned back to Charles. 'Spredlegsir,' he snapped.

Charles parted his legs obediently, relieved that he had seen those 'B' movies and could thus interpret the request. There was some heavy-handed patting which made him wonder a bit about Brojinski, but it was over swiftly. 'He's clean, cap'n.'

The captain found the Press pass in his wallet and studied it suspiciously. 'What is the purpose of your visit, sir?'

'I understand,' said Charles, feeling ridiculous again, 'you have had an eventuality.'

The captain seemed unsurprised by the word. 'That is the case, sir. So what is the purpose of your visit?'

Charles began to appreciate why Mr Juby had found his telephone conversation so exasperating. 'We are naturally interested to know why the base is in a state of emergency.'

'That is *not* the case, sir,' said the captain firmly. 'We are not in a state of emergency. We are in a state of precaution. That is quite a different situation.'

'Quite so.' The exasperation was growing. 'But it was enough to make you sound the siren, and we'd rather like to know why.'

'We sounded the siren,' explained the captain with a great display of patience, 'because it is a standard precautionary measure in the event of an eventuality. Sir.'

Charles played his trump card. 'I am here at the invitation of the Duty Press Officer. He has talked to my editor and authorised my visit. Would you please let him know that I am here.'

The captain looked again at the Press card. It bore his name and confirmed his membership of the National Union of Journalists, but admittedly the photograph was not a good likeness. It had been taken by the wedding photographer rather hastily in a spare moment between receptions. 'Let me just check your identity, sir. This picture could be anybody.'

'My name is Charles Benson, my editor is Mr Juby, and I work for the *Toftham and Wettleford Journal*. It is the leading newspaper in this area.' This was not an idle boast; the Journal was the *only* newspaper in the area.

'So it's a local paper, sir?' The captain seemed to mellow. 'You're not connected with any of those London papers? The *Sunday Herald*, for instance? We've had bad vibes from the *Sunday Herald*.'

Charles remembered that the Herald had recently run a campaign against American servicemen for spreading unsavoury social diseases among the female populace of Britain. He also remembered that as a local correspondent he had sent occasional stories to the Herald himself, but it seemed unnecessary to say so.

'You got it,' he said. He was back in the B movie again.

'Wait here with Brojinski, sir.' The captain went into the guardhouse and Charles leaned on the bonnet of the Vibrator, trying to look nonchalant. Brojinski stared fixedly at him, poised for any false move.

'OK'. The captain came back and handed him his wallet and Press card. 'You're in, Mr Benson. Welcome to Marford Heath. Brojinski, take Mr Benson to Major Wortheimer's office on B Block. Don't go via Number Three Hangar; take the long way round. There you go, Mr Benson. Have a nice day.'

Brojinski climbed into the passenger seat, making the Vibrator tilt alarmingly. Hastily, Charles climbed in too, bringing it to a more even keel, and he drove underneath the raised barrier and through the gates, feeling he had achieved a major journalistic coup.

'Take a right here, sir, then a left, then another left.'

He remembered the captain's instructions to Brojinski. 'Why can't we go via Number Three Hangar, sergeant? Is that where they've got the eventuality?'

'No comment sir,' said Brojinski firmly. 'All questions to Major Wortheimer, sir. Take another left, then a right. That's it.'

They pulled up outside a Nissen hut bearing the legend 'Information Office'. Brojinski led him through an anteroom, rapped on a door labelled Duty Press Officer, and half-ushered, half-marched him inside.

'This is Benson, Major. Comes from the Tufty and Nettlesoup Times, or sump'n. Says you're expecting him.'

Major Wortheimer rose from his swivel chair, removed his cigar, and extended a welcoming hand. He was in shirtsleeves, small, plump and balding, with an instant smile. 'Come in, Chas, come in. Good to see you. Make yourself comfortable; have a cup of coffee. OK Brojinski, that's it.'

Brojinski gave a looping salute and turned to the door, ignoring Charles. 'Have a nice day,' Charles murmured, but he did not seem to hear.

'Take a seat,' said the major, filling a mug from the coffee pot behind his desk. He passed over the mug and pushed a huge jug of cream across the desk with a sugarbowl to match. 'Now what can I tell you?'

34

This is more promising, thought Charles. He settled into a chair, put down the coffee, and took out his notebook. 'Well, major,' he started.

'Call me Theo, Chas. Everybody calls me Theo.' The major waved his cigar expansively. 'Named after Teddy Roosevelt, remember? But I can't take Teddy. Just call me Theo.'

'Well, Theo . . .' For the third time that morning Charles felt fainly ridiculous. 'I'd just like to know what's happening here.'

'Yeah, sure. What sort of thing did you want to know?'

Charles could feel the exasperation rising again. 'Well, there's the siren, and the state of precaution, whatever that means.'

'That's all quite straightforward,' said Theo genially. 'We've had an eventuality. I explained all that to your Mr Juby.'

Charles could not take any more of it. It was time to take the initiative. He leaned back in his chair and took a sip of coffee.

'Rumour has it,' he said casually, 'that there's a mutiny in your bomb store, and half the population of East Anglia is about to be wiped out.'

Major Wortheimer's jaw dropped.

'Alternatively,' Charles continued cheerfully, 'the Russians have parachuted into the base, taken the commanding officer hostage, and demanded you hand over your entire stock of nuclear weapons. Then there are others who say a warhead has been stolen and a Soviet spy is trying to smuggle it out of the base in his trousers, and you're looking for a man with a pronounced limp so Brojinski can frisk him . . .'

The major had been listening intently at first, but as the theories got wilder he relaxed again and puffed comfortably at his cigar. 'OK, Chas, great stuff. You want an official comment on all that? Negative. That's it, negative.' He removed the cigar from his mouth. 'You want an unofficial comment? Forget the mutiny and the Russians and the spy with the limp. But stick around. Something may turn up.'

'You mean you'll be able to tell me something soon?'

Theo shrugged. 'I mean something may turn up. Who knows?'

Charles leaned forward. 'Would it be something connected with Number Three Hangar, perhaps?'

The major did not flicker. 'Could be Number Three Hangar, or Number Nine Bomb Store, or the canteen in C Block. Who knows? But you're welcome to stick around. Have another coffee.'

Charles had a great many more coffees during the next few hours. He also had two large hamburgers on a cardboard plate at lunchtime and some rather awful sauerkraut in a paper bag. He read all the newspapers in Theo's office, English and American, and a few back

35

numbers of *Life* magazine. And he rang Mr Juby every hour on the hour, to tell him that something might turn up, but nothing had yet. The official explanation remained unchanged: there was a state of precaution because of an eventuality.

Major Wortheimer sometimes chatted, sometimes worked on the papers on his desk, sometimes sent for more coffee. Two or three times he put on his jacket and left the office, in response to a telephone summons. Each time when he returned Charles asked him eagerly for any news. The reply was always the same. 'Negative.'

After lunch there was a sudden burst of telephone activity. The major had two phones on his desk and both of them came into action. His dual conversations all followed the same pattern. 'Negative to that . . . No comment at this time . . . That I couldn't say . . . No, sir. Negative. Sure, if you wanna make the trip, glad to see you.'

In a brief lull he nodded across to Charles. 'Seems your buddies in Fleet Street are getting kinda excited.' Charles's heart sank. Somehow the word had got through Mr Juby's cordon and the heavy battalions were on their way.

The mention of Fleet Street reminded him that the *World's Press News* was still lying in his car, and the deadline for the application was fast approaching. It had to be in the post that afternoon to have any hope of reaching the BBC in time. While the major continued to battle with his telephones he borrowed a sheet of paper and an envelope, collected the magazine from the car and wrote out his application, quoting the vital reference number. He asked Theo if there was a post-box nearby.

'Sure, there's one just outside the door here.' Theo gave him his instant smile. 'Won't do you much good if it's urgent, Chas – no civilians entering or leaving the base at the moment, except for gentlemen of the Press like yourself. That box won't get emptied today.'

'Then how about one of your chaps taking it out for me and posting it outside?'

'Sorry, Chas. All personnel are confined to base.'

Charles stared at him incredulously. 'And this is just a state of precaution? What happens in a state of emergency?'

'In a state of emergency,' said Theo quietly, 'you wouldn't be here at all, Chas, and nor would I. You'd be kept off the base altogether – and I'd be down one of those bunkers. So things could be a lot worse. Have another coffee.'

'Supposing I go and post it myself,' suggested Charles desperately. 'I could be back in the base in ten minutes.' But he knew that was out of the question, and Theo put it into words.

36

'That's up to you, Chas. Just be a pity if you weren't here when something comes through. Specially with all your buddies on the way.'

'I'd hardly call them buddies,' Charles muttered, but he took the point. Gloomily he stuffed the envelope in his pocket and held out his mug for more coffee.

It was tea-time when the first buddy from Fleet Street reported at the gate. It was also the time of the last post from Toftham, which gave him double cause for depression. He had missed one boat and looked like being left behind in another.

Theo took the call from the guardroom. 'Which paper did you say? Jeez, it would be. Never mind, we'd better have him in here, where I can keep an eye on him. Send him along.' He put the phone down and looked across at Charles. 'You know a guy called Groyne?'

Charles shook his head. But he was wrong. A few minutes later Brojinski appeared, escorting a perspiring little man with a pork-pie hat on the back of his head and cigarette ash down his lapels. It had been six years since Charles last met him, but he remembered him instantly, though he had never known his name. This was the *Sunday Herald* reporter who had covered the East Coast floods from the comfort of the Red Lion bar in Wettleford.

'Bill Groyne,' announced the newcomer, advancing on the major with his hands deep in his pockets. 'What are you Yanks up to this time, then? Going to blow us all to pieces?' He gave the familiar guffaw which Charles remembered so well, though it ended now in a rasping cough.

Theo was unperturbed. He gave the *Sunday Herald* man his usual instant smile. 'Come on in, Bill. Glad to see you. Just call me Theo, everybody does. How about a coffee?'

'How about a gin, Theo?' Groyne leered hopefully. 'Sun's getting near the yardarm, I'd say.'

Theo spoke gently, as if to a fractious child. 'We don't have a yardarm, Bill. This is an Air Force base, not Navy.'

The fractious child remained fractious. 'All right, what about a sundowner then? Doesn't the Air Force know about sundowners?'

'The American Air Force,' said Theo cheerfully, 'is like the British Empire used to be. The sun never sets on it. Have a coffee.'

Bill Groyne gathered himself for another attack and Charles felt that in the interests of Anglo–American relations it was time to intervene. 'I can recommend the coffee, Mr Groyne. I've drunk a couple of gallons of it and I've managed to survive.'

Groyne looked at him for the first time. 'Do I know you? Face seems familiar.'

'We met during the floods. You told me you couldn't understand why people didn't run out of the way instead of getting drowned.' Charles tried to keep his voice steady. 'Pretty slow, you thought Norfolk people must be. You made a great impression.'

Groyne remained unconcerned. 'I remember. Terrible pub, that was. Ran out of gin the second night, or so they said. I've often wondered. Unfriendly sort of cove, that landlord.'

Charles could have told him, but refrained. The unfriendly landlord, normally a most congenial host, had found the easiest way of shedding his Fleet Street guests.

'Never mind, son. Water under the bridge now. Or water over the bridge in that case.' The guffaw and the cough silenced any reply.

'Nice to see a reunion of old friends,' said Major Wortheimer blandly. 'Have some more coffee . . .'

More journalists started to arrive. Bill Groyne knew most of them; Charles knew none at all. More chairs were brought in, the major sent for more supplies of coffee, the room steadily filled up with bodies and cigarette smoke. Each new arrival brought in by Brojinski had the same genial reception. 'Good to see you. Make yourself comfortable. Have a coffee.' And in answer to their questions they all got the same genial reply. 'Well now, I'd sure like to help you, but negative, I'm afraid. Stick around, though. Something may come up.'

The last arrival was rather different, an elegant young man about Charles's age wearing an immaculate lightweight summer suit and a tie bearing some sort of crest. The hair was neatly brushed, the shoes gleamed, the creases in the trousers were knife-edged. Over his arm he carried a dark overcoat with velvet round the collar. Brojinski, astonishingly, was carrying his case.

'Thank you, sergeant, that's very civil of you. I think that'll be all.' The voice was smooth, and precise, and strangely familiar.

As the newcomer edged his way through the crowded room towards the major's desk Charles saw that his case was actually a box, dark green and very solid. He swung it adroitly to clear his way through the throng. To get past Bill Groyne, Charles noted with approval, he caught him quite neatly behind the knee.

'Major Wortheimer? Good of you to see me. My name is Quentin Milton, BBC News. A pleasure to meet you.'

The major found himself out-courtesied, but he tried hard. 'Nice to meet you too, Quentin. Have a coffee. Take a chair if you can find one. Maybe you know one or two people here.'

Quentin Milton surveyed Bill Groyne and his associates and smiled briefly. 'Oh yes, I know them. Except for this gentleman.' And he came across to Charles and proffered a hand. 'Milton, BBC.'

'Yes I know,' said Charles. 'I recognised the voice. Sorry, you must get fed up with people saying that.'

'Not at all,' Quentin assured him. 'When people stop recognising the voice I'll know I'm on the way out. And you are. . . ?'

'Benson, Charles Benson.' He took a deep breath. '*Toftham and Wettleford Journal*. Just the local paper, I'm afraid.'

'No need to apologise, dear boy. Best place to start.' Quentin gave him a friendly grin. 'I seemed to miss that rung somehow. I went straight to *The Times* from Cambridge. But I could have done with that experience you're getting – most of the other chaps came in that way.' He paused. 'Hang on, now. Did you say Toftham? Do you know a Mr Juby?'

'Good grief.' Charles was constantly surprised by the extent of Mr Juby's contacts. 'Don't tell me his network spreads into the BBC too!'

Quentin looked puzzled. 'Not exactly. Friend of mine called James North works for television documentaries. He came up to Norfolk with some dreadful woman producer a few years ago to interview a woman who wouldn't send her children to school. The husband turned up out of the blue, sent the children off to school, and effectively killed the story. James always suspected your Mr Juby had a hand in it. I gather he didn't take to this lady producer.'

'You could well be right.' Charles remembered that visit too. Mr Juby had contacted the husband so he was there when the producer called at the house. It had been a lively encounter in which the self-important lady from London had fared rather unhappily; the story was still sometimes repeated with relish in the farmers' bar.

'Come to think of it, James mentioned you too. I'd forgotten your name – but you don't forget a name like Juby. I gather you and James got on rather well.'

'We did indeed.' Charles wondered if it was a good moment to mention his own aspirations, but thought better of it. No doubt every local reporter who met Quentin said he would like to join the BBC.

Quentin meanwhile had opened the top of the green box and revealed it to be a sort of portable tape recorder. He produced a microphone and a spool of tape from the pockets of his overcoat, threaded the tape onto the machine, plugged in the mike and pressed the knob.

'One, two, three,' he enunciated clearly. The group with Bill Groyne looked round, nudged each other knowingly, and turned away again.

'One, two, three,' came the voice out of the tape recorder as he pressed another knob. He turned to Charles. 'There we are, then. Ready for action. Now what actually is going on?'

'Not a lot,' said Charles, but he told him what he could, about the siren and the mysterious 'eventuality', and the 'state of precaution' which had cooped him in this office for the best part of the day. He mentioned his suspicions about Number Three Hangar, so far unconfirmed.

'It's a start,' said Quentin encouragingly. 'Have you tried it out on the good major?'

'All he says is "negative". That's not a lot of help.'

Quentin shook his head. 'Surprising how significant "negative" can sound in this sort of situation. You can say it as if you really mean it, or you can say it as if you're just saying it. Let's give it a try.' He picked up his tape recorder and headed for the major's desk.

Theo removed his cigar and rose from his swivel chair as Quentin approached. How nice to have that sort of effect on people, Charles thought enviously. Nobody ever got up for me.

'I wonder if I can record a brief interview with you, Major?'

Theo shrugged. 'You're very welcome, Quentin, and I'd really like to help, but I have nothing to say that I haven't said to everybody already.'

Quentin smiled disarmingly. 'Then I'm sure you wouldn't mind telling me again. That's splendid.' He turned to the group of reporters around Groyne. 'Thank you, gentlemen. A little hush, please. Much obliged.'

The conversation was grudgingly reduced to a few mutters. Quentin stood beside the major with the tape recorder on the desk before them, pressed the knob, and went into action. And Charles was fascinated to see that he was no longer the affable guest making polite conversation with his host, but the crisp, authoritative interviewer whom Charles had heard so often on the radio.

'Major Wortheimer, why is this base in what you call "a state of precaution"? The phrase sounds rather ominous.'

'I wouldn't say ominous, Quentin.' Theo was going to continue, but as he paused Quentin chipped in. 'Then what *would* you say, Major, if not ominous? You've increased security on the main gate, you're allowing no civilians in or out, you've confined all military personnel to base, and you have sounded a warning siren to alert the neighbourhood. Wouldn't you say that was ominous?'

'No I wouldn't,' said the major a little sharply. Charles had not heard him speak sharply before. 'This is the normal precautionary procedure if there is an appropriate eventuality.'

'An appropriate eventuality?' Quentin repeated the phrase solemnly. 'Presumably involving the nuclear weaponry on the base?'

'Negative,' said the major more comfortably. He was back on home ground.

'You mean it doesn't involve nuclear weaponry?'

'I mean negative, Mr Milton. Just that.' He was no longer calling him Quentin.

'Then it's nothing to do with Number Three Hangar?'

The major hesitated for only a moment, but it was enough. 'Negative,' he said, but somehow it no longer sounded convincing.

'So you can categorically assure us that absolutely nothing is wrong in Number Three Hangar, and nuclear weaponry is not involved?' And before the major could answer Quentin added swiftly: 'You appreciate that if you say "Negative", Major, that means "No, you cannot give that assurance".'

The major glared. 'I know what negative means, Mr Milton. I have nothing further to say at this time.'

'So you cannot give that assurance?' Quentin persisted.

'I have nothing further to say at this time,' the major repeated.

Quentin smiled at him sweetly and switched off the recorder. 'Much obliged, Major. Very kind of you to talk to me. Can I get you a coffee?'

The group of reporters had been taking a few notes, but they seemed unimpressed – particularly Bill Groyne. 'Bit of a *negative* interview, eh Milton?' And one or two of his companions joined in the guffaw. But Quentin seemed well satisfied, and Charles could understand why. Most listeners hearing that interview would be fairly convinced that something rather nasty had been happening in Number Three Hangar.

Quentin returned to him and started winding back the tape. 'Nice chap, the major,' he murmured, 'but I'm afraid he has the old problem. The more you deny something, the less people believe you. And if you don't actually deny it, they're convinced it's true. Can't win, really.'

'So what happens now?' asked Charles.

'That was the easy part.' Quentin took the tape off the machine. 'Now I've got to get it on the air. It's all right for these chaps, they've only got tomorrow's paper to think about. They needn't start filing for hours yet. And the awful Groyne's paper doesn't come out until the day after tomorrow. I need to get this on "Radio Newsreel" at seven o'clock this evening, so that gives me about an hour to get to the nearest studio. How long does it take to get to Norwich from here?'

Charles did a quick estimation. 'About forty minutes, with luck, if you don't get stuck behind too many tractors. Have you got a car?'

'There's a taxi waiting outside the gate. Local chap. Can't understand what he says much, but I expect he knows the way to Norwich.'

Charles was much impressed. 'You mean you've had a taxi waiting all this time outside the gate? That's going to be jolly expensive. They're inclined to whack it up in these parts for waiting around – particularly for foreigners.'

'I rather suspect he will. But that's the Corporation's worry, not mine. If I can get this on tonight's Reel it'll be worth it.'

'Will you be coming back?' asked Charles rather wistfully as Quentin picked up his coat. A long evening with Bill Groyne and his friends stretched ahead.

'If it's still going on by the time I've sent this lot down to London then I suppose I'll have to,' said Quentin reluctantly. 'But I can't see anything's going to happen at this stage. If we *were* in for a major disaster it would have happened by now. My guess is they've just been carrying out some sort of check and they'll call off all this nonsense once the check's finished. All the more reason to get this on the air before the whole story fizzles out.' He grinned at Charles. 'If there is a bang I should be able to record it quite clearly in Norwich.'

Charles had a sudden inspiration. He felt for the envelope in his pocket. 'Assuming you go straight back to London, could you drop this in for me? If you do hear a bang, of course, don't bother.'

Quentin glanced at the address on the envelope and chuckled. 'Do you know, I thought you were the first chap I'd ever met on a story who didn't want to join the BBC. And here you are, one jump ahead already.'

Charles shook his head. 'Actually I'm one jump behind. The application's got to be in by tomorrow. I thought I'd had it, being stuck here.'

'Fear not,' said Quentin grandly. 'Your missive is safe with me.' He called across to Major Wortheimer. 'Major, I wonder if you'd be good enough to ask Sergeant Brojinski to escort me back to the gate.' Then he turned back to Charles. 'Actually, you needn't have worried about the application arriving late. They always allow a few days' grace. This isn't the harsh world of commerce you're dealing with, dear boy. This is the BBC.'

They were all listening to 'Radio Newsreel' in Major Wortheimer's

42

crowded, smoke-filled office, and they had just heard the major's final unconvincing 'Negative' when the announcement came over the Tannoy outside.

'Now hear this. Now hear this.' The major turned off the radio with some relief. 'Precautionary restrictions are lifted as of now. Repeat, restrictions are lifted with immediate effect. All functions will return to normal. Repeat, normal.' Quentin Milton, it seemed, had been right.

'OK, gentlemen, that's it. Glad to have had your company. You'll find local taxis waiting at the gate. Enjoy your journey.' The major started bustling the reporters towards the door.

'False alarm, then?' asked Bill Groyne.

'If that's the way you like to play it, then that's OK by me. Now gentlemen, I'm shutting up shop, unless anyone would like some more coffee?'

Nobody wanted more coffee. Sergeant Brojinski appeared in the doorway and led the reporters off towards the main gate. But Charles, whose car was still parked outside, remained behind for a final word of thanks to Theo for his hospitality.

'No sweat,' said the major, much more cheerful now the others had disappeared. He started gathering up the empty mugs and cardboard cups. 'Sorry you had to wait so long, Chas. We could have wrapped it up a couple of hours ago, but your buddies from London had come a long way. It seemed a pity to send them straight back again.'

Charles felt a little bitter. 'So it really was a false alarm – just a waste of everybody's time.'

'Not entirely.' The major was putting on his jacket. 'This is off the record, Chas, but you've had a long wait, and you're a local so you know the score. We really did have an eventuality. A group of your guys from Marford village were digging up the roadway outside Number Three Hangar, and they went through a power cable that operates the hangar doors. We couldn't open the doors until they'd repaired it, then we had to check everything was OK inside in case it *hadn't* been just an accident. But if we told that to everyone, those guys would look kinda stupid, and we wouldn't look too clever either. So let's make it a false alarm, huh? Then nobody gets their butt kicked.'

Charles felt a little better. 'I think you may find the story gets out anyway, Theo. If it does, don't blame me. Mr Juby has a lot of friends in Marford; he'll find out eventually.'

'By that time,' said the major comfortably, escorting him to the door, 'your London buddies will have found something else to chase. Don't give it another thought.'

'I won't,' Charles assured him. His thoughts were already returning to the envelope he had given Quentin Milton. He hoped Quentin would think about it too when he got back to London. 'Thank you again, Theo. I hope we haven't been too much trouble.'

Major Wortheimer waved his cigar and gave his instant smile. 'Negative, Charles. Negative.' And as they parted: 'Have a nice day . . .'

Charles wrote his story of the false alarm at Marford Heath air base, with a few colourful touches about his day-long vigil in Major Wortheimer's office, then went to find Mr Juby in the farmers' bar. He gave him back his copy of the *World's Press News*.

'I hope you found it useful,' said Mr Juby, sipping his special. 'By the way, I heard that fellow Milton on the wireless. No doubt you had a chat with him?'

'No doubt,' said Charles guardedly.

Mr Juby gazed into his tankard. 'Must be a good job that, travelling about in style, having a few words with folk on a bit o' tape, then back to the stoodio for a nice cup o' tea. Not a bad life, eh?'

'I don't think it's quite like that, Mr Juby.' Charles tried not to sound too involved. It was time to change the subject. 'How did you get on with Len Cloppett?'

'Well, he hent too happy about the public meeting, but he can't do much about it now. We'll have to watch him, though. Tricky as a sackful o' ferrets is Len. He can do a fair amount of damage if he tries.' Mr Juby paused and took another sip, then added innocently, 'Very near as much damage as George Perkins' cousin did with his pewmatic drill.'

Charles sipped his pint too. He guessed what Mr Juby was driving at. 'George Perkins' cousin? Now would he live out at Marford and work at the air base?'

'That he does, boy, that he does.' Mr Juby gave Charles a knowing look. 'So we can learn a lesson from that, I reckon. Let's say we'd better be in a state of precaution, like, when we have the meeting. There might be an evenchewality . . .'

FOUR

Charles was working his way through Page Four of his application form, 'Honours, awards, degrees and other qualifications', when a coach pulled up in the market-place and the passengers poured off. They were an interesting assortment. Some of the men were in sober business suits carrying briefcases, others were in sports jackets and brightly coloured pullovers carrying copies of the *Daily Mirror*. One or two of these were looking rather dishevelled and seemed slightly unsteady on their feet. The women ranged from the elegant to the festive; neat suits and blouses rubbed shoulders with floral dresses and cardigans, and smart leather handbags bumped against carrier bags bulging with Thermos flasks and knitting. To Charles's startled eye it looked a cross between a business delegation and a works outing. Then he saw the Birmingham address on the back of the coach and all became clear.

Under 'Honours, awards, degrees and other qualifications' he wrote with a flourish: 'Matriculated with distinction in English.' Then he put the form in a drawer and prepared to welcome the guests. They would have three or four hours to kill in Toftham before the meeting, and it was early closing day, but Mr Juby had suggested the timing of their arrival personally. 'Give 'em time to absorb the atmosphere.'

While most of the party milled about uncertainly beside the coach in the otherwise deserted square, two of the dark-suited men made their way towards the Journal office. Charles went down to the front office to greet them, but the younger of the two greeted him first. 'How're yew a-goin' on then, boy?'

He was disconcerted by the broad Norfolk accent, when he had been expecting the flatter vowels of the Midlands, but the newcomer, seeing he had made his impact, dropped back into more usual speech. 'Just wondered if I could still do the accent. I'm Jimmie Renshaw, late of the *Thetford Journal*, currently with the *Birmingham Post*. You must be the boy Charlie.'

'Blast, if it hent the boy Jimma,' replied Charles in kind.

Jimmie grinned. 'Not bad for a furriner.' He shook his hand and introduced his companion, a sharp-featured man with a bright red tie.

45

'This is Reginald Morris, chairman of the Labour group on Birmingham Corporation.'

Charles was a little puzzled. 'Glad to see you, Mr Morris, but I thought this was just an informal meeting to let people get to know each other. I don't think we were expecting anyone from the Corporation.'

'I daresay you weren't.' The voice was sharp and unmistakeably hostile. 'Len Cloppett thought it might be a good idea if I came along, just to make sure everyone gets a fair picture.' The thin lips smiled, but the eyes did not join in.

Charles nodded thoughtfully. First move to Len Cloppett.

'We don't have any reception committee, I'm afraid. I'm sure the chairman of the meeting would have been happy to meet you if he'd known you were coming.'

'I'll meet him soon enough. I'll find Len first. We've a thing or two to talk about before the meeting.' Charles started to suggest where he might find him, but Mr Morris needed no assistance. 'I know where Len is, round at the Labour Club. He told me where it was. I'll see you later, Mr Renshaw.' He left the office and set off purposefully across the market-place.

Jimmy gave an apologetic shrug. 'I could hardly stop him coming, I'm afraid. And now he's here I think he'll expect to be up on the platform and given a chance to speak. He'll speak anyway, of course. Quite a forceful character, our Reg.'

Charles nodded agreement. 'We'd better warn Major Burney –Mr Juby's with him now. Meanwhile I hope the rest of your party can find something to do for the next few hours. I'm afraid everything's closed on Wednesdays, even the teashop, and the pubs don't open until six. They could always go to the Regal, of course; it's Veronica Lake this week.'

'So I saw when we arrived.' Jimmy grinned. 'I think that was showing in Birmingham about six months ago. But I'm sure they'll enjoy absorbing the atmosphere.' Charles recognised Mr Juby's phrase.

They looked around the market-place. Some of the women off the coach were peering into shop windows or looking at the photographs of Veronica Lake outside the Regal. One group had disappeared inside the Dog and Partridge, presumably attracted by the single AA star over the doorway and hoping to find a cup of tea, but the first of them were already re-emerging, their thirst unquenched. The Dog and Partridge did not go in for afternoon teas.

There were optimistic members of the coloured-pullover brigade

46

hanging about outside the three other pubs in the market-place, perhaps assuming that opening time followed the city pattern and came at five-thirty. At the Fleece, in particular, they would have a long wait; Jim Bloxham, the landlord, rarely opened his doors before seven, and as he was running the bar at the Jubilee Hall that evening it was unlikely he would bother to open at all.

Others had seated themselves disconsolately on the seat by the war memorial, where a couple of the ladies were already ensconced with their knitting. The men in the business suits had mostly wandered out of the market-place, presumably to weigh up the commercial possibilities of the surrounding properties. A couple of them had been to see the cattle market and were already returning. Charles watched them trying to wipe their shoes clean on the grass around the memorial; they had obviously absorbed more of the atmosphere than they intended.

'I gather Mr Juby is not too keen on this overspill plan,' said Jimmie Renshaw at his side, surveying this scene of inactivity.

'I think you could say that. But I'm not entirely sure he's right.'

'Nor am I.' Charles raised an enquiring eyebrow, and Jimmie shook his head. 'I know it's supposed to have been the ruin of Thetford. I thought so myself at first – that's why I left. But really you can't stand still for ever in this sort of town, not these days. Either you bring in new jobs and new blood or places like Toftham will just become museum pieces. The young people are leaving the villages already; soon they'll be leaving these little market towns too, if there isn't more to offer them. I don't say overspill is necessarily the right answer. That's a bit drastic for me, that's why I'm helping out Mr Juby – and he helped me a lot in the old days too. But Toftham can't be the same in twenty years' time as it is today. Either it'll grow and have more industry and new estates and supermarkets, or it'll shrink, like the wool towns did when the wool trade moved up north, and you'll be left with this big old empty market square, and a few antique shops, and a lot of retired folk sitting in the sun talking about the old days. Which Toftham do you fancy, Charles?'

Charles was silent for a moment. He had not heard the argument put so convincingly before. 'To be quite honest,' he said, 'I don't really fancy either.' He ushered him towards the stairs. 'If you'd like to make yourself comfortable, in Mr Juby's office or mine, I've got a form I must finish filling in before tonight . . .'

Toftham Jubilee Hall had not been so packed since the last night of the

Drama Society's production of *Harvey*, in which Freddie Pendleton had scored such a spectacular success as Elwood P. Dowd, philosophical custodian of the invisible white rabbit. Freddie compensated for the more macabre aspects of his job as the town's principal funeral director by playing the fool both on and off the stage; he had once made Charles disgrace himself by giggling at a funeral under the eyes of the family mourners. He took all the leading comedy roles in the local productions and *Harvey* had been his latest triumph. For some weeks afterwards, as a personal tribute, Charles had included a Mr Harvey in the list of mourners at every funeral in which Freddie was involved. Not even Mr Juby had spotted it.

In the centre of the stage this evening, however, instead of Freddie and his invisible rabbit, Major Clarence Burney was seated behind a table draped with the legend: 'Sponsored by the *Toftham & Wettleford Journal* and the *Birmingham Post*'. Alongside him was the very visible and unrabbit-like figure of Mr Reginald Morris. Jimmie Renshaw sat with Charles at the Press table just below the stage. In the front row were George Flatt, Clerk to Toftham Council, Len Cloppett, Harry Hurn, and other members of the Council. There was also a stranger sitting next to Len Cloppett, whom Charles had not seen before; he was fairly certain he had not been on the Birmingham coach. The Birmingham contingent occupied the next three rows; some of the women were already knitting.

Major Burney rapped on the table. 'Good evening, ladies and gentlemen. Thank you for your excellent turnout this evening, and we are particularly pleased to welcome our guests from Birmingham. Perhaps they would kindly make themselves known.'

The three rows of guests grudgingly rose from their seats and acknowledged the equally grudging applause from those behind. The men in the business suits bowed slightly or just nodded, one or two beer-glasses were raised among the coloured pullovers, who had at last found a bar that was open, and one of the women waved a half-knitted sock. Enthusiasm was noticeably lacking on either side.

Major Burney continued, as they resumed their seats. 'I'm glad our visitors have had an hour or two to take a look around our little community. I hope they've been able to absorb the atmosphere of this historic market town, so rich in tradition and ancient custom . . .'

He was interrupted by his neighbour at the table. 'You don't need to go into all that, Mr Chairman. Birmingham has quite a bit of history too, you know. There's nothing so special about that.'

' 'Ear 'ear,' shouted somebody in the third row. 'You tell 'im, Reg.'

There was some scattered applause from the Birmingham contingent and the half-knitted sock was waved in encouragement.

In the front row, Harry Hurn rose and turned on the group behind him. 'Bet you hent got a chutch what was built by the Normans,' he said loudly. 'Nor a market that goes back to King John, nor a set o' bells that's been rung every Michaelmas morning for five hundred year . . .'

'Now wait a minute,' said one of the business-suited men in the row behind him, also rising. 'Didn't you know that Birmingham is mentioned in the Domesday Book? Didn't you know we've had our Bull Ring nearly as long as you've had your market? Didn't you know our St Martin's Church goes back to the thirteenth century? A big city can still have its historical significance, you know. We didn't just start from scratch yesterday.'

'But that's what you want us to do now, hent it?' George Perkins was shouting from the back of the hall. 'You reckon you can turn us into another little Birmingham, startin' from scratch. Never mind us small shopkeepers trying to make a livin', you want to bring in the chain stores and the supermarkets and the do-it-yourselfs and all that squit. That hent for the likes of us.'

'At least you'd be open on a Wednesday afternoon,' retorted a shirt-sleeved man with a half-empty glass in the second row. 'Or at least you could get a cup of tea and a bun when you want it, and the pubs would open at the proper time . . .'

'You tell 'em, mate,' roared his neighbour. 'They don't know they're living, this lot. Right lot o' yokels we've got 'ere.'

The rest of the hall erupted. There was much shouting and arm-waving from the rear rows, and the three rows from Birmingham shouted and waved back. Charles spotted Freddie Pendleton, who was sitting just behind the visitors, pick up a carrier bag belonging to one of the knitters and invert it over the head of the shirt-sleeved man with the glass. The woman with the half-knitted sock spotted him also and turned on him furiously, brandishing a knitting-needle and uttering incomprehensible cries. Harry Hurn and Len Cloppett were arguing fiercely in the front row with George Flatt trying to restrain them. And somewhere at the back of the hall Charles caught sight of Mr Juby, leaning against the wall with his arms folded, legs crossed, a seraphic smile on his face. The meeting of minds was under way.

Complete mayhem seemed about to break out, but Major Burney, who had been tapping on the table, not too forcefully, for some time now, produced a parade-ground roar that could be heard clearly above the racket in the hall.

'THAT'S ENOUGH!' Everyone turned towards him, and the lady with the sock stopped brandishing her needle. 'Be silent, the lot of you. Pull yourselves together and sit down.'

Beside him, Reginald Morris lent unexpected support. 'That's right,' he shouted at the Birmingham contingent, 'you shut yer row. We're here for a proper discussion, not a shouting match.' As the noise subsided he turned to Major Burney. 'I suggest we forget about the history, Mr Chairman, and talk about the future.'

'Hear hear!' shouted Len Cloppett from the front row. Harry Hurn seemed about to shout back, but contained himself.

'Thank you for your advice, Mr Morris,' said Major Burney sharply. 'This is a matter of great concern to our town, and I am not surprised that feelings run high. Everybody should have their say, and I am sure we have all noted with great interest the views expressed by your colleagues from the floor of the hall.'

'They're not my colleagues,' Reg Morris snapped back. 'Half of them are here to see if there's money to be made out of this town, and the other half are here for a free day out. I'm here because I think this overspill plan could help the working people in your town and mine. There'd be better facilities for your people, and there'd be jobs enough here for some of mine too, and they'd all have modern houses to live in, and room to move, and a better life.'

The protests began to build up again in the Toftham audience, but it was a shout from one of the Birmingham group which took the edge off Morris's argument. 'You speak for yourself, Reg. I wouldn't come and work in this dump if you built me a bleedin' palace.'

The hubbub broke out again and Charles glanced at Mr Juby at the back of the hall. The seraphic smile was still in place; it was all going according to plan.

'Mr Chairman! Point of order!'

This time it was Len Cloppett's shout that silenced the noise. Major Burney eyes him suspiciously. 'I'm not sure we need points of order at an informal meeting like this, Mr Cloppett, but go ahead.'

Len waited for the last murmurs to die away before continuing. 'May I propose, Mr Chairman, that we hear an independent speaker, who can give us some useful facts and figures from his own personal experience about the effect of overspill development. I think it may assist us in our deliberations.'

'And who might that be?' Major Burney looked round the hall. 'I'm afraid everybody here tonight seems to be somewhat partisan, one way or the other.'

Len indicated the stranger sitting beside him. 'This gentleman is a civil servant and therefore able to give impartial advice and an unbiased view, and what's more, there is no one here who is in a better position to know about this subject. Mr Flatt knows him very well, of course, and it is through his good offices that we have persuaded him to join us. This is Mr Evans, the Town Planning Officer for Thetford.'

'Thought I recognised him,' muttered Jimmie, and Charles looked again towards the back of the hall. Mr Juby still had his arms folded and his legs crossed as he leaned against the wall, but the seraphic smile had disappeared. Len Cloppett had pulled one out of the bag.

Major Burney stood up and waved the Town Planning Officer for Thetford onto the platform. 'Good of you to give up your time, Mr Evans. Perhaps you'd care to join us up here, then everyone can hear what you have to say.'

Mr Evans, quietly and simply, explained how Thetford had been developed into an overspill town. It had been a long, detailed negotiation involving the town council and the London County Council, in which every interested party had had the chance to take part. He summed it up in a sentence. 'It took three years from the first letter being written to the first brick being laid – but when we laid it, nobody raised a voice against it.'

Now the town had new recreational facilities, new schools, new sports grounds. It also of course had new factories, new housing estates and new people, but he felt the locals had come to terms with the Londoners and the town had not lost its identity. It was still growing and it would continue to do so for another decade, but it was planned growth instead of haphazard sprawl, and the town's prosperity grew with it. The Thetford overspill plan had been a daring project, said Mr Evans, but it had worked.

When he finished and sat down the hall was silent. Even the Birmingham party had been listening closely. Major Burney cleared his throat. 'We're very grateful to you, Mr Evans, I'm sure. Of course a great many of us here know Thetford very well – and we knew it very well before all this happened. Perhaps we have our own view on it, but you have put your view very clearly. Are there any questions from the hall?'

'Never mind questions,' said Len Cloppett, rising again from his seat in the front row. 'As you say, Mr Evans has put the facts very clearly. Now before we forget what he's been saying, I move we vote on whether we are in favour or not of Toftham becoming an overspill town.'

'Hold you hard,' cried Harry Hurn, jumping up too. 'We didn't come here to vote, we just came to exchange views. A vote don't mean a thing.'

'It'll be a useful expression of public opinion to guide the council in its deliberations.' Len rattled out the words as though he had rehearsed them with care.

'Quite right,' interjected Reg Morris from the platform.

'Now don't you start again,' roared Harry Hurn. 'We don't need the likes of you to tell us what to do.'

Major Burney rose hastily. 'That'll do, gentlemen. I think Mr Hurn is right. I see no point in a vote at this meeting. We should each give the matter some thought in the light of what we've heard tonight and tell our council representatives how we feel in due course. Any further discussion or questions? No?' He was obviously eager to close the meeting before any further uproar broke out.

'Mr Chairman,' came a familiar voice from the back of the hall. 'I have a question for Mr Evans, if thass in order.' Mr Juby had unfolded his arms and was holding his pipe aloft.

Major Burney nodded towards him, looking rather surprised, and Charles could understand why. It was rare for Mr Juby to make any sort of public utterance, particularly on a contentious occasion like this. He must feel desperate measures were needed.

'Am I right in recalling that Mr Evans was Town Planning Officer in Thetford before all this came about?' Mr Evans, on the platform, nodded. 'And at that time the town had something under 5000 people?' Mr Evans nodded again. 'And by the time thass all finished that'll be nearer 17,000?' Again Mr Evans agreed.

'Well now,' said Mr Juby, and paused to puff his pipe, 'I know we've had a very impartial report from Mr Evans, and as a public servant he hent got no axe to grind, but hent that a fact that a Town Planning Officer for a town with 17,000 people fare a sight better than in a little town of 5000?'

'Yes, of course,' said Mr Evans rather coldly. 'There are different grades, as in any other local government department.'

'Ah,' said Mr Juby, pausing again to let the point sink in. Then, having taken a few more puffs, he waved his pipe genially towards George Flatt, who had turned round in the front row. 'That sounds like good news for you, George, wouldn't you say?'

'Nice one, Mr Juby,' muttered Jimmie Renshaw as laughter broke out around the hall. Major Burney stepped in before George Flatt could reply.

'Thank you, Mr Juby. I think on that lighter thought we'll end the meeting. I'd like to thank the sponsors for bringing us all together, and thank you all for attending, particularly our friends from Birmingham. You'll find your coach waiting outside. I hope you will take back with you pleasant memories of Toftham . . .' – he paused and gave a warning glance at Reg Morris in case he attempted to interrupt – 'our historic and ancient little market town. Goodnight to you all.'

Which is precisely, thought Charles, where we came in.

As the Birmingham ladies gathered up their knitting and followed their menfolk out to the coach he asked Jimmie how he thought the evening had gone.

'I'd say that was a fairly even match. The first half all one way, and the second half all the other, then a late rally at the end.' Jimmie gathered up his notes from the Press table. 'Frankly, I don't think it'll make a lot of difference either way. Reg Morris has got as much influence in Birmingham as all my little Fred Karno army put together, so that'll balance out at my end, and I imagine your Len Cloppett and Harry Hurn balance things out here. But the decision won't be taken by any of them, it'll be a lot higher than that, and it'll be decided on government policy and investment budgets and unemployment figures and the like. They won't take much notice of meetings like this, I'm afraid, even though we'll give it a good show in the Post and no doubt you will in the Journal. And I have to say . . .' – and he grinned at Charles – 'I know this is close to heresy in Toftham, but I don't think they'll take much notice of Mr Juby either.'

They shook hands and Jimmie went off to make his farewells to Mr Juby and catch the coach, while Charles left the hall and returned thoughtfully to the Journal office. As he passed the Post Office he remembered that the envelope containing his BBC application form was still in his pocket. He had delayed posting it until after the meeting, in case anything happened to change his mind.

'Pity,' he murmured to himself – and put it in the box.

The next few weeks were something of an anti-climax for Charles and Mr Juby, though for different reasons. Apart from a formal acknowledgement of his application, Charles heard nothing more from the BBC, and Mr Juby's antennae failed to detect any further moves in the overspill saga, either in Toftham or Birmingham. Len Cloppett was keeping a low profile and there was no word from Jimmie Renshaw.

They each dealt with their frustration in their own way. Mr Juby sought solace in the farmers' bar, while Charles spent much time driving round the Journal's reporting area, ostensibly in search of stories, actually enjoying the countryside in the summer sunshine and meeting the acquaintances he had made in the villages. Whatever happened in Toftham itself, these little clusters of flintwalled cottages tucked away in the rolling fields and woods of High Norfolk never seemed likely to change.

He kept away from Remingham, with its memories of the delectable Rebecca, but there were other places which could be relied upon to produce a ninety-year-old blacksmith with memories of the horse-and-wagon days, or a collecter of unlikely curios with a tale to tell, a pub about to change hands or a schoolteacher due to retire. At worst there was always a parochial church council meeting or a beetle drive in the village hall. He prided himself that he had never failed to find a story of some sort in every village he visited, and even after seven years there were still isolated hamlets which he knew nothing about, and which were untapped territory for the Journal.

He came across one of these unfamiliar village names on the fading map in Mr Juby's office. It was printed in such tiny type he found it difficult to make out.

'What's this little place, on the far side of Tittlesham?' he asked Mr Juby, pointing at the minute speck on the map.

Mr Juby did not bother to look up. 'There hent nothing the far side of Tittlesham, not so far as we're concerned. That's on the boundary with the West Norfolk office. You go beyond Tittlesham, you're trespassing, boy. They won't like that in King's Lynn.'

Charles studied the map more closely. 'According to the Journal boundary line this place is just inside our patch. Looks like Something-Parva . . .'

'That'll be Godborough Parva. You don't want to bother with that. God-forsaken Godborough, they call it in those parts. Nothing's ever happened there since the Black Vicar were there, back in the Twenties.'

'The Black Vicar?' Charles was intrigued. 'You mean Godborough had an African parson? That'd be something for High Norfolk.'

'I don't see why.' Mr Juby was a little put out. 'We had a maharajah down at Elveden in the old days; they called him the Black Prince, when he weren't about. And there was a Red Indian princess out at Heacham on the coast – married one of the Norfolk gentry who went out to America, and he brought her back as the squire's lady. Hent you heard o' Pocahontas?'

'All right, so this is a very cosmopolitan county,' said Charles soothingly. 'Now where did the Black Vicar come from? Nigeria, perhaps? Kenya?'

'I think he come from Camberwell for a start. Or it might have been Clapham.' Mr Juby paused for a moment, enjoying Charles's bewilderment, then he explained. 'They dint call him Black because he was that sort o' black. It was what he got up to in the church. Strange goings-on there was, chickens and goats and all that mumbo-jumbo. Rum owld do, that were; but then thass a rum owld village. Nobody there seemed to mind what he got up to at night-time, so long as he took a service each Sunday morning and buried 'em proper when they died.'

Charles was astonished. 'You mean black as in black magic? Here in Norfolk, only thirty-odd years ago?'

My Juby chuckled. 'Never mind thirty year ago, Charlie boy. There's still some of it about if you get out in the littler villages. But they're a bit more careful about it these days; the bishop don't seem to take to it.'

'And what about your Black Vicar? What happened to him?'

'Well, I doubt nothing would have happened to him if he hent tried it on at Tittlesham as well. Old Nicholson up at the farm got to hear of it and found him up to his little games in Tittlesham church, and he turfed him out himself. A younger man he was then, o' course. He tell him if he catch him at it again he'd open up the old stocks in Godborough and lock him in for a day or two, till he mend his ways.' Mr Juby chuckled again. 'We call him Nick for short, but he hent Old Nick, thass for sure, and he hent got no time for that sort o' squit. The Vicar, he gets the message, and soon afterwards he ups and goes off to somewhere in Lincolnshire. I dessay he was more appreciated up there. Rum folk in Lincolnshire.'

'Sounds like a great story,' said Charles rather enviously. Mr Juby snorted. 'Don't you believe it, boy. Not in those days, it weren't. My father was running the paper then; a decent God-fearing man he was, he wouldn't want to put ideas in people's heads printing something like that. He wrote a nice little piece about the Vicar when he left, saying how much he'd be missed in the parish. I expect he were too; as I recall it took a fair time to get another parson for Godborough Parva.'

'I can imagine,' said Charles. 'I suppose he'd have to scrub all that blood off the altar for a start.' Mr Juby did not seem amused, so he hastened on. 'Do they have a Vicar there now?'

'Thass been joined up with Tittlesham for years. The Vicar lives in Tittlesham and the big old Vicarage at Godborough has been derelict since before the war. I don't think the church is in much better state –

there's only a handful of folk left in the village these days, and I doubt they do much church-going except for Harvest and Christmas.'

'It sounds worth a look anyway.' Charles stared at the map to memorise the route to Godborough. He had long since given up relying on signposts, which were either broken off or turned round to point in the wrong direction. It might just be accidental, but Norfolk villagers liked their privacy. 'I was going over to Tittlesham this afternoon to have a chat with Mrs Boggis at the Stores. I might take a look at Godborough Parva while I'm there – just have a browse round.'

Mr Juby nodded without much interest and headed for the door; lunchtime was approaching. 'You'd better come and have a glass first. Who knows what grisly horrors you may find in God-forsaken Godborough. But don't expect to hear much about the Black Vicar in the village. Real old Norfolk folk they are out there, boy – niver know narthin about narthin . . .'

As they went through the front office Anthea intercepted them. 'There's a letter been delivered for you, Charles. It looks rather important.'

For a moment Charles thought it must be from the BBC, and his heart leapt. Then he saw it had come by hand, and the heart subsided. The BBC might pay for taxis to wait indefinitely for its reporters, but it could hardly run to a personal delivery service for its potential ones.

The envelope was large and square and impressive. So was the card inside, with the addition of gold edging and embossed print. It advised Charles Benson Esq. that his presence would be welcomed by the Master and members of the Mid-Norfolk Foxhounds at their Annual Hunt Ball. Dress, white tie. Decorations would be worn. Carriages at 3 a.m.

'Blast boy, you come up in the world.' Mr Juby was looking over his shoulder at the card. 'You been hob-nobbin' with the gentry, then?' Charles detected a note of disapproval, but he seemed impressed nonetheless. 'Our Charlie's going to the hunt ball, Anthea. Now you find a good-sized pumpkin for him, thass a good girl. He can't go to the ball in that terrible old car.'

'How exciting, Charles. You must be absolutely thrilled.' Anthea was positively bubbling with excitement herself, and it occurred to him that some faint glimmer of hope might be flickering within her angular frame. He hastened to douse it. 'The invitation's only for one, I'm afraid. Anyway, I doubt very much I'll be going; I've no idea why they've asked me.'

'Oh, but you must, you must,' urged Anthea, still bubbling, and

Charles mentally apologised for misjudging her. She was obviously delighted for him.

'How can I, Anthea? I don't have even the white tie, let alone all the gear that goes with it. And I certainly can't afford to hire one. Come on Mr Juby, let's have that drink.' He led the way out of the office.

Mr Juby paused for a moment to pat Anthea's shoulder, which was already starting to heave. 'Never you mind, gel. We hent got too many pumpkins in Toftham, but I can find a fancy suit for him, thass for sure, even if I have to get the folk in Norwich to pay for it. Thass a legitimate expense, I'd say. If the Journal can supply a black tie for funerals it can supply a white one for hunt balls.'

He drew himself up to his full five-foot eight and waved his pipe, wand-like, above his head. 'Fear not, the boy Charlie *will* go to the ball . . .'

Mrs Boggis in the Tittlesham Stores shook her head emphatically. 'No, we don't have much to do with them Godborough folk. Funny lot they are out there; never did get on with 'em.'

Charles nodded understandingly. 'All to do with that Black Vicar, I suppose.'

Mrs Boggis stared at him, then unxpectedly burst out laughing. 'That duzzy old fule? We din't pay no attention to him and his conjurations. Mr Nicholson soon sent him packing. No, thass the war that done it; we hent spoken to 'em much since the war. Thass a pity we got to share the parson with 'em these days, but he got the sense to spend most of his time over here. He only take one service a month at Godborough.'

Charles picked up her reference to the war. 'What was this wartime problem, Mrs Boggis? Did Godborough have a lot of conscientious objectors, or did they cheat on the rationing, or what?'

She looked puzzled. 'Whatever are you on about, Mr Benson? I hent talking about the last war.'

Now it was Charles who was puzzled. 'The Great War, then?'

'Course not. They lost some men in the Great War, just like we did, and all the other villages hereabouts. They even had a bomb drop on Godborough from one of them German airships, killed poor old Henry Fitt right outside his cottage. A great argument they had, deciding whether to put his name on the war memorial. There's some said he weren't killed on active service, so he weren't illegible like, and there's others said it was due to enemy action, so that was good enough. They put his name on eventually, but right at the end after Willie Whiting instead of alphabetical. I tell you, they're rum owld folk in Godborough.'

Mrs Boggis had wandered off the point again, but Charles led her back.

'If it wasn't the last war or the Great War that caused the trouble, then which war was it, Mrs Boggis?'

'Why, the Civil War of course. What else would it be?' She saw he was still bewildered. 'Tittlesham and all about us here was for Cromwell, like everybody else with any sense to 'em, but those folk in Godborough, they reckon they liked having a king spending their money for 'em and a lot of the men went off to Lynn and joined up with the gentry that live at Hunstanton, them Lestranges. Still live there, they do – I never did understand how they managed to keep a-goin' even after they lost. I tell you, Mr Benson, I wouldn't go to Hunstanton for a holiday; I wouldn't give 'em the satisfaction. And for that matter, I wouldn't go to Godborough. They're hully quare folk in Godborough, and no mistake.'

For a moment Charles thought this must be another of Mr Juby's little jokes, and he had primed Mrs Boggis to tell him the tale. But there was no mistaking the genuine anger as she talked about the Lestranges and the men from Godborough who went to fight for the Royalists, and he realised this was no joke. Black magic was not the only relic of the past that had survived in High Norfolk.

'Well, I think I'll chance a visit there anyway, Mrs Boggis. At least they should be friendly once they know that I'm a Charles too.' It was an attempt to lighten the atmosphere, but he might have known she would take him seriously. 'They're such fules over there, Mr Benson, they wouldn't know what king they'd been fighting for. You mind how you go with them folk; they don't see many strangers over there.' She leaned over the counter and tapped his chest. 'Trouble with them is, you know, they lives in the past.'

'Ah,' said Charles. 'Quite so.'

Back in the Vibrator he had to consult his map again to find the road to Godborough Parva; as he expected, none of the signposts in Tittlesham indicated which way to go. Mrs Boggis had given the impression it was on another planet, but it was only three miles away, along a succession of winding lanes which grew narrower the further he went, with tufts of grass growing up the middle. The familiar High Norfolk landscape of barley and beet fields gave way to an area on the map called Godborough Heath, an open stretch of unkempt common land where the gorse and nettles had apparently been untouched by human hand or foot.

His first sight of Godborough itself was a squat church tower on a slight ridge ahead, and alongside it a gaunt-looking house which was presumably the derelict Vicarage. Below them a ragged-looking wood covered the ridge and ran down into a fold of the land, and as he drove closer he saw a cluster of pantiled roofs at the foot of the ridge which marked the village itself. This must be one of the Black Death villages, he thought, originally grouped around the church at the top of the hill until the plague wiped out most of the villagers and the rest moved away and rebuilt their homes in the dip below, with the protection of the wood in between. The original cottages must have crumbled and disappeared; only the medieval church remained, and the Georgian Vicarage which had been built beside it and was now deserted too.

He drove out of the heathland straight into the village street. Indeed the first cottages had the gorse and nettles almost reaching their back doors. All the closed doors and windows made it seem like a ghost town, but Charles was used to that. In these isolated little communities the men were out working in the fields, the children were at school in the nearest sizeable village, and the women, if they were not confined indoors, had probably been collected by bus to work in the nearest egg-packing station, or wherever there were potatoes to be lifted or fruit to be picked. Even so, knowing Godborough's macabre history, Charles found the silence and the emptiness of this lonely little settlement quite disturbing.

His normal routine when he made his first visit was to call at the village shop, but there was no sign of a shop in Godborough Parva, just a venerable postbox in the wall of one of the cottages, the red paint flaking off its rusty 'V.R.'. But at the far end of the street, where it petered out into a rough track, he spotted a faded sign swinging from what looked like just another cottage, but must be the village pub. It bore the portrait of a handsome man with an aquiline face, a long black wig and a neat pointed beard. 'The King's Head,' it said underneath, and Charles had no difficulty working out which king it was. The sign had obviously been there for many years, but when he pulled up outside he saw that the wording over the door was quite new. It announced that Richard Cattermole was licensed to sell intoxicating liquors on these premises.

He got out of the Vibrator and knocked on the door, with no great hope of getting a response. In rural Norfolk, pub landlords like Mr Cattermole generally worked on the land during the daytime and only appeared behind the bar in the evenings. At lunchtime the front door might be left unlocked to satisfy the brewers, and the landlord's wife might cope with any customers, but lunchtime was considered a time for eating, not drinking, and Charles knew by now that in most country pubs food had a very low priority.

In the middle of the afternoon he was even less likely to find anyone around, but surprisingly he heard footsteps inside, then bolts being drawn and a key being turned, and then the rattle of a chain. When the door eventually opened he expected to see a wizened old crone clutching a broomstick, but it was actually a plump lady in a pinafore, armed with nothing more sinister than a carpet sweeper.

'Sorry about all that,' she said cheerfully. 'We have to keep the place locked up properly out-of-hours even though there's never anyone about: we've got quite a lot of stock in the cellar and the brewers insist. What can I do for you? We're closed for drinks of course, but I could make you a pot of tea.'

Much impressed by such a friendly reception Charles followed her into the bar. Instead of the usual battered tables and plain wooden benches the tables were highly polished, the seats were comfortably padded and there was even a vase of flowers on the bar.

'I'm just tidying up after last night,' she explained. 'It was the village domino competition – we had quite a crowd in.'

This was not quite the image of Godborough that had been painted by Mrs Boggis, or indeed Mr Juby. Nor was the King's Head an average Norfolk pub. Over a cup of tea and an excellent home-baked scone he learned why. Richard Cattermole and his wife were 'foreigners' from the Surrey commuter belt. Like so many others they had dreamed of a pub in the country, but unlike most of the others they had actually found one. The dream had retained a hold on reality; Mr Cattermole had opened his own office in King's Lynn as an accountant, driving to work through the empty Norfolk countryside instead of the congested South London suburbs, while his wife looked after what trade there was during the day. In the evenings he presided behind the bar while Mrs Cattermole made sandwiches or cooked snacks for whoever wanted them. It had taken time for the villagers to get used to them, but trade was just starting to build up and their latest venture, the domino competition, seemed to have finally broken the ice.

Charles saw the makings of a story here, though it was not the one he had come for. He could see the headline now: 'Newcomers Revitalise Village Pub'.

'So how long has it taken?' he asked, getting out his notebook.

'About six years, getting on for seven,' said Mrs Cattermole – and he put it away again. She smiled: 'Things take a little time to change around here.'

Charles tried another tack. 'Do you get much custom from Tittlesham?'

'None at all,' she said firmly. 'I wouldn't expect to.'

'You know about this Civil War business then?' He reached for his notebook again as a new headline came to mind: 'Descendants of Cromwell's Men Still Boycott King's Head.'

'Oh, that.' She seemed surprised. 'Of course, the brewery warned us about that, but why should they come over here for a drink along all those little lanes when they've got two pubs of their own? I don't think there's much of a story for you there.'

Regretfully he had to agree. He played his final card. 'What about the Black Vicar? Did they tell you about him too?'

Mrs Cattermole nodded. 'They don't talk about him much in the village. We only mentioned it once in the bar, and everybody seemed to go a bit quiet. I think they were quite fond of him really, and they rather resented somebody from Tittlesham getting rid of *their* Vicar.'

'Perhaps they still hanker after a little black magic,' suggested Charles, half-jokingly.

'That's nonsense,' said Mrs Cattermole sharply, a little too sharply, it seemed to Charles. 'It was all a long time ago.' But he remembered her own words: things take a little time to change around here.

'I think I'll take a look at the church anyway. There's always something interesting in these old country churches.'

She did not seem too pleased at the idea. 'There's really nothing up there. Nobody goes near the place, except once a month when the Vicar comes from Tittlesham – and then there's only one or two. I wouldn't waste your time with it – there's nothing there you'd want to put in the paper.'

'I've come this far, I may as well.' The more she protested, the more determined he became to visit the scene of the Black Vicar's activities. 'What's the quickest way up there? Through the wood, I suppose?'

Again Mrs Cattermole seemed anxious to put him off. 'I wouldn't go through Old Jem's Wood if I were you. It may look quicker but the path's overgrown and you may lose your way. If you must go up there, then follow the track around the outside of it. That's the way the Vicar goes. He doesn't like Old Jem's Wood too much – that's not meant for strangers.'

Those six years in God-forsaken Godborough must be having an

61

effect, thought Charles. She's beginning to talk like the locals. But he hastened to reassure her. 'I'll take the track round the wood. It's a nice afternoon – pity not to make the most of the sunshine. I'll leave the car here and walk.'

Mrs Cattermole, looking curiously relieved, followed him to the door. The carpet sweeper was propped beside it, and he was prompted to ask one more question.

'Don't you find it a little boring here all day on your own? There can't be a lot of passing trade – there's nowhere to pass to.'

She smiled a little wistfully. 'It does get lonely sometimes, but I'm hoping we can encourage more people to come and see us. I could do bar snacks at lunchtime and teas in the afternoon – we've got a nice little garden out the back if they'd like to sit outside.' She opened the door for him and they went out into the deserted lane. 'It's a lovely quiet spot for people to get away from things for a while. That's why Richard and I are so happy here; but it would be nice to share it with a few visitors who'd appreciate it.'

'You could always advertise,' he suggested, but she shook her head. 'That's too expensive for a little place like this – and anyway I don't think our neighbours would much appreciate that. They'd think we were trying to turn Godborough Parva into some sort of Yarmouth!'

'I'll spread the word in Toftham anyway,' Charles promised. And if the church yields anything about the Black Vicar, he thought privately, then he would spread the word much wider than that.

He said goodbye and set off along the track towards Old Jem's Wood – whoever Old Jem might be, he thought, and wished he had asked, though Mrs Cattermole had seemed rather touchy on the subject. As he reached the wood the track divided, one fork winding off round the outskirts of the wood, the other disappearing into the trees. He glanced back and saw Mrs Cattermole still watching him from the doorway of the pub. All right, Mrs C, he said to himself, I'll save Old Jem for the walk back, and he waved to her cheerfully before taking the outside path.

He reached the derelict Vicarage first, a gloomy roofless ruin surrounded by a tangle of brambles and nettles which must once have been the garden. He attempted to force a way up the front path but the brambles had grown right across it, and a notice on the front door said firmly: 'Danger. Falling Masonry. Keep Away.' It seemed a good idea.

The churchyard next to the Vicarage looked almost as overgrown as the garden, the gravestones nearly buried among the long grass and the nettles. He thought he could see another grave just outside the dilapidated lychgate, a long shape half-concealed in the undergrowth, but when he looked closer he saw it was made of wood, not stone, and when he cleared away some of the weeds he realised it was a set of stocks, still locked by an ancient padlock covered in years of rust. This must be where Mr Nicholson threatened to put the Black Vicar, Charles recalled. It would take Old Nick himself to budge that padlock now.

As he walked through the churchyard to the porch something flew out past his head. He was relieved to see it was only a martin which had been nesting over the noticeboard. Just one notice was on the board, almost illegible beneath the bird droppings; it confirmed that Holy Communion was celebrated here on the first Sunday of the month by the Vicar of Tittlesham with Godborough Parva.

He pushed the door open. It creaked nosily, as he knew it would. There ought to be bats flying about the ceiling, but there was no sign of life in the church, just signs of death: stones sunk in the floor, cracked memorial tablets on the walls, a dark stained-glass window behind the altar dedicated to someone whose name he could not read. There was an ornate rood screen, a lectern bearing a wooden eagle, some elaborate bench-ends carved with curious beasts and birds. At one time this must have been a very handsome little church, but the plaster was peeling off the walls, there were cobwebs in the roof, the carpet before the altar was frayed and dusty, and the white altar cloth was grey.

He peered into the vestry that opened off the chancel. It was bare and unwelcoming; there were a few flower vases on the floor but none of them showed any sign of recent use. The good folk of Godborough Parva, thought Charles, did not put themselves out too much for their parson from Tittlesham.

But this hardly added up to a story. Neglected churches were unfortunately not uncommon in Norfolk. Hopefully he removed the altar cloth and examined the stone underneath, but there were no signs of bloodstains or knifemarks or even the odd feather. He lifted the carpet too, but if there had been any sinister markings beneath it they had long since been removed. The strange carvings on the bench-ends might have been significant except they had been put there many centuries before the Black Vicar came, by some medieval artist with a taste for the bizarre.

Charles retreated to the doorway and surveyed the empty pews of this sad little church. He realised now why Mrs Cattermole had not wanted him to see it. For anyone hoping to attract tourists to Godborough Parva the church hardly gave much encouragement – and she was probably a little ashamed of its sorry condition. Abruptly he decided that he had had enough of God-forsaken Godborough – and the quickest way back to his car and the road out of the village was straight through Old Jem's Wood.

A path from the churchyard gate led down into the trees, and it was easy to follow it at first, with the sun shining through the branches overhead. Then he came to a choice of tracks and he took what looked like the direct one, but soon it petered out and he had to kick his way through the underbrush, with the trees becoming taller and thicker around him until the sunshine was obscured and it might have been dusk.

He was not too worried. If he kept going downhill, he reasoned, he must emerge near the village in due course. But the wood was certainly a lot denser than he expected and the undergrowth was getting more difficult to force a way through.

Suddenly he stepped into a clearing, with the sunshine lighting it up like a little amphitheatre in the heart of the wood. It made him blink for a moment after the gloom of the trees, and as he paused something brushed against his face. He put his hand up to push it away, thinking it was a dangling branch. But what he touched was soft and feathery and black. It was a dead crow, hanging by the neck.

He ducked and backed away from it, and as he turned he found his face within inches of another. But this one had been dead much longer; little living things were crawling all over it.

Sickened, Charles hurried away from the two corpses into the centre of the clearing, but there was no getting away from the crows. There were a dozen or more, strung up from the trees all around him. And not only crows, there were magpies and other birds he could not identify, and little animals that could have been weasels or stoats. He had heard of children hanging puppies or kittens, but this was much more methodical slaughter, and the bodies had been hung at regular intervals around the clearing, as if guarding it against intruders.

As the full extent of his discovery dawned upon him there was a violent rustling in the undergrowth just behind him. It was too much. He made a dive for a gap between the dangling birds and found himself on a path leading straight down the hill. Surprisingly it was not at all overgrown; and it led directly down to the fork where he had waved to Mrs Cattermole.

He came out into the sunshine almost gasping with relief. Below him, outside the King's Head, he saw her sweeping the front doorstep; he had no doubt she had been waiting there for his return. He pulled himself together and walked down to her.

'That's quite a wood you've got there,' he said, a little coldly. 'Very strange decorations on the trees, for instance. No wonder you didn't want me to go in there.'

She shrugged quietly. 'They're Old Jem's birds,' she said. 'They don't do anybody any harm, but they don't look too pretty, I know. I'm sorry.'

'Pretty? They're disgusting.' Charles blushed at the memory of his flight from the clearing, but at least he had not imagined all those dangling corpses. 'What's going on in that wood? Something very nasty by the look of it. Your Black Vicar would be proud of Old Jem, whoever Old Jem might be. Perhaps he was one of his assistants in the old days.'

Mrs Cattermole looked at him in astonishment. 'Old Jem? He's never been near the church since he was christened, I shouldn't think. What on earth are you talking about?'

'That clearing in the wood, and those dead things hanging all round it, all neatly spaced out, like some sort of ritual. It's eerie enough in the daytime. It must be really weird at night. That's when this sort of thing goes on, isn't it?'

Her astonishment changed to comprehension. And much to Charles's discomfiture, Mrs Cattermole started to laugh. 'You reckon Old Jem's been up to a little black magic in that wood? Now he'd really love to hear that! Old Jem the Black Magician of God-forsaken Godborough . . .' She couldn't stop laughing.

'So who is he, then? And what's he doing with those crows?' Charles was getting very exasperated.

'Why, he's Mr Nicholson's gamekeeper of course. That's where he breeds his pheasants. Didn't you see any of them?' He remembered the commotion in the undergrowth. 'He hangs up the crows and the magpies and the like to scare off the others from taking the eggs. I'm told it's an old gamekeeper's trick in this part of the world. Maybe he reckons they keep trespassers away from his pheasants too. I must say it seems to work!' And she started laughing again, so heartily and with so little malice that Charles had to join in too – though he realised he had lost another good story.

'If you'll stretch a point over the licensing hours,' said Charles at last, 'I could really do with a beer. And I'm going to get some news out of Godborough Parva, even without the Black Vicar and Old Jem and the Civil War.' He took out his notebook again, and this time he kept it out.

'Now then, about that dominoes competition. I'll take the names of the winners . . .'

FIVE

'Oooh!' cried Anthea ecstatically. 'Charles, you look lovely.'

'I suppose it's not too bad,' he conceded, blushing slightly. And indeed the white tie and tails made him look quite dashing. He had come into the office to show off his borrowed plumage before setting off for the hunt ball, and Anthea was enormously impressed.

'Just like Fred Astaire,' she sighed. 'You have exactly the right figure for it.'

'Sort of weedy, you mean?' He saw her expression change and went on hastily. 'This collar's a bit of a killer. Every time I turn my head it feels as if it's sawing it off.' He had had quite a battle getting it on at all, with the studs refusing to penetrate the stiffly-starched holes, but he had won in the end, and the thumb-mark he had left behind in the struggle was fortunately concealed beneath the bow. The waistcoat had also presented a challenge. Every waistcoat he had previously encountered did up at the front; this one had to be fastened together at the back. The intricate network of straps and braces was concealed now beneath the tailcoat, but he was very conscious of all the fastenings around his waist and shoulders. He was convinced that one sudden movement could dislodge something vital and the whole complicated ensemble would collapse around his feet.

'You be careful with all that fancy gear, boy. Thass all got to go back tomorrow.' Mr Juby had come down from his office and was eying his protegé critically. 'You spill anything on that shirtfront, you'll have to pay to get it cleaned. And don't forget what they said at the shop: if you can show off that label on the inside pocket, that'll please them a treat.'

The label said: 'On Hire from Ace Clothiers, Norwich', and Charles had absolutely no intention of allowing anyone the merest glimpse of it. Ace Clothiers did hire out suits without this tell-tale label, but they allowed a slight discount on those which bore it, and Mr Juby always liked a bargain.

'Now listen,' he told Charles as he brushed a few specks off his shoulders. 'I only got Norwich to pay for all this squit by telling 'em you were going to write one of your hooman interest articles about the gentry up at the Hall, so make sure you find something civil to say about them. I know you don't get on too well with 'em normally.'

'That's not true. It's the butlers I don't get on with.' The memory still rankled of his first visit to Remingham Hall on his old delivery bike to enquire about a burglary, when Lord Remingham's butler had advised him to use the tradesmen's entrance. At least he couldn't do that tonight.

'I was thinking of that young Henry Burton, that lad of Lord Burton's. There weren't no love lost there, as I recall.' Mr Juby chuckled, and Charles could only shrug in agreement. Henry Burton had been one of Rebecca's suitors and he had always considered him an obnoxious young snob, but their paths had rarely crossed since Rebecca had become engaged to a fellow student in Newcastle and disappeared from the Norfolk scene.

'He's not exactly typical. At least, I hope not.' Charles straightened his tie a little belligerently. 'If they're all like that tonight I'll leave them to it and you can try and get your money back.'

'No, you stick it out, boy. It'll be an education for you.' Mr Juby gave him a congratulatory pat on the back. 'Tonight you're the society correspondent of the *Toftham and Wettleford Journal*; you mind you don't disgrace yourself.' He pointed him towards the door. 'Now let's get our moneysworth out of that monkey-suit. You come over to the Dog and Partridge and give 'em all a good laugh.'

Charles drove the Vibrator through the massive gateway of Remingham Hall and followed the stream of cars up the drive. He was glad of the couple of pints he had had with Mr Juby; he felt less intimidated by the long queue of gleaming limousines, most of them driven by uniformed chauffeurs. He had given the old Vauxhall a dust-down to get rid of the worst of the mud, but if he removed too much he knew that pieces of mudguard would start falling off. As it was, the front bumper had come loose on the way from Toftham and it was rattling noisily above the usual thumps and groans of the engine.

A team of estate workers were ushering the cars into neat rows on the grass beside the drive, just before it broadened out in front of the Hall itself. That semi-circle of immaculate gravel was presumably reserved for the more important guests. There had been rumours that one of the Royals might be coming over from Sandringham; in fact that was one of the arguments that Mr Juby had put to the office in Norwich. 'Can't have a Royal there with no one to keep an eye on 'em. Suppose they take a drop too much and fall down the stairs?'

Charles followed the directions of a grizzled figure in tweed jacket and highly polished brown gaiters, and parked the Vibrator cautiously beside a splendid Rolls-Bentley. He huddled in the driving seat with his head well down as the occupants climbed out, the men in hunting pink, the women in long dresses and furs in spite of the mild evening. They cast amused glances at the dilapidated Vauxhall, but Charles hoped they could not see who was in it.

As they moved away towards the Hall somebody tapped on the car window. 'You can get out now, sir.' And the grizzled man in gaiters opened the door. 'It's Mr Benson, isn't it?'

Charles straightened up, blushing, and admitted that it was.

'Thass a rare good piece you wrote about Cousin Herbert and the gal Aggie. You found out things about them we never knew ourselves. You must ha' got along with 'em hully well together.' He helped Charles out of the car. 'I put that writin' o' yours in the family scrapbook to keep for the little 'uns.'

It was a moment for Charles to treasure. Readers of the Journal rarely expressed any approval of his efforts, they only contacted him if he had got something wrong. 'You must be an Eke, then?' he enquired, but it was a pretty safe bet in Remingham, even without the mention of Herbert and Aggie's golden wedding.

'Thass right. I'm Nelson Eke. I'm one of his lordship's game-keepers when I hent parkin' cars.' Nelson leaned towards him and lowered his voice. 'You need a good bird during the season, you let me know and I'll see what I can do.'

Charles thanked him, and surveyed the elegant couples walking towards the Hall. It was another sort of bird he could do with tonight, he thought wistfully. But he was relieved that he had found an ally in this alien world.

'Would you happen to know if any of the Royals are coming over from Sandringham tonight?' If anyone knew, he suspected, it would be someone like Nelson Eke.

The gamekeeper pursed his lips. 'Not for me to say, really. But I did see a couple o' young fellers in city suits ferretin' round the grounds this afternoon. That might mean suffin'.'

'That might indeed.' Charles had covered enough local visits by the Royals to know that discreet young men in city suits checked out the venues first. He had no great hopes of seeing a royal somersault down the stairs, but just a royal presence was enough to justify the suit. He thanked Nelson and headed for the Hall.

At the top of the broad stone steps leading to the open front doors he paused to look back at the vista which Lord Remingham enjoyed from his porch. The drive stretched away through the parkland to the distant entrance gates, past the ornamental lake which had been created by a much earlier Lord Remingham to improve the view. He had also demolished the servants' cottages which had stood inside the park and moved them into new homes beyond the gates so that they no longer cluttered the landscape. Charles remembered Mr Juby telling him about it.

'Nice noo cottages they went into, better'n the ones they moved out of, no doubt, but nobody asked 'em if they wanted to go, and they finished up with a mile extra to walk to work.' And he had added darkly: 'His Lordship hent as drastic as that these days, but he still owns the whole village, along with a lot more o' this part of Norfolk, and he still employs most of the people who work there. He can get rid of 'em any time he like. It's still a foodal society once you get out into the country areas, Charlie boy, make no mistake about that.'

Standing on the steps of Remingham Hall, Charles needed no convincing. There was the park with the rows of gleaming cars, and behind him, through the open doors, was the vast entrance hall where the guests were sipping their champagne, the light from the massive central chandelier sparkling on the glasses and the jewellery. It all seemed a million miles from the farmers' bar.

'Your name, sir?' He turned to the door and found a lofty figure with shiny black hair was ushering him in. Charles recognised him immediately; it was the awful butler.

'It's all right, I've got a ticket,' he said defensively, and thrust it towards him. The butler raised a disdainful hand.

'I'm sure you have, sir. I just require your name to announce you.' And he gestured towards the reception line in the hall.

Charles blushed. 'Benson,' he mumbled. The butler leaned forward enquiringly and he repeated it more loudly. 'Charles Benson.'

The butler bowed graciously; a little too graciously. 'Would that be Sir Charles Benson, sir? Or Lord Benson, perhaps?'

Charles caught the mocking glint in his eye, and realised that the recognition had been mutual. The butler must have remembered his previous visit on the old delivery bike and was not going to let him forget it. But Charles had learned a lot from Mr Juby since then on how to cope with officious butlers. The two pints in the farmers' bar were quite a help too.

'You know very well I'm Charles Benson from the Journal,' he said sharply. 'Now what's your name?'

The butler looked a little startled. 'I'm Harcourt, sir. I'm the butler.'

'What Harcourt?' demanded Charles, producing a pen and scribbling on the back of his ticket. 'Fred Harcourt? Sid Harcourt?'

'Just Harcourt, sir. That is quite sufficient.'

'Very well, Mr Harcourt. How long have you been in Lord Remingham's employ?' Charles found himself imitating the crisp, authoritative radio voice of Quentin Milton. It seemed to work. The butler answered more civilly.

'Twenty-eight years, sir. I came here as a pantry-boy.' He coughed. 'Why do you need to know, sir?'

Charles did not reply immediately, but finished writing on the ticket. Then he surveyed the butler with as much loftiness as he could muster. 'It's always useful to have this kind of background information. I never know when I may need it. Now you had better go ahead and announce me; we're holding up the queue.' He turned away from Harcourt and started to walk towards the reception line, feeling very pleased with himself.

'Now, now, Benson, you mustn't bully poor Harcourt. He's only doing his job.'

He recognised the sardonic voice behind him and his elation evaporated. He must have made rather a fool of himself in front of the Honourable Henry Burton.

'And I'm only doing mine, Mr Burton,' he retorted, and immediately felt like a rookie policeman trying to hand out a parking ticket. He glared at Burton's immaculate evening suit, the snowy white waistcoat, the ruby shirt-studs, the hand-tied white tie, and felt his own network of straps and braces rubbing against his back. It is at this sort of moment, he thought, that something will snap and the whole lot will fall apart.

'May I suggest you do it at a rather more convenient time, then? It would be quite pleasant to get in out of the draught.' Henry Burton indicated his companion, a ravishing blonde who had already removed her fur wrap to reveal an expanse of bare arms and shoulders above a plunging neckline. She gave him an icy smile. Its iciness had little to do with the draught, and Charles blushed again.

'Yes, of course.' As he clumsily stuffed his invitation back into the inside pocket of his jacket the 'On Hire' label became clearly visible. Henry Burton and the blonde did not need to say anything, they just looked at the label, and then at each other, and then at the ceiling.

Harcourt, probably unintentionally, came to his rescue. 'Mr Charles Benson,' he announced, and Charles felt himself propelled gently towards the reception line. The only face he recognised was the host, Lord Remingham.

'Evening, Burton, hope you enjoy the evening. Have you met the Master?' He ushered him towards his neighbour, a splendid figure in hunting pink, who in turn ushered him towards his wife. She ushered him towards the Deputy Master, and the Deputy Master ushered him towards *his* wife. It all happened with the smoothness and precision of a car conveyor belt. Carried along with the others in the queue he shook each hand, mumbled incoherent greetings to each unknown face, then thankfully accepted a glass of champagne from the waiter hovering at the end of the line. At least he had not tripped over, or sneezed, or exposed his 'On Hire' label again.

His relief must have been obvious. 'Have another, sir,' said the waiter sympathetically, and he did. Maybe the evening was on the turn.

He was content at first to lurk in the hallway, watching Henry Burton have long conversations with the reception party while the guests behind him fidgetted impatiently. Then, with his third glass of champagne, he ambled into the main ballroom, where the older guests were dancing sedately to foxtrots and waltzes; and with his fourth glass he strolled nonchalantly up the imposing staircase to another vast chamber where a much noisier band was playing the latest hits and the younger set were disporting themselves energetically around the floor. He gathered from the conversations around him that this was popularly known as the Debs' Room, and there actually seemed to be some unescorted girls in little groups, chatting among themselves.

Maybe, he thought, as he grasped a cocktail sausage in one hand and the fifth champagne in the other, maybe the evening is going to be an astonishing success after all. He did not even worry particularly when the sausage fell off its stick as he attempted to bite it, and dropped onto the carpet at his feet. Without hesitation he side-kicked it under a chair.

'You should be playing for the Canaries.' Again the voice behind him was familiar, but this time he felt disbelief instead of dismay, because this was a very different voice from Henry Burton's. It was warm, and friendly, and definitely female. He turned and stared into the deep blue eyes. After six years the hair was cut shorter and the figure was attractively fuller, but nothing else had changed.

72

'You've still got the freckles, then,' he said inanely, and Rebecca smiled and nodded. 'And Harry Hurn still cuts your hair far too short,' she responded, and he smiled and nodded too. Smiling and nodding was about all he felt capable of. This was the first time he had seen her since the party at the Old Rectory when she had announced her engagement.

Automatically, he tried to observe the niceties and held out his hand. He realised it was holding the champagne glass and tried to transfer it to his other hand, but that was still holding the cocktail stick. It seemed logical to drain the glass before disposing of it on a nearby table, and the cocktail stick followed the sausage under the chair. Now unencumbered, he politely shook her hand and tried to think of something intelligent to say.

'It's good to see you,' was all he could come up with.

'You too,' said Rebecca. 'I'm glad you were able to come.'

'You knew I'd been invited?' As he asked, he had an inkling what the answer might be, but it seemed too good to be true.

'Daddy arranged an invitation for you. He thought it might be rather a nice idea.' Dr Bateman, Charles now recalled, was honorary medical officer to the Mid-Norfolk Foxhounds. But the doctor had never thought it would be rather a nice idea before. The inkling was confirmed; she must have put him up to it. But he was still mystified.

'What about you? When did you come back to Norfolk?' For the first time he glanced at her left hand. She was wearing a couple of rings, but none on the fourth finger.

'I've been back a few weeks now, but I haven't got around to seeing anybody yet. Daddy thought this might be a good opportunity to, well, mingle, I suppose.'

'Mingle?' Charles repeated the word with a certain distaste. It really had been Dr Bateman's idea, then, not Rebecca's, and he had been invited along as a mingle-ee. 'You shouldn't have any problems mingling with this lot.' He gestured towards the groups of girls around the walls and the exuberant dancers on the floor. Henry Burton, he noted, was well to the fore. 'You've got a right lot of minglers here.'

'Now don't start that again, as soon as we meet.' She frowned slightly. 'I know you never got on with Henry and the others, but they're really quite reasonable people.'

The only real row they had had, Charles recalled, was when he had complained about her 'county' friends, who seemed to have even less time for him than he had for them. He had done it wrong again.

'I'm sorry, you're quite right. I should have grown out of all that by now. But why haven't you been out mingling before?'

'It's a little difficult to explain.' She hesitated, and as a waiter passed with another tray of champagne Charles took a couple of glasses. 'Don't talk about it now if you don't want to. It's good to see you anyway.' He handed her one of the glasses. 'Cheers, Beccy.'

That's my fifth, he thought, as they both sipped their glasses. To hell with it; now I'm going to stop counting.

The band had launched into a leisurely Sinatra number, and couples were shuffling slowly round the floor, sometimes so slowly that any movement was imperceptible. The lights had dimmed. It might be worth a try.

'You'll remember I'm a rotten dancer, but I can walk very slowly forwards, if you don't mind walking very slowly backwards!'

She smiled. 'I suppose that's one way to mingle,' she agreed, and they moved onto the crowded floor. Charles put a tentative arm around her, they started shuffling very slowly round the room, and as they shuffled – and mingled – her story gradually came out.

The first year of the engagement, when they were finishing their degrees at Newcastle, was a halcyon time of parties, studying, and more parties. They both scraped through with second-class PPEs – philosophy, politics and economics – but while Rebecca wanted to find a job her fiancé only wanted to return to the family estate in Northumberland. His father offered him the Dower House and a share in managing the estate; her role would be junior lady of the manor. His family disapproved of working wives.

Rebecca was still determined to make use of her degree if she could, but in the weeks before the wedding she soon discovered that vacancies in rural Northumberland for postgraduate philosophers or embryo economists were thin on the ground; there was certainly no scope for a potential politician in a community almost as 'foodal' as Norfolk. She gave up the search, resigned herself to a life of elegant leisure in the Dower House, and hoped for the best.

The best failed to materialise. It became apparent that her husband did what he was told by his parents, and his parents had only two things to tell him. He must take over the estate when his father died, and she must produce an heir to take over after that. He spent most of his time around the tenant farms, she spent most of hers at coffee mornings and afternoon teas, or fending off heavy hints from her in-laws. Boredom and resentment led to friction, then antipathy, and finally open warfare. Seeing the danger signs she determined there would be no children involved, and that made matters worse. Separation became inevitable.

Rather than return to her parents, who knew nothing of the growing rift, she spent a couple of abortive months in Newcastle searching for a job, but Newcastle was already well supplied with PPE graduates and she was forced to admit defeat again. She told them the whole story, and came back to Remingham. Since then she had stayed at home and kept away from her old friends. Until tonight.

She told him all this in a matter-of-fact way as they edged through the throng of other couples, and she often had to pause and wave cheerfully as somebody recognised her and shouted a greeting, but the closing stages of the story must have been painfully fresh, and when he heard a slight catch in her voice Charles instinctively held her closer. She immediately pulled away.

'I don't think that was quite Daddy's idea when he suggested inviting you,' she said gently. 'He always considered you a rather well-behaved young man.' She smiled at him. 'And so did I. That's why I agreed to come. I knew you'd understand.'

'You mean I'd know when the mingling had to stop?' He was not sure whether to feel gratified or disappointed.

'Well, you'd know better than, say, him!' She nodded across the room towards Henry Burton, who was closely intertwined with his ravishing blonde. He spotted her over the blonde's shoulder, and after a momentary look of surprise he nodded enthusiastically back. Charles scowled and steered Rebecca in the opposite direction, towards the door.

'In that case I think I ought to escort you for the rest of the evening, just to make sure you don't have to over-mingle. It's the least I can do for Dr Bateman.' And he led her towards the nearest wine waiter.

The rest of the evening passed for Charles in a happy blur. The champagne seemed inexhaustible, he coped with the buffet with enormous aplomb, and when they danced again he seemed to move on air. At some stage Rebecca took him to meet Dr and Mrs Bateman in the more sedate surroundings of the lower ballroom, and they both seemed pleased to see him. Henry Burton, happily, was fully occupied with his blonde and did not cross their path again. They talked inconsequentially of nothing in particular, and Charles did not get back to more personal topics until they found themselves sitting on the stairs in the early hours, eating platefuls of eggs and bacon and drinking black coffee.

The temperature of the Hall had risen considerably during the evening, and some of the younger men had removed their tailcoats and ties, but Charles kept his firmly in place, conscious of the telltale label on the inside pocket, the unlovely assortment of straps and braces round his back, and the thumbmark under the bow. Not even the champagne had made him forget all that. So he sat on the stairs in a rosy glow brought on by the heat, the champagne, and a confusion of emotions.

'What do you plan to do now?' he asked as they sipped their coffee. 'Are you going to look for a job somewhere else?'

She shook her head. 'I've had enough of that for a while. I just want to stay out of the way in Remingham and try to get back to normal, while the lawyers sort something out. As far as I'm concerned, Norfolk is going to be good enough for me in future.' She looked at him a little quizzically. 'It's obviously good enough for you too, or you wouldn't still be here.'

'Ah,' said Charles, remembering his BBC application. Norfolk had certainly not been good enough of late, but tonight it looked a lot more attractive. Here was another complication, just when he thought he had made up his mind.

'I've enjoyed Norfolk enormously, but I think I'll have to make a move some time,' he said cautiously.

'What on earth for?' She seemed genuinely surprised. 'You're well settled into a good job, it's a lovely area to work in – and Mr Juby can't go on for ever.' She was voicing the arguments he had gone through so often already, and doing so with considerable conviction. It sounds as though she wants me to stay, he thought. That would be the most convincing argument of all.

'We'll have to see. I don't think I want to stay in Toftham indefinitely. It might be an idea to try something different.'

'That's what I did,' said Rebecca bitterly. 'Look what happened to me.'

'It's not quite the same thing.' There seemed little similarity between joining the Northumbrian aristocracy and joining the BBC. Though on second thoughts . . .

Dr Bateman came up the stairs, carrying a wrap. 'Time we were going, Beccy. Good of you to look after her, Charles.'

Rebecca smiled at him too as they got up. 'Yes, thank you, Charles. I've had a lovely evening.'

'When can I see you again?' he asked quickly.

'Do you mind waiting until I contact you?' She could see his disappointment. 'I still have things to think through; it all takes a little time.'

He nodded reluctantly. 'I could drive you home,' he offered, but it was clear Dr Bateman had other plans, and Rebecca was already putting on her wrap. 'This,' she said gently, 'is where the mingling has to stop.' She kissed him quickly on the cheek, Dr Bateman shook his hand, and the two of them started down the stairs.

'By the way,' said Rebecca, turning for a moment, 'I love that label. An Ace Clothier for an ace reporter. Very clever.' She waved, and was gone.

Charles lingered to drink another large coffee, then made his way out of the Hall and down to the dwindling lines of cars. Dawn was just beginning to silhouette the trees in the park, and there was enough light to see the ramshackle outline of the Vibrator among the sleek monsters around it. He headed for it cheerfully and stood beside it with the door open for a few moments, to make sure everyone knew it was his. He bowed graciously as some of the other guests went by, and when he saw Henry Burton and the blonde climbing into an E-type Jaguar in the row behind him he took out the Vibrator's starting-handle and raised it in mock salute.

As he did so the gaitered figure of Nelson Eke appeared beside him. Judging by the ruddy glow of his cheeks, reminiscent of Mr Juby after a couple of specials, Charles guessed that not all the champagne had got as far as the guests.

'Everything all right, Mr Benson?'

'Absolutely splendid, Nelson. Couldn't be better.'

Nelson looked rather surprised. 'Thought you'd be disappointed, with no Royals turning up. Must have changed their minds, I suppose – or maybe those smart young fellers in the city suits found suffin' nasty in the flowerbeds.'

Charles had completely forgotten about the Royals. He had also forgotten he was supposed to be writing a 'hooman interest' story about the ball. He had found more than his share of human interest that evening, but not for general publication. He had a sudden inspiration.

'Tell you what, Nelson, I wasn't really interested in the Royals. I was hoping to get your memories of these hunt balls: how this one compares with those before the war, perhaps, or something about the guests who used to come here.'

'Never mind the last war, I remember before the Great War.' Nelson leaned comfortably against the bonnet of the Vibrator. 'I was a lad then, working in the stables. Used to hold the horses' heads while all the grand folk got out their carriages. The whole village gathered by the gates to see them drive in, all in their oldest clothes and lookin' rare miserable, they did, so they might get an odd copper thrown to 'em.' Charles listened, entranced. 'Then up here at the Big House, while their lordships and their ladyships were dancing away in the ballroom, their servants would be drinking ale down in the kitchen with the maids, and the footmen would be picking up little bits o' tittle-tattle upstairs and coming down to tell 'em, and they'd pass it on to the grooms, and us lads would be in the stables listening to the grooms telling each other, and adding little bits extra. Some rare tales I heard in those days, Mr Benson, tales you wouldn't believe if you read 'em in the papers.'

Charles reached for his notebook and sat down contentedly on the running-board.

'Try me, Nelson,' he said.

'HUNT BALLS OF YESTERYEAR: THE VIEW FROM THE SERVANTS' HALL' filled the entire centre page in the Journal that Friday. Charles had written a few words about his own impressions as an introduction, gently implying that those who attended hunt balls had not changed much in their behaviour over the years, then he had set out Nelson Eke's memories of his boyhood encounters with the gentry. He had toned down some of the more lurid stories and disguised some of the names, but they still made good reading.

It did occur to him that Lord Remingham might take exception to his gamekeeper reminiscing so freely, but he had been careful to omit any anecdotes about the Reminghams themselves, and when he checked with Nelson later on Friday morning he was relieved to learn that his lordship had apparently been having a good chuckle over the Journal at the breakfast-table. That piece of information had come down to Nelson via Harcourt and the kitchen staff, just as it always had.

At lunch-time Mr Juby took him across to the Dog and Partridge for a celebratory drink. The evening dress had been safely returned to the Ace Clothiers, after the grease from the running-board had been sponged off by Anthea. Charles did not know it, but she had first checked the shirtfront and collar for lipstick; her failure to find any accounted for her willingness to deal with the grease.

'You got Nelson going with those tales of his,' said Mr Juby over his first special. 'That weren't quite what I was expecting but you did well to find suffin to write about, with no Royals there an' all. That suit were money well spent, I reckon.' He paused and gazed into his glass. 'I hope you reckon so too, Charlie boy. I do hear you had a very convivial evenin' with the gal Beccy.'

Charles grinned complacently. 'You do hear correctly, Mr Juby. As always.'

'Well, I knew she were back home, o' course, but I didn't reckon she'd go dancin' for a while. Had a very bad time with that feller up North, so they say.'

Charles stopped grinning. 'Do they really? And who's "they"?'

My Juby chuckled. 'Now, now, boy, you hent the only one can hear an odd tale or two below stairs. Remember all those waiters around when you and Beccy were dancin' and she were talkin' her head off to you? Course you remember them; you kept 'em hully busy, by all accounts.'

Charles blushed. Mr Juby's knowledge of his activities and conversations was as comprehensive as ever. And there was more to come.

'That were a nice idea of Dr Bateman to get you two t'gether. Maybe you'll feel a little more settled now.'

'Settled?' This was something quite new from the Juby data bank. 'What makes you think I'm unsettled, then?'

'Thass obvious, boy, hent it.' Mr Juby put down his glass and turned to face Charles. 'Mopin' about the place the way you do, waiting for the post to come, then mopin' again after it's been. I reckoned when you wanted another look at that *World's Press News* you was planning to go for the BBC job. You hent ever wanted to look at it before, and thass the only thing in it might interest you.'

Charles was not too surprised that Mr Juby knew about his application, but he was a little hurt at his lack of concern. 'You don't seem very bothered about it.'

'Well o' course I'm bothered.' Mr Juby turned back to his special. 'I spent a lot o' time knocking some sense into you all these years; thass a pity if I have to start all over again with some other young fule from the city. But you bin here long enough to know if you want to stay or not, and if you don't want to, then thass best you do go, boy. You just need to make up your mind, then you bide by it. Thass no good ditherin' and flatherin' about like some daft owld mawther.' The accent had thickened; Mr Juby obviously felt more deeply about Charles's possible departure than he liked to admit.

'That's not entirely up to me. I've done my bit. It's up to the BBC now. And they've hung about so long I should think they've got somebody else by now.' And he wouldn't be all that sorry, he added to himself privately. Rebecca's return had rather changed the situation.

Mr Juby shook his head. 'They'd have written and told you if they don't want you, boy. Very polite they are at the BBC, so I hear tell.' He drained his glass. 'Come on, Charlie, drink up and have another, I reckon you're still in there with a chance.'

And once again Mr Juby was right. Next morning a letter arrived inviting Charles to present himself at Broadcasting House for a written test and a trial recording, prior to possible interview by the Appointments Board at a later date. The cost of the rail fare (second class) would be refunded, together with any other reasonable expenses incurred, in accordance with the enclosed scale.

The mills of the British Broadcasting Corporation were beginning to grind.

SIX

Charles paused on the pavement as the office workers jostled past him, and gazed up at the forbidding frontage of Broadcasting House. It loomed over him like the blunt prow of a great stone ship, with the carving of an elderly gentleman and a small boy in place of a figurehead over the doors. This was the citadel he had come to conquer, he mused, an Aladdin's cave of unknown terrors and delights. It could be a yawning cavern into which he disappeared without a trace, or the gateway to fame, fortune and a two-thirds pension after forty years' service.

As the metaphors grew wilder a sturdily-built, middle-aged man in a smart blue blazer and regimental tie came out through the doors and stopped briefly beside him. 'Ugly-looking pile, isn't it?' The voice was deep, slightly husky, and unmistakeable. 'But if you're really pushed, it's not a bad place to make a living.' He walked off down Regent Street, leaving Charles grinning inanely after him, much gratified that he had been spoken to by Jack de Manio, already well-established as a popular national figure after two years on his breakfast-time programme. Feeling a lot bolder he went in through the swing doors and made for the reception desk, hoping for more encounters with famous folk on the way.

Nobody took the slightest notice of him. Nor indeed did the ladies behind the desk, who were much engaged with telephones, clipboards and message pads. He tried to contain his growing impatience as the moments ticked away. His train had been late and he had just five minutes before his appointment for the written test and trial recording. Three of them had passed before one of the ladies came off the phone and he managed to catch her eye. With some relief he explained who he was.

The relief was soon dispelled. 'You're in the wrong place, Mr Benson. Just take a seat while I find a commissionaire to take you.'

'How far do I have to go?' asked Charles, now close to panic.

'You'll be all right. They always get you here much too early.' But Charles was not convinced. The day was obviously doomed.

'This way, sir.' The burly, uniformed figure led him back through the doors into the street, and they waited on the kerb by a pedestrian crossing as the traffic roared past, with Charles getting more and more jumpy.

'Shouldn't they stop for us?' he demanded at last.

'They will, sir, they will,' the commissionaire assured him, with the calm of a man who was quite content to stand at pedestrian crossings all day, if need be, or at least until the end of his shift. Charles looked at his watch and could wait no longer. He stepped out onto the crossing.

The effect was dramatic. Tyres squealed, brakes screamed, drivers shouted, and the long line of traffic in Portland Place came to a shuddering halt. Charles's first instinct was to leap back on the pavement, but the commissionaire, acting on his behalf, raised two eloquent fingers towards the nearest drivers, gave Charles a gentle shove, and followed him in triumph across the road.

'Do you do that sort of thing often, sir?' he asked admiringly as they reached the far kerb.

'If necessary,' said Charles as crisply as he could, trying to keep the quaver out of his voice. He had quite forgotten how terrifying the London traffic could be.

They went into an anonymous-looking building opposite Broadcasting House. Only a discreet plaque beside the door indicated that this was BBC property. Glancing along the row of buildings before he entered, Charles noticed that most of the other front doors bore plaques too. The Corporation seemed to own quite a substantial slice of Marylebone.

His guide handed him over to a colleague behind the desk, who ticked his name off on quite a lengthy list. 'Was that you who caused all that excitement outside, sir?' Charles confessed that it was. 'That really showed 'em, sir. Very impressive that was. Sir Greville thought so too. He was just coming in the door at the time; he had quite a laugh.'

'Sir Greville?' enquired Charles. 'Don't tell me he's after this job too?'

'Not exactly.' The commissionaire grinned appreciatively at the thought. 'Sir Greville is the chairman of the Appointments Board. You may get to see him in due course. But for the moment, sir, please follow me.'

As they walked along the corridor Charles looked at his watch apprehensively. 'Don't you worry, sir,' said his escort, just as the receptionist had done in Broadcasting House. 'They always get you here too early. It allows a little time for holding up the traffic, and suchlike . . .'

He opened the door at the end of the corridor, into what looked like a dentist's waiting-room. Chairs lined the walls, most of them already occupied. A large table in the centre was piled with magazines. Cardboard cups were everywhere.

Charles surveyed the dozen or so occupants of the room, who glanced up at him briefly before returning to their conversations or their magazines. 'Are these all for the same vacancies?' he muttered to the commissionaire.

'This is today's batch, sir. We had the first lot yesterday, and there's some more tomorrow. Seems a popular sort of job you're all after.'

Charles nodded gloomily. 'It does indeed.'

'Make yourself at home, sir. There's still a fair time to wait. I'll get you some coffee.'

Charles selected an early number of *The Listener* from the table – at least it made a change from *Punch* – and took a seat in the corner, where he could survey the opposition. Some of the applicants obviously knew each other and were chatting over their coffees. Others had brought their own reading matter, and a couple were combining their efforts on a crossword. All of them looked enormously confident and calm.

He retreated behind his *Listener* and mentally reviewed the preparations he had gone through for the test; they already seemed hopelessly inadequate. The written paper, he assumed, was some sort of general knowledge exam – 'wide knowledge of current affairs', the advertisement had said – so he had spent all his spare moments in Toftham Public Library, poring over every newspaper and magazine he could find. He realised now, with a sinking heart, that the reports and articles he had read were probably written by the people in this room. None of them looked as if the previous evening's assignment had been the annual general meeting of the Tittlesham & District Bowls League.

'I think you should have read that page by now. If your arm's gone numb I can turn it over for you.'

His next-door neighbour was looking at him solemnly over a pair of rimless glasses. Charles blushed and shook his head. 'Nice of you to offer, but I think I can manage. Do we have much longer to wait?'

'I gather from one of the chaps who was here yesterday that they allow about half-an-hour's grace for latecomers. Apparently some people have to get here from way out in the sticks. But I thought I'd better be here on time, just in case they've changed the system overnight. My name's Dickie Johnson – Extel.'

'Charles Benson.' He paused and grinned. 'From way out in the sticks. Norfolk, actually.'

Dickie Johnson grinned too. 'Sorry about that. It's just that these jobs seem to go mostly to Fleet Street chaps, or some high flier from the universities. I'm glad they're spreading their net a bit wider.'

Charles was not sure whether to feel encouraged or depressed. He decided not to think about it. 'It's nice to meet someone from Exchange Telegraph after all these years. I'm one of your local stringers, but we don't get much to send the national agencies from Toftham.' He automatically pronounced it 'Tarf'm', and the agency man smiled.

'You'll have to go easy on the Norfolk accent up here. I know Wilfred Pickles gets away with that sort of thing reading the news, but they don't seem to like it from reporters.'

'I'll remember to stick to standard Wembley Park English,' Charles promised. 'Thanks for reminding me.' He looked round the rest of the room. 'What about all these chaps? Are they all from London?'

Dickie glanced round too. 'Yes, I think so. That's Henry Blackman from the *Guardian*, and next to him is Giles Bellinger from *The Times*.' He named some of the others as well, and Charles recognised some of the bylines in the newspapers he had studied so carefully. He had feared as much.

'But I shouldn't let that worry you,' said Dickie as he ended the list. 'I know at least two of them have broad Cockney accents, and I think that chap in the far corner has got quite a bad stutter when he gets rattled. They should fall at the first fence.'

A middle-aged woman in a smart blouse and skirt walked briskly into the room, carrying the inevitable clipboard. All conversation stopped.

'Good morning, gentlemen. Thank you all for attending. Would you please answer your names.' She called the roll and paused only once, when the applicant sitting in the far corner had some difficulty with 'P-p-present'. She looked at him sharply and made a note by his name. 'Told you so,' murmured Dickie. 'Hasn't even reached the first fence.'

'Follow me, please.' She led the way at a lively pace to another room set out with individual tables and chairs. On each table was a pile of blank paper and, to Charles's surprise, a typewriter. She marshalled them into the chairs and stood before them.

'This will be quite straightforward. We would like you to write a report on any news story you have covered in recent weeks. Not more than a thousand words, double spacing, one side of the paper only. You

84

have exactly one hour. Then we shall ask you to record your reports in the studios next door.'

Charles was flabbergasted. This was not what he had expected at all. The others, however, were quietly inserting the first sheets of paper into their typewriters, and Dickie Johnson was already hammering the keys. No doubt the Fleet Street candidates knew all about this procedure from those who had done it before, but not even Mr Juby had been able to get word of it in Toftham.

He gazed at his typewriter and desperately reviewed his most recent contributions to the *Toftham & Wettleford Journal*. The Tittlesham and District Bowls League hardly seemed appropriate; nor did the two funerals he had attended the previous afternoon. His mind went blank.

All the other typewriters were now in action. No doubt, thought Charles, dramatic stories are unfolding of international air disasters or wars or famines, of political coups or industrial unrest, and while they are writing about Harold Macmillan and Hugh Gaitskell I am stuck with Len Cloppett and Harry Hurn. But the names reminded him that perhaps there was just one event which had a certain significance beyond the bounds of Toftham.

In his remaining fifty-five minutes he wrote the story of the Great Toftham Overspill Debate, setting out as fairly as he could the arguments for and against, the impact that sudden expansion would have on a small town, its benefits and its dangers, the risk of stagnation if it failed to happen. And he ended with the public meeting in the Jubilee Hall, trying to give a flavour of the backstage manoeuvrings of Mr Juby, as well as the more bizarre incidents at the meeting itself. He wrote with much more frankness than usual, since it would never be seen by readers of the Journal – or by Mr Juby.

At the end of the hour they were taken one by one to the studios. As the order was alphabetical Charles was one of the first. He found himself alone in front of the first BBC microphone he had ever seen, a bulky affair on a heavy stand in the middle of the table. He attempted to pull it towards him and was amazed at its weight.

'There's no need to move it, Mr Benson,' said a disembodied voice from somewhere in the ceiling. 'It should be at the correct distance. Just read a few words for level, please.'

Charles read a few words, as levelly as he could. 'Thank you,' the voice interrupted. 'Just relax and enjoy yourself, Mr Benson. Watch for the green light, then go ahead.'

The green light came on and he started reading. What had seemed a very lucid account when he wrote it now sounded terribly complicated when he heard himself reading it. Some of the sentences, he realised, were far too long, without a comma to take a breath. The name of Len Cloppett, taken for granted in Toftham, sounded so ridiculous when said out loud that he felt an urge to snigger. On the other hand the account of the shouting matches at the meeting, which looked quite amusing on paper, sounded singularly unfunny when addressed to this awesome microphone.

He emerged from the studio sunk in gloom. At least he had not stumbled over any of the words, he told himself desperately, and he had stopped himself saying 'Tarf'm,' but those seemed the only plus points

'How did it go?' asked Dickie Johnson as they passed in the corridor. 'Norfolk, here I come,' he replied resignedly, and the Extel man laughed sympathetically. 'Before you go way back to the sticks, there's a pub called the Dover Castle just round the corner. If you'd like to wait for me there, we'll see what we can do about the rest of that letter we got from the Board.'

Charles looked at him blankly.

'You remember,' said Dickie as he went into the studio. 'That line about "incurring reasonable expenses" . . .'

It was two weeks before the next letter came. To Charles it seemed like two years. He managed to deal with the routine meetings and dinners that came his way, and Mr Juby did not press him unduly, but when he read some of his own reports in the paper he felt guilty at how clumsily he had thrown them together. He decided to stay well clear of Remingham; apart from Rebecca's request that he should not contact her first, he needed to know more about his chances in London before seeing her again.

Anthea brought the letter up the stairs to him. It had the BBC insignia in the top corner, and not for the first time he wished that mail could be delivered direct to his tiny flat over Mr Pollitt's shop, but there was no separate letter-box and anything sent there went straight into the shop and could lie around in Mr Pollitt's back room for days.

'I think this is what you've been waiting for,' she said without looking at him, and ran off down the stairs. She was not supposed to know about the BBC job, but the earlier letters had not gone unnoticed, nor his trip to London, and since then she had been permanently plunged in private grief.

The letter was signed by Sir Greville Taylor, chairman of the Appointments Board. It invited him to attend the Board for interview the following week. It also advised him that he would be required to undergo a screen test at Alexandra Palace three days after that. And would he now give permission for the Corporation to take up his references with his head office in Norwich. The mills were grinding faster.

Charles found himself back in the same waiting-room, but this time he was on his own: the candidate ahead of him was already with the Board. Among the copies of *The Listener* on the table he found a copy of *Radio Times*, and he browsed through the pages of familiar photographs and names. Who knows, he thought, one day . . .

Dickie Johnson came into the room, absently polishing his glasses. He put them on when he saw Charles and held out his hand. 'So Norfolk didn't want you back?'

'I wouldn't say that. They'll be deeply grieved to see me go.' Actually the Norwich office had unexpectedly offered him quite a substantial rise in the last week; a complete coincidence, they assured him, he was due for it anyway, but he found it difficult to believe them.

'So how did you get on?' he asked. Dickie took his glasses off again and polished them. 'Who knows? They're all so polite it's difficult to know what they're really thinking. But I can give you one tip: the chap who sits on the end of the table, he's from the Civil Service Commissioners. He's there to make sure you're not a Communist trying to infiltrate the Corporation. So if he asks you what paper you read regularly, for God's sake don't say the *Daily Worker*!'

The businesslike lady in the neat blouse and skirt appeared in the doorway and asked Charles to follow her. 'See you in the Dover Castle,' said Dickie as he went out. 'They haven't queried those reasonable expenses yet.'

Sir Greville Taylor, at the centre of the table, was grey-haired, distinguished, and very much in charge. He introduced the other members of the Board, but Charles did not register who they were or why they were there. All he did notice was that the one on the end, who represented the Civil Service Commissioners, appeared to be in a deep sleep.

'Now Mr Benson, what makes you think you'd be a valuable asset to the BBC – apart from being able to halt the traffic?' Everyone at the table smiled, except for the somnolent Civil Servant; presumably Sir Greville had told them about the incident at the pedestrian crossing. Charles hoped it augured well.

'I'm sorry if it seemed a little reckless, sir. I was late for my first appointment here.'

'Not at all. Shows the right spirit. I thought it was only *In Town Tonight* that could stop the mighty roar of London's traffic.' There were smiles along the table again, but now Sir Greville waved his hand and dismissed the matter. 'Apart from that, what else can you offer?'

Charles tried to tell them. Afterwards he could not remember a word that he had said, or anything else he had been asked, except when the Civil Servant at the end of the table stirred slightly, opened his eyes, and enquired, 'What newspapers do you read, Mr Benson?'

'The *Daily Telegraph* and the *Sunday Times*, sir,' said Charles firmly.

'Ah,' said the man at the end. He made a note on his pad and closed his eyes again.

'Thank you, Mr Benson,' said Sir Greville. 'Incidentally I was interested in that overspill plan for Toftham. It would be a pity to turn it into a Birmingham suburb.'

'You know Toftham, sir?' Charles was amazed. Most people he had met so far in the BBC had hardly heard of Norfolk, let alone one of its smaller market towns.

'My wife's family live in Norfolk. Have done for quite a while, actually. She's quite appalled at the idea.' Sir Greville leaned forward. 'What's your own personal view, Mr Benson? It was difficult to tell from the piece you wrote.'

'That was the idea, sir,' said Charles carefully, trying not to sound too pompous. He was relieved when Sir Greville smiled.

'Quite so, Mr Benson. Admirably put. Good day to you – and thank you for your time.'

Charles went back to the waiting-room to pick up his coat. Giles Bellinger from *The Times*, immaculate in double-breasted blue suit and Old Etonian tie, was studying one of the aged copies of *The Listener*. He looked up as Charles came in.

'Aren't you the one from Norfolk? I'd no idea they were considering fellows from the provinces these days.' The tone was identical to Henry Burton's; Charles's hackles rose.

'I suppose they thought they'd make a gesture to their more distant listeners. We can pick up the Overseas Service quite clearly on a good day.'

Bellinger nodded solemnly. 'It must be quite a link with civilisation. Tell me, what sort of chaps have they got on the Board? I know Sir Greville, of course, but who else?'

Charles had a mischievous thought. 'The only one I knew was the chap at the end of the table. He represents the unions on the Appointments Board. He's quite a Red, from what I hear. He asks this trick question about what paper you read; I said the *Daily Mirror* and he seemed quite impressed.'

He left before Bellinger could question him further. Not quite cricket, he thought, but Mr Juby would be proud of me. And he made for the Dover Castle.

'That didn't take too long, eh,' said Dickie Johnson, ordering him a pint. 'But I gather it's only a matter of form really. They have to go through all this rigmarole to make it look fair. Then they'll finish up with the Director-General's nephew, or someone like Giles Bellinger, or whoever it was they were going to take on anyway.'

Charles's spirits slumped again. 'I thought I was doing rather well, really. They were all very civil to me.'

'That's what the BBC is all about, my rustic friend, being civil, just like the Civil Service, except the BBC is civil to a few million people at a time. It has the added advantage that it can't hear what all those people are saying back, so it doesn't look uncivil when it ignores them. As for jobs, everyone knows that normally they wouldn't look twice at anyone who hadn't been to Oxbridge. It's only that there's a few people at the top of the News Division these days who want reporters who've actually done some basic reporting, instead of graduates who've gone straight into leader-writing. That's the only reason you and I are still in the running.'

Charles was getting thoroughly depressed. He rather wished he had given the Dover Castle a miss. 'It hardly seems worth while wasting another day on this screen test.'

'Don't you believe it,' said Dickie cheerfully. 'There are some good pubs around Alexandra Palace. We can always pile up some more "reasonable expenses" . . .'

Alexandra Palace, perched on top of its hill overlooking the North London suburbs, seemed even more daunting to Charles than Broadcasting House. It was massive enough when the Victorians built it as an entertainments centre for the bourgeoisie. Then part of it was taken over and expanded by the BBC for its television service, and apart from a break during the war years – when the Germans invaded Poland the service shut down abruptly in the middle of a Mickey Mouse cartoon – it had been adding bits ever since, not least the mast on top of the main tower, which Charles had seen on the screen so often at the start of Television News. Looking up at it from the main door it seemed as lofty as the Eiffel Tower – and a lot less stable. He hastened inside.

One of the BBC's army of commissionaires led him through a maze of corridors to a bleak barn of a studio; there were just two chairs and one camera tucked in a corner. Again, Charles did not know what to expect. Even Dickie's knowledge did not extend to the screen test, since he knew nobody who had reached this stage before, and that at least was slightly encouraging. Charles assumed he might have to recite something into the camera, and he had spent much of the previous evening in his room over Mr Pollitt's shop, reading his test piece about the Toftham overspill into the mirror. He had even practised a whimsical raise of the eyebrow when he came to the funny bits.

Again he was hopelessly off the mark. A bored young man in corduroys, a tattered pullover and headphones escorted him to one of the chairs. In the other, looking even more bored, was Quentin Milton. They had not met since the vigil at the Marford Heath air base, and Milton seemed quite pleased to see him.

'Ah, dear boy, nice to see a familiar face. I never did hear that bang, so I assume you escaped unscathed?'

Charles was puzzled. 'What are you doing here, Quentin? You can't be applying for the job – you've already got it.'

'It's a little chore I get landed with sometimes, when business is quiet. I act as a guineapig for the young hopefuls. I'm afraid you've got to interview me for a few minutes while our masters gaze upon you through yonder camera.'

'But what do I interview you about?' Charles was still not clear what was expected of him.

'That's the tricky bit,' said Milton. 'You've got to imagine I am the general secretary of the National Union of Railwaymen. Do you think you can manage that?'

Charles could not imagine anyone who looked less like a union secretary, but he nodded cautiously.

'The idea is I've just come out of a national executive meeting which has been discussing the latest pay offer. You've been waiting outside to find out what we've been up to. It's the ancient art of door-stepping, one of the more tedious facets of BBC reporting. But at least you haven't had to wait two hours in the rain before I've come out. Now Joe here will fill you in with the technical stuff.'

Joe here, the bored young man in the headphones, stepped forward. 'You've got three minutes, Mr Benson. When you have two minutes left I do this.' He languidly raised two fingers. 'When you have one minute left I do this.' He held up one. 'And when your time is running out I do this.' He drew the finger, still languidly, across his throat. 'Everything quite clear?'

'Absolutely,' said Charles. He could feel panic coming on.

'Ready to go, Nigel,' said Joe. He paused, then raised a hand in acknowledgement to the unseen Nigel. 'Mr Benson, Nigel thinks you might look the teeniest bit more comfy if you sat back in your chair and perhaps crossed your legs, instead of gripping the chair-arms like that.'

Charles hastily let go of the arms, sat back and crossed his legs. An expanse of naked leg appeared between turn-up and sock.

'Basic equipment for a television interviewer: long socks,' said Quentin lightly. 'But don't worry about it now – they won't be looking at your legs. At least, they ought not to be, but you can never tell with Nigel.' He turned to the camera. 'Isn't that so, Nigel?'

'Nigel says very funny, and can we please get on with the interview?' said Joe a little coldly. 'Here we go, then. Quiet, everyone. Thirty seconds from now.'

Charles had half a minute to collect his thoughts and plunge himself into the complex world of industrial relations. The first question was obvious enough: 'What has the executive decided, Mr Milton?' But what about the second question, and the third. . . ?

'Ten, nine, eight . . .' Joe had started the count-down. This was really quite awful.

'. . . seven, six, five . . .' It was worse than awful. It was a nightmare.

'. . . four, three . . .' Oh God, this was it.

'So what has the executive decided, Mr Milton?'

'My execkertive,' said Quentin grandly, 'has decided to call a national strike of all our members as from midnight tomorrow night.'

'Oh, really?' It was all he could think of.

'Yus, really.' Quentin could see Charles was floundering, and generously kept talking. 'We shall be advising all our branches accordingly and forthwith, either by telephone or special delivery or by personal contact. We shall ensure the instruction reaches them in good time to take universal simultaneous action and show solidarity throughout the union.'

The few extra seconds were invaluable. Charles had had another thought.

'Isn't this going to have a disastrous effect on the travelling public?'

Quentin gave an almost imperceptible nod of approval. 'My execkertive wishes to express its regrets for any inconvenience this may cause, but we wish to make it clear that this is the fault of the Railways Board and not of my members.'

Charles began to get the hang of things. He also remembered Quentin's technique with the major at the air base.

'It's all very well expressing regrets, Mr Milton, but surely you need public opinion on your side if you are going to get anywhere in this dispute, and would you not agree that this action is going to antagonise a great many people?'

'That is a risk we must take,' said Quentin crisply. He had apparently decided that Charles no longer needed any help.

'Regardless of the fact that people rely on the railways to get to work and make a living, or to visit sick relatives, or to take a holiday they've been looking forward to for months?' Charles was surprised to find he was actually beginning to enjoy himself. He was startled when Joe raised two fingers to him, then remembered it was merely the two-minute signal.

'We express our regrets,' repeated Quentin firmly, 'but we are sure they will understand we have no alternative to taking industrial action at this moment in time.'

'But surely it is better to stay at the negotiating table until common sense prevails?' Charles was not only enjoying it, he was finding himself using the jargon. He glimpsed a hint of a smile from Quentin.

'That is a matter for my execkertive, and they take the view we have reached the end of the road. The Board's offer is derisory.'

'But if you refuse to negotiate with them further, how can you expect them to make a better offer? It seems to me you are just forcing them to dig their heels in.'

'And what makes you think you know more about pay negotiations than I do, young man?' Quentin had decided it was time to turn nasty. 'I don't try to tell you your job, now don't you try to tell me mine, not a young whipper-snapper like you.' Charles got the message; he had gone beyond the bounds of normal BBC courtesy. He back-pedalled.

'It just looks like common sense to me, Mr Milton. But I'm sure you have the best interests of your members at heart.' He was relieved to have found another platitude, and groped for a further question. 'But are you certain you have their full support on this?'

'My execkertive is fully empowered to take this decision under the rules of the union, as confirmed in Resolutions forty-three and forty-four at the last annual conference.' Quentin rattled it out with such conviction that Charles hardly felt able to argue. He tried another tack.

'Won't they lose a great deal of money if the strike goes on for any length of time?' Joe held up a finger in apparent admonition, but Charles realised what he meant.

'My members are loyal to the union and they will back their execkertive all the way. What's more, we have a very substantial strike fund which we intend to make full use of. My members will not go short.'

Charles spotted an opening. 'So your members will not go short, while the general public are suffering all manner of inconvenience and possible hardship?'

'My execkertive,' repeated Quentin, 'regrets any inconvenience. But when I say my members won't go short, of course the strike pay won't be as much as full pay, but it'll be enough to get by on.'

He attacked again. 'What about their wives? Will they think it's enough to get by on? Have you asked if they fully support this action? They'll be the ones that have to cope with the housekeeping bills.'

'No doubt they'll do the best they can.' Charles detected the defensive note, and he remembered Quentin's technique at the air base when Theo had reached this stage.

'But you're not really worried what they think about it. It's just a matter for your members.'

'That's not what I said. Of course I'm interested in what they think about it.'

'Then why didn't you ask them before you decided on the strike?'

'Ask the wives? That's not the way these things work, young man.'

Charles saw Joe place his finger against his throat, and went for the jugular himself.

'So how do you know you've got the wives' full support?'

'I just know, and that's it.'

'Without asking them?'

'Yes, without asking them.'

'Thank you very much, Mr Milton.'

'And thank you too, Counsel for the Prosecution,' chuckled Quentin, as Joe indicated the recording was over.

Charles mopped his brow. What with the studio lights, the unaccustomed concentration, and the general tension, it had been an exhausting three minutes. But he felt a curious exhilaration too. 'Do you think I overdid it a bit?' he asked, hoping for reassurance. It came, but not in the way he expected.

'You did go over the top, dear boy, no doubt about that. But I shouldn't let that worry you. No one takes much notice of what you actually say in these test interviews. You mainly come here so that

Nigel can make sure you look sufficiently winsome in front of the camera. I should think you'll do. Lots of sincerity and righteous indignation. They'll love it.'

Nigel's voice came over the studio loudspeaker. 'Don't tease him, Quentin, there's a dear. Thank you so much, Charles. Just the teeniest bit too macho, perhaps, but it made lovely television.'

'There you are,' said Quentin. 'That means he liked your legs. Now I'll take you for the next test. It's a lot more gruelling than this one.'

'Oh Lord.' Charles was appalled. 'I thought it was all over.'

'Not quite,' Quentin led him towards the studio door. 'We're going to the canteen for some BBC coffee. The test is to drink it without throwing up.'

Whether it was because Nigel liked his legs, or the Civil Service liked his taste in newspapers, or Sir Greville liked his firm handling of the Portland Place traffic, Charles would never know, though he suspected that the Norfolk connection through Sir Greville's wife may have helped. Three weeks later – three agonising, interminable weeks – another letter arrived from the BBC. There was a great deal of small print about staff establishment and annual increments and roofs of grades and terms of service 'and conformity with such rules and regulations as may at the time be in force', and much of it was incomprehensible, but the gist of it was clear.

He had got the job.

SEVEN

'Well done, Charlie boy. I thought you'd show those London folk we
hent so daft in Norfolk.'

Charles had come up to Mr Juby's office to tell him the news, and by
Norfolk standards Mr Juby was effusive in his congratulations, but
there was obviously something on his mind. He was reading a letter
that had arrived in the same post as Charles's, and it bore the
letterheading of the Birmingham Post.

'Bad news?'

'Not good, boy, not good. This is from the boy Jimma. That Reg
Morris who came to the meeting from Birmingham, seems he's talked
his committee into going ahead with working out the overspill plan.
They're getting in touch with Norfolk County Council, and the
Department of This and the Ministry of That, and God knows who else.
If they get that lot a-goin' there'll be no stoppin' 'em, thass for sure.'

Charles shrugged. 'It looks as though it's out of our hands then.'

Mr Juby bristled. 'That may be out of your hands, boy, now you're
off to London, but it hent out o' mine. I've got a couple o' weeks before
the next meeting of Toftham Council, thanks to our Jimma sending me
the word. I'll make good use of 'em before Len Cloppett has a chance to
push anything through at this end. Just give me a while to think,
Charlie. You'd better go and start your packing.'

'I'm not leaving for a month yet. I'd still like to help if I can.'

'Right you are then,' said Mr Juby crisply. 'There's old Albert
Hewitt out at Tittlesham, he's been winding the church clock for fifty
year and they're making a presentation to him this afternoon. It'll be a
clock, more than likely. And you'll need to see Mrs Boggis while you're
out there, she's late with her British Legion report again. And John
Nicholson's foreman out at the Manor Farm there, he tell me he's got
some noo-fangled idea about planting Christmas trees on his little
scutes o'land where narthin' else'll grow. He reckon there'll be worth a
bob or two in a few year's time. You get that little lot sorted out for me,
boy, and that'll be all the help I'll need.' And Mr Juby leaned back in
his chair and started purposefully filling his pipe.

'Should I tell anyone about this BBC job yet?' asked Charles.

95

'Thass up to you, boy. I hent said a word, but they'll know in Norwich o' course, and that'll soon get about. You tell who you like.'

There was only one person Charles wanted to tell, and he was not sure how to go about it. Rebecca had still not contacted him, but in spite of her request he felt the situation was urgent enough for him to call her. He debated whether to invite her out for a meal, or just ask to call and see her. Should he drop her a note or phone? Should he explain why he needed to see her, or keep her guessing until they met? He spent some time staring out of his office window trying to plan his campaign before eventually picking up the phone. But he need not have worried.

It was Mrs Bateman who answered. Beccy had gone away to stay with friends, she explained; she was not sure for how long. But she had left a message for him in case he tried to contact her; she would definitely telephone him as soon as she came back.

Charles put down the phone and stared into space again. Would she be back before he left in a month's time? Should be write her a letter and ask the Batemans to forward it? Did she care either way? And was there any point in it, even if she did, with him in London and her in Norfolk . . .

'Hent you gone yet, boy?' Mr Juby was in the doorway, his pipe going full blast. 'Thass time you were in Tittlesham, or you'll be late for that football club meeting tonight. Du yew get a-goin' instead o' sarnickin' about in the office like an old mawther.'

Charles noted the pipe smoke and the broadened accent. Mr Juby must have devised a way of countering the move by Reg Morris. 'Have you had an idea then?'

Mr Juby nodded vigorously. 'That I have, boy, that I have. I tell you what we're going to do. We're going to have a referendum.'

'You mean some sort of town vote?' Charles was sceptical. 'That'll take ages, even if the Council agrees to hold it.'

'We hent goin' to ask the Council, we're goin' to hold it ourselves,' said Mr Juby gleefully. 'The *Toftham Journal* Referendum. We'll print the forms in this week's paper and say they got to be handed in by next Wednesday. Then we'll get the result in on the Friday, and still be ahead of the Council meeting. Blast me, that'll put a pritch up Len Crockett's backside.' He was hugely pleased with himself.

'But what makes you so sure that most people will vote against the overspill? And what difference will it make anyway? The Council can still vote in favour – they won't be bound by a vote like that.' The plan seemed full of flaws.

'I know the sort o' people who buy the Journal,' said Mr Juby confidently. 'They'll vote against it all right. Len Cloppett's lot, the only paper they buy is the *Mirror*, and there's not many of them even read that, they just look at the busty young mawthers. And if Len catches on and buys up a few score copies of the Journal, that'll seem a fare bit rum, wunt you say? Thass vote-rigging, Charlie, and we can't have that.'

'But that still doesn't mean the Council has to abide by it,' objected Charles.

'Don't be so duzzy stoopid, boy. That'll let Harry Hurn off the hook, don't you see? He dussent vote against this overspill squit at present, or folk'll say he's just feared o' the competition. But if he can say thass the wish of the town, like, then he can vote against it and no one can't say narthin'. And if it come to a casting vote, the Vicar can say the same. Then our Mr Morris'll have his work cut out, and no mistairk.'

'I'm not sure that a referendum on those lines is a very democratic procedure,' said Charles dubiously.

'Democratic?' Mr Juby snorted derisively. 'You hent got to London just yet, boy. This is Norfolk you're in, not the House o' Commons. Come you on t'gether.' And he headed off down the stairs, with Charles at his heels.

As they went through the front office they saw Anthea crouched over her desk, her head in her hands; she was sobbing quietly. Mr Juby looked at Charles, and Charles shrugged helplessly. She must have guessed the contents of the latest BBC letter.

Mr Juby went over to her and put an arm round her shoulders. 'Hold you hard, Anthea,' he said gently. Charles could not remember hearing him speak gently before. 'I'll give you a clip o' the lug dew you don't stop a-blarin'.'

She looked up at him, then across at Charles, and subsided in tears again.

'Close the office after we gone, gal, till you feel right again. We'll get by without young Charlie, never you fear.'

As they left the office Mr Juby gave Charles a nudge. 'If we had a referendum for Benson for Prime Minister, thass one vote you're sure of, boy. Now you get goin' to Tittlesham, 'fore you break any more young mawthers' hearts.' And he headed for the farmers' bar.

'ARE YOU IN FAVOUR OF TOFTHAM BEING AN
OVERSPILL TOWN FOR BIRMINGHAM?
YES or NO?
PLEASE PUT YOUR "X" IN APPROPRIATE BOX.'

The referendum form occupied most of the front page of the Journal, and produced an immediate response. The forms started coming in as soon as the office opened, nearly all of them with an 'X' in the box marked NO. Mr Juby spent much of the morning in the front office, keeping an eye on the returns, and his beam broadened as the pile of NO votes steadily increased. It remained in place even when Len Cloppett came in waving a form with YES written right across it in red ink.

'This stoopid referendum of yours don't mean a thing,' he snapped at Mr Juby, slapping the form down on the counter. 'Things are moving up in Birmingham, you know. We only need the County Council to give the word at this end, and all these bits o' paper won't be worth tuppence.'

'We'll see, Len, we'll see. We're all the servants of public opinion, hent we?' And Mr Juby beamed on. But Charles had overheard the exchange and when Len had left he asked him about the County Council's position. Could they overrule a local decision?

'We'll have to see.' The beam had faded now that Len had gone. 'That all depends what the Coltons and Gurlays decide. There's no telling how they'll take to it. If it hent in their own back garden they may not give a toss either way – but if it means more business for them they might quite fancy it. There's narthin' I can do about the gentry.'

'Surely the Coltons and the Gurlays shouldn't be able to decide on their own,' protested Charles, but without much conviction. They were the leading business families in Norfolk, not as deeply rooted as some of the landowning 'county' but involved in Norwich's commercial prosperity for a century or more, and a considerable power in the land. Both families were well represented on the County Council, and the voting rarely went against them. Mr Juby shook his head and repeated what he had said before. 'This hent democracy, boy. This is Norfolk.'

As the days went by the NO votes continued to arrive in substantial numbers, with only a handful in favour, and Mr Juby was able to head the front page on the following Friday: 'TOFTHAM SAYS "NO" TO OVERSPILL'. He was well pleased with himself, and Charles was pleased for him too, but by now he was much occupied in his own affairs. The mills of the BBC were grinding out advice, instructions and information at an increasing pace. There were forms to sign, documents to digest and appointments to keep.

There were more visits to London to see the Corporation doctor, the Corporation pensions department, the Corporation personnel director. Not least, there was the matter of finding somewhere to live. His parents were still in Wembley Park, within easy reach of Broadcasting House on the Underground, but he had no desire to return to the parental roof after seven years away; and he guessed they were no keener to have their peaceful routine disturbed.

The Corporation welfare officer sent him a list of possible quarters in the Marylebone area, but even a single room cost twice as much as his flatlet over Mr Pollitt's shop, and a one-bedroomed flat the same size was out of the question. He eventually decided on the smallest and cheapest room on offer, somewhere in the hinterland behind Oxford Street, with use of bathroom on the next landing. There were rental agreements to be completed, deposits to be paid, occupation date to be arranged. He had never dreamed it would all be so complicated; the preliminaries to taking up a job at the BBC were a full-time job in themselves.

Meanwhile the news soon got out in Toftham, perhaps through Anthea, perhaps through an unguarded word during a convivial evening in the farmers' bar. Charles was quite gratified that most people seemed sorry to see him go. Some he hardly knew stopped him in the market-place and shook his hand. At his last meeting of Launford R.D.C. Lord Remingham actually wished him well on behalf of the members and he got a round of applause. And when he made his final tour of the villages Mrs Boggis at the Tittlesham Stores insisted on making an announcement to her customers. 'Our Mr Benson's goin' on the wireless.' She said it with personal pride. 'I've known him since he fust came to Norfolk, when he didn't know narthin' about narthin'.'

'And now I know narthin' about suffin,' Charles responded, and was relieved when they all laughed. 'But it's not just the wireless, Mrs Boggis. I'll be on the television too.'

He thought that would impress them, but Mrs Boggis shook her head in disgust. 'Never mind that noo-fangled telly. Nobody take no notice of that in these parts, Mr Benson. But the wireless, now that do count for suffin . . .'

On the day of the Toftham Council meeting Charles was on one of his excursions to London, this time to the BBC personnel department, which also turned out to be the BBC perks department. He returned to Toftham with a stopwatch, a staff card entitling him to a free copy each week of *Radio Times*, and the promise of a brand-new Morris Minor as soon as he took up his post. The days of the Vibrator were numbered.

He got back just before closing time and made straight for the Dog and Partridge, eager to tell Mr Juby about his latest acquisitions. When he entered the farmers' bar Mr Juby was on his customary stool sipping his customary special, but the atmosphere of gloom that hung over him was almost tangible. Charles remembered the Council meeting.

'Oh dear.' He took a seat at the bar beside Mr Juby. 'Didn't it go well, then?'

Mr Juby looked at him morosely. 'Oh yes, it went very well. They voted against taking any further action.'

Charles was baffled. 'What's wrong, then? Why all the gloom? Isn't that what you wanted?'

'Yes, o' course,' Mr Juby snapped. 'But it don't stop there. Len Cloppett has been writing to the chief planning officer at the County Council.' He took some papers out of his pocket and consulted one of them. 'He gave me a copy of it – all fancy phrases he learned from that Reg Morris. He says the referendum hent constitutional and there was unfair pressure on council members, and any decision they made under such circumstances should be disregarded. I never read such a load o' squit.'

'Well, the chief planning officer may think it's a load of squit too,' said Charles consolingly, but Mr Juby waved another letter at him. 'No he don't, thass the trouble. He's writ back saying he takes Mr Cloppett's point' – he had put on his mock-gentry accent – 'and he quait agrees that the tighn of Toftham was not consulted fairly, and the result was improper and unsighnd. The Council was not bighnd by it and it should have been kept off the agenda. Duzzy old fule.'

'So now it's up to the Coltons and the Gurlays, I suppose. You'll just have to hope for the best, Mr Juby.' In an effort to change the subject and cheer him up, he looked ostentatiously at his new BBC watch. 'Do you notice anything in particular about this?'

'Course I do,' said Mr Juby. 'Thass time for another round . . .'

On the day before he was due to leave Norfolk, Charles took the day off. It was a Thursday, the quietest day of the week, and anyway he was finding it increasingly difficult to concentrate on whist drive winners and darts league results. He was also anxious to keep clear of Anthea on his last day – the prospect of her tearful farewell had been haunting him for weeks. So with Mr Juby's permission he drove out of Toftham in the Vibrator for the last time. He had already agreed to sell it to a young farm foreman who had just moved into the district and knew nothing of its failings. 'It only needs a good clean-up,' he had told him, 'and it'll look as good as new.' He did not add that it would then probably fall to pieces; at least he had learnt that much in Norfolk.

He headed for the coast and pulled up on the summit of the hill above Branham Staithe. This was where he and Mr Juby had paused on the night of the East Coast floods and looked down on the lights of the village as the gale howled round them and the breakers pounded against the shore. An hour later, as they stood on the quay at Branham, the waves burst through the sea defences and over the dunes, flooding the marshes and sweeping into the village itself, so they had to run for their lives while the sea swept over the quay and smashed against the cottages that lined it. Charles had spent much of the night helping boatmen to rescue stranded villagers through their bedroom windows, in those cottages which still stood, and taking them to the village school on higher ground. He had made some good friends that night; whenever he revisited the village he was always sure of a warm welcome.

There was no gale blowing today, just one of Norfolk's 'lazy winds': 'thass too lazy to go round yew, that go straight thru' yew, boy.' It was enough to whip up white breakers beyond the marshes, but the clouds were high and he could enjoy the view right along the coast in both directions, a vast expanse of green and brown and grey, with a touch of blue on the horizon. Nobody else was about, not even on the coast road below him, just some sheep grazing on the marshes and a flock of seagulls swooping overhead.

This is what he would miss, he thought, the space and the silence and the vast Norfolk sky. He drove slowly down into Branham, where the damaged cottages had been restored or rebuilt, and as he strolled along the peaceful quayside and exchanged greetings with some of the boatmen, he knew he would miss these friendships too, founded on the camaraderie of that night. But high drama like the East Coast floods was mercifully rare in Norfolk, and Branham Staithe had settled back into its normal sleepy existence. He drove out of the village full of nostalgia but with no regrets. It was time to move on.

At lunch-time he arrived at the King's Head in God-forsaken Godborough. He had not been back since his eerie experience in Old Jem's Wood during the summer, and he was curious to know how Mrs Cattermole's plans were progressing. Another car was already parked outside, and when he went into the bar he found a couple sitting at one of the polished tables tackling large platefuls of ham and salad.

'Welcome back.' Mrs Cattermole was polishing glasses behind the bar. 'Would you like to see the menu?'

He was much impressed. To find food in a village pub was unusual enough; to find a choice of food was luxury indeed. It looked as though she had created a modest oasis in Norfolk's gastronomic desert.

'If I'd known you'd got this far,' said Charles, 'I'd never have taken a job in London.'

While he enjoyed the home-made vegetable soup and the cheese and pickle sandwiches he chatted with the couple at the other table. Mrs Cattermole's husband had been spreading the word about the King's Head and its pub lunches among his office contacts, and these were two of his clients who had come out to sample them. They were just as impressed as Charles; the word would continue to spread.

In a mellow mood he made his farewells to Mrs Cattermole and promised to tell the folk in London there was excellent fare available in no-longer-God-forsaken Godborough. In years to come, he thought as he drove across the heath, when every village pub in Norfolk serves bar lunches, I hope they'll remember it was Mrs Cattermole who led the way.

The sun had come out and the wind had dropped, and there were all the signs of a golden winter afternoon, with that specially clear light which brought so many artists to East Anglia. He decided there was one more moment of bitter-sweet nostalgia to savour before the returned to Toftham. At the next fork he took the road to Remingham.

He pulled up outside the church where John Cranmer had met so much opposition over his idea of family services, though the opposition had melted once Lord Remingham had expressed approval. Maybe he would see John again in London. It was an encouraging thought. He switched off the engine, and then he heard a sound which had once made his heart leap, the sound of a horse whinnying in the stable at the Old Rectory. Rebecca's horse Thunder had whinnied like that just before she arrived home, even when nobody else knew she was coming. Thunder had gone to fresh pastures when she moved to the North, but now there was a horse at the Old Rectory again, and that meant Rebecca had to be there too.

It was Mrs Bateman who answered the door, and for a moment he feared he must be wrong, but she smiled and ushered him into the lounge. 'Beccy's been trying to contact you all day,' she said. 'She got back this morning with her new horse. I'll tell her you're here – she's just changing out of her riding things.'

When Rebecca came in he felt as awkward as on the day he came to take her on their first picnic. The gaps between their meetings had been too long. But she came and took his hand with a welcoming smile, and after the tiniest pause she kissed him on the cheek.

'It's good to see you again,' she said. 'I'm sorry I missed you this morning; I did ring the office two or three times but nobody seemed to know where you were. And every time the girl answered the phone and I asked for you she started crying. It was really rather embarrassing. What have you been up to with her?'

'Absolutely nothing,' Charles assured her. 'I'm afraid that's why she's upset.'

'Then you've been saving yourself for me,' she said solemnly.

'It wasn't that difficult,' he admitted, and she shook her head wryly.

'Gallant as ever. Good old Charles.'

They sat on the sofa together and Charles launched into polite conversation. 'I gather you've got a new horse. What's this one called?'

She smiled. 'It had to be Lightning, didn't it? Even though he's not nearly as fast as Thunder. I've just been showing him the local scenery.' She paused. 'I took him down to the riverbank where we had that picnic. Do you remember?'

'Oh yes,' said Charles. 'I remember.' He paused too, then decided to chance it. 'It's a pity you've just been down there – I was going to suggest we might take a stroll that way. It's a marvellous afternoon.'

She jumped up. 'What a nice idea. I was hoping you might suggest it. I'll get my coat.'

Left on his own for a moment, Charles danced a little jig of delight.

They drove in the Vibrator to where the drift led away from the lane towards the river, then walked along it between the high hedges, which were bare now that winter had come. They could glimpse the fields on either side, the brown earth freshly ploughed and harrowed. When they reached the brow of the ridge the hedges ended and they stood looking out across the river valley at the broad sweep of Norfolk countryside. When they had first stood there the fields were green with young sugar beet and barley. Now they were brown, and the clumps of trees had shed their leaves, but the water-meadows below them were still bright green, and the river flowing through them sparkled blue in the sunshine.

'The last time we were here,' said Charles, 'you wanted to race me to the river, you on that damn great horse and me on my old delivery bike. I didn't stand a chance against Thunder; you ought to give me a return match.'

'Right,' said Rebecca briskly. 'Race you to the river.'

They ran down the slope and across the water-meadows, with Charles just a few yards ahead. He headed for the little wooden bridge that spanned the river, and just before they reached it Rebecca made a sudden spurt; they arrived neck-and-neck.

'You nearly had me there,' he gasped, hanging on to the little hand-rail of the bridge.

'I doubt it, but it's nice of you to say so.' She was panting too. Her hand on the rail was close to his.

'There was something else that happened, the last time we were here,' he said slowly, and took her hand.

'Yes,' she said. 'I remember.' And they kissed, long and tenderly, the first real kiss for six years . . .

A little while later, as they leaned on the rail and watched the river flowing beneath them, Charles said abruptly: 'I expect you've heard I'm leaving.'

She did not look at him. 'Yes, Daddy told me something about it. But he didn't know exactly when.'

'Actually, it's tomorrow. This is my last day in Norfolk.'

She said nothing for a few moments. They both kept their eyes on the water.

'I suppose,' she said eventually, 'this is what they call Sod's Law.'

He nodded glumly. 'I know what you said about this being a marvellous area to work in, and what a pleasant job I've got, and Mr Juby won't last for ever, but I've got to give this a go, Beccy. It's a tremendous opportunity. Some of those chaps in Fleet Street would give their last bottle of gin for it.'

'You're quite right, of course.' She picked up a twig, dropped it in the water and watched it drift away downstream. 'But if it doesn't work out right, or if they don't like you down there, or worse still if you don't like them, if it all turns out to be an awful mistake, don't be afraid to come back.' She turned and looked straight at him. 'We're all very fond of you, you know.'

He smiled a little wryly. 'I ought not to start thinking about packing it in before I've even started. But if it all falls around my ears I'll know where to come for a shoulder to cry on. A gorgeous freckly shoulder . . .'

They kissed again, but this time it was not a kiss of reunion, it was a kiss of farewell. They walked quietly back to the car, and he drove her back to the Old Rectory.

When he pulled up to let her out she kissed him again, but it was just a swift brush on his cheek. 'Good luck, Charles,' she said. 'Keep in touch.'

'That I will, gal,' he said lightly in his best Norfolk accent. 'Fare y'well t'gether, me old booty.'

She smiled briefly. 'You still can't do it properly, but I'm sure it will make them laugh in London.'

Then she was out of the car and up the drive, and as she disappeared past the stables he could hear Lightning welcoming her home.

He parked his car in the market-place, where the young foreman would pick it up next morning. It was six o'clock. The Journal was shut and the Dog and Partridge was open, but he let himself into the office, hurried past Anthea's empty chair with a sigh of relief, and climbed the stairs to his office for the last time. He looked around for some memento to take with him, but the room was just about as bare as when he arrived, except for the extra chair he had bought at the auction and he could hardly take that.

Then he saw the roughly scrawled notice which Mr Juby had made him put on the wall on his first day with the Journal. It was still pinned up behind his desk, faded and tattered and extremely dusty, but still quite legible. 'INITIALS ARE SACRED', it said, the first maxim of local reporting that Mr Juby had drummed into him.

He took it down, folded it carefully and put it in his pocket. 'If the next chap needs telling,' he murmured, 'you can write him out a new one.' And he gave the room a wave, and went downstairs.

In the front office he paused by Anthea's desk, feeling rather guilty. He really should have said goodbye. He found a piece of paper and wrote: 'Thanks for everything, Anthea. Love, Charles.' He paused, then added six big crosses. I hope that makes you feel a little better, he thought. It had made him feel better anyway. He left the note on her desk, locked the office behind him and headed for the Dog and Partridge.

'Here's the young marster,' cried Mr Juby from his corner stool as he entered the farmers' bar. 'Get a pint or two down you, boy, we're having a celebration.' Indeed he had obviously been celebrating for some time, even though the bar was not supposed to open until six. Opening hours had little meaning for Mr Juby when he felt like a special.

'I know you're pleased to see me go, but this is ridiculous,' said Charles as he raised his glass.

'This hent narthin' to do with you a-goin', boy, but never mind, we'll celebrate that too.' He took a long draught of his special.

'So what are we celebrating, then? Has Reg Morris decided he doesn't want to invade us after all?'

'Better'n that, boy, much better'n that. Blast me if the County Council hent told 'em what they can do with their stoopid overspill notions. Toftham hent sootable, they say. It would ruin the character of the town, they say. Thass better to have natural expansion than drastic development, they say. So get stuffed, they say, and thass what we say too.'

There were cheers around the farmers' bar, and Charles joined in. He had never expected the County Council to turn it down. 'Len Cloppett's letter didn't do any good after all, then?'

Mr Juby chuckled. 'Len Cloppett hent no match for them Coltons and Gurlays, boy. They read his letter, then they read what the Chief Plannin' Officer wrote back, and they drop on 'im like a ton o' muck. Old Fred Knock's boy, he works at County Hall, he say he hent never heard narthin' like it. He were listening outside the door and he say there was one of 'em, she really let fly at that plannin' feller. You hent any right to send letters like that without our authority, she say. There hent been proper discussion, she say. Blast, she give him a rare rollicking, so Fred's boy say. He were right glad he weren't in that feller's shoes.' He chuckled again and called for another special.

'Who's this "she" he was talking about?' Charles was surprised that it had been a woman who led the onslaught. There were not many women on the County Council.

'It was that Miss Gurlay what married some smart city feller from London. She's a Lady something now, but she still talks like a Gurlay, by all accounts.'

An unlikely thought occurred to Charles. It could be just a coincidence, but . . .

'You don't happen to know what her husband's name is, I suppose?'

'Some plain sort o' name. Nothing special. His fust name was a rum 'un though. Suffin' like Gravy, that sound like. Now however did they come by a name like that for a young 'un? "Thass the boy Gravy," they say. Never heard narthin' so daft.'

'It's not quite Gravy, it's Greville,' said Charles quietly. 'Sir Greville Taylor.' He had a clear picture of the distinguished grey-haired chairman of the Appointments Board whose wife had been so appalled at the Toftham overspill plan.

'Thass the one.' Mr Juby had had too many specials to wonder how he knew, though no doubt it would puzzle him later. 'If you run across him down in London you tell him his missus done a fine job.'

'I certainly will.' Charles debated whether to reveal the whole story of his test piece but decided against it. This had been Mr Juby's personal campaign and he should get the credit. He emptied his glass. 'Time for another round, I think.'

'That it is,' agreed Mr Juby. 'And incident'ly, thass a very fine watch they give you down in London. They must be rum owld folk at the BBC. Most places they give you a watch when you leave, not when you start.'

Much, much later Charles and Mr Juby emerged into the empty market-place. It was a clear, crisp night and they both paused to savour it, the star-speckled sky, the fresh clean air, the moonlight gleaming on the cobbles. Then Mr Juby turned and shook Charles's hand. It was the first time they had shaken hands since he arrived in Toftham.

'Good luck, young Charlie. You done a good job in these parts, you'll do a good job down there in London, there's no doubt o' that.'

'Goodbye, Mr Juby. And thank you for teaching me how to do it.'

'Never you mind about that.' Mr Juby gave a final parting chuckle. 'I reckon we hent seen the last o' you yet, boy. Norfolk's a rum place for droring folk back.' He started off across the square, then paused, and turned, and raised a hand.

'Fare y'well t'gether,' said Mr Juby. And Charles was on his own.

EIGHT

'Come in, Charles. Welcome to the finest news-gathering organisation in the world. Bar none.'

The burly, shirt-sleeved figure behind the desk leaned forward and grasped Charles's hand, then waved him to a chair. 'Sit down, make yourself comfortable. I just need to give you a bit of a briefing before you meet the team. What's the weather like in Norfolk?'

'It's a bit chilly, sir,' Charles admitted.

'Generally is, as I recall. Had a squadron there for a while during the war. It seemed to me it was either raining, or freezing, or both – never knew whether to wear gumboots or skates. Incidentally, never mind the "sir". None of that stuff here.'

Robert Corby was Head of Reporters and Correspondents, and the 'sir' had been automatic. Such an illustrious-sounding title seemed to warrant a proper respect from a newcomer to the Corporation, and his new boss was the sort of commanding figure who qualified for a 'sir' anyway.

'Thank you, Mr Corby. I'll remember.'

'No, no, just make it Bob. We're all members of the same team here, you know. When I'm not around I gather they call me Uncle Bob – Bob's your uncle, what?' He laughed explosively, then became more serious. 'They also call me the HORC. You'll find the Corporation's very keen on initials. Sometimes you get a curious combination; there's one of my colleagues here, used to be an amateur boxing champion, now he's Head of Current Affairs Magazine Programmes, and the poor devil's known as Head of CAMP. But HORC isn't far off the mark, as it happens. You've heard of eyes like a hawk, Charles? I think it's fair to say I don't miss much.' And he jerked his arms briskly, as if shooting his cuffs clear of his jacket sleeves, though his jacket was hanging over the chair. It was apparently the signal for getting down to business.

'Here's the situation, Charles. We have a number of specialist correspondents: Parliamentary, industrial, air, Royals. You won't be much involved with any of them unless they need someone to do a bit of leg-work. You'll be in our pool of general reporters, which may not sound as glamorous, but you're just as important as the correspondents are, and in some ways you need to be a lot sharper. They know all about their particular subject, but you've got to know something about everything – or at any rate, sound as if you do, for long enough to do the interview or write the report. Some of it'll be boring, especially to start with when you're doing the dogsbody jobs, but once you're in the Fire Brigade you'll find plenty to keep you on your toes.'

He saw Charles's puzzled look. 'The Fire Brigade is what I call my "A" team. Able to go anywhere in the world at the drop of a hat, whatever the story is: mine disaster, plane crash, volcano blowing up, war breaking out . . .' Bob Corby was out of his chair now and pacing the office. 'This is where the Corporation can beat all the competition, Charles. There's no quicker way of reporting a news story than radio. Those boys in Fleet Street have to phone their copy to the office, then it has to be subbed, and set, and printed, and distributed. We can broadcast the story on the spot, where it happens, while it's still happening. That's real reporting, Charles, and now you're a part of it.'

Charles was a little bewildered by Bob Corby's energetic enthusiasm. It was not exactly the Juby approach. But then Mr Juby had not urged him to use his Christian name at their first meeting. In fact, in all his seven years in Toftham he had never even discovered what it was.

He felt he ought to demonstrate that he was taking an intelligent interest. 'I suppose,' he ventured, 'television takes it on a stage further?'

Bob Corby gave a caustic snort which not even Mr Juby could have matched. 'Television? Don't you believe it. By the time they've shot their film and sent it back to be developed, then edited and scripted, by the time they've got anything on the air we'll have done the on-the-spot live report, the interviews, half-a-dozen up-dates and wrapped up the whole story. No, it's all much too cumbersome over in television; radio's the finest medium for news, Charles, take it from me.' And he shot his cuffs with great finality.

'But I thought we were supposed to do television reporting as well as radio?' The HORC must have noticed the disappointment in Charles's voice, and nodded understandingly. 'It seems much more glamorous, doesn't it? Don't worry, my boy, you'll have your chance to join in the play-acting at Ally Pally. You'll do a three-month spell up there once you've learned the ropes here, then you'll go on the rota with the rest of the team. But don't get carried away by the hair lacquer and the greasepaint, Charles. The real reporting work is done right here.'

'I understand,' said Charles, but he didn't. He had assumed the

BBC was one united organisation, with radio and television working together to get the best results. He still had a lot to learn . . .

'Here's your brief from Editor, News.' The HORC handed him two sheets of foolscap and picked up the phone. 'I'll get Quentin to take you along to your office and show you round; I gather you two have met already. One of the best chaps in the team, Quentin. But then they're all good men or they wouldn't be here. I'm very proud of them all, Charles, and I'm sure I'll be proud of you too.'

'I hope so,' mumbled Charles, but Bob was already talking on the phone. 'Quentin, I've got your friend Charles Benson here, just arrived from Norfolk. The poor chap's nearly thawed out but I expect he could do with a cup of tea, then perhaps you'd take him along to Fred to get a Midget, and show him anywhere else that might be useful. I'll see you both in the Club for a drink at lunchtime.' He put down the phone. 'Does that sound all right to you?'

'That's fine, sir. Er, Bob.' He rose to his feet and found himself almost standing to attention.

'Good man. Make sure you get everything you need from the admin people. There should be a car waiting for you at the garage, and you'll need to make sure your jabs are up to date, and you'd better make your number with the ladies in Facilities. Any problem, let me know; the door's always open.'

Charles was not sure where the garage was, or who gave him the jabs, or why there were ladies in the men's facilities, but Quentin arrived before he could ask, and Bob Corby raised a hand in farewell. As he followed Quentin out the door he noticed that the HORC was shooting his cuffs purposefully as he eyed the papers on his desk.

'Uncle Bob's been giving you the full treatment, then?' Quentin led the way down the corridor. 'All that Fire Brigade routine, no doubt, and the finest news-gathering team in the world, and never mind those ponces at Television News . . .'

'Just about,' agreed Charles. 'He doesn't seem to have much time for television.'

'Newfangled nonsense, he reckons. Turning reporters into performing seals, more interested in fancy camera angles than reporting the news. You'll find a lot of the old-time radio men feel that way. But at least Alexandra Palace is the other side of London and they can slang each other at a distance. It's when there are two departments at each other's throats in the same corridor that you have to keep your head down. For instance, keep clear of the Current Affairs lot; they don't get on with the News Division at all.'

'What's the difference between news and current affairs?' asked Charles innocently. 'They sound much the same thing.'

'What's the difference?' Quentin raised an eyebrow. 'Dear boy, you do have a lot to learn. News Division's job is to report the news; Current Affairs' job is to tart it up into a pretty package, add a few elegant trimmings and put it on the air a couple of weeks later. It's like saying is there any difference between a newspaper and a glossy magazine. Lucky you didn't try that one on Uncle Bob. He reckons the C.A. in Current Affairs stands for Complete Arses.'

They had climbed three flights of stairs and were in what looked like the attics of Egton House, the venerable office block round the corner from Broadcasting House which was the headquarters of BBC News. Charles had been disappointed that he was not in B.H. itself; he had looked forward to marching through its portals displaying his BBC staff card, while lesser mortals queued up at the reception desk. Instead his arrival had passed quite unnoticed; none of the lesser mortals had ever heard of Egton House.

'This is your office, dear boy. Or rather, half of it is.' Quentin ushered him into a gloomy little room with one small window, two tables and chairs, a telephone, and very little else. To Charles it seemed a couple of steps down the career ladder from his old office at the Toftham Journal. 'You'll be sharing it with the other new chap. He won't be starting for another fortnight, so if I were you I'd take the desk by the window. It may be a little draughtier but at least you can see what you're doing.'

Charles shook his head. 'I think I'd better let him have that one; he has to wear glasses already.' Dickie Johnson had been the other successful candidate. They had met once or twice during Charles's excursions to various administrative corners of the BBC and they had incurred some quite unreasonable expenses at the Dover Castle. He was glad they would be sharing the same room, even though it was so pokey.

He went over to the window and looked down into the narrow back street below. A couple of mangy cats were exploring a heap of rubbish. 'I shan't miss much of a view anyway.'

Quentin looked over his shoulder at the foraging cats. 'Doesn't quite compare with Toftham market-place, eh?' And Charles, with a twinge of nostalgia, had to agree.

'Never mind, dear boy. I'll show you one of the more attractive features of Egton House, something that Toftham can't compete with. Come and meet Prudence.'

He led the way past more little offices, and Charles recognised some of the names on the doors: John Burns, Ray Colley, Leonard Parkin, David Holmes. He had heard them reporting many times from various troublespots around the globe. The seedy little offices hardly lived up to Bob Corby's 'finest news-gathering organisation in the world', but the names suddenly made it a reality.

The name on the last door was unknown to him, but it looked the most impressive of all: 'Miss Prudence Bentworthy-Smythe'. Beneath it, less impressively, it said 'Reporters' Secretary'. Quentin tapped on the door and led the way in.

'Prudence, this is Charles, the first of our two new boys. You've got a fortnight to knock him into shape before the other one arrives.'

The vision behind the desk rose and held out an immaculately manicured hand. 'It's jolly nice to meet you, Charles. I do hope you like it here.'

'I'm sure I shall,' said Charles enthusiastically. This gorgeous creature with blonde hair down to her shoulders, big blue eyes and perfect figure accentuated by a tight-fitting sweater, this was a bonus he had not expected. He could not see the legs behind the desk but he had no doubt they matched the rest.

'Prudence is not too hot on typing, as you can see by the length of those nails, but she's a great morale-booster,' said Quentin. 'She's also marvellous at dealing with complaints.'

Charles remembered his Friday mornings placating dissatisfied readers of the *Toftham & Wettleford Journal*, but he was still a little surprised. 'Are there many complaints from listeners, then?'

Quentin answered for her. 'Not listeners, dear boy, they're usually as good as gold. But if the admin people complain about our expenses, or the garage boys complain because we've bumped our cars, or the pensions department complains because we haven't filled in the right forms, then we pass them on to Prudence and in a trice she has them eating out of her enchanting little hand. So who cares about the typing?'

'I'm not all that bad at it,' Prudence assured him. 'I'm just getting the hang of this white stuff that blots out the mistakes. It all takes a little time, that's all.' She smiled delightfully; the teeth were perfect too.

'Pru will put you right about leave applications, and how you get an advance from the cashier, how much you can charge for an overnight, all the really vital aspects of BBC reporting. The only thing you have to worry about is the actual broadcasting – and that's the easy bit. Now we'd better leave her to grapple with the white stuff – I think the manufacturers must have made a fortune since she discovered it.'

Quentin led him reluctantly out of the office as Prudence gave him another dazzling smile and reached for the bottle of Tipp-Ex. 'God knows how she got through the typing test when she applied for the job,' he said as they walked back along the corridor. 'Rumour has it the chap who was supposed to be testing her finished up by doing the typing himself. I don't believe that, of course.' They started descending the stairs. 'It's more likely that Daddy plays golf with the Director-General. But however she got in, she's an absolute godsend as far as we're concerned – quite apart from her decorative value.'

'And presumably in great demand?' Charles suggested tentatively.

'Very true.' Quentin became more serious. 'Too much so for her own good, unfortunately. She's a very innocent soul, you know. I honestly don't think she realises what an impact she makes. She's only nineteen, this is the first time she's been away from the country seat down in Dorset, and she's landed straight into this den of wolves.'

'Is it as bad as that?' asked Charles, remembering those well-known names on the doors.

'Oh, most of our chaps are safe enough. We're nearly all married for a start, so I suppose we ought to be. But there's a lot of people around in this business I wouldn't trust if they were married with ten kids, even if they were handcuffed to the desk and wearing a bag over their heads. She was nearly caught out once or twice when she first arrived, before we realised what was going on. So we formed the P.P.P., dear boy: Pru's Protection Patrol. There's generally a few of us around in the offices, and of course you have to get past them to reach Pru. We just keep a friendly eye open when there are visitors; it seems to work quite well.'

Charles nodded thoughtfully. 'And how about single chaps who work on the same floor?'

Quentin laughed. 'We keep a particularly close watch on them, dear boy. Now, enough of the lovely Prudence. This is the continuity suite. Come and see a real live broadcaster at work.'

The real live broadcaster, a raddled-looking man of indeterminate age in a rolltop sweater, was sitting in a tiny studio, immersed in a leather-bound volume of the works of William Wordsworth, while an orchestra played Beethoven on the loudspeaker behind him. He looked up as they entered, glanced at the clock and raised a warning finger. Charles was about to greet him, but Quentin gave him a nudge just as the music ended and a red light came on over the studio door.

The announcer laid aside his Wordsworth, selected a script from the table, and in beautifully polished tones advised the nation that it had been listening to the final movement of Beethoven's Emperor Concerto, played by the London Philharmonic Orchestra conducted by Sir

Adrian Boult. He then announced the delights that would be on offer at the same time the following morning, and introduced the Daily Service. An organ started playing over the loudspeaker, the red light went out, and he rose to greet them.

'I hope we're not disturbing you,' said Charles as he offered his hand.

'Always delighted to have company in my padded cell. Even Wordsworth can pall after a few hours, and I've got fifteen minutes to kill before the next break – unless somebody decides to blow up All Soul's.' The mellifluous voice with the immaculate enunciation made even the small talk sound like poetry.

'They sometimes call Adrian and his colleagues the workhorses of the BBC,' said Quentin, 'but I prefer to think of them as stud bulls. You can put anything in front of them and they'll work their way through it.'

Adrian did not seem at all offended, just amused. 'Wouldn't you say your metaphor was a trifle . . . inappropriate?' he suggested gently.

Quentin laughed. 'On second thoughts, you're absolutely right, dear boy. Come on Charles, or you'll be taking his mind off his work; he'll have to make do with Wordsworth. If you ever dreamed of being a pop star, come with me and I'll show you where you'll be cutting your first record.'

They waved goodbye to Adrian as he returned a little reluctantly to his leather-bound volume, and headed off down the corridor. Charles imagined it was a joke about making records – he had assumed that everything would be on tape – but the next cubicle they entered had black discs littered around the machines. Quentin noticed his surprise.

'Yes, we still cut discs here, two at a time, then if they want to leave out something in the middle they can do a jump cut – they switch from one record to the other. If you have to take something out of a tape recording it means literally cutting it with a razor-blade, and the old stagers here reckon there's a danger of losing something vital, and they say the tape can stretch and the quality can deteriorate. But mostly they're very worried because it takes a split second for the tape to run up to the right speed when you start it, whereas you can drop the stylus onto a record while it's spinning and it starts immediately. You'll find they get very fussy about the odd second in the BBC. It may seem a bit perfectionist, but it's surprising how long a second can seem when there's nothing coming out of the radio.'

'So what about the tape recorder you had at Marford Heath?'

'Thank goodness, they let us use recorders now when we're out on the road. It's not so long ago we had to go out with a recording car and two engineers to cut the discs – a real pantomime, that was. It wasted a lot of time and money.'

'And records, I suppose? At least on tape if you make a mistake you can re-use it. What happens if you make a mistake on a disc?'

'You chuck that pair away and start again,' said Quentin, pointing at the discards in the waste-bin. 'So it's very simple really; you don't make mistakes. But you're right, it's much easier on tape. Give me the Midget every time.'

'Bob Corby talked about a midget. Don't tell me he runs along behind you with the tape recorder?'

Quentin chuckled. 'It's a nice idea, but the Midget *is* the tape recorder. Mind you, it's only a midget by comparison with the equipment you need to cut discs; it's actually a hell of a weight if you have to carry it any distance. But at least you can be fairly mobile – and if the Fleet Street lads are in front of you and you want to get past, you only need to catch one or two of them behind the knees with a Midget and it's amazing how a path opens up. Let's go and see Fred. It's time you got a little practice yourself.'

Fred was the elderly engineer in charge of the Midget store. He soon made it clear to Charles it was not a job he enjoyed. 'You can't beat discs for sound quality,' he told him morosely as he put a recorder on the counter. 'I dunno why they let you play about with these things. Recording is a job for an engineer, not a lot of bleedin' amateurs.'

Quentin sighed. 'Now, Fred, we had all that from the unions and it's all been sorted out. Nobody's going to lose their job over it.'

'It's not a matter of jobs, it's a matter of standards, young Quentin.' Fred was genuinely angry. 'You start putting out second-best recordings, next thing you know you'll have second-best programmes – and second-best reporters, come to that. If you've got something worth saying, you want people to hear it said properly; not too much base or over-mod. or your s's coming through like a steam-kettle. And like as not, sooner or later you'll press the wrong button on this machine and wipe the whole tape. Then where are you? You couldn't go wrong with a disc and an engineer to look after it.'

'That's a very good warning,' said Quentin placatingly. 'Wiping the tape is one of my nightmares. Perhaps you'd show him which buttons he *should* press.'

Fred grudgingly explained the controls of the Midget to Charles, how to adjust the tone and the volume, how far away to hold the microphone, what the needle should be indicating on the input meter, how to attach the little handle to wind back the spool.

115

The handle seemed rather primitive amongst all the other technology. 'Why isn't there a re-wind button?' Charles asked.

'You're better off without one,' Fred snapped. 'It would use up all your batteries winding back a couple of tapes. Here's the button you need to worry about, the one marked "Record". If you try and play back the tape and you press that by mistake, that's how you wipe the lot. I'll give you a FAWD, just to remind you.'

He produced a red label, licked it, and stuck it beside the 'Record' button. 'There we are: FAWD. That should make you watch out for that button.'

'Fred's been in the BBC too long,' Quentin explained. 'He's got this obsession with initials too. FAWD stands for Fred's Anti-Wipe Device; it's almost infallible.'

'Mind how you go with it,' warned Fred as he pushed the Midget across the counter. 'They're built strong, these machines, but they don't like being banged about. I expect young Quentin's told you his trick for getting through crowds, but don't go thumping people too hard with it. There's no point getting to the front of the crowd, then finding your recorder won't work. And one more thing.' Fred picked up the microphone that plugged into the Midget. 'When you're doing an interview don't wave this backwards and forwards between you like a conductor's baton. It makes people nervous, and it isn't necessary. You hold it steady, midway between you, then you'll get the same level all the time.'

'They seem to do it quite a lot on television,' Charles ventured.

'That's because on television they've got a real engineer with the cameraman to balance the level,' snapped Fred. 'You've got to do your own balancing, and that's the way to do it.'

Quentin was getting restless. 'Thank you, Fred, we'd better get on. Charles, you've just had a FICOM – Fred's Instant Course on Midgets. You are now a qualified Midget operator: congratulations.'

Charles thanked Fred, signed for the Midget, and lifted it off the counter. Taken unawares by its unexpected weight he bumped it noisily against the counter leg. Fred said nothing, but his sigh could have been heard all over Marylebone.

'Congratulations again,' said Quentin. 'You're the first reporter to be given a FICOM and fail the first test before you get out the door. We'd better get going before Fred does something unpleasant to you with that microphone.'

The BBC Club was based in the old cocktail lounge of the Langham Hotel, just across the road from Broadcasting House, once patronised by Lily Langtry and the then Prince of Wales, now yet another bastion of the Corporation's Marylebone empire. As Quentin and Charles went in, the centre of attention at the bar was a voluble little man bizarrely dressed for a London winter in khaki drill trousers and open-necked shirt. A bush hat trimmed with a band of leopard-skin was placed prominently on the bar beside him. He was in the midst of a lengthy story which seemed to require much dramatic gesturing, interspersed with realistic sounds of battle.

'Oh Lord,' murmured Quentin. 'The White Hunter's back from safari. Let's stay down this end of the bar.' But it was too late. The White Hunter had spotted them and waved them over.

'Come and join us, Quentin, and bring your friend. I've just got in from Lagos – great story on the fighting in Kwara Province. It should make the lead tonight.'

'No chance,' said Quentin. 'Kwara Province won't mean much to the chap on the Number Nine bus. I doubt if he's even heard of Lagos. Spare a moment to meet Charles Benson here – he's just emerged from the Norfolk bush to join us. Had a hell of a time getting past the elephants in Thetford Forest. Charles, this is Ronnie Horton, teller of interminable travellers' tales and specialist in very small African wars.'

Charles recognised the name and the face. The last time he had seen Ronald Horton on television he was reporting dramatically on Mau Mau atrocities in Kenya. Now presumably the Kikuyu had quietened down for a bit and he had gone in search of trouble elsewhere.

Ronnie shook his hand briefly, then insisted on resuming his story. 'So I was doing this piece to camera with plenty of guns going off in the background, fair amount of smoke billowing about, the odd patch of grass on fire, all the signs of a really good punch-up. I was just giving it the finishing touches, some nice evocative stuff about a flame being kindled which could set the whole of West Africa ablaze, real front-line reporting, then damn me if this little black kid ambles across in front of me, right between me and the camera, leading a goat! About six years old he is, and he just stands there and giggles at me, with all this racket going on around us, then the goat wanders up to me and craps all over my feet.'

Even Quentin had to laugh. 'I hope the cameraman kept filming – it should be a good one for the Christmas party.'

'I think he was laughing so much he got the shakes,' said Ronnie. 'Never mind, I gave the kid a couple of bob to take the goat away, and

117

we did the whole thing again. I think you'll find it looks quite impressive on tonight's news.'

Quentin laughed again. 'Let's hope they don't use the wrong version.' Then he added quietly to Charles, 'On second thoughts, let's hope they do.'

They got themselves a beer and a sandwich and took them to a corner table well away from the White Hunter. They were just finishing them when Bob Corby came briskly into the bar and headed straight for them. 'Glad I caught you, Charles. You're in business. I've got a job for you.'

'Right, sir, er, Bob.' Charles leapt up, poised for action. He could see Ronnie Horton at the bar, still recounting his adventures. Perhaps it would be his turn next.

'Sit down, there's a good chap. No need to get so excited. It's not until tomorrow. I'll just get myself a beer.'

Charles subsided, and Quentin patted his shoulder as the HORC headed for the bar. 'You'll get used to Uncle Bob's touches of drama. He doesn't get out on the road himself, so he can't compete with Ronnie's stories, but he gets what excitement he can from issuing the orders.'

'Was he ever a reporter?' Charles asked. 'I know he was in the RAF, but that's about it.'

'To be quite honest, he's never actually been a journalist at all, though I think he'd dearly like to be. He was in the BBC before the war as an S.M. – studio manager. Then when he came out of the Air Force he moved up to news producer, and when we began to take on more reporting staff and someone had to keep us all in order he invented this new job of Head of Reporters. That meant he was the HOR for a bit, which didn't sound too savoury, so he expanded the job to include correspondents, and the HOR became the HORC. You'll find the BBC is a great place for inventing new titles and building up empires, and Uncle Bob is a past-master at the game.'

Quentin glanced quickly at the bar; the HORC was still paying for his drink. 'I think he'd like to take over the new training department as well, so he can be in charge of instructors in addition to reporters and correspondents. Then he'd be HORCI. How do you fancy that, Charles, being briefed by HORCI, the Last of the Mohicans . . .'

'Right, Charles, this is it.' The HORC, as yet I-less, sat down opposite them. I know what's he going to do now, thought Charles, and he was right. Bob Corby shot his cuffs.

'There's a job to be done for tomorrow's South-East Region News. How does that strike you?'

It did not strike him at all. He had never heard of South-East Region News. 'That sounds absolutely splendid,' he said.

'Of course you won't have heard of it in Norfolk, but it's the region with the biggest audience in the country. All of London and the Home Counties and a few more besides. A very good outlet for us, even though Quentin is inclined to mock it.'

'It's the BBC's version of a provincial evening paper,' explained Quentin. 'I'd say about half a step ahead of the *Toftham and Wettleford Journal*.'

'Don't forget that's where you did *your* first story,' said the HORC sharply. 'And very nervous you were too, as I recall, even though it was only a round-up of Bank Holiday train services.' He leaned across to Charles. 'I tell you this, and Quentin should know it too; whether you're doing a travel round-up for South-East Region or covering a major plane crash for Radio Newsreel, they demand the same accuracy, the same attention to detail, the same professionalism.' This could almost be Mr Juby talking, thought Charles, except Mr Juby never shot his cuffs.

The HORC became Uncle Bob again. 'Now then, here's what they want. There's a group of Swedish fishing boats coming into Folkestone tomorrow on some sort of goodwill mission. The public relations chap at Folkestone is very keen to give us any help we need – he always likes to get one up on his opposite number in Dover. So he should lay on everything for you, and as it's your first time out we'll send a news producer with you to give a hand with working the Midget. You'll have all day to play with, so it shouldn't be too much of a rush. Drop in on the ladies in Facilities this afternoon and they'll have everything ready for you.' He finished his beer and rose. 'I shall look forward to hearing it tomorrow night, Charles. Good luck.'

Bob swept out of the Club, and Charles turned to Quentin for guidance on that final instruction. It was the second time he had heard the reference and it still seemed to make no sense. 'These ladies in the facilities. Why are they in there? I thought they only had women in men's loos on the Continent.'

Quentin laughed delightedly. 'They'll love that. I don't think they've been confused with lavatory attendants before. The Facilities Unit is certainly there for our convenience, dear boy, but not quite the way you mean. They are the ladies who book our tickets for us and look up train times and contact the people we're going to meet, and generally nurse and cosset us. They're really a throwback to a more civilised era, when news-gathering involved carrier pigeons and the Morse Code. I think

119

the BBC is the only place where they could still survive. Unique, dear boy, utterly unique. Finish your beer and I'll take you to meet them.'

There were half a dozen ladies in the Facilities office, all of mature age, neatly dressed in sensible two-piece tweeds, with a quite impressive scattering of pearl necklaces and gold bracelets. They spoke softly and elegantly, and they all had pot plants on their desks, but no sign of a typewriter. Typing, it seemed, was not approved of, perhaps because of the noise; the Facilities Unit was very quiet indeed. Even the telephones did not have the temerity to ring, they had little lights on them instead. The papers and files on the desks were all in neat piles, and Charles noticed one or two oldfashioned wooden pencil-cases like the one he had at school. It was a scene of enormous calm and tranquillity. He had once had to visit the Toftham Ladies' Sewing Circle, and the atmosphere seemed much the same.

Even Quentin seemed affected. He introduced Charles to the nearest lady almost in a whisper, and Charles just mouthed a silent hello.

'You must be the Folkestone fishing-boat story, Mr Benson.'

'I am indeed,' agreed Charles, just stopping himself from adding 'ma'am'.

'How very nice,' said the Facilities lady. 'I'm so fond of Folkestone. We always used to take our holidays there before the war; such a nice beach, and the sun always seemed to shine.' She smiled at him sweetly, and Charles wondered if she was about to offer him a buttered scone and a cup of Earl Grey tea. Instead, she indicated another lady on the far side of the room, who was writing slowly and carefully with a slim gold fountain-pen. 'Miss Murchison is dealing with that for you. She's just finishing off the travel details, and I'm sure she's looking forward to meeting you. We like to meet you all personally, just in case there are any special requirements – whether you like to travel facing the engine, for instance, and which paper you like to have waiting for you at the hotel, and anyone you'd like contacted if you're sent off suddenly – that sort of thing. It's such a help if we know these things, then we don't have to keep asking.'

They walked as quietly as they could across the room. Charles heard his shoe squeaking and looked around nervously, but none of the ladies was ill-bred enough to react. They merely smiled gently at their pot plants after he had gone by.

Miss Murchison finished writing as they reached her and put the sheet of paper into an envelope which already seemed quite full. In an immaculate rounded hand she wrote on it: 'Mr Charles Benson. Documentation for Folkestone assignment.'

She handed the envelope to Charles as if she was entrusting him with her life's work. 'I hope you'll find it's all there, Mr Benson. First-class return ticket, the time of your train, the platform where you'll be meeting your producer, the telephone number of the public relations officer in case he misses you at the station, a street map of the town so you can find his office if necessary, information from the Swedish Embassy about the background to the visit, the name of the Swedish skipper who will act as spokesman – we've checked that he speaks English well enough for you to interview him – a tide table for that part of the coast which suggests you should go aboard at about 2 p.m. if you are going to avoid quite a long climb down from the quayside, and the phone number of a local taxi service in case the PRO cannot take you back to the station. I hope we haven't forgotten anything vital.'

Charles was about to reassure her, but Quentin chipped in. 'I think you have, Miss Murchison. What about a list of reputable restaurants for Charles to have lunch?'

Charles thought he must be joking. Miss Murchison obviously did not.

'Lunch is kindly being arranged by the public relations department,' she said solemnly. 'But if by any chance they fail to do so, there is a selection of restaurants marked on the street map. I think you'll find they are all acceptable.'

He took the envelope in something of a daze, and stammered his thanks. 'Quentin is absolutely right about Facilities,' he added. 'It's quite unique.'

'No, Mr Benson,' said Miss Murchison gently, 'it is not *quite* unique. There can be no degrees of uniqueness, as I am sure you know. I think you mean we are *simply* unique. But then,' – and she smiled at him serenely – 'so is the BBC.'

NINE

Charles looked again at the station clock and again checked Miss Murchison's brief. 'Your train leaves Platform 9 (nine) at Victoria Station at 09.32 hours, arriving Folkestone 11.13 hours. It is not necessary to change, this is a through train. You and Mr Benjamin Gunn, news producer, have been reserved window seats in a smoking compartment in Carriage C, which you will find in the first-class section at the rear of the train. Mr Gunn will meet you at the ticket barrier on Platform 9 (nine).' Then Miss Murchison had added a footnote which was both reassuring and disturbing: 'Nota Bene: Mr Gunn is not likely to arrive before 09.30 hours. He is inclined to cut things a little fine.'

Mr Gunn was cutting things very fine indeed. The clock said 9.28 and Charles was facing the nightmare decision of either missing the train or embarking on his first assignment unassisted. The hand of the clock moved on with a jerk to 9.29, and the ticket collector showed signs of closing the barrier. Charles decided he would have to go it alone.

'Hang on! I'm with you.'

A little round man with a purple face was running towards the barrier, waving his newspaper. He wore a flat cap and a heavy tweed overcoat and he looked very hot indeed. Charles waited for him as the collector punched his ticket and the hand of the clock jerked on to 9.30. Miss Murchison had judged it just right.

'Mr Gunn?' he enquired, unnecessarily.

'None other,' gasped the little round man; he hardly came up to Charles's shoulder. They hastened along the platform, Charles walking as briskly as his Midget would allow, Mr Gunn almost running to keep up. They boarded Carriage C, found their compartment and collapsed into the window seats just as the guard blew his whistle.

'There we are, spot on.' The little man was getting his breath back, and his purple cheeks were resuming a more normal shade. 'Very important to get the timing right in the BBC – I expect they've told you that.'

'Yes, they have,' said Charles a little coolly, 'but I thought it only

122

applied to broadcasting, not catching trains. I didn't think you'd make it.'

'Oh, I always make it.' The little round man sounded enormously complacent. He took off his heavy tweed coat, then the heavy tweed jacket beneath it, then the pullover underneath that, and put them all on the seat beside him. He was not quite so round without them, but he was definitely little.

He surveyed the empty compartment. 'There's never anybody on these trains going out of London at this time of day. If they left it to me to do the booking I'd go second-class and make a bob or two. But Facilities have their routine and nothing'll budge them.'

Then he nodded at the Midget which Charles had put on the floor. 'I should keep that on the seat if I were you. The vibration of the floor can play the devil with the speed mechanism of the spools. If Facilities really wanted to spend the Corporation's money sensibly they should reserve an extra seat for tape recorders. I expect Fred gave you one of his FICOMs. D'you think you've got the hang of it?'

'Yes, I think so.' Charles had spent most of the previous evening practising on the Midget, reciting Miss Murchison's brief into the microphone, putting questions to imaginary Swedish fishermen, then playing it all back. His voice had sounded far too low and funereal at first, and he had done the whole thing again in a higher key, so that he sounded like a schoolboy whose voice was just breaking. After a number of other attempts he carefully wiped the tape so it did not find its way into any Christmas parties, and decided to hope for the best.

'I expect Fred told you not to wave the mike under people's noses, but he's only used these things in studio conditions. If there's much noise going on you have to hold the mike good and close to whoever's talking and turn the level down on the recorder. I'll look after that end for you, as it's your first go. Just enjoy your day out – and incidentally don't bother about the Mister Gunn or Benjamin. It's only the Facilities ladies who call me that. It's just Ben Gunn.' He saw Charles start slightly, and gave a sigh. 'I know. Now you're going to ask me where Long John Silver buried the treasure. Get it out of your system.'

'I wouldn't dream of it,' lied Charles.

'Pity. Because then I'll tell you, "The same place the monkey buried the nuts. Now get the hell out of my cave." Never mind, I expect we'll go through the same routine with the P.R.O. at Folkestone. Very jolly fellows, P.R.O.s.' And Ben Gunn sniffed, and buried himself behind his newspaper.

Charles gazed out of the window and watched the London suburbs

123

give way to the hop-fields of Kent. It was a clear, crisp winter's morning and for a moment he thought wistfully of the days he had spent puttering around the Norfolk countryside in the Vibrator, meeting the familiar characters in the villages, arriving back in Toftham in time for a pint with Mr Juby in the farmers' bar. Here he was on his way to meet a lot of people he didn't know, whom he was never likely to meet again, in the company of a Midget tape recorder and a rather abrupt little man called Ben Gunn. Had it all been a ghastly mistake?

The door of the compartment slid open and the guard came in to check their tickets. He saw the recorder with the BBC News label on it and nodded appreciatively. 'Never miss the news,' he told Charles. 'Always listened to it during the war when we were out in North Africa, the only news we could trust out there. Are you gentlemen off on a story, then?'

'As a matter of fact, we are,' said Charles. He chose his words carefully, while Ben Gunn remained hidden behind his paper. 'There's something going on in Folkestone we're going to look into. You should hear it on the News tonight.' He did not mention it was the South-East Region News; somehow there was not the same ring about it.

'Fancy that. I'll be listening,' the guard assured him. 'May I ask your name, sir?'

'I'm Charles Benson and this is the news producer, Mr Gunn.'

'Charles Benson, eh? I'll be able to tell the wife I've met you.' He ignored Ben Gunn; the wife was presumably not so impressed by news producers. He clipped the tickets, thanked Charles again and carefully closed the door behind him. Charles settled back in his seat in a rosy glow; it had not been a ghastly mistake after all.

'There's your first moment of glory, then.' Ben Gunn gave him an amused look over his paper. 'Something going on in Folkestone we're going to look into, eh? Maybe those Swedish fishermen are smuggling heroin or gun-running, or they're planning an invasion. It should be quite exciting.'

Charles blushed. 'It seemed a pity to spoil his enjoyment,' he said without much conviction. 'Anyway, who knows? Maybe it *is* an international drug-smuggling plot. I can't think of any other reason why a lot of Swedes would want to come to Folkestone.'

'Very true, Charles, very true.' Ben nodded solemnly. 'We should have asked Facilities for a sniffer dog.'

He returned to his newspaper and Charles read Miss Murchison's brief for the umpteenth time. The visitors were actually on a goodwill mission from the Swedish port of Malmo. In the evening there was to be a presentation to the Mayor by the leader of the party, and the Council would then be entertaining them to dinner. That would all be too late for South-East Region News, so Charles was asked to record a short introductory piece with background actuality of harbour noises, leading into an even shorter interview with the English-speaking skipper about the gift for the Mayor and what he thought of Folkestone. Total duration, two minutes, thirty seconds.

It all sounded highly respectable and not a little boring. Charles suspected that he had been chosen for it because if he messed it up nobody would greatly miss it. Even if he got it right it was hardly an indispensable item; Quentin had warned him that South-East Region always asked for more items than they could use, just as a precaution. And if there was a good last-minute item he would almost certainly be crowded out. He began to wish he hadn't given his name to the guard.

'How did you get to Victoria?' Ben Gunn asked suddenly. He had a notebook out and was jotting down figures.

'By Underground, of course. Why?'

'Then you're in pocket. If you are carrying a Midget you are entitled to a taxi, to protect it from possible damage in public transport. Actually I think you're entitled to a taxi anyway, especially if you're late – and I'm *always* late. You can put down thirty bob.'

Charles nodded dumbly. His real BBC training had just begun.

'Then there'll be lunch. You get the official allowance for that. I don't think we'll quite make an evening meal out of it – you need to be out until after 20.00 hours and we're due back at 5.30.'

'But according to Facilities the P.R.O. will be buying us lunch,' Charles objected.

'Of course he will. That's his job. But BBC allowance regulations are quite clear: if you are out on an assignment between the hours of noon and 2 p.m. you are entitled to lunch allowance. If we put down on the expenses sheet that the P.R.O. had given us lunch, that would look as if he was bribing us to give him free publicity – which of course he is, but there's no need to put it on paper.' Ben Gunn looked at him solemnly. 'After all, we have to preserve our integrity.'

'Quite so,' said Charles. 'But the fact remains that Facilities know we're not paying for our lunch.'

'Quite so,' mimicked Ben. 'But Facilities and the accounts department are on two different floors, which in the BBC means they're in two different worlds, and mercifully never the twain shall meet.'

He consulted his notebook again. 'Now then, we'll have to offer hospitality to this Swedish captain you're talking to, that's only civil.

We could put down a pound or two apiece for that. And there's always his crew to think of. We ought to look after them properly, that comes under international relations. The BBC's very keen on that.'

'But we shan't even meet them until after lunch, and it'll be a tight squeeze to catch the train anyway. There won't be time to do all that.'

Ben sighed and put down his notebook again. 'There's nothing in BBC regulations about how long it must take to buy a man a drink. If the entire crew of any fishing boat put their mind to it I'll bet they could drink five quids-worth of beer in a couple of minutes. We just need to give them a bottle or two, just for appearances, then we must make sure we get a crew-list from the skipper so we can quote a few names.'

Charles was beginning to get the picture. 'Surely we could just make up the names. The boats'll be back in Malmo before they get a chance to check.'

'Now, now.' Ben shook his head reprovingly. 'That wouldn't be very honest, Charles, now would it. It also wouldn't be very sensible. The BBC has a stringer in Malmo; if they were feeling awkward in Accounts and asked him to pop down to the harbour and check, we might have a problem. You must take warning from Colonel Jaczinski.'

'Jaczinski?' The name meant nothing to Charles.

'Colonel Jaczinski used to feature regularly on the expenses of one of our more illustrious correspondents,' Ben explained. 'No need to tell you *his* name; everyone in B.H. knows the story. He used to put down five pounds each month for entertaining Jaczinski, the military attaché at the Polish Embassy. Very useful contact, he used to say. Then some new broom took over in Accounts and started checking. He got in touch with the Embassy to find out why the Colonel merited so much hospitality. And of course there was no such person; he didn't exist.'

'So the illustrious correspondent got the high jump?'

'As it happens, he didn't.' Ben Gunn chuckled. 'He was an old BBC hand. He heard on the grapevine they were making enquiries, so when he got hauled in and they told him there was nobody called Jaczinski at the Polish Embassy he just registered shocked surprise. "That's dreadful," he said. "The fellow I've been entertaining must be an imposter. I shall not meet him again." He actually got away with it – he *was* a very illustrious correspondent. And thus another piece of BBC folklore was born.'

Ben grinned, then raised a warning finger. 'But nobody could get away with it twice, Charles. So always remember Colonel Jaczinski; he passes this way but once.'

126

The train arrived at Folkestone a few minutes early, but their host was already waiting for them by the barrier. Peter Kettering, public relations officer for Folkestone Council, positively overflowed with professional bonhomie. He greeted them like old friends.

'Welcome to Folkestone, Charles. Welcome, Ben. Splendid of you to come to our fine little town, I suggest we have a cup of coffee at my office, then I'll take you on a little tour of the attractions here, just to give you the feel of the place, then we'll have a bit of lunch at the Victoria. That's very handy for the harbour, so we'll be able to meet those Swedish chappies at around two o'clock.'

'Yes, of course, it'll be high tide,' said Charles casually. 'It'll be easier to get on the boats.' Kettering looked impressed, and Charles mentally thanked the meticulous Miss Murchison.

'Quite right, Charles. I see you've been doing your homework. Always the mark of a good reporter.' Ben Gunn spluttered slightly but Charles ignored him, and so did Kettering. 'Now my office is just round the corner – we'll walk there, if it's all right with you. Let me carry that for you.' He took the Midget and led the way out of the station, with Charles and Ben following a few paces behind.

'What's the point of the grand tour?' asked Charles quietly. 'We're not doing a story about Folkestone's tourist attractions.'

Ben shrugged inside his tweed overcoat. 'No point at all so far as we're concerned, but he'll be able to tell the Council he's made the most of having a BBC news team in his grip for a couple of hours. He's got *his* expenses to worry about too. Anyway, it'll pass the time until lunch – and we should get a pretty good one at the Victoria.'

Charles remembered their earlier conversation. 'He hasn't asked you about the treasure yet. You'd have lost that bet.'

'True,' admitted Ben. 'Maybe he knows it doesn't pay to bite the hand that publicises you. He's a better P.R. man than I thought.'

His prediction about the lunch at the Victoria was more accurate. It turned out to be excellent, and by then Charles felt he had earned it. On Kettering's tour of the town he had dutifully admired the Leas, and Kingsnorth Gardens, and the East Cliff Golf Links, and the Martello Tower, and the cliff lift, and the amusement park, and even the museum and library. So he enjoyed his smoked salmon, his Beef Wellington, and his crêpes suzettes. He was also much tempted by the wine that the P.R. man pressed upon him, but he wisely heeded the warning glances of Ben Gunn. However, he mused to himself over the coffee, the life of a BBC reporter was not exactly an unhappy one.

'Two o'clock, gentlemen,' said their host. 'Time to go.'

The Victoria was only a few yards from the harbour, and this time Charles said he would carry the Midget himself, but rather regretted it. Its weight seemed to have doubled. Ben noticed his expression and grinned. 'They always feel heavier after lunch,' he said. 'I'd like to help, but I've got all this beer.' He had generously bought three bottles.

The Swedish boats were bobbing about by the harbour wall. In spite of Miss Murchison's skilful timing there was still quite a drop to the decks. A rusty metal ladder led down to the nearest boat, and Charles eyed it with misgiving. Then he noticed the man in the smart blue suit and the large chain of office, waiting on the quayside to greet them.

'I didn't expect the mayor to be here,' he muttered to Peter Kettering, feeling quite flustered. The infallible Miss Murchison had failed to mention any worshipful spectator. Worse still, perhaps he expected to be interviewed.

Peter Kettering beamed cheerfully. 'He did say something about dropping by if he was in the area. Happy coincidence, eh?' And he slapped Charles heavily on the back. Charles rocked slightly, but managed a smile. It seemed unlikely that the mayor made a habit of wandering around the harbour in his best suit and full regalia, but he could hardly refuse to meet him. He looked questioningly at Ben Gunn, who shrugged back.

'You may as well interview him now he's here. We can always drop him if we've got too much.'

'But what do I ask him? I hadn't planned any questions for the mayor, just the skipper.'

'You're the reporter; that's your problem.' Ben smirked. 'Ask him if there's much drug-smuggling in Folkestone. And I'll go wuff-wuff.'

Kettering introduced Charles and the mayor greeted him warmly. 'Welcome to our fine little town, Mr Benson.' It seemed to be the standard Folkestone greeting. 'I thought I'd make sure that Peter was looking after you all right. And I might be able to help if you need an interview about the work of the Council and its services to the towns-people.'

He turned to Ben Gunn. 'And you must be the cameraman, I assume? Did you leave your equipment in the Victoria? I'll get Peter to go and fetch it for you.'

'No, I'm not a cameraman, Mr Mayor,' said Ben coldly. 'I am a producer. A *radio* producer. This item is for *Radio* News.'

The mayor seemed considerably put out. 'But when Peter said BBC News I assumed it was for television. Are you sure they're not coming?'

Charles saw that Ben's face was achieving an even deeper shade of

128

purple that when they first met, and this time it was not caused by running. He hastily stepped in. Much too hastily.

'Let me introduce you properly, Mr Mayor. This is Ben Gunn.'

He recognised the mayor's reaction, and his heart sank. But it was too late.

'I say,' said the mayor. 'Perhaps you can tell me where Long John Silver has hidden the treasure . . .'

Charles shuddered as Ben Gunn, now almost apoplectic, opened his mouth to speak. It was Peter Kettering, the professional P.R. man, who saved the day.

'I think Mr Benson would very much like to interview you, Mr Mayor. Perhaps we could get that done straight away – I'm sure you've got other pressing duties.'

Charles took the cue. 'Yes indeed, Mr Mayor. If we could just step over here in the lee of the wall. The wind won't be quite so noisy for the Midget.'

'The Midget?' The mayor looked again at Ben Gunn and started to smile, but Charles hustled him away, avoiding Ben's eye. 'This is a Midget tape-recorder. It's just a name we give it. Shall we stand over here?'

He did not dare ask Ben to operate the recorder, even though it was his first-ever interview; it might be asking for trouble. Instead he adjusted all the knobs with great care, counted up to five into the microphone, played it back successfully, cleared his throat, and asked his first question on behalf of BBC Radio News.

'Mr Mayor, can you please tell me about the work of Folkestone Council?'

The Mayor could, and did. Charles had no need to think of any further questions. Several minutes later he made his second and final contribution to the interview. 'Mr Mayor, thank you very much.'

He did not bother to wind back the tape. He took it off the spool, put it in its box and threaded a new one on to the recorder. On the box he discreetly wrote: 'Wipe'. He was beginning to learn . . .

When they rejoined the others the colour of Ben's face had nearly returned to normal; Peter Kettering had been working hard to restore diplomatic relations.

'How did it go?' asked the P.R. man a little apprehensively.

'Absolutely splendid,' Charles assured him. 'The mayor was most . . . fluent. Now may we go aboard? I think we're getting a little pushed for time.' According to Miss Murchison's schedule they were due to catch the 15.32 train to London.

'By all means,' said Kettering with visible relief. 'The skipper should be waiting for us.' He started to lead Charles towards the ladder, but Ben intercepted them.

'I think it'll be a lot simpler if the skipper comes up to us. It'll be quite a job getting down that ladder with' – he paused and glared at the Mayor – 'a Midget.'

'But wouldn't it be more appropriate to do the interview on board?' asked Charles. 'I think that's what Miss Murchison had in mind.'

'And so you shall,' said Ben reassuringly, 'at any rate so far as the listeners are concerned. You'll get the same actuality in the background up here as you would down there. There's no point in risking your neck – and worse still, risking the tape recorder. All you have to say is, "Here I am on board . . ." and there you are, on board.'

'But surely that's cheating?' Even as he said it he remembered Ronnie Horton's dramatic front-line despatch, in the company of the unconcerned small boy and his goat. Even the old hands used a little leeway.

Ben merely raised an eyebrow. 'I prefer to call it adapting to circumstances. If there's an easy way and a hard way, why pick the hard way?'

A large blond gentleman in a blue jersey emerged on the deck below them in response to a hail from Peter Kettering, and as he climbed the ladder Charles silently rehearsed his introduction. 'I'm standing on board one of the six Swedish fishing smacks which are here in Folkestone Harbour on a goodwill visit from Malmo. With me is the skipper' – he glanced at Miss Murchison's brief – 'Olaf Svensen, who is leading the Swedish party.'

The large blond gentleman had reached the top of the ladder and was looking round the group uncertainly. Charles stepped forward. 'Captain Svensen?'

The Swede unexpectedly shook his head. 'The captain, not feeling too good. He had very big dinner, I think.' He beamed at them. 'He tell me I talk to BBC instead. Klaus Olafsen, first mate.'

Peter Kettering, the ever-professional P.R.O., leapt in.

'Glad to meet you, Mr Olafsen. Welcome to our fine little town. I'm sure you'll do splendidly, won't he, Charles?'

'I'm sure,' agreed Charles. But nothing seemed to be working out quite as planned. 'I suppose you do speak English, Mr Olafsen?'

'Of course I speak the English.' Mr Olafsen looked offended. 'This is what I speak now, yes?'

'Yes, of course,' Charles said hastily. 'If you'll stand here beside me,

I'll just do a little introduction, then I'll ask a couple of questions.' He handed over the Midget to Ben. 'As soon as you're ready, Ben, I'll get going.'

'Right, I'll just test it.' Ben put it on the ground and pressed the 'Record' knob. There was a pause. 'Hang on, the spool's not turning.'

He twiddled the other knobs, then pressed 'Record' again. Nothing happened.

'What's wrong with it?' Charles could sense his BBC career crumbling around him.

'I'm not quite sure. I'll just check the batteries.'

'The batteries?' An awful realisation dawned. He remembered all the time he had spent the previous evening recording different styles of voice, over and over again. And then there was that interminable interview with the mayor, which he had not bothered to check. Of course, the batteries . . .

'They're just about dead.' Ben glared at him from behind the Midget. 'What the hell have you been playing at, Charles? You only got the damn thing yesterday.'

'Perhaps they were faulty,' lied Charles. 'What do we do now?'

'If you need batteries,' said Peter Kettering helpfully, 'there's an electrician's shop not too far away. I could soon nip round there.'

'Marvellous,' said Charles with enormous relief.

The mayor interrupted. 'It's early closing day. They'll be shut.' He said it with some satisfaction, and it soon became clear why. 'I'm afraid you'll have to fill up the time with the material you've already got.'

Charles thought of the material, and shuddered.

'Calm down, everyone.' Ben was groping in the pocket of his capacious tweed overcoat. 'Crisis over. I always carry some spares. Perhaps you will too in future, Charles. It's pretty basic.'

Charles blushed. He felt he was back in Mr Juby's office, being reprimanded for putting the wrong initial in a funeral report, except that this reprimand was a lot more public. Again it was the professional P.R. man who smoothed the situation.

'I'm sure Charles has a lot of things to think about on occasions like this. He's very fortunate to have an experienced producer working with him. Eh, Mr Mayor?'

'All set to go,' said Ben before the Mayor could reply. 'Quiet, everyone.' He pressed the 'Record' knob, and this time the spool began to turn. 'Go ahead, Charles.'

'Right,' said Charles, and cleared his throat. The others waited expectantly. 'I'm standing on board one of the six Swedish fishing sacks

. . . Sorry, I'll start again. I'm standing on board one of the six Swedish swishing macks . . .'

The first mate of one of the swishing macks interrupted. He seemed puzzled. 'Excuse, your English no damn good. We stand on harbour, not boat. You have wrong word, yes?'

Charles was about to explain, but Ben cut in. 'Never mind all that, and never mind the blasted fishing smacks. We'll leave the introduction to the newsreader. Just do the interview, Charles. Time's getting on.'

'Right,' said Charles, trying not to look as flustered as he felt. 'Here we go.' He glanced at Miss Murchison's brief. 'Now, Captain Svenson . . .'

'Not Svensen, Olafsen,' said Olafsen. 'Not captain, first mate. Now what you ask, please?'

There was a subdued snigger from the direction of the mayor. It spurred Charles on. Anything would be better than having to use that terrible interview.

'Mr Olafsen, how did this visit come about?'

The large Swede looked at him blankly and shrugged his shoulders. 'I not know. Nobody told me.'

Charles gulped, and tried again. 'Mr Olafsen, you must be delighted to be part of this link-up between Folkestone and Malmo.'

There was another shrug. 'I not care much. I get paid, I come.'

'Dear God,' said Charles.

'We're still recording,' said Ben, crouched over the Midget. 'Have another go.'

Charles desperately reviewed his list of planned questions. There must be one that this monosyllabic Swede could answer.

'Mr Olafsen, how long are you staying in Folkestone?'

This time, at last, he got a positive reply. 'Not long, I hope. You have very dull town here. Dead as a doorknob, yes?'

It was Peter Kettering who saved the day. He had been listening with increasing concern; the final comment about Folkestone was too much for him.

'Could I just interrupt a moment, old chap?' He waved to Ben to stop the tape recorder. 'May I make a suggestion, Charles? I know it's teaching granny to suck eggs and all that, but I wonder if you could put your questions one at a time, then Ben stops the tape after each question, and I tell Mr Olafsen what to say, then you record the answer. I'm sure Ben can edit out the pauses without too much of a problem, then the whole thing should flow quite reasonably. What do you think, Ben?'

Ben nodded. 'It looks like the only way. There won't be time to do the editing when I get back, but I expect I can manage on the train.' He gave Charles a significant look. 'I *have* remembered to bring a razor-blade and some editing tape.'

Kettering beamed. 'Is that all right with you, Charles?'

'Yes, please,' said Charles. 'I mean, yes, by all means, no problem. That's if Mr Olafsen agrees.' Mr Olafsen, they gathered, did not give a damn either way.

So Charles asked a question, and Ben switched off the tape, and Peter Kettering told Mr Olafsen what to say, and Ben switched on the tape, and Mr Olafsen said it. Then Charles asked the next question, and Ben switched off the tape, and Peter told Mr Olafsen what to say, and Ben switched on the tape, and Mr Olafsen said it . . .

Peter Kettering drove them back to the station and they caught the 15.32 by the comfortable margin, according to Ben Gunn's standards, of five minutes. During the journey Ben toiled away with his razorblade and editing tape, while Charles composed the introduction for the newsreader, and licked his wounds. To his great relief it was a different guard on the train; after his day of humiliating near-disasters he could not have faced his first and only fan.

When they got back to Broadcasting House Ben offered to take the tape and the script to the South-East Region office, and Charles gratefully agreed. He had no wish to answer any questions about his first assignment, nor did he want to be around when Ben told the story of their day. He suspected that a new piece of BBC folklore had just been created, and he was the star.

Instead he went to his empty office and lurked there until it was time to listen to the South-East Region News on the 'Internal', the ring-main speaker in every office. By the time it started he was almost wishing that his piece would not be used.

It seemed his wish would be granted. The bulletin was almost over when the announcer started reading his introduction. Charles had a copy in front of him and he started to follow it, interested to hear how he coped with the 'six Swedish fishing smacks'.

'In Folkestone this evening the mayor is holding a reception for a party of Swedish fishermen on a goodwill visit from Malmo. Our reporter Charles Benson has been to Folkestone harbour where they had just arrived in' – there was the tiniest of pauses, then the calm voice continued – 'half-a-dozen Scandinavian trawlers.'

It was Charles's first experience of BBC professionalism. The second came when the interview with Klaus Olafsen was played. In spite of the rocking train Ben Gunn had done a masterly job with his razorblade. The questions sounded crisp and intelligent, the replies came smoothly and fluently. There was no hint of the fraught atmosphere on the quayside. The honour of Folkestone, of the Swedish fishing fleet, and of the BBC's newest recruit had been preserved.

Charles could find nobody in the Dover Castle that evening who had heard the interview, and his debut seemed to pass almost unnoticed. But next morning a telegram arrived for him at Egton House, from Peter Kettering. 'CONGRATULATIONS,' it said. 'FIRST-CLASS INTERVIEW STOP MUCH APPRECIATED BY ALL HERE STOP DO COME AGAIN.'

No doubt about it, Charles realised: Peter Kettering was a very good P.R.O.

TEN

'So, my rustic friend, how does it feel to be part of the finest newsgathering organisation in the world?'

'I find it's given me an allergy to Swedes,' replied Charles obscurely, as Dickie Johnson settled himself at the desk beside the window. There had been two or three modest assignments since the Folkestone near-fiasco, and they had all gone smoothly, but the memory still rankled. 'I presume you've just had your indoctrination from Uncle Bob?'

Dickie jerked his cuffs in the familiar gesture. ' "It's a great team, Richard. I'm proud of them all. I'm sure I shall be proud of you too." It's stirring stuff – I kept expecting I'd have to stand up and salute the flag.' He looked round the bleak little office. 'I must say it was rather more inspiring than this is. Even Exchange Telegraph ran to a coffee machine.'

'We have something much better than a coffee machine,' Charles assured him. 'We have Prudence.'

In his first fortnight in Egton House he had discovered just how valuable Prudence was. Ben Gunn may have given him some useful tips about expenses, but she showed him which forms to put them on, how to phrase them in the correct BBC jargon, and where to send them. She introduced him to her Aladdin's cave of a stationery cupboard, where he could find anything from a rubber band to a year's supply of carbon paper.

She explained how to time his arrival in the canteen to be just ahead of the main queue, and where to draw his free copy of *Radio Times*. She even persuaded him to put in his first leave application, though it seemed to him a little premature. They were taken in rotation, she explained, and if he waited too long he would finish up with a fortnight in November and a couple of weekends next March.

What he valued more than all this, though, was her unaffected, almost naïve friendliness, which she displayed not only to him but to anyone who came into her office. He could quite understand why Quentin had formed the P.P.P.; her guilelessness made her very vulnerable. The system seemed to work: if any newcomer, including himself, spent any length of time in the office, one of the other reporters would wander in to ask for a packet of paper-clips or a telephone number.

He explained all this to Dickie as best he could, before taking him along to meet her. Quentin had been sent off to the West Country for a couple of days and he had been deputed to show Dickie round.

As they walked into her office Prudence was stretching up to the top shelf of the stationery cupboard, trying to reach a pile of folders. Her sweater had ridden up from her skirt, leaving an entrancing gap in between. Standing on tip-toe, with her arms stretched above her and her blonde hair falling back over her shoulders, she seemed to Charles like a young goddess about to take flight.

'Wow,' said Dickie beside him, and Prudence turned quickly.

'Thank goodness you've come, Charles. I'm really not quite tall enough for this cupboard. Could you possibly get those folders down for me?'

Both of them dived for the folders. Dickie got there first, took them down and handed them to her. 'It's a great pleasure,' he said, gazing at her at close quarters. Charles edged him aside.

'This is the latest new boy, Dickie Johnson. I'm just showing him the ropes.' He tried to sound like an old hand, but Prudence giggled. 'You hardly know your own way round yet, Charles. But you're very sweet.'

She turned back to Dickie. 'I do hope you like it here. I'll help all I can.'

'I think this place is absolutely marvellous,' said Dickie with great enthusiasm. 'Can I help you down with any more folders? Or carry these somewhere for you? Or would you like a cup of tea, or dinner tonight perhaps, or we could try a theatre . . .'

'Hang on, hang on.' Charles took him by the arm. He had just enrolled himself in the Prudence Protection Patrol. 'We're due to pick up your Midget from Fred, and he's not a man to be kept waiting. I'm sorry about all that, Pru; he's been in Fleet Street too long. It'll take a little time to train him up to BBC standards.'

'That's quite all right. I think he's rather sweet too.' And she gave Dickie a smile which brought a look of dazed rapture to his face. He allowed himself to be led, unresisting, from the room.

'I should think twice before trying that on again,' said Charles rather sourly as he led him away. 'You could make yourself very unpopular along this corridor.'

Dickie did not seem to hear him. 'What an absolute stunner. Did you see that figure? And those legs? And that smile?'

'It's time you came down to earth,' said Charles crisply. 'Come and see Fred.'

Later that morning, when they had completed their tour, they returned to their office to find a note awaiting Charles. If Mr Benson could spare a moment, the HORC would like a word.

'You stay out of Pru's office for a bit,' he warned Dickie, and Dickie nodded absently but made no comment. As he headed for Bob Corby's office he hoped the P.P.P. was on full alert.

'Ah, Charles, come in. I thought I'd just check with you about a little job I'm lining up for tomorrow. Is that the only suit you've got, or do you have something a little smarter?'

Charles looked down at the suit. It was the one he used to wear at major funerals in Toftham, and the one he wore for the Appointments Board and his appearance in front of the camera at Alexandra Palace. He had also worn it each day since he had joined the Corporation. It was in fact his only suit.

'I'm sure I can get another one if necessary,' he said. 'What sort of suit do you have in mind?'

'The sort that doesn't look as if it spends all its time carrying coffins, my boy. But there's no time for that. Just see if you can get a crease in those trousers; then it shouldn't look too bad.' The HORC consulted some papers on his desk. 'Now you said in your original application, under "reporting experience", "extensive coverage of royal events". Is that so?'

Charles gulped. He had once been to the Sandringham Flower Show and seen the Queen Mother in the distance, and he had been in the crowd at Wettleford when the Queen and Prince Philip drove through on the way to Norwich. He had distinctly seen them wave.

'Absolutely,' he said.

'Good. Then you'll know what to do tomorrow.' And the HORC shot his cuffs. 'South-East Region want a straight one-minute-thirty on the Queen and the Duke visiting Hendon and Edgware. Godfrey normally handles these things but he's on leave at the moment. Do you think you can cope?'

Charles gulped again, and nodded. Godfrey, he knew, was the BBC's Court Correspondent, a figure almost as well-known and certainly as imposing as the Royals themselves. He was staggered to find himself moving in such elevated circles. But Bob Corby soon put it in perspective.

'There's really nothing to it. Everything's laid on for you by the Palace: background information, transport, a copy of anything the

137

Queen says, details of her dress. You'll be spoon-fed from start to finish. The trickiest part will be getting a crease in those trousers.'

He picked up a card from the desk and passed it over. 'Here's your accreditation card. Facilities will tell you where to meet the Palace Press Officer and you'll get the rest then. You'll come back afterwards to record your piece in the studio, but you ought to take your Midget with you. I doubt there'll be an assassination attempt in Hendon – or even Edgware. But you'd look rather silly if there was, and you had no recorder with you.'

He paused, then said more gently: 'There really is nothing to worry about, Charles. Just go where they tell you to go, and stand where they tell you to stand, and move on when they tell you to move on. The Palace organise these things rather well, you know. They've been doing it a long time, even if you haven't.'

Charles thanked him and turned to go. But the HORC hadn't quite finished. 'Just one more thing, Charles. Don't forget to take some spare batteries . . .'

Outside the door Charles looked at the accreditation card. It was pale green and very discreet. Under the royal crown it advised whoever it might concern that Mr Charles Benson was authorised to be granted facilities as a BBC observer in the special Press party when the Queen and the Duke of Edinburgh made an official visit to Hendon and Edgware. It was signed by R. Colville (Commander), Press Secretary to HM The Queen.

Much elated, Charles hurried to Facilities to pick up his brief. It was again Miss Murchison who had prepared it for him, but this time it was unusually short. It merely asked him to join the Press party outside Hendon Town Hall at 10 a.m., where he would be fully briefed by the Palace Press Office.

'Good luck, Mr Benson,' said Miss Murchison. Then she coughed delicately as he started to leave.

He paused. 'Is there something else?'

She coughed again. 'Well, Mr Benson,' she said hesitantly. 'Will you be wearing that suit?'

Charles was taken aback. 'As a matter of fact, I will. Is that all right?'

Miss Murchison produced a visiting card from her desk drawer. 'I think you may find this quite useful, if you'll forgive me saying so. It's only just round the corner in Great Portland Street. You go down Langham Street, turn right, and it's four doors down. They do quite a lot of work for us – they're very reliable.'

Charles looked at the card, and blushed. But in its way it was as valuable as the green card he had been given by Bob Corby. It said: 'Harry Cohen, Tailor & Cutter. Suits altered, cleaned and pressed.' And Miss Murchison had underlined the next words: 'Trousers pressed while you wait'.

'Thank you, Miss Murchison. I'll go round this afternoon.'

She picked up the telephone and smiled at him sweetly. 'I'll let them know you're coming. And in case you're wondering – yes, you can put it on expenses.'

When he got back to his office Dickie was sitting by the window, staring into space. He jumped slightly as Charles came in.

'Sorry, miles away.' Charles recognised the slightly dazed look.

'Have you been chatting up Prudence again?'

Dickie gave a modest shrug. 'I wouldn't put it quite like that. I just thought I'd better stock up on stationery while I had a little time to spare. Funnily enough I'd only been there a couple of minutes and one of our distinguished colleagues came in and started a long discussion on how to apply for a replacement staff car. Seemed to go on for ever, so I gave up after a bit and left them to it.'

'I trust he doesn't get one. I was supposed to get my staff car last week and they said there weren't any to spare.' But he wasn't too worried; the conversation with Prudence was probably just a ploy. He was glad the P.P.P. was functioning so well.

'So what did the HORC want?' asked Dickie, and he told him about his royal assignment. Dickie was unimpressed.

'Thank God I missed that one. What a bore. All you have to report is who she shakes hands with, what she's wearing, and who gives her the bouquet. You could write it without leaving the office.'

'You've done a lot of these, then?' Charles was rather put out.

'No, that's Tweedledee's job – he's the ExTel Court Correspondent. You'll have the pleasure of meeting him and Tweedledum tomorrow – that's the other Royals man, from the Press Association. They like it if you bow slightly before you address them.'

'I'll remember.' He was beginning to wish he hadn't mentioned his 'extensive coverage of royal events'. But Dickie had not quite finished.

'Incidentally, you're not going to wear that suit?'

Charles's first encounter with the problems of royal reporting occurred a hundred yards from Hendon Town Hall. When his taxi reached a junction with the main road its way was blocked by a row of metal railings, a small crowd of spectators and several much-bemedalled

139

policemen. The largest of them, with the most medals, approached the taxi and the driver looked at Charles in his mirror. 'What's 'appenin' 'ere, Guv? You bin a naughty boy?'

'Don't worry,' said Charles confidently. 'I'll get us through.' He wound down the window and greeted the policeman genially. 'Good morning, officer. I'm from the BBC, accredited to Buckingham Palace.' He waved his little green card.

The taxi-driver looked quite impressed. The large policeman did not. 'Sorry, sir, no vehicles allowed beyond this point. We have to keep the main road clear for the official procession. You'll have to walk the rest of the way.'

'But I have this tape recorder with me,' objected Charles. 'It's really quite a weight.'

'Sorry, sir, those are the orders. But you look quite fit.' And the policeman pointedly opened the door.

Charles paid the driver, who was now even less impressed than the policeman, and he was led to a gap in the railings. 'That's your route, sir, straight up the road. The Town Hall is that large building on the left. I don't think you can get lost.'

Charles didn't think he could either. Once he was on the main road there was no way off it. It was lined with metal railings, and the metal railings were lined with people. More policemen with more medals were spaced in front of them. The Town Hall would have been difficult to miss on a normal day; today it was festooned with flags and bunting and highly-polished soldiery.

He started his lonely pilgrimage, every eye in the crowd upon him. Thank goodness, he thought, that Miss Murchison had sent him to Harry Cohen, Tailor & Cutter. He had worked miracles with the steam press, and the creases in his trousers could have sliced bacon. In a rush of over-confidence he waved to the crowd.

It was an obvious mistake. A group of schoolchildren, perhaps assuming he was the first of the Royals on an informal walkabout, waved their flags and gave him a ragged cheer. Other spectators, seeing the flags waving, surged against the railings to find out what was happening. The policemen, taking their cue from an inspector who had also been misled by the cheering, sprang to attention as Charles approached.

He had covered about fifty yards, feeling acutely embarrassed, when the inspector on the Town Hall steps realised his error and stood his men at ease. As Charles reached the Town Hall he barred his way.

'No need for all that showing-off, sir,' he said coldly. 'Our job is difficult enough on these occasions without people trying to make us look foolish. May I check your identity, please – and I'll have a look at that tape recorder.'

While the crowd watched curiously the inspector spent some time studying the green card and comparing it with Charles's BBC staff card and his driving licence. He then examined the recorder, asking questions about the function of each knob and demanding a demonstration of how it worked. There were some ribald comments from the spectators, and Charles became increasingly flustered. He hoped desperately there was nobody there from Toftham.

'That seems to be in order,' said the inspector at last. 'You'll find the Press party at the top of the steps. I suggest you stay with them and don't wander off on your own again. It'll make life a lot simpler for all of us.'

'Thank you very much,' said Charles, not sure what he was thanking him for but deeply relieved to be escaping from the public spotlight. He tried to part on a conciliatory note. 'I think your men are looking extremely smart.'

The inspector was not to placated. 'They've also been standing there the best part of an hour, and they're due to stand there for another hour yet. So may I suggest you don't cause them any further aggravation.'

Charles gave up.

When he reached the top of the steps the Press party was easy to identify, a little huddle of bored-looking men and women, some with cameras, all with a large folder marked 'Royal Visit to Hendon and Edgware'. The women were quite elaborately dressed, the male reporters less so, the cameramen less than that. The exceptions were two dapper figures standing slightly apart from the rest, wearing dark suits and bowler hats and carrying tightly-furled umbrellas. One had an old-fashioned wing collar, and his tie was impaled with a large diamond pin. They might have been Army officers in mufti or members of the Diplomatic Corps, but Charles guessed they must be Tweedle-dum and Tweedledee.

He approached them and in spite of himself gave a vestige of a bow. 'I'm Charles Benson, BBC. Would you be from the news agencies?'

They surveyed him carefully, and again he was grateful to Harry Cohen, Tailor & Cutter. 'Good morning,' said the one with the wing-collar. 'Yes, I suppose you could put it like that. We are . . .' – and he repeated the words distastefully – 'from the news agencies.'

'I suppose Godfrey is sitting this one out?' enquired his companion, and Charles explained he was on leave. He glanced across at the Press group. 'Is Commander Colville about? I'd like to get one of those folders.'

The couple exchanged sad smiles. 'I don't think you'll find Richard running about with folders on these occasions,' said the wing-collar, who seemed used to speaking for them both. Charles did not know if he was Tweedledum or 'dee, but on the principle that his colleague preferred to remain 'dum, he decided the wing-collar was 'dee, and mentally christened them thus.

A young woman in an unobtrusive jacket and skirt emerged from the group carrying an armful of folders. 'Mr Benson?' she asked. 'You may find this useful.' She opened one of the folders and flicked briskly through its contents. 'There's the history of Hendon and Edgware since the Romans built the road here. Details of the Town Hall, when it was built and how much it cost and the materials used . . .' She looked up briefly. 'The Royal party will only spend a few minutes in the building but the information is there if you want it.'

She riffled through more papers in the folder. 'Here are the statistics about the hospital they're visiting, the services it offers, number of patients, cost per bed, biographies of the Matron and the senior staff and the patients they'll be talking to. And here are the details of the sailing display on the Welsh Harp where the tour finishes. This sheet gives a full list of the councillors and officials and other local figures who will be introduced to Their Majesties, and of course a complete timetable of the day's events. And this is your personal briefing; it shows the position you've been allocated at each venue, and the number of the car you'll be travelling in. I'll be getting the details of the Queen's dress from the lady-in-waiting when the royal party arrives. I'm afraid we don't release that beforehand.'

'Naturally not,' said Charles. 'It must be a State secret.' And he laughed, hopefully. The young woman did not laugh. Neither did Tweedledum or Tweedledee. They just looked at him.

'If you'd care to join the rest of the Press, Mr Benson, it'll be time to take up our positions shortly. I trust that, apart from the description of Her Majesty's dress, you have everything you require?'

Charles was tempted to say there was enough in the folder to write a fair-sized book, never mind one-minute-thirty for the South-East Region News, but he didn't think that would make them laugh either.

'I think I'll manage,' he said, and joined the main group. The young woman followed him across.

'Ladies and gentlemen, could we have the "writing" Press behind these railings over here, and the "photo" Press behind the railings over there.'

This corralling routine was obviously familiar to the others, and they moved dutifully to their pens, except for 'dum and 'dee, who remained precisely where they were, leaning casually on their umbrellas. Charles dithered for a moment, certain that Godfrey would have remained there too. Then he caught the eye of Tweedledum; he had rarely encountered an eye so uninviting. With as much dignity as he could muster he joined the 'writing' press.

He found himself much more at home. There were one or two rather superior women writers who kept very much to themselves, but most of the reporters were from the local Press in Hendon and Edgware, and although at first they were wary of his tape recorder and his BBC pass they became a lot more friendly when he revealed how recently he had been covering whist drives and funerals for the *Toftham Journal*.

He was discussing the relative merits of rural and suburban reporting with a cheerful young man from the *Hendon & Finchley Times* when it started to rain, lightly at first, then more steadily, until it became quite a downpour. Along the main road umbrellas went up and policemen donned their capes. The guard of honour of the Town Hall steps, unprotected from the elements, became damp, then wet, then sodden. The reception party inside the foyer could be seen putting on macintoshes and plastic hat covers. Under the partial shelter of the porch the Press group muttered among themselves.

'Looks like Queen's weather again,' observed the cheerful young man, still determinedly cheerful. 'They say it always rains for important royal visits. At least it shows Hendon must be in the big league.'

Charles nodded gloomily, trying to work out how he could keep both the Midget and the Press folder dry in the eventual dash to the cars, let alone the crease in his trousers. He noted with some satisfaction that Tweedledum and Tweedledee were no longer leaning casually on their umbrellas but were standing underneath them. It must have taken some time to furl them so immaculately, and now they would have to do it all over again.

There was the sound of cheering from the crowd along the route and the royal car came in sight, a glass-topped Rolls with the Royal Standard flapping damply on the bonnet. A considerable procession of cars followed behind, some empty, some full, all with numbers on their windscreens. Charles quickly checked his folder. He had been allocated Car Number 4, the first of the empty cars. The three ahead of it, according to his list, contained a Lady-in-Waiting, an equerry, the Lord Lieutenant of Middlesex, the Chief Constable, and the folder-free Commander Colville.

The reception committee emerged reluctantly from the Town Hall, the Queen and Prince Philip emerged (probably just as reluctantly but they did not reveal it) from the Rolls, and they converged in front of the Town Hall beneath a small forest of umbrellas, while the saturated guard of honour presented arms and the crowd loyally cheered and waved their flags. Introductions were hastily made and hands shaken, then the Queen rather briskly inspected the sodden ranks of soldiery, escorted by an officer with drawn sword. 'More useful if it was an umbrella,' muttered the cheerful young reporter to Charles.

Everyone then moved as fast as dignity allowed into the shelter of the Town Hall, where according to Charles's folder the Queen and Duke would sign the visitors' book, admire sundry paintings and inspect the Council chamber.

The photographers followed the royal party inside, hoping for something better that just shadowy figures under umbrellas, and Charles prepared to do so too. Then he noticed that Tweedledum and 'dee were already heading rapidly down the steps towards the row of parked cars.

Again, for the second time that morning, he dithered. He had ample information about the Town Hall in his folder without trailing around the Council chamber in the wake of the royal party. But suppose a councillor went berserk and attacked the Duke, or the mayor tripped over his robes and somersaulted down the stairs, or a painting dropped off the wall and fell on the Queen's foot. His nerve broke, and he went inside.

Nobody went berserk, the mayor remained upright and the paintings stayed firmly on the walls. He was too far behind to see anything anyway. All he achieved was a note from the the lady-in-waiting, via the young woman from the Palace Press Office, which described the Queen's dress as aquamarine. This was the most useful information he had acquired so far; in his notebook he had put 'sort of greeny-blue'.

The Press were led out of the Town Hall ahead of the royal party, and made a dash through the rain for the cars. Clutching his Midget and folder and notebook Charles headed for Car Number 4. Tweedledum and 'dee were already esconced in it, their refurled umbrellas at their feet. He opened the door and started to climb in.

'My dear chap, I don't really think there's room in here for you and 'that machine,' said Tweedledee firmly. He was quite right; the umbrellas occupied most of the floorspace.

'I'll go in the front, then,' said Charles, preparing to do so.

'I think you'll find the young lady from the Palace Press Office will be sitting there.' Tweedledee smiled at him sweetly. 'I'm sure you'll find there's much more room in the other cars.'

Yet again, Charles dithered. If he had been the BBC's real Court Correspondent he would have told them to put the umbrellas on the rear shelf or even in the boot, which would then create enough room for him and his recorder. But he wasn't, and he didn't.

'See you later, then,' he said, as nonchalantly as he could, and set off up the line of cars, leaving the door wide open. He took some consolation from seeing Tweedledee having to lean out into the rain to close it. A tiny gesture of defiance, but satisfying nonetheless.

The next two cars were already full of photographers, and the two after that were full of lady reporters. Car Number 9, the last in the queue, looked quite crowded as well, and Charles was desperately thinking of hitching a lift in the police car at the rear of the procession when the cheerful young man from the *Hendon and Finchley Times* opened the rear door and beckoned him inside. 'There's just about room,' he said, 'so long as you have that recorder on your lap.'

By now very wet, and getting wetter, he was only too grateful to climb into Number 9 and wedge himself alongside the other two occupants of the rear sear, with the recorder, folder and noteback heaped on his lap. It was impractical in this constricted position to write down any notes on the events so far, but he made a few mental ones for the future. First, if he had to choose between a recorder and an umbrella, he would carry an umbrella. Second, if he had to choose between staying with the Royals and getting a seat in a car, he would get a seat in a car. Third, if he had to choose between royalty in Hendon and Swedish fishermen in Folkestone, he would go to Folkestone.

'I suggest when we get to the hospital you leave that thing in the car,' said the cheerful young reporter, indicating the Midget. 'I'm not quite sure what you expect to do with it anyway. I wouldn't recommend trying to snatch an interview with the Queen. I understand that's a beheading job.'

It might shake those two in the front Press car, thought Charles, but he put the thought aside. 'It's just for emergencies, but I think I'll take it anyway. One of the patients might have a go at the Duke with his crutch.'

'And you'd record the Duke's response?' The young reporter chuckled. 'They'd never dare broadcast it.'

The procession had been driving slowly up the Edgware Road; a transformed Edgware Road, completely empty of traffic, just lines of spectators on each pavement who had gathered in goodly numbers in spite of the downpour. Charles could not have stirred sufficiently to wave even if he wanted to – and after his previous experience he had vowed never to wave to anyone ever again – but the other occupants of the car waved happily, and the crowd waved happily back. He began to feel a little better; this royal reporting had its moments. Then the procession pulled up at the hospital, with the rear cars well outside the main gate. As Charles clambered out of Number 9 clutching his tape recorder he caught the eye of a small boy at the front of the crowd.

'Look, Mum,' the boy shouted, pointing at Charles with his Midget. ''Ere's the plumber come to mend the bog.'

Charles sighed as the crowd guffawed. Royal reporting had its other moments too . . .

He caught up with the main party and dutifully followed them through the wards, the Midget getting heavier at every step. The photographers were assembled at set points to take pictures of the Queen at a bedside, or inspecting equipment, or chatting to nurses, and the reporters clustered around after she had moved on, asking what she had said and what they had replied. Everyone seemed to be getting something out of it except the representative of South-East Region News.

As he lugged the Midget into the children's ward at the rear of the entourage he wished, not for the first time, he had taken the local reporter's advice and left the damn thing in the car.

He glanced at the programme in the folder as he edged inside the door. 'Children's ward: welcome by the children.' It sounded as unexciting as all the rest. Then the welcome began, and after a few seconds he hastily plugged the microphone into the recorder and started adjusting the knobs. The welcome was in fact a musical one: the children had gathered in a group at one end of the ward and were singing a happy little song of greeting, children in wheelchairs and bandages and splints and plasters, all singing with great enthusiasm and charm, to the obvious delight of the Queen.

He started recording, but he was surrounded by reporters, at the far end of the ward from the children, and the needle on the Midget hardly registered.

'Excuse me, excuse me,' he whispered, and edged his way forward, but he was still in the middle of the group when the singing ended and the Queen started to chat to the children. He went out of the ward into the corridor, wound back the tape, and with some apprehension played it over.

His apprehension was well-founded. The singing could be faintly heard in the distance, but it was almost blotted out by the rustling and shuffling of the people around him. There were also frequent clunks as the microphone knocked against handbags and notebooks, and worst of all was his desperate 'Excuse me, excuse me'. The recording was not merely 'below broadcast quality', as the engineers would have said; it was a complete disaster.

The cheerful young reporter from the *Hendon and Finchley Times* had been listening behind him. 'Hardly does the little pets justice, does it?'

'Might as well not have bothered,' Charles gloomed. 'It was about the only thing worth bringing this wretched machine for, and I've messed it up. If I play that tape back at the office they'll fall about.'

'But surely there's no great problem?'

'No problem!' Charles was getting irritated. 'Of course there's a problem. It's unusable.'

'I know *that* is,' said the young reporter, more cheerful than ever, 'but now you can do it properly. You can ask the kids to sing it for her again.'

'I can't do that!' Charles was aghast. 'How can I go up to the Queen and say, "Excuse me, Your Majesty, I cocked up that recording, would you hang on for a couple of minutes while they welcome you again?" You're crazy.'

The young reporter sighed. 'I don't mean they should do it for real. Wait until she's gone into the next ward, then ask them to sing it just for you.'

Charles remembered Ben Gunn's comment at Folkestone about a hard way and an easy way. This might well be the easy way. But there still seemed a snag. 'They've had their moment of glory; they're not likely to do it all again just for me.'

'It's not just for you, it's for the BBC. That's a very different thing – you're in the big league now. I think you'll find they're only too delighted. And if they're not then the nurses will be. They'll make sure they do it again.'

Charles did not have to appeal to the nurses, just the ward sister. He explained he had been too far away to record the song but he was most anxious that it should be heard by a much wider audience, and without hesitation she called the children together again, told them they were going to sing for the BBC now, which was very nearly as important as singing for the Queen, and would they round off the song with a special cheer for this nice gentleman from BBC News. When he eventually caught up with the rest of the party as they were leaving the hospital, the cheer for the nice gentleman was still echoing in his ears.

Back in Car Number 9, with the tape re-wound and safely in its box, he thanked his young adviser from the *Hendon and Finchley* and settled himself as comfortably as he could between his two companions. The rain continued to pour down, but the crowds still lined the streets, and he even felt relaxed enough to acknowledge the cheers as they drove by.

'Make the most of this,' said the young reporter. He no longer seemed quite so cheerful. 'It's going to be hell at the Welsh Harp.'

He remembered the Welsh Harp from his young days in Wembley Park, an unexpectedly pleasant stretch of water in the suburban environs of the Edgware Road and the North Circular. He had no idea how it got there, but the Press folder made it all clear. It was actually a reservoir, fed by the River Brent, and much used by local sailing clubs. There was to be a sailpast in honour of the Queen, who would view it from the adjoining playing fields. The idea must have seemed very picturesque to the planners of the visit, as they sat in their warm offices, probably back in the summer: white sails drifting against a blue sky, the waters lapping against the grassy bank, and a canvas-canopied platform for the royal party to watch the sylvan scene.

The royal party squelched across the mud to the platform and gratefully sheltered under the canopy. The Press were shepherded into an enclosure nearby, which lacked a canopy or any other protection from the elements. The waters of the lake did not exactly lap, they splashed quite violently against the bank. And the white sails were hardly visible against the dark grey of the sky.

'At least they've managed to keep the Royals dry,' murmured Charles, trying to protect the Midget under his coat, but only succeeding in getting his trouser legs even wetter than before. Not that it mattered any longer. The weight of the Midget on his lap during the car-rides had created creases which Harry Cohen, Tailor & Cutter, could not have imagined in his worst nightmare.

The young reporter tapped his arm. 'I'm not so sure,' he said, and indicated the canopy over the royal dais. The rain was not all dripping off the edges; a considerable quantity was accumulating in the middle. And the canopy was sagging quite dramatically – just above the royal heads.

The party on the platform seemed oblivious of the impending disaster, but it had not gone unnoticed elsewhere. Charles saw first one

148

photographer, then another, then the whole group edge their way discreetly towards the platform. This humdrum tour of Hendon might yet produce the picture of the year.

'I should have your tape recorder ready,' advised his young mentor. 'If that lot comes through the canopy there should be some quite interesting reactions.'

The word had gone round the rest of the Press group, and as Charles plugged in the microphone he could sense the growing air of expectancy around him. Even the ladies in the party – who had been getting more and more miserable as the mud oozed over their shoes and their damp hair stuck to their foreheads – were showing signs of animation. Charles could not spot Tweedledum or 'dee; maybe, he thought with some satisfaction, they have already gone back to their car.

Perhaps the increased excitement among the Press conveyed itself to the Duke, or perhaps it was because he was taller than his neighbours and thus closer to the sagging canvas, but Charles saw him suddenly glance up and obviously realise what was about to happen. He turned to his equerry and gave a significant look upwards. And then, Charles could have sworn, he indicated the cameramen, who by now were within a yard or two of the platform.

Charles was not quite sure of the duties of an equerry, though the folder had done its best to explain. 'An equerry was originally the officer in a royal household responsible for the horses, ('equerry' is derived from the Latin word equus), but these days he fulfils a more formal role as the officer attendant upon the sovereign or the sovereign's consort.' He had assumed from his small experience in Norfolk that the sovereign and her consort were actually protected by discreet gentlemen in city suits from the Special Branch, and that the magnificently-uniformed figure in the royal party was just there for additional decoration. But it now became clear that the Press folder had got it right, and he had got it wrong.

The equerry discreetly borrowed a furled umbrella from the dignitary next to him, reversed it so that he was holding the ferrule, raised it in the air until the handle was against the sagging canvas, then thrust it firmly upwards.

Charles got his recording all right, but it was not the sound of a waterfall bursting through the canvas onto the royal shoulders, as he had rather hoped; it was the picturesque language of the cameramen around the platform, who got the full force of the deluge as the water poured off the sides of the canopy.

The equerry looked round at them and shrugged apologetically, while the others on the platform affected not to notice what had happened and continued to watch the sailing on the lake. But Charles was certain he saw the Duke catch the equerry's eye and give the faintest flicker of a smile.

Back in the South-East newsroom Charles located Ben Gunn, told him what had happened and played over both his tapes. Ben listened to the singing in silence, but the chorus from the cameramen had a much more gratifying effect.

'The chief sub must hear this,' he said when he had stopped laughing. He told the chief sub and played the tape, and the chief sub laughed as well. Then they called the editor and went through the tapes again, and the editor laughed at the cameramen loudest of all.

'So you'll use it, then?' asked Charles, basking in his unlikely triumph.

'Don't be ridiculous,' said the editor. 'We can't use that language on the air. Anyway the Palace would be on us like a ton of bricks –and Godfrey would have a fit. Save it for the Christmas party, Charles. But we'll use thirty seconds of the kids singing, and you can do a nice descriptive piece about the smiling faces above the splints and how the Queen enjoyed it all. Our women listeners will love all that. And don't forget to mention what she was wearing.'

The chief sub patted Charles on the back. 'That was a good move, getting in close enough to the kids to record them as clearly as that. How did you manage it?'

Charles gave the credit where it was due. 'I had a little help,' he said, 'from a chap on the *Hendon and Finchley Times*.'

As he left the office Ben Gunn caught up with him and gave him a knowing grin. 'That quality on the singing tape was much too good to be true – no background noise at all. There couldn't have been anyone else in the ward when you recorded that, let alone the Queen.'

Charles gazed at him solemnly. 'Haven't you heard of the easy way and the hard way? That was the easy way.'

Ben nodded appreciatively. 'Glad you're getting the hang of that, young Charles.'

'I'm getting the hang of quite a few things,' young Charles replied. 'For instance, that chap I mentioned on the *Hendon and Finchley Times*. I never did find out his name, but he ought to be worth some hospitality, wouldn't you say?'

'I would,' said Ben Gunn. 'And tell you what. After the bulletin I'll come and help you drink it.'

ELEVEN

Dickie Johnson threw down his Facilities brief on to the desk, tilted back his chair and stared out of the window at the sunlit blank wall on the other side of the road.

'This is getting ridiculous. It's another anniversary exhibition. That's the third in a fortnight. First it was an anniversary of steam engines, then it was an anniversary of Dr Barnardo's, now it's an anniversary of lifeboats.' He glanced again at the brief. 'Did you know, my rustic friend, the first lifeboat was called *The Original* and it was launched exactly 170 years ago this year? Not 169 years, or 171, but the magical 170. There's something to hold the front page for.'

'You'd have been quite glad to see it if you'd been drowning at the time,' said Charles absently. He was studying his own brief from Facilities. 'At least you're getting out of town. I've got a fascinating tour of a block of flats in Lambeth with Princess Margaret. There are times I wish I'd never recorded those kids singing for the Queen. Uncle Bob seems to think I can produce something like that every time a Royal appears.' He riffled through the documents in the brief and waved the green card from Clarence House. 'I'm beginning to collect these like cigarette cards. It would be nice to see what's going on in the real world.'

There was a distinct atmosphere of discontent in the fusty little office at the top of Egton House. Charles and Dickie had been sharing it for nearly four months, and in that time they had become the South-East Region's most regular performers. Meanwhile from the offices along the corridor their colleagues had set out on all manner of dramatic news assignments – or so it always seemed. Worst of all, every few weeks a bush hat with a leopard-skin band would appear in the doorway, and beneath it was Ronnie Horton with another tale of epic adventure in foreign parts.

'At least with the Royals everything is written out for you, and you get driven around in comfort, and there's a chance of a decent meal thrown in,' grumbled Dickie. 'All I get at these exhibitions is a catalogue and a nice cup of tea; then they ask when the television people are going to turn up. And anyway, the Maritime Museum at Greenwich is hardly "getting out of town".'

'But you do have something different to talk about each time,' Charles grumbled back, 'even if it's only an antique lifeboat. What happens with the Royals? They shake hands with half the local population, then cut a ribbon or lay a stone or plant a tree, then a quick wave to the crowd and it's back to the Palace to get their brief for the next one. What a life for them.' He shook his head sadly. 'Think of it. Every morning, the Queen finishing breakfast and saying to herself, "Pack up your troubles in your glass-topped Rolls and smile, smile, smile." '

'Never mind,' said Dickie. 'That was great stuff from the cameramen you recorded at the Welsh Harp. Maybe one day you'll get something like that on the air. It was a much better story than those kids.'

'Not a hope,' said Charles gloomily. 'I don't think we'd mention it even if the Duke threw a bucket of water over each individual photographer. They can't even take a picture of a Royal if they're holding a glass of gin. That reduces the scope a bit in one or two cases, I can tell you.'

He waved his brief again. 'Still, I seem to have made a little progress. I've actually got details of Margaret's dress in advance. Now I know why we had to sign the Official Secrets Act. Do you think the Russians might cough up a few roubles if I told them the princess is going to be in cerise with matching accessories?'

'If they're anything like me,' said Dickie, 'they wouldn't know a cerise from a magenta. They'd say she can wear any colour she likes so long as it's red.'

A soft voice interrupted from the doorway. 'There's quite a difference, actually. Cerise is a gorgeous dark cherry colour, and magenta is a very deep purplish red, like this skirt. It's rather nice, isn't it?'

They both leapt to their feet to welcome Prudence, and they duly admired the skirt, but it was the rest of the ensemble that really caught the eye. Spring had arrived, and her white blouse had been chosen for coolness rather than modesty. As always, she looked quite enchanting.

Dickie ushered her to his chair, with a curiously proprietorial air, 'Come and sit by the window, Pru. I think you'll find it cooler.' He perched on the desk beside her, while Charles sulkily returned to his own.

'Actually I did know the difference.' He had looked it up in the faint hope of enlivening his report from Lambeth on the morrow. 'Cerise

153

comes from the French for cherry, and magenta is named after a town in Italy where there was a particularly bloody battle.'

Prudence was impressed. 'That's fascinating, Charles.'

Charles preened. 'I must say this is a great job for picking up useless information. Dickie's about to become an instant expert on the history of lifeboats.'

Dickie took the cue. 'The first lifeboat was launched in 1790 and they called it *The Original*. And when it first went into the water they all shouted "Original's In!", and the parson refused to bless it.'

'Is that really true?' asked Prudence, looking up at him wide-eyed.

'I shouldn't think so,' Dickie admitted, 'but it might cheer up the South-East Region News.'

She pouted. 'I see. You're just being silly again.'

'Again?' It was Charles who seized upon it. 'What do you mean, again? How has he been silly before?'

She smiled across at him. 'Now you're being silly, Charles.' Then she smiled up at Dickie, and it seemed to Charles it was quite a different kind of smile, much more intimate. Dickie smiled back at her, and Charles glared at them both. The Prudence Protection Patrol seemed to have been slipping.

'Steady, my rustic friend.' Dickie grinned at him cheerfully. 'You seem to be going slightly magenta – or is it cerise?' And he and Pru exchanged smiles again. 'Now, Pru, what tidings do you bring us? Of great joy, I trust?'

Pru stopped smiling. 'Well, not entirely. I shall be sorry to see you both go, in spite of your silly jokes.'

Dickie stopped smiling too. 'My God, don't tell me we're fired? If someone's been listening in to us, I was really only joking about those anniversary exhibitions. I really love them.' Charles didn't laugh: he suddenly remembered Bob Corby's warning, 'They say I've got eyes like a HORC . . .'

'Now you're being really silly,' said Prudence. 'You're only going to Parliament for three months, and Charles is going to Alexandra Palace. Then you swap places. You ought to be quite pleased.'

Charles relaxed again. 'I certainly am. That's great news. I wondered when Uncle Bob would let me have a crack at television.'

'It won't be as great as all that.' Dickie countered. 'You'll spend those three months on *Town and Around*. That's just South-East Region News with pictures. You haven't escaped from the Royals yet, I'll guarantee. And don't forget it's only black-and-white television. You'll still have to say what colour the dresses are.'

154

'From my experience of Royal engagements,' said Charles loftily, 'the television people never send a reporter, just a cameraman. They're only interested in the pictures. No, I might even be let loose on a lifeboat exhibition. Who knows?'

Dickie got off his desk and took Prudence's arm. To Charles the little touch seemed far too familiar. 'Thanks for reminding me Charles, I need a new notebook to take to that exhibition tomorrow. Have you got one in your magic cupboard, Pru?'

'Of course.' She let him lead her to the door, then called across to Charles. 'Is there anything you want? Notebook, pencils, typewriter ribbon?'

'A shotgun would come in handy,' said Charles savagely. He caught a glimpse of the puzzlement on her face, then they were gone.

He sat brooding behind his desk. In the last few months he had often daydreamed about the delectable secretary, and he had no doubt that many of his colleagues along the corridor had done so too, married or single. But he had taken it no further than that, and so far as he knew, neither had they. Now it seemed that the Prudence Protection Patrol had a problem. He was not sure how far Dickie had got, but judging by the masterful way he had escorted her out of the office it must be considerably further than everyone else. Maybe, he thought, it was time to throw his hat into the ring as well.

On the other hand, maybe it was time to write to Rebecca. The thought had not occurred to him since his arrival in London, because nothing much had happened which seemed worth writing to her about. In Norfolk she would not have heard his efforts on the South-East Region, and he was not entirely sorry. Dickie had mocked *Town and Around* for merely being the South-East News with pictures, but the South-East News itself seemed little more than the *Toftham Journal* with voices. He might be in the finest news-gathering organisation in the world, but it was not much use trying to convince her of that when the sort of news he had gathered was interviewing Swedish fishermen in Folkestone and recording children's songs in deepest Edgware.

'Anyone about, Charles? I rang your secretary's office a little while back but she doesn't seem to be there.' Bob Corby was in the doorway, looking a little flushed from his climb up the stairs. Again Charles was reminded of Mr Juby. But the thought was quickly replaced by apprehension. The HORC rarely visited the reporters' corridor personally.

'She must have been in here when you rang. I think she should be back in her office now.' He hoped he was right.

'Well, I'm glad I've caught you, at any rate. Your Midget is all charged up, I trust?'

'Oh yes, of course.' He hoped he was right about that too.

'Good. Get off down to Marble Arch straight away. That marathon walker from Cornwall is just heading up the Edgware Road. He's got here a lot quicker than we expected. I gather he's somewhere in Maida Vale at the moment; if you get your skates on you should just catch him when he finishes the walk at the Arch.' The HORC shot his cuffs briskly. 'The Reel want an interview back by seven. Away you go.'

Charles was delighted. This would be his first item on *Radio Newsreel* – the first time one of his reports would be heard back in Norfolk. He thanked the HORC, picked up his Midget and made for the door. Then he turned back to his desk, took some spare batteries from a drawer and waved them rather smugly at Bob Corby before stuffing them in his pocket. Uncle Bob acknowledged the wave with a mock bow of approval as he hurried out of the door.

For once there was an empty taxi cruising through Portland Place and he scrambled aboard. 'Edgware Road, please. Quick as you can.' This was more like it.

The cabbie pulled away from the kerb, but slowly. 'Whereabouts in Edgware Road do you fancy?' he asked, eyeing him pityingly in the mirror. 'Edgware Road, Marylebone, or Edgware Road, St John's Wood, or Edgware Road, Maida Vale, or Edgware Road, Cricklewood . . .'

'Somewhere near Marble Arch,' said Charles hastily. 'Not too near. Perhaps half a mile up.' He thought he would intercept the marathon walker while he was still on the move.

'I've never had a fare ask for half a mile up the Edgware Road,' grumbled the cabbie. 'Ain't you got the address, mate?'

'There isn't any address.' He saw the cabbie's expression in the mirror and tried to explain. 'I'm meeting a man there somewhere. He's just walked from Cornwall.'

'I see.' The cabbie spoke very slowly. 'You are meeting a man somewhere in the Edgware Road who's just walked from bleedin' Cornwall.' He shook his head sadly. 'Are you sure you don't want Marble Arch, mate? You seem to be short of a few marbles yourself.'

'Just get me to the Edgware Road, please.' Charles tried not to sound too exasperated. 'I might miss him.'

'You might indeed, guv'nor. There's quite a lot of people in the Edgware Road and I daresay most of them have walked from Cornwall.' But he speeded up a little and drove down Wigmore Street

156

into Portman Square and then on to the Edgware Road. 'Will this do you?'

They were only a couple of hundred yards from Marble Arch, but Charles had had enough. 'This'll do fine.'

As he handed over the fare the cabbie offered a parting thought. 'If you ever find this geyser, tell him he needn't walk back to Cornwall. I'll drive him back, special rate.' He was still chuckling as he drove away.

Charles started walking up the Edgware Road with his Midget, away from Marble Arch. The earlier he met the marathon walker, the more time he would have to interview him. But as he plodded along the pavement through the rush-hour crowds, doubts began to assail him. There was none of the preparatory excitement he had got used to on his royal assignments, no railings along the kerb, no policemen, no clearing of the streets. Edgware Road seemed its usual noisy, crowded, fume-filled self. Had Uncle Bob got it right?

He had reached Sussex Gardens, about the half mile from Marble Arch that he had originally planned, when he saw signs of activity ahead. A police car with a flashing blue light was approaching, very slowly, and there seemed to be quite a crowd behind it. He mentally apologised to Uncle Bob, plugged the microphone into the Midget, checked the knobs, and waited.

As the police car got nearer the other passers-by around him noticed it too. They paused, and pointed, and in a few moments Charles found himself part of a jostling throng, none of whom seemed to know what they were jostling about. He struggled to stay close to the kerb, at considerable risk of being shoved into the traffic that was still driving past. As the police car drew level he was very nearly pushed underneath it. For the first time Charles appreciated all the cosseting he received on royal visits; this was a taste of life on the other side of the barrier – without the barrier.

The policeman in the passenger seat waved him back. The Royals might warrant rows of railings and bemedalled officers every twenty yards, but apparently a marathon walker from Cornwall only rated one policeman waving an arm out of a car window. It was sufficient for most purposes, but it was no help to Charles. As the car moved on the crowd surged into the road and he was forced to surge with it. He caught a glimpse of a tight little circle of very large, broad-shouldered men marching along behind the car with the marathon walker in the middle of them, then they had passed him too and he was left behind among people who had spotted his microphone and were demanding to know what the hell it was all about.

Desperately, he shoved his way past them into the long queue of cars and buses that had formed up behind the marathon walker and his escorts. He bumped into the bonnet of a bus and narrowly avoiding having a wheel go over his foot. As the bus-driver shouted furiously at him he leapt back into a cyclist who became entangled with the Midget, and the cyclist shouted at him too. Wait till I get out of this, thought Charles wildly as he dived for the kerb. This'll knock Ronnie Horton's front-line stories into a leopard-skinned bush hat.

The marathon walker was getting further and further away. Charles gave up trying to dodge through the traffic and started forcing his way along the crowded pavement. This was much more successful, largely because he made use of Quentin's advice about the Midget's usefulness in crowd control. After one or two trial swings he got the rhythm going nicely, and scythed his way through the crowd quite briskly – just like Ronnie, he thought, hacking his way through the jungle with a machete. The system only failed once, when a burly pedestrian in front of him turned round unexpectedly and caught the full force of the Midget on his knee-cap. Charles apologised hastily as his victim bellowed in agony, then forged on. When he looked back a few seconds later the burly pedestrian was hobbling after him, waving his arms. He swung the Midget even more energetically; now he had two reasons for moving fast.

He managed to draw level with the minders quite near the corner where the sceptical cabbie had originally dropped him. He wished he was still parked there to see him meet the man who had walked from Cornwall. As the little group marched briskly along behind the police car he pressed the 'Record' button on the Midget and ran alongside.

'I'm from the BBC,' he gasped to the nearest minder. 'I'd just like a quick word with your man as he finishes the last few yards.'

'No chance, mate.' The minder placed a large hand on his shoulder. 'He's only just going to make it as it is. He's in no state to talk to anyone. You can see for yourself.'

Charles looked at the man in the centre of the group. He was stumbling along on shaky legs, his eyes shut and his mouth wide open. It looked as if the minder was right.

'If he stops concentrating on keeping those legs going he'll probably fold up. You wouldn't want to wreck the whole walk at this stage, now would you?' The grip on his shoulder became firmer. 'Why not come and see us later this evening when he's had time to get over it?'

'But that'll be too late,' pleaded Charles.

The minder started minding in earnest. 'Just keep clear, mate,' he said, and gave Charles a firm shove. He stumbled on the kerb and nearly fell. By the time he had recovered, the minders and their charge had moved on and he was separated from them again. He heard a burst of cheering further ahead as the group reached the junction with Bayswater Road and started on the home straight to Marble Arch. The crowd around him heard the cheering too and joined in.

Charles looked down at the Midget. The tape was still going round. He elbowed his way across the pavement and wedged himself in a shop doorway. The needle on the Midget was registering far too high, and he remembered Ben Gunn's warning: 'If there's a lot of background noise, turn down the level and talk right into the mike.' Sending up a silent prayer he turned down the level, gazed into space, and talked right into the mike.

'And there he goes now, this remarkable man from Cornwall, at the end of his epic walk, with the cheers of the crowd urging him on. When I spoke to one of his escorts a few moments ago as they came within sight of their goal he was full of confidence that the walk would be completed successfully, and he's been right.' He tweaked up the volume control on the Midget, ever so slightly, still hoping for the best. 'You can hear the cheers growing as this gallant marathon man takes the last few paces, and there he is, mounting the steps of Marble Arch. He's made it! Just listen to the crowd . . .'

He kept the tape running as he edged out of the doorway, and tried to look over the heads of the people who were filling the road between him and Marble Arch. To his relief he saw the walker being carried shoulder-high by his minders, waving limply but triumphantly to the crowd. The gamble with the commentary had worked.

He returned to the shelter of the doorway, re-wound the tape and played back the opening words. 'And there he goes now this remarkable man from Cornwall . . .' The level was right, the cheers could be heard clearly in the background; thanks to Ben Gunn and a little creative reporting, it was all there.

Then he glanced back along the Edgware Road. A burly figure with a pronounced limp was approaching, waving his arms and shouting. Charles switched off the tape and slung the Midget over his shoulder. It was high time to get back to the office.

Radio Newsreel was already on the air when he reached Broadcasting House, and he went straight into the control cubicle and dictated an

159

introduction for the newsreader while the producer listened to the tape. 'No interview, then?'

'The poor chap was at his last gasp – I hadn't the heart,' said Charles, half-truthfully.

'Pity,' said the producer. 'People are always talking about a last gasp. We've never actually recorded one. Never mind, this'll do. Some quite nice actuality there; and the commentary will just about pass. It's only thirty-five seconds. We'll drop it in at the end of the programme.'

Charles sat in the cubicle in a happy daze as his tape was broadcast to the nation. It had all been worthwhile: the argument with the taxi-driver, the long walk up Edgware Road and the long struggle back, the flight from the burly man with the bruised knee-cap, the brush-off from the minder, and the final gamble in the shop doorway doing his commentary 'blind'. He had got thirty-five seconds on *Radio Newsreel*, and all was right with the world.

He hurried back into Egton House and climbed up to the reporters' corridor, hoping to find someone who had heard it, but the place was deserted. He even checked in Prudence's office, but he knew she left much earlier than this. He was turning to leave when her telephone rang. With any luck, he thought, it's a listener ringing to congratulate me – maybe someone in Norfolk. But it was not a listener, it was Bob Corby, and his tone did not sound at all congratulatory.

'Glad I caught you, Charles. Come down to the office.'

He came down to the office. The HORC was waiting for him, and he had the Marble Arch tape recording in his hand. 'Come in, Charles. Let's listen to this again.'

He played it as far as the final passage. 'And there he is, mounting the steps of Marble Arch. He's made it!' Then he switched it off.

'Tell me, Charles,' he said quietly. 'Have you ever been to Marble Arch?'

'Yes, of course,' said Charles, much alarmed but not sure why. 'That's where I did that commentary.'

'Then they must have rebuilt it since I went past this morning,' said the HORC icily. 'It didn't have any steps then for this fellow to "mount", and I rather doubt there are any there now. Where did you get those damn steps from, Charles?'

Charles took a breath. 'Well, actually, I suppose I was a little way back. It was difficult to see exactly what was happening.' He groped for an explanation. 'Maybe they put up a platform specially for him.'

'No they didn't. I checked with the police at the station there. They told me that's why he was carried shoulder-high after he finished. It was the only way the crowd could see him. You don't seem to have mentioned that.'

Charles wished the floor would swallow him up. 'I'm sorry,' he said miserably. 'It really was terribly difficult to see what was happening. I got stuck at the back.'

'That's what I thought.' The HORC seemed to relax slightly. 'And I know it's a tempting thought that the listeners can't see what's really happening. I think Ben Gunn calls it the easy way and the hard way.' Charles nodded dumbly. 'Now listen, Charles. I agree it doesn't matter too much if you say you're on the deck of a boat when you can't be bothered to climb down off the quayside, and sometimes it does no harm to ask people to repeat something if you didn't record it properly the first time, like those children at the hospital, when you were first starting with us. But if you're supposed to be doing an eyewitness commentary and you say something's happening when it isn't, then that's dangerous, Charles, and I don't advise it.'

The HORC paused and shot his cuffs, and Charles's heart sank into his boots. Here comes the *coup de grâs*, he thought. But the tone was gentler than he expected.

'So far as this item is concerned, you have a couple of things going for you. Not many people will remember whether Marble Arch has got any steps or not, and I can't imagine many of them will bother to phone the police and check. So with any luck not many people know you've made an arse of yourself, and with more luck, very few of them will bother to ring us up to say so. There are one or two newspaper columnists who'd have a field day with a boob like that, but I doubt they heard it. They'd all be in the pub by then. So you've probably escaped this time, Charles, but please don't try it again.'

'I won't,' promised Charles, and really meant it.

'Good. That's that, then.' And the HORC became Uncle Bob. 'Come on, I'll buy you a drink in the Club.' He led the way to the door, opened it and ushered Charles through.

'Careful,' he said. 'Mind the step . . .'

They were half-way through their second pints, Bob Corby had embarked on reminiscences of his RAF days in Norfolk, and Charles was beginning to feel a little better, when he had another nasty jolt.

'Anyone here called Benson?' It was the barman. 'Urgent phone call for Mr Benson.'

It had to be the editor of *Radio Newsreel*, or the Head of News, or even,

161

why not, the Director-General. He put down his glass. 'I'm Benson,' he called to the barman, who pointed to the telephone cubicle.

Uncle Bob guessed what he was thinking. 'Don't worry too much. Maybe they haven't bothered to check like I did. Try them with the "special platform" story.'

Charles went to the cubicle, took a deep breath, and picked up the receiver. 'B-Benson here.'

The voice that replied would have been welcome at any time; at this moment it was the voice of an angel.

'Found you at last,' said Rebecca. 'It's terribly difficult getting hold of people at the BBC. They put me through to your secretary's office, and there was no reply, but they just left me hanging on so I had to ring off and start again. Then they tried *Radio Newsreel*, and there was no answer there, and they left me hanging on for ages again. Then I asked for the canteen, and they'd never heard of you there, but they suggested you might be in the Club. Then they said they couldn't get the call transferred so I had to ring off again. It would have been quicker to come down and look for you myself.' She sounded rather exasperated, but that didn't worry Charles.

'Marvellous,' he burbled, and then hastily qualified it. 'I mean, marvellous that you did find me, and marvellous to talk to you, and what a marvellous idea to come down.' He had been lifted from despair to near-delirium.

'There's no chance, I'm afraid.' The exasperation had faded, and he detected a note of real regret. She went on quickly. 'But I thought I must talk to you to tell you how good you were this evening. I've been waiting for ages to hear you on the radio – I listen to *Radio Newsreel* most nights but I must have missed all your other reports. Were they all as exciting as that?'

Charles remembered the Swedish fishermen and the children at the hospital. 'Perhaps not quite as exciting. This was my first on-the-spot commentary; I'm glad you liked it.'

'I'm sure everybody down there is terribly pleased with it,' said Rebecca enthusiastically.

He hesitated. 'Well, fairly pleased. I've just been having a drink with the HORC, so he can't have thought it was too bad.'

'The Hawk?'

He told her about Bob Corby and the BBC's mania for initials. Then he told her about the royal engagements he had been covering, which impressed her considerably more than he had expected. He told her about his seedy little room behind Oxford Street, and about Dickie

162

Johnson and the office they shared, and about his forthcoming three months at Alexandra Palace. He did not tell her, though he was not sure why not, about the ingenuous Prudence and the P.P.P.

Then it was Rebecca's turn. 'You'll be glad to hear I've managed to get a job in Toftham. They've taken me on as assistant almoner at the hospital. They've never had one before. I think actually it was Daddy who suggested it, and nobody was quite sure what I was supposed to do when I started, but it turns out there are all sorts of problems the patients have, with their sickness payments and allowances and so on, and I've been round to see quite a few of their families and helped a bit there. I think I'm really being quite useful.'

'I'm sure you are.' He didn't know whether he was glad to hear the news or not. He had half-hoped she might get bored at home and come to look for a job in London. But she certainly sounded happy; Daddy must have sorted things out rather well.

'And how is your father? And Mrs Bateman?'

'They're fine, but they won't be if we talk much longer. All these calls to different corners of the BBC must have cost a fortune already.' She paused. 'Do write and tell me what you're up to sometimes; it'll probably be even more difficult to find you at Alexandra Palace than Broadcasting House.'

He promised to write, and she promised too. He was just about to say a reluctant goodbye when she interrupted him. 'Hang on. Dad wants to say something.' There was a pause, and he could hear Dr Bateman's voice in the background. She came on the line again. 'He says he doesn't remember seeing any steps on Marble Arch, and are you sure you got it right?'

'Yes, of course,' said Charles calmly. 'They built a special platform . . .'

TWELVE

The greeting was familiar, but not exactly the one he had expected.

'I suppose you haven't got another suit?'

Charles was in the cameramen's rest-room at Alexandra Palace, feeling like a new boy in the prefects' common-room. The head prefect, or senior cameraman, was eyeing his suit with some distaste, and he looked down at the carefully creased trousers and neatly-buttoned jacket. They had just come back from Harry Cohen, Tailor & Cutter, and considering the suit's long service at Toftham funerals, followed by its new career attending minor Royals, he thought it looked reasonably spruce.

'What's wrong with this one?' he asked defensively.

'It's too dark, of course, much too dark. You'll just come out on the screen as a black blob, except for that white shirt, and if we tweak up the exposure to lighten the suit, then the shirt'll blind us. If you haven't got another suit with you, have you got another shirt?'

'I'm afraid not.' Charles had got used to carrying spare batteries for the Midget, but nobody had told him about spare shirts.

'Well, at least we can do something about that God-awful tie.'

Charles blushed. He had given a lot of thought to his choice of tie for his first appearance on television, and decided to wear his old school tie, a brightly-striped creation in gold and maroon. He hoped it would not only impress any other former pupils or masters who recognised it, but also catch the eye of the casual viewer. It had certainly caught the eye of the senior cameraman.

'You can't wear a thing like that when you're in front of camera, it'll distract attention from what you're supposed to be reporting. Everyone will be staring at the tie wondering what the colours mean: is it the Grenadier Guards or the MCC, or little Wallop Primary School, or just a practical joke? You need to wear something plain and simple. If you haven't got a plain and simple tie then I should go out and buy a few; I'm sure you can devise some way of getting the money back on expenses.' He had a quick glance round his colleagues. 'Meanwhile you can switch ties with Bert. He'll be the cameraman you're out with today. That all right, Bert?'

Bert was a morose-looking individual sprawled in one of the dilapidated armchairs, deep in the *Daily Mirror*. He looked up from the paper and surveyed Charles with even less enthusiasm than the senior cameraman.

'Me again? Gawd's-truth, why do I always catch the new ones? Anyone'd think I was a bleedin' nursemaid.' The broad Cockney voice was full of disgust.

'You catch the new ones because of your innate patience and charm,' said the senior cameraman. 'You also do quite a good rescue job if they cock it up.' He turned back to Charles. 'This is Bert Filby. He's not as offensive as he tries to make out, but I should do what he tells you and make sure you buy him a beer whenever you get the chance. He's a good enough cameraman to make that suit look quite reasonable, but if you get on his wrong side you'll find he can fix the lighting so you've got bags under your eyes the size of suitcases, and the rest of you will look fit for scaring crows.'

It was the most useful piece of advice Charles had been given since he arrived at Alexandra Palace this morning. In fact nobody had bothered to advise him at all. He had felt a certain thrill of anticipation as he drove up the hill through Alexandra Park in his BBC Morris Minor, and parked by the massive Victorian building with its anachronistic mast, but his arrival seemed to make no great impact.

The editor of *Town and Around* had given him a brief welcome, enquired how much he knew about musical boxes, and when he admitted he knew nothing at all, said that was fine, he'd start with an open mind. He gave him a newspaper cutting, told him to report to the senior cameraman, and as an afterthought, wished him luck. It seemed an undramatic way to start a television career, but he hoped this casual approach meant that the editor had complete faith in him. Now he realised it just meant that he had complete faith in the senior cameraman.

'So where've we gotta go, mate? It'd better not be out in the sticks again; I had a day on some bleedin' fruit farm in Sussex yesterday. Got bitten to hell.'

Charles looked at the cutting and hastened to reassure his new mentor and guide. 'It seems to be a pub in Leytonstone. Is that all right?'

Bert Filby climbed out of his chair and folded his paper. 'Leytonstone ain't too marvellous, but I like the sound of the pub. You done well – what's y'name?' Charles told him. 'Right, you done well, young Charlie. Just for that, I'll lend you me tie.'

The tie was frayed and a little greasy, but it met the senior cameraman's criterion – it was plain and simple. Charles took off his own and handed it over, and Bert eyed it dubiously. 'If my missus sees me in this she'll think I've joined the ruddy Masons. Make sure we don't forget to swop back when we've finished.'

He started putting it on, and turned to the figure in the next armchair, who was engrossed in the *Daily Telegraph* crossword. 'Come on, Euclid, we're off to lovely Leytonstone with young Richard Dimbleby 'ere. Charlie, this is Euclid; he's my sound recordist. He does the translating for me if we meet someone who talks too posh.'

Euclid put aside his newspaper and rose to shake Charles's hand. He was in his late fifties, tall and well-groomed. Alongside the dumpy and rather rumpled Bert Filby he looked rather like a British version of Abbott, to Bert Filby's Costello.

'His name isn't Charlie, Bert, it's Charles.' His voice was as well-groomed as his clothes. 'How do you do, Charles, delighted to meet you. I hope you enjoy your stay here. My name isn't Euclid, of course, it's Harold Yukely-Brown, but Bert insists on Euclid and I've got rather used to it now.'

'I expect I'll get used to Charlie again,' said Charles resignedly. 'It's nothing new.'

'If it's any consolation,' Euclid added, 'Bert isn't really Bert, of course. He's Hubert, would you believe. That's a useful thing to know if he turns difficult.'

The senior cameraman waved them towards the door. 'So now you've all been properly introduced, off you go.' He grinned at Bert. 'I must say you look terribly dashing in that tie.'

Bert made a rude gesture, and the three of them left the rest-room and headed for the car park. On the way, Charles explained why they were going to Leytonstone. 'It all seems fairly straightforward. There's this chap in the pub who collects unusual musical boxes. According to the local paper there's a remarkable variety, all different shapes and sizes and all playing different tunes.'

Bert grunted. 'You think that's straightforward, Charlie? I got news for you, mate. That's one of the most fiddlin' jobs they could've dreamt up for us. Bleedin' musical boxes!'

'Let me explain why Bert is a little miffed,' said Euclid gently. 'With a straightforward interview we just film the interviewee, then do the cut-aways and that's that. But if we have to illustrate the interview with items like musical boxes, then we have to film each box separately and arrange the questions so that the interviewee talks about each one for the same length of time, then we can overlay the shots of the boxes on the interview. Right?'

Charles hesitated. Cut-aways? Overlay? 'I think so,' he said doubtfully.

'Then there's an extra complication, because as there's music involved I have to record each musical box at the right level so that the music can be mixed into the interview between the questions, with a nice fade-in and fade-out. There's really quite a lot to think about, I'm afraid. But we'll show you what to do.'

'We *always* show 'em what to do,' said Bert gloomily. 'Bleedin' nursemaids, that's what we are.' They had reached the car park. 'Now then, do you think you can find Leytonstone on yer own, young Charlie, or do you want to follow me?'

'Isn't there room for the three of us in your car?' asked Charles, indicating the capacious Humber that Bert was unlocking.

'If you reckon to get into that back seat you're welcome to join us, mate. But unless you cut off yer legs and tie 'em on the roof, I don't fancy yer chances.'

Charles looked through the window. The back seat was invisible beneath bulky camera cases and sound equipment. 'And don't suggest putting all that in the boot, because the boot's full up too.' Bert opened it up to show him the tripods and lamps that were crammed inside.

'Perhaps I'll take my car,' said Charles. 'You carry on; I'll follow you.'

Euclid nodded. 'Good thinking, Charles. But I hope you've got a street map in case you get left behind. Bert does like to drive rather fast.'

Bert liked to drive very fast indeed. Charles had his work cut out to keep the Humber in sight as it weaved through the North London traffic, paying little regard to pedestrian crossings, traffic lights or the blood pressure of other drivers. When they crossed yet another set of lights with the amber turning to red, and yet another group of pedestrians leapt back on the pavement at their approach, Charles had a nostalgic vision of the empty lanes of Norfolk where he used to trundle along so peacefully in the Vibrator. The poor old thing would have shaken itself to pieces in this hectic dash, but fortunately the Morris Minor was only a few months old, with a lively acceleration, and when Bert eventually drew up outside the Talbot Arms in Leytonstone, Charles was only a few seconds behind.

'Well done, Charles.' Euclid was climbing out of the passenger seat, a little shakily. 'You've passed the first test. I rather suspect Stirling

Moss here was hoping to shake you off. He doesn't usually behave quite as madly as that.'

Stirling Moss smiled complacently. It was the first time he had smiled all morning. 'Come off it, Euclid. You know as well as I do, if yer chasin' a news story you gotta get there ahead of the field. We done it often enough.'

'But in this case,' said Euclid patiently, 'you can hardly call it an urgent news story, and there wasn't any field, just Charles. And he's supposed to be on our side.'

Charles decided it was time to prove it. 'Let me buy you a drink,' he said, and let the way into the Talbot Arms.

The accuracy of the newspaper cutting was immediately evident. The walls of the saloon bar were lined with shelves, and the shelves were lined with musical boxes, of every conceivable shape and pattern. But the handful of customers perched on their stools by the bar had their backs to this impressive display and were more interested in the beer than the boxes. Charles paused to consult the cutting, then approached the large lady behind the bar and ordered three pints. As she filled the glasses he asked if he could speak to Mr Glissop.

'What for?' She eyed Charles and his companions suspiciously. 'You're not from the Excise people, are you?' Behind him, Bert guffawed. He smiled at her gently.

'Not at all,' he assured her. 'We're from Television News.' It was the first time he had announced himself in this way, and the words rolled splendidly off the tongue. She did not seem too over-awed.

'Oh, *that* lot. I thought they were pulling our legs when they rang up.' Then she leaned forward eagerly across the bar. 'Have you got Robert Dougall with you, then?'

'I don't think Mr Dougall comes out to do this kind of interview,' said Charles coldly. 'Anyway, we're not from the main news, we're from *Town and Around*.' You can't win, he thought. Whenever he had introduced himself as a radio reporter he had been asked where the telly people were. Now he was with the telly people they wanted to know where Robert Dougall was. He wondered who they asked for when they met Robert Dougall; Muffin the Mule, probably.

The large lady decided to make the best of it. 'Gerry,' she yelled behind her, 'there's the people here from the telly to look at your boxes. They're from *Town and About*.'

'*Around*,' corrected Charles. '*Town and Around*.' But she had already lifted the flap of the bar and was heading for the shelves.

'Right, then. Which ones do you want me to show you?'

He was taken unawares. 'Aren't they Mr Glissop's boxes? I was rather expecting to talk to him.'

The large lady sniffed. 'They're his boxes all right, but I have to keep 'em dusted and show 'em off whenever a customer asks to hear one, and I have to clobber anyone who tries to pinch one. I reckon I've got as much right to be on the telly with 'em as he has.'

Charles looked despairingly at his camera crew. Bert was smiling for the second time that morning, but it was the smile of a nursemaid whose fractious charge had been startled into silence by a stranger peering into its pram. He merely sipped his beer, and it was left to Euclid to come to the rescue.

'Of course we shall be delighted to film you, madam, perhaps dusting the boxes or playing one or two of them. We can see you play an important part here. But may we just have a word with Mr Glissop first? We'll get that out of the way, then we can interview you at your leisure.'

The large lady, greatly mollified, went behind the bar again to seek out Mr Glissop, leaving Charles staring at Euclid in blank amazement. 'I'm not really going to interview her, am I? We don't want two of them, surely?'

'That's up to you, Charles,' said Euclid quietly, returning to his pint. 'Either you can do the interview and we use a French lens, or we get a sudden call from the office when you've finished with Mr Glissop and we have to dash off.'

Charles was still not clear. 'How do you mean, use a French lens?'

Bert drained his glass and put it ostentatiously on the counter. 'No bleedin' film in the mag, mate, that's a French lens. And for that little tip, I think you owe us another drink.'

There was an interruption. 'I'm Mr Glissop. Good morning.'

The voice came from behind the bar, but Charles could not immediately spot the person that went with it. Then he realised that Mr Glissop's head was just visible above the counter.

'Good morning, Mr Glissop. Come through.' Charles lifted the flap, but it was hardly necessary. Mr Glissop, it was now apparent, was very short indeed; his head came level with Charles's chest.

'Gawd's-truth,' muttered Bert Filby. 'More problems.'

Charles knew what he meant. They would look a bizarre couple in front of the camera, with him towering over his tiny interviewee. He could also understand why the large lady dusted the musical boxes and took them down when required; Mr Glissop could hardly reach the shelves.

'Can we manage, Bert?' he asked.

Bert sighed. 'I said you might have to cut off your legs. Never mind, we'll have you both sitting down, so we'll get your 'eads nearer the same 'eight, and you'll have to decide the boxes you want to talk about, and we'll put 'em on a table beside yer, so 'e can point to 'em or pick 'em up. That all right with you, Shorty?'

Charles shuddered, but Mr Glissop was obviously used to being addressed thus. He probably had plenty of customers like Bert. 'It'll save us getting a ladder,' he said cheerfully, and Charles breathed again.

'That's the stuff,' said Bert. 'Now, Charlie, you get yourself sorted out with what you're going to ask our friend 'ere, and get a couple of chairs and a table, and line up the boxes you fancy, while we get set up. But don't forget – you still owe us that pint.'

The large lady produced the chairs and a table while Bert and Euclid fetched their gear from the car. Charles inspected the shelves with Mr Glissop and made his selection. It was a difficult task; most of the boxes were worth looking at, and even those that weren't could still produce some pleasant tunes. He finally decided on eight, and set them out on the table.

'Do you think these'll do, Bert?'

Bert had been busy setting up his camera and tripod. He glanced at the table, then turned his eyes to the heavens. 'Have a heart, Charlie. This ain't a bleedin' half-hour documentary. We've got three minutes at the most. You'll need the first minute to talk to Mr Glissop about how he started collecting boxes and how much they're worth, and do they ever get nicked by the customers, all that sort of thing, then he'll need to talk about each box we show, and we'll 'ave to play a little music on each one just to show they work, that's about forty seconds a box, I'd say. So how many boxes is that, Charlie? 'Ow's your arithmetic?'

'We need three boxes,' said Charles humbly.

'Wrong. We need four boxes. Always do an extra one, that gives 'em the chance to chuck one out, back at the Palace. If you only give 'em three they'll still chuck one out, just to show who's boss. That'll leave you with two and you lose half a minute, and the producer'll have to find a filler to make up for it, he'll cuss you sideways. Got it?'

'Got it,' said Charles. And before Bert could speak again: 'And that's another pint I owe you.' Bert permitted himself another smile.

Charles discarded four of the boxes and waited expectantly. 'Shall we start?'

170

The smile disappeared. 'Start? 'Ow the 'ell do we start without a Sparks? You reckon you're dazzlin' enough without one?'

Again it was Euclid who explained. 'We have to wait for the lighting man. We can't shoot interiors without lights.'

'But I thought you had a light,' protested Charles. 'I saw it in the boot of the car.'

Euclid remained patient. 'We have one hand-held lamp for emergencies. It's not enough to light a set-up like this. It'd be all stark highlights and deep shadow. And anyway the battery wouldn't last long enough. We have to have a Sparks with the proper equipment.'

'So where is the Sparks? Shouldn't he be here by now?' Charles was getting the feeling, an unpleasantly familiar feeling, that this was not going to be his day.

Bert was heading back to the bar. 'I expect they told 'im to be here the same time as us, but if he's got any sense he knows it takes time to chat people up and get the gear set up. He shouldn't be more'n a coupla minutes – just time to have one of those pints you owe us.'

It took a little longer than that. Bert had finished that pint, and Charles was wondering how steady the camerawork would be after his third, when a van pulled up outside and a man in white overalls climbed out. He was looking quite flustered.

''Ere we go, 'e'll say he was held up in the traffic,' Bert forecast, half-way through the third pint. 'They always say it's the traffic. You watch.'

The lighting man appeared in the doorway. 'Sorry, folks. Got held up by the traffic.' Bert guffawed over his glass and the new arrival turned on him sharply. 'I was, chum, and that's a fact. There's a bloody great jam down the Whitechapel Road. You can go and look if you don't believe me. D'you think I'd have missed a beer if I could have got here quicker?'

'All right, Sparks, all right.' Bert obviously considered this a convincing argument. 'No need to lose your wool, mate, you're in plenty of time. You get your gear and we'll have a pint waiting for you.'

He sounded unusually conciliatory, and as the Sparks went back to his van Euclid explained why. 'That's another lesson, Charles. You already know a good reporter keeps on the right side of his cameraman. Now you know a good cameraman keeps on the right side of his Sparks. It's all to do with unions, you see. They're quite a militant lot in the electricians' union. Put their backs up and they're quite liable to walk out on us, and then the cameraman gets the blame.'

171

Charles nodded. 'Thanks very much. I suppose that's another pint I owe you.'

'I gotta better idea,' said Bert. 'You buy a pint for the Sparks.'

Another quarter-hour passed while the Sparks set up his lights under Bert's benevolent eye. The handful of customers had got very bored with all the preparations, but there were still enough left in the bar to provide a little mocking applause as Charles at last took his seat opposite Mr Glissop. Euclid clipped a neck-mike to Charles's plain and simple tie, and another to Mr Glissop's. It occurred to Charles that as the camera was right behind him, pointing over his shoulder at Mr Glissop, he need never have changed ties at all, but this was no time for another lecture on the duties of a television reporter. Instead he glanced through his notes, smiled reassuringly at Mr Glissop, and prepared to ask the first question.

'Hang on,' said Bert behind him. 'How many questions before we get to the first musical box, Charlie?'

'Well,' said Charles, 'I thought, three. On the lines of, how did you come to collect musical boxes, how much is the collection worth, and have you had any stolen.'

He heard Bert chuckle. 'Brilliant, mate. Great minds, eh? I couldn't have done better myself. Just remember to stop after you've asked them, so I can change position, right? All set, Euclid? OK, Sparks? Off you go, then. Running.'

'Running?' Who was supposed to be running?

'Gawd's-truth!' He could not see Bert's expression behind him, but he could imagine it. 'The film, Charlie. The film's running. For Gawd's sake get on with it.'

So Charles got on with it. He asked his three questions and Mr Glissop, to his relief, gave sensible answers. Then he stopped obediently, and there was a long pause while Bert moved his camera and the Sparks re-aligned his lights. 'Off you go, then. Running.' And with an effort he got his mind into gear again and asked about the first musical box. Mr Glissop picked it up.

'Hold it, mate. I can't follow you if you move that too fast. Pick it up slower, eh? Right-oh, Charlie, ask him again. Running.'

Charles asked him again. Mr Glissop leaned down very slowly, took the musical-box off the table and lifted it gingerly.

'It ain't goin' to bite yer, mate. You look as if you've picked up a rattlesnake. Do it again, eh? Not quite so slow, and talk to Charlie while you're doing it. OK, Charlie, ask him again. Running . . .'

At the third time of asking there was no interruption from Bert, and

Charles hopefully asked about the next box. Mr Glissop picked up the next box, and talked about it. He asked about the third and the fourth, and still there were no interruptions as Mr Glissop went through the same routine. 'Thank you very much,' said Charles, with enormous relief. 'That's it, Bert. That's the lot. Did we do OK?'

'That was fine,' said Bert, turning off the camera and wandering over to them. 'But you needn't have bothered to pick 'em all up, it was only the first one I wanted. We'll overlay all the rest with close-ups of the boxes, so we don't have to see you going through all that pantomime. It was just the words we wanted.'

Pity you didn't tell us before, thought Charles, then remembered they had talked about overlaying the interview before they left Alexandra Palace. He should have told Mr Glissop. He got up and started taking off his neck-mike. 'That's me finished, then?'

'Not yet, Charlie, there's the cutaways. You keep out the way while I do these close-ups of the boxes. And I'll need our friend here to switch 'em on at the right time, OK?'

Mr Glissop stayed in his chair while the camera and lights were moved yet again, and Charles paced about at the other end of the room. If this had been a radio interview, he thought, I'd have been in and out of here hours ago. He had never realised that it all took so long. No wonder Bert had objected when he called it 'straightforward'. And he still wasn't finished. What the hell were these cutaways?

'Right, Charlie, we're ready for you. Come and sit down again. We don't need you any more, Mr Glissop. Well done, mate.'

Charles sat down opposite Mr Glissop's empty chair, while Bert moved his camera to face him. From behind him he heard Euclid ask quietly, 'I suppose you know what cutaways are?'

'I haven't the remotest idea,' confessed Charles miserably.

'Nuffin' to it, Charlie.' Bert was studying his exposure meter. 'Just ask the same questions you asked before, so we can cut you in if we need to. This is your moment of glory, mate; the punters 'aven't seen you yet, except for the back of yer left ear.'

He was still studying the exposure meter. 'Gawd's-truth, you gotta shiny face, mate. Let's see if we can tone it down a bit.' He turned to the large lady, who was still hovering behind the bar. 'Hey, missus, got any powder?'

As she went off Bert came over to have a quiet word with Euclid. 'That reminds me. Once we've done the cutaways you'd better check with the office, right? We don't want to be messing about all afternoon.'

Euclid nodded understandingly. 'No problem.'

173

'Excuse me,' said Charles. 'But those questions – who am I going to ask? Shouldn't Mr Glissop be here?'

'You're much better off without Mr Glissop,' said Bert firmly. 'We don't want any answers, just the questions. If you've got him sitting in front of you, either he'll answer them automatically and waste a lot of our time, or else he'll giggle, which will also waste time, or worse still, *you'll* giggle, which'll really cock things up. You'll find it's much easier without having Shorty staring at you; just talk to the chair.'

The large lady reappeared and to the delight of the remaining customers she vigorously powdered Charles's face, until Bert and his exposure meter pronounced themselves satisfied. Bert took up his position behind the camera. 'Right, Charlie, look a bit higher, that's a good lad – he wasn't as short as all that. OK, Euclid? Right, away you go.'

'So, Mr Glissop,' said Charles earnestly to the chair, feeling a monumental fool. 'How did you come to get interested in collecting musical boxes?'

A shout came from behind the bar. 'I told you, it was when I was in the Army.'

'Somebody put a bag over his bleedin' 'ead,' said Bert wearily. 'Go on, Charlie, still running.' He paused. 'Go on, Charlie.'

But Charles's mind had gone blank. This so-straightforward interview had got completely out of hand. He looked around desperately for some way of escape.

'How much, Charles. How much is the collection worth?' The gentle prompting came from Euclid, crouched over his recording equipment. Charles repeated it, and stopped again, helplessly. Euclid prompted him with the next one too.

'Right, Charlie,' called Bert, after he had successfully repeated the third question. 'Now give us some noddies.'

Charles just stared at the camera. He was completely baffled.

'That's very charming, mate, and I'll put it in for this year's Frozen Face award. But now can I have the noddies?'

Again he heard Euclid's discreet murmur. 'He just wants some nods, Charles. Look as if you're agreeing with the answer – or at least understanding it.'

Charles nodded understandingly at the chair, then nodded in agreement, then just kept on nodding.

'That'll do, Charlie, we don't want yer bleedin' 'ead to fall off.' Bert switched off the camera and straightened up. 'We'll make you another

174

Larry Olivier yet. Save the lights, Sparks. Euclid, you'd better check with the office.'

Charles ostentatiously thanked the chair for its trouble and bowed to the mocking applause at the bar. Now it was over he felt rather gratified as well as relieved. Being the centre of attention, if only as the butt of Bert's heavy humour, was not entirely unenjoyable. 'If you're still open, Mr Glissop, I think we'll have another round.'

'Wait a minute,' said the large lady. 'What about me?'

'We're just coming to you,' Charles assured her. 'Just as soon as our sound recordist has made his phone call.'

The sound recordist returned, looking suitably dramatic. 'We've got to get going, chaps. Big story just broken the other side of Walthamstow. We're the nearest crew.'

'Right,' said Bert promptly. 'It's a wrap, then. Let's get the gear in the car.' And he started dismantling the tripod.

'Walthamstow?' interrupted one of the customers, a large man with a stubbly beard and straggly long hair. 'What's happening at Walthamstow, mate? That's where I live.'

Euclid hesitated for only a moment. 'You don't keep a ladies' hairdressing salon, by any chance?' The man with the stubble and the straggly hair gave a snort. 'What do you think, guv'nor?'

'Quite so,' said Euclid serenely. 'Well, there's a ladies' hairdressing salon on fire in Walthamstow. We're got to get over there straight away. I'm glad it's not yours.'

The man with the stubble returned to his beer and Bert hurriedly got the caravan on the move. 'They won't need you at Walfamstow, Sparks – quite enough light there already by the sound of it. Thanks very much, that was fine. Now Charlie, give me a hand with this gear. Sorry, lady. Maybe next time. I'll just nip out and take some exteriors.'

While Bert got his pictures outside the Talbot Arms, Charles hastily carried out the equipment, eager not only to escape the angry eye of the large lady but also to get his first television report back to the developing room at Alexandra Palace; he had not seen himself on film before. He was on his way out to the car with the tripod when the customer from Walthamstow tapped him on the shoulder.

'Oi, guv, I don't reckon you made as good a job of that as the last time.'

Charles stopped dead. 'The last time? How do you mean?'

'We had that chap Michelmore come out here a week or two back. Did a piece about those musical boxes with little Gerry here, same as you have, only he asked a lot more questions and they took pictures of a lot more boxes.' He nodded towards the large lady behind the bar. 'Funny thing was, they didn't have time to interview her neither. Right narked she was.'

But Charles was not worried about the large lady's disappointment. He was right narked himself; his first television report had already been covered on the *Tonight* programme by Cliff Michelmore. Why hadn't they known that at Alexandra Palace? And why hadn't the wretched Mr Glissop warned them before they started?

He went across to where Euclid was packing up his equipment. 'We've been wasting our time here. We'll have to scrap the whole thing. They've already done it on *Tonight*.' He felt furious with Mr Glissop, the large lady, the customer from Walthamstow and Cliff Michelmore in just about equal measure.

Euclid remained unperturbed. 'These things happen, old chap. *Tonight* is based down at Lime Grove. Nobody at Alexandra Palace watches what they do down there, and even if they did, that wouldn't stop us doing the same story if the editor fancied it. As it happens he's very keen on musical boxes. This is the third collection we've done this year. They'll never dare to drop it.'

'Not even if somebody tells him it's just been done by Michelmore?'

Euclid shook his head confidently. 'He'll say they had a different audience. They say the same thing about us. Don't worry, Charles, your little masterpiece will still see the light of day. Now give me a hand with these cases, there's a good fellow.'

Charles was still not quite satisfied. 'Surely they should have told us here?' He glared at the top of Mr Glissop's head behind the bar. 'He should have mentioned it when they phoned from the office.'

'Well, the lady did say she was surprised, if you remember.' Euclid shrugged. 'But anyway, why should they? It's all good publicity for the pub; the more times it appears on television, the better they like it. You can't blame them if the BBC's a little lacking in internal communication. You'll find it's a common failing in the communication business. I expect that cutting you've got has been going the rounds of all the departments; maybe Blue Peter will be along next.'

He gave Charles a friendly pat. 'You're in a distinguished queue for your first assignment – just behind Cliff Michelmore and just ahead of Valerie Singleton. There's something to tell your grandchildren.' He picked up a couple of cases and gave them to Charles. 'Come along now. Walthamstow calls.'

176

The musical box item went out on *Town and Around* the following evening. It started with an exterior shot of the pub, then a general view of the boxes on the shelves while the announcer read the introduction, then the interview. There was a brief glimpse of Charles's ear, as Bert had promised, before the camera zoomed in on Mr Glissop for the first three questions. Then there were close-ups of three musical boxes with the voice of Mr Glissop describing them, and his hand appeared occasionally to start and stop them. It ended with another outside shot of the pub and the last musical box playing 'Abide with me' while Bert artistically tilted upwards to finish on the rooftop and the clouds scudding past above it, a little touch which Charles had known nothing about.

As for Charles himself, none of the cutaways was used and they had even cut out his questions about each of the boxes – Mr Glissop's explanations sounded quite adequate on their own. Indeed Mr Glissop came across as quite a seasoned performer, whereas Charles's left ear, what one saw of it, displayed no outstanding histrionic talents.

But then, unlike Charles, Mr Glissop had done it all before.

THIRTEEN

'It's you again, then,' said Bert gloomily, as Charles parked his Morris Minor beside the camera crew's Humber. Euclid, in the passenger seat, looked up from the *Telegraph* crossword and gave him a friendly nod.

''Fraid so,' said Charles cheerfully. 'Fate has dealt you another dastardly blow.' He had been out with them several times since his inauspicious debut with the musical boxes, and he had got used to Bert's grumpiness. With only a few days left before he returned to Egton House, he felt quite sorry to be leaving it behind.

'Not a bad little gaff they got 'ere,' observed Bert, and Charles had to agree. They were parked beside the massive wrought-iron gates of Petling Hall, set in a twenty-foot high stone wall that stretched away down the road in both directions until it disappeared around distant bends. Through the gates they could see the immaculate gravel drive leading to the Hall itself, a stately pile of such imposing proportions that beside it, thought Charles, Remingham Hall back in Norfolk seemed little more than a holiday cottage. It was not a bad little gaff at all.

'Have you let them know we're here?' he asked, nodding towards the porter's lodge beside the gate.

'That's your job, mate. You're the one who does the talkin'. I just turn the bleedin' 'andle.' It was obviously one of Bert's bad days.

Charles knew better than to argue. He got out of the car and knocked on the door of the lodge. The man who answered was dressed in tweeds and gaiters, and presumably doubled as gamekeeper and custodian of the gate. He looked at Charles, then ostentatiously looked at his watch.

'If you're the television people you're ten minutes late. His Grace doesn't like to be kept waiting, you know. Stay there while I open the gates. And don't drive too fast up the drive – it disturbs the gravel.'

This was not the sort of reception that Charles had grown used to during his travels with television crews. Most people they visited were delighted to see them. He found that some were actually beginning to recognise him, even if they couldn't remember his name. On the rare occasions he was asked for his autograph he always wrote it very carefully and clearly, so that no one could confuse him with another

Charles, Charles Wheeler, a television reporter of considerably greater renown. It was quite a jolt after such gratifying experiences to be greeted at Petling in much the same way as Lord Remingham's butler had received him when he was on the *Toftham Journal*.

'What's the matter with him?' he murmured to Euclid as they waited for the gates to be opened. Euclid did not bother to look up from his crossword. 'I expect he's a little put out that His Grace is planning to open the house to the public. Lowers the tone, you know, destroys the mystique. I'll bet his family's worked here for umpteen generations, fending off the peasants beyond the gates, and he doesn't fancy them having the run of the place now.' He looked up briefly. 'And so far as he's concerned, we're just peasants with a fancy camera.'

'Come along if you're coming,' called the gatekeeper. Only one of the gates was open; presumably he only opened them both for visiting royalty, or His Grace himself. Bert edged the bulky Humber through, muttering to himself. Once he was clear he accelerated sharply and gravel flew in all directions, a considerable quantity rattling against the gatekeeper's gaiters.

'Hey, you!' the man shouted furiously after the Humber. The only response was a wave out of the driver's window, with two fingers predominant. Bert, like Charles, was unused to surly receptions, but unlike Charles he was quite prepared to match it.

'Sorry about that,' said Charles as he drove gingerly through the gate. 'I think he was just anxious not to keep His Grace waiting any longer.' He had not the faintest hope that the gatekeeper would believe him, and indeed he was barely past before the gate was slammed shut, perilously close to his rear bumper.

By the time he had got to the Hall, driving so cautiously that not a single pebble was dislodged, Bert had parked at the foot of the broad stone steps leading up to the front door and was slumped behind the wheel, immersed in a crumpled *Daily Mirror*. 'I know,' said Charles as he got out of his car, 'I'm the one who does the talking.'

He started climbing the steps, filled with foreboding. This looked like being Remingham Hall all over again. He started working out what he would say if the butler tried to send them round to the tradesmen's entrance. The simplest thing, he decided, was just to call for Bert.

The need did not arise. He was half-way up the steps when the door opened, and instead of a supercilious butler he was greeted by a genial figure in his late sixties, in baggy flannels and a rumpled sports coat, with a tie which had slipped slightly askew. But the tie, as Charles recognised after his duties with the Royals, belonged to the Guards,

179

and the patrician face with the welcoming smile was undoubtedly that of the Earl himself.

'Good morning, and welcome to Petling. I hope you've had a pleasant journey.' He came down the steps and shook Charles's hand. 'You must be Mr Benson. Good of you to come.'

'Not at all, sir.' Charles was greatly relieved. He wished the gatekeeper had been there to take a lesson from His Grace. 'It's good of you to have us. I hope we shan't be too much of a nuisance.'

'No, no, it's really quite exciting.' The Earl smiled a little wryly. 'After all, we've got to get used to a lot of new faces coming to the Hall. It'll be good practice for me.' He accompanied Charles down the steps again and greeted Bert and Euclid, who had laid aside their papers and were now out of the Humber.

'Good morning to you, gentlemen. I assume you're with Mr Benson.'

'Not exactly,' said Bert. 'Mr Benson is with us.' But he shook the Earl's hand fairly civilly.

'Now what would you like to do? Have a look round first, to get an idea of the place? Or better still, why don't we discuss your plans over coffee?'

'That sounds more like it,' said Bert firmly, and again Charles did not attempt to argue. It meant that another half-hour would be taken up before the first camera case was unloaded, but he knew better than to stand between Bert and his refreshment.

The Earl led them up the steps, through the splendid hallway and along a gallery which seemed to stretch into the next county, lined with tapestries and paintings and the occasional suit of armour. The ceiling was decorated with intricate plasterwork, and the floor was marble.

'This is one of the rooms we'll be opening to the public,' the Earl explained. 'When we were children we used to play a sort of indoor cricket in here, but that's about all it's useful for. It's much too long, there's not enough light from the windows, and it's almost impossible to keep warm. But I hope people will enjoy having a look at it; there's some quite decent paintings to see too.'

Euclid had paused to look at one. 'Rather more than quite decent, Your Grace. I'd say magnificent. This Jacob de Wet here. Didn't he do all the portraits of the Scottish kings at Holyrood? Then he decorated the chapel at Glamis. I didn't know there was much of his work outside Scotland.'

'Quite right.' The Earl chuckled. 'One of my shrewder ancestors commissioned that one when the Scots had their backs turned. I think poor old Jacob was a bit strapped for cash at times. He spent years painting that chapel for the Strathmores and all they paid him was ninety quid and his keep. No wonder he did a bit of moonlighting on the side.'

Charles chipped in. 'Perhaps we could work that little story into the interview, sir? It's a nice bit of background colour. And we could overlay some shots of the painting and this part of the gallery. What do you think, Bert?'

'I suppose so,' said Bert grudgingly. 'But I'll have a hell of a job with me tripod on this marble.'

'I'll find some mats for you, if that would help,' offered the Earl, and Bert agreed, quite graciously, that it would. Charles was relieved to note that his irascible colleague was beginning to mellow under the Earl's genial approach – though he suspected that the Earl had suggested the mats as much to protect his marble floor as to stop Bert's tripod slipping. No matter, things were working out rather better than he had expected after their unpromising reception at the gate. His Grace, it seemed, was more pragmatic than his gatekeeper about opening the Hall to the public.

They continued down the gallery with Bert chatting amiably to the Earl, and Charles fell behind with Euclid. 'Thanks for pointing out that picture,' he murmured. 'How did you know all that stuff about Jacob de Wet?'

Euclid smiled quietly. 'It's amazing what you can pick up from the *Telegraph* crossword.' When Charles raised a disbelieving eyebrow he added casually: 'I did study art for a time. Thought I might even make a living from it. But de Wet isn't the only painter who got a bit strapped for cash.'

'I'd no idea.' Charles glanced ahead at the stocky figure alongside the Earl. 'I wouldn't have thought that Bert was the most compatible company for an artistic temperament.'

'Compared with starving in a garret,' said Euclid calmly, 'he's better company than Michaelangelo and Rembrandt rolled into one.'

The Early ushered them into an ornate drawing-room and settled them in armchairs which were so uncomfortable they had to be extremely valuable. 'I'll just organise the coffee,' he said. Charles glanced at the elaborate bell-pull beside the fireplace, but the Earl shook his head. 'No use pulling that thing. It hasn't worked for years. Excuse me, gentlemen.' And he left the room.

'Seems a nice enough bloke.' Bert took the cushion out of his chair, dropped it on the floor beside him, and sprawled back with one leg over the arm. 'That's better. Dunno why they bother with those things.'

The cushion was velvet, elegantly embroidered with the Earl's coat of arms, and there were gold tassels on each corner. It would not have looked out of place on a royal throne, but it did look very out of place on the floor, and Charles wondered desperately how he could retrieve it before the Earl returned, without offending his touchy colleague. Euclid was ahead of him.

'Let's have a look at that cushion, Bert. I can't quite make out the coat of arms.' Bert tossed it across and Euclid placed it carefully on his lap. Not for the first time, Charles was glad to have him around. The cushion was still on his lap when the Earl returned.

'Coffee's on its way. Belinda will be bringing it in a few minutes. Now would you care to discuss what you have in mind?'

Charles explained. After his experience with the musical boxes he had never regarded an assignment as 'straightforward' again, but this one really did seem to be fairly simple. The Earl was opening his ancestral home for the first time, and the brief was to interview him about the history of the Hall and why he had decided to open it. The answer, he guessed, was shortage of cash, but maybe he could provide some awesome statistics. They would need some overlay shots of the State Apartments, and he had to do a twenty-second introduction to camera against an appropriate background, preferably out of doors. Well, the sun was shining, there was plenty of good material to film, and the Earl was obviously anxious to co-operate. It really seemed an ideal set-up; there shouldn't be anything to cause problems. Indeed, the only hazard was that it could turn out to be rather boring.

Then in came Belinda.

Charles had been expecting a housekeeper or a maid, but Belinda was carrying the tray of coffee with the supreme self-confidence of a young lady who was mistress of all she surveyed. She was poised, self-possessed, and about eight years old.

'Ah, Belinda, come and meet these gentlemen from the BBC.' The Earl waved towards them. 'Gentlemen, this is my granddaughter Belinda. She's staying with me while her parents are on safari in Africa.'

Euclid was already on his feet and Charles, after a moment's hesitation, rose also. Bert, deep in his cushionless armchair, waved a hand.

'How d'do, gentlemen. I'm very pleased to meet you.' The voice was clear and regal, the intonation just right, the vowels immaculate. Belinda could have been the Queen welcoming her Prime Ministers at a Commonwealth conference. Charles could visualise a tiara instead of the Alice band round the long straight hair, and a ceremonial sash across the simple blouse and skirt.

She took the tray to each of them, and by the time she reached Bert's armchair he was on his feet too. She had that effect. Finally she reached the Earl, and as he took his cup she spoke to him firmly.

'I hope you're going to show them the Gainsborough in the Blue Room, Grandfather. That's my favourite. And you ought to tell them about that Russian sword that Great-great-grandfather brought back from the Crimea, and there's that awful portrait of the first Earl wearing that silly armour that makes him look like a Roman.'

'I'll show them, Belinda,' he assured her. He smiled across at Charles. 'Belinda knows as much about this house and the family as I do. That's why she wouldn't go to Africa with her parents. She said she'd rather stay here with me, and all the other old relics.' He put an arm round her and beamed at her fondly.

''Ang on.' Bert had been listening to her, quite fascinated. 'Mind if I 'ave a quick word with Charlie-boy, guv'nor? I think I might 'ave an idea.'

'Not at all.' The Earl looked a little disconcerted, but his courtesy was unshaken. 'Would you wish Belinda and me to leave the room?'

'Good Lord no, sir.' Charles was acutely embarrassed. 'I'm sure it's not all that private. What's this idea you've got, Bert?'

'All right, then. 'Ow about doing the interview with Little Lady Fauntleroy 'ere instead of 'is Lordship? That'd be a bit different, mate. They'll love it back at the Palace.'

Charles gulped. 'I don't think that was quite the idea, Bert. We're supposed to be talking to the Earl about his reason for opening the house, and all that sort of thing. Belinda couldn't very well do that.'

'You can do that in one question to 'is Lordship,' snapped Bert. 'Then he can 'and over to young Belinda to do the tourist guide bit, and we're away.'

Charles was about to protest again, but this time the Earl interrupted. 'That sounds rather a jolly idea to me. Belinda, are you game? Mr Benson will go round the State Apartments with you and ask you some questions, and you can tell him all about the Gainsborough and the Russian sword and that awful portrait.'

Belinda did not reply straight away. She frowned slightly with concentration, as she gave the proposal serious thought. The room fell silent, and Charles found himself poised anxiously for her reply. Beside him he sensed that Bert, if not exactly poised, was keen to hear it too. Euclid was smiling quietly to himself, still nursing Bert's cushion.

The little girl looked up at them, and the frown disappeared. She gave Charles a delightful smile. 'I think,' she said, 'that sounds absolutely supah.'

Charles beamed back. 'So do I, Belinda. Bert, you're a genius. Let's get the gear.'

Back in the cutting room at Alexandra Palace that afternoon quite a crowd gathered round the editing machine to see the rough cuts of the film, as word got round of Charles's unlikely interviewee. They watched, quite spellbound, as the self-possessed eight-year-old led him through the Long Gallery and told him the story of the de Wet painting, then showed him the Russian sword that had been brought back from the Crimea, talked about her favourite Gainsborough – 'Isn't it supah?' – and finally pointed out the painting of the first Earl in his Roman armour, all the time giving a running commentary which Charles hardly needed to prompt.

'Doesn't he look just too appallingly frightful,' said the regal young voice, the vowels almost too good to be true, as they stared up at the portrait. In the cutting room Bert looked at the senior cameraman, who looked at the editor, who looked at Charles.

'It's a gem,' said the editor. 'It's an absolute gem.'

Everyone else murmured agreement. Charles tried to be modest. 'I'm afraid I'm looking a little dazed in some of those shots.'

The editor patted his back. 'Don't worry, Charles. You look exactly right.' He leaned over the film editor who was operating the machine. 'We'll drop the Earl and give the whole spot to Belinda. Let's just have a look at the intro and see if it still fits.'

They had a look, and it didn't. Charles was standing in front of the Hall, considerately positioned by Bert so that none of the chimneys grew out of his head, and sufficiently off-centre to show the steps leading up to the front door. As usual when he did a piece to camera, he looked a little sheepish.

'Here at Petling Hall the door behind me will be opened to the public for the first time in the Hall's 500-year history, and visitors will be able to see treasures which have never been put on view before. Their host is waiting for us now.'

The camera followed him as he turned and climbed the steps. Halfway up, on a discreet cue from Euclid, the Earl appeared in the doorway and extended a welcoming hand.

'Hold it,' said the editor. 'Where's Belinda?'

'I introduce her later,' Charles explained. 'After the interview with the Earl.'

'What good's that?' demanded the editor. 'You'll have lost all the viewers by then, Charles. I can hear the sets being switched over from here to Dungeness.' He pondered for a moment, while Charles was grateful that his blushes could not be seen in the darkened cutting-room. It had all seemed so straightforward at the time. Whoops, there was that word again . . .

'Got it,' said the editor. 'We'll give this a more personalised approach. Charles, you'll do a live introduction in the studio.'

'Live?' Charles gulped. 'In the studio? I've never done anything live in the studio in my life.'

'Now's the time to start,' said the editor. If he had been Bob Corby, thought Charles miserably, this was when he'd shoot his cuffs. 'Write a thirty-second script, saying the Hall's being opened to the public because the Earl needs the money – he took a couple of minutes to say that, so we've saved that much time already – then go on to explain you've been to the Hall and met this remarkable young lady, and she offered to show you round her ancestral home. Then we'll run the film. We'll give it three minutes thirty.'

'But it didn't quite happen like that,' protested Charles. 'It was actually Bert's idea.'

The editor stopped him. 'Do you want to say that in your intro? I owe it all to Bert, my genius of a cameraman? Come on, Charles, be realistic. That young lady has a mind of her own, she didn't need Bert to prompt her. I gather from Euclid she probably planned the whole thing before she came in with the coffee.' Charles began to understand; the gratification of appearing on television was almost universal, even for an eight-year-old. The editor continued. 'Didn't she reel out all that stuff in front of you about the Gainsborough and the Russian sword and that too appallingly frightful portrait? It was just that Bert took the bait before you did, and the Earl fell for it too. I gather she even had the nerve to make you sweat a bit before she agreed.'

Charles remembered the frown of concentration, the tension as they waited for her decision, the relief when she agreed. The crafty little schemer.

'Never mind all that. It's worked out all right in the end. Just get your intro written or there won't be time to put it on teleprompt.' The editor waved a hand to the little crowd around the editing machine. 'Thanks, chaps. That's absolutely supah!'

185

The *Town and Around* studio in the bowels of Alexandra Palace had two chairs behind a long desk, two cameras in front of it, a seat by the cameras for the teleprompt girl, and not a lot more. Charles had often peered into it through the control room window and watched news-readers introduce a filmed report in their familiar calm voices while somebody shouted through their 'deaf-aid' earphones, 'Three . . . two . . . one . . .'. Somehow they always reached the last word of the introduction on the '. . . one . . .'. He had watched them read the words on the teleprompter as if they were doing it all from memory, addressing the camera like an old and trusted friend. Then once the film was running they switched their gaze to the script on the desk and read from that. As soon as the cameras were back on them again they had returned to the teleprompter, discreetly turning the pages of their script while they read, so the correct page was on top when they next had to look down. It all looked very effortless and completely routine. But now he was sitting in one of those newsreader's chairs, and he had never felt so terrified in his life.

'Right, everyone, rehearsal please. Charles, dear boy, how nice to see you again.'

He recognised the voice over the studio loudspeaker. It was Nigel, the director who had handled his television test interview with Quentin Milton.

'Now, Charles, if you could look just the teeniest bit more cheerful, I think it might not be quite so frightening for the viewers.'

Charles gave a ghastly grin. 'Is that better?'

There was a pause before Nigel's voice came over the loudspeaker again. 'I think perhaps, dear boy, I prefer the glare. Just try not to think about it, there's a good chap. Now I think we have time for a quick run-through with the teleprompter before Mike comes in. Is tele-prompter there, Joe?'

Joe was the studio manager, the same bored young man who had been at the test interview. 'Not a hope, Nigel. It's the lovely Rhoda. She'll still be doing her toe-nails.'

As he spoke the studio door opened and a well-proportioned girl in a flimsy blouse and a very short skirt strolled in. She was holding something that looked like a roll of toilet paper, but Charles realised it was the script for the teleprompter. 'It's all right, Joe, the toes are all finished. I had to get them right for Charles's debut.'

She smiled at Charles as she leaned against one of the cameras and wiggled ten red-painted toes in his direction. He smiled tentatively back, and a gleeful cry came over the loudspeaker.

'That's it, dear boy, that's a really lovely smile. The old ladies will simply adore you. You'll be inundated with knitted sweaters and home-made toffee. Don't change a single dimple.'

Charles nodded towards the camera and waved an acknowledgement to Nigel in the control room, but he was much more interested in Rhoda. He had seen her sometimes in the newsroom and the canteen, and he had noted how attractive she always looked, with or without the red toenails, but television seemed to be a magnet for attractive secretaries and news assistants and teleprompter operators, perhaps because they hoped eventually to appear in front of the cameras themselves. He had not got too involved with any of them during his three months at the Palace, assuming they all had commitments already with the more permanent residents. But Rhoda, it seemed, knew his name, she knew this was his first live appearance – and she knew how to take his mind off it.

'Is this about the right height for you?' She had put the roll of paper behind the magnifying lens in the teleprompter and was waiting to adjust it on its stand. This involved leaning over the stand towards Charles, and the flimsy blouse drooped dramatically.

'That's fine,' he assured her, his mind more on the blouse than the teleprompter. She arranged herself on the low seat beside the camera and stretched her legs out underneath the teleprompter stand. Charles gazed along the length of them, from the red-painted toe-nails to the glimpse of lace below the tiny skirt. 'That's absolutely fine,' he murmured again.

'Are you still with us, Charles?' Nigel's voice over the loudspeaker sounded a little impatient. 'Perhaps you're dreaming of all that home-made toffee. Or are you in some sort of trance?'

Joe the studio manager leaned over Charles's microphone. 'It's only Rhoda doing her Hedy Lamarr act. He'll get used to it.' He walked across to Rhoda and gave her tiny skirt a tug, in a hopeless attempt to conceal some of her thigh. 'You really shouldn't distract the poor boy like this. Why can't you wear jeans like all the other teleprompt girls?'

Rhoda looked up at him, then down at her legs. 'I should have thought that was obvious,' she said blandly.

'Hear hear!' said Charles feelingly, and Rhoda gave him a big smile and winked. But Joe had not finished. 'Make sure you've tightened up the screw properly on that teleprompter. Remember what happened last time with Bob Dougall? It started slipping down the stand half-way through the bulletin and the poor chap almost had to get down behind his desk to read it.'

'He didn't seem to mind,' said Rhoda calmly. 'As I recall, I was wearing this same skirt at the time.'

'All right, then,' snapped Joe. 'So what about the time you knocked against the stand and set it swinging, and Dickie Baker looked like a metronome trying to keep up with it?'

'Children, children.' Nigel was sounding more exasperated. 'Can we get on with rehearsal, please. Let Charles have a run-through on the teleprompter; we haven't time to run the film.'

Charles reluctantly took his eyes off Rhoda's legs, and stared at the teleprompter. The roll of paper only had three or four words on each line, and only three or four lines were visible behind the lens. All he could see was:

> BENSON: Petling Hall in
> Surrey, which has been
> the ancestral home for
> five hundred years of

'Stand by, then,' said Joe. 'Ready, Charles? Three . . . two . . . one . . .' He waved his hand.

'Petling-Hall-in-Surrey-which-has-been-the-ancestral-home-for-five-hundred-years . . .' he gabbled. The words in front of him, which had begun to move slowly upwards when he started speaking, moved faster as Rhoda operated the control button to try and keep up with him. As the words revolved faster, Charles felt they were getting ahead of him and started reading faster too. Rhoda realised he was speeding up, and she speeded up the teleprompter to keep up.

Around the studio Joe and the camera operators and assorted studio hands watched in fascination as Charles and Rhoda came down the home straight neck-and-neck.

'. . . so-Belinda-took-me-on-an-escorted-tour-of-the-State-Apart-ments-and-showed-me-some-of-her-favourite-items-cut-to-film.'

There was a moment's silence, then a raucous cheer from one of the studio hands and everyone else joined in.

'Thank you, Charles.' Nigel no longer sounded exasperated, just quietly resigned. 'Quite a tour de force, dear boy. My only problem is that you've read that thirty-second intro in just under fourteen seconds. If we do the whole programme at that speed I'm afraid we'll finish ten minutes early. I think just the teeniest bit slower, if you can bear it. Why not take a little break now and get your breath back?'

Gratefully Charles left the newsreader's desk and wandered out of the studio. In the cluttered corridor he slumped into an armchair which was sometimes used for studio interviews, and tried to pull himself together. For the first time in his life he wished he smoked. Instead he twiddled a pencil between his fingers, an old habit that had stayed with him since his schooldays. He was still twiddling it when Rhoda came out of the studio and sat herself on the arm of his chair.

'Don't worry,' she said. 'That always happens the first time. They shouldn't have made fun of you like that. You must remember that *you* don't have to follow *me* – I follow you. You read at whatever speed you find comfortable, and I'll make sure I'm there with you.'

Charles smiled up at her weakly. 'You sound like Ruth: "Whither thou goest, there shall I go also." I'll try and remember.'

She patted him gently on the shoulder. 'You do that, Charles. And after the show, if thou goest into the bar, then if it's all right with you, there shall I go also.'

She rose to leave him, then paused. He was still twiddling his pencil. 'Does that make you feel more comfortable?'

He hastily put it in his pocket. 'I suppose it does. It's a silly habit. I must stop doing it.'

She shook her head. 'No, it might be a help in the studio, just for the first time. Your hands will only be in shot for the first moment or two, then the cameraman will tighten to a head-and-shoulders, so you can twiddle away after that to your heart's content, without anyone being able to see.'

She started to walk away, then paused again. 'Anyway, it's a better idea than having a couple of pints first, like some of your colleagues.' She smiled at him over her shoulder, gave a little wave, and went off down the corridor.

'Thank you,' he called after her. 'Actually, that wasn't what I had in mind. Quite the reverse.' And he went in search of the nearest 'gents'.

When he returned to the studio the other newsreader's chair was already occupied. Michael Aspel was sorting through his script. He looked up as Charles came over and gave him a welcoming grin. 'Is this your first "live"? Good luck, old son. I'm sure it'll go well. Rhoda will look after you.'

From her low seat beside the camera, her legs again stretched out distractingly beneath it, Rhoda gave him an encouraging wave. 'Whither thou goest,' she called.

He sat down beside Mike Aspel and wished for a moment that *Town and Around* could be seen in Norfolk. Suppose Rebecca could watch him sitting next to one of the best-known figures in television, sharing the same desk, facing the same cameras. He had not been in touch with Rebecca lately; at this rather crucial moment he was surprised to find she was quite vividly in his thoughts.

Next to him Mike was patting a stray hair into place, adjusting his tie, straightening his jacket, brushing a speck of dust off his sleeve. If Charles hadn't known that he had sat in front of the cameras hundreds of times before, he would almost have thought he was nervous. Mike sensed what he was thinking.

'You're quite right. We always get a little jumpy before the start. Bob Dougall always says that the day you stop feeling nervous before a broadcast is the day you should pack up and go. It means the old adrenalin has stopped flowing, and it'll show. So don't worry about feeling keyed up, old son; that's the way you should be.'

'Stand by, studio. Thirty seconds.' Nigel's voice was no longer exasperated, or resigned, just cool and firm. 'Good luck, everyone. Here we go.'

The item about Petling Hall was the last in the running order. He sat there quietly, enormously impressed, as Mike Aspel's 'jumpiness', if that is what it was, evaporated when the red light on the camera went on. He read his script smoothly, not a word fluffed, not a cue ending too early or too late. But as his own item got nearer, Charles felt his heart begin to pound, and the sweat broke out on the back of his neck. Then Rhoda caught his eye, and he saw she was holding up a pencil and waggling it at him significantly. At first he had no idea what she meant; then it dawned. By the time it came to his cue he had picked up his own pencil and was twiddling it vigorously. His heart was still thumping, and the sweat was still there, but somehow he felt better.

'And now for tonight's special report,' announced Michael Aspel. 'Here's Charles Benson.'

Out of the corner of his eye Charles saw Joe's hand go down. In front of him the familiar words appeared on the teleprompter. Rhoda's legs were still stretched out beneath it, but he did not give them a thought. Instead he was remembering what she had said: 'Whither thou goest . . .'

So he went.

'Petling Hall in Surrey, which has been the ancestral home for five hundred years . . .'

Up in the control room Nigel gave a sigh of relief. 'Three words a second – that's more like it. If he keeps that up we can hit the film bang on.' He had not bothered to ask Charles to wear an earpiece. He guessed that he had problems enough on his first 'live' without any '. . . three . . . two . . . one . . .'

Thirty words before the end of Charles's intro he gave the cue: 'Run telecine'. On one of the screens in front of him the numbers began to revolve as the telecine came up to the right speed: ten . . . nine . . . eight . . . seven . . . On another screen Charles was still reading, and Nigel muttered softly at it: 'Don't change speed, dear boy.' And Charles didn't.

'. . . so Belinda took me on an escorted tour of the State Apartments, and showed me some of her favourite items.'

'Cut to film,' called Nigel. The numbers on the film ended at the same moment. Up came the picture of Belinda leading Charles down the Long Gallery, and up came the clear little voice with the impeccable intonation and the almost too-perfect vowels, precisely on time.

'Great,' said Nigel over the loudspeaker. 'Charles, we'll make a star of you yet.'

Down in the studio Charles sank back in his chair. He felt as though he had climbed the Matterhorn in the space of thirty seconds, single-handed. No, he thought, not single-handed. There had been a helping hand on the other end of the rope. He beamed across at Rhoda; ten red-painted toe-nails wiggled back.

Joe stopped him as he tried to get up. 'Wait until the end of the programme – you might trip over something vital. And enjoy this film. It's good stuff.'

And indeed the studio crew were watching the screens, quite engrossed, as the self-possessed little girl led a bemused-looking Charles from the de Wet painting to the Russian sword, and from the Russian sword to the Gainsborough, then the portrait of the first Earl in his Roman armour.

'Doesn't he look just too appallingly frightful?' The studio crew, and Joe, and Rhoda, and even Mike Aspel, fell about. Up in the control room Nigel was watching delightedly too. 'Never mind making a star of dear Charles,' he said. 'With that little darling I could take Hollywood by storm.'

The closing credits came up on the screen, and in the studio the 'On Air' sign went off. Mike slapped Charles on the back as they got up from the long desk. 'She's great, young Belinda. Brilliant of you to handle the story like that. And the studio spot was fine too.'

Charles was in a happy haze of exultation, something he had never experienced before. 'Thanks very much. I really quite enjoyed the

191

studio bit, once I got going. It can't be a bad life, this news-reading business.'

Mike grinned, and shook his head. 'Don't you believe it,' he said, and Charles realised he was not entirely joking. 'This is no job for a grown man.' Then he waved cheerily as he headed for the studio door. 'I'll bet you feel like a drink. See you in the Club.'

'You will indeed,' said Charles, much gratified.

'Now wait a minute,' said a voice behind him. 'Whither thou goest, there shall I go also.' And Rhoda took his arm, and led him out of the studio.

He did not think of Rebecca again that night.

FOURTEEN

'Right,' said the HORC. 'You've done your spell with South-East Region, you had three months at Alexandra Palace, you've been down at Westminster long enough to know the difference between a Conservative and a Socialist. I think you're ready for a Party Conference.' And he shot his cuffs.

Charles was not enormously thrilled. His tour of duty at the Houses of Parliament had not only taught him the difference between Left and Right, but the difference between politicians and ordinary people. They were charming, and fluent, and when they wanted publicity they were extremely helpful. They also belonged to the best club in London, and as a temporary member of the Parliamentary Press Gallery he had enjoyed listening to their off-the-record stories and joining in the friendly off-duty gatherings in the bars and the tea-rooms, which were in such marked contast to the pitched battles they waged in the Chamber.

On the other hand, he had learned that in interviews they could talk a great deal and say nothing at all. They could adapt any question to fit the answer they wanted to give, and he lacked the experience to pin them down. On the whole, he much preferred ordinary people. The two senior BBC men at Westminster, Roland Fox and Conrad Voss Bark, had piloted him through the treacherous shoals of Parliamentary procedure, and tried to convince him that the howls and barracking and schoolboy humour during Question Time were all part of a noble and historic tradition, but he finished his Parliamentary stint with some relief, hoping to return to a more normal world. Now he was being tossed back among the politicians again.

'I hope you like Scarborough,' said the HORC. 'The conference organisers seem to. It's got both the big conferences this year. As you're a fortnight senior to Dickie you can take first pick and he can do the other one. He'll just finish his television stint in time. So, which do you fancy: Gaitskell or Macmillan?'

'I'll take whichever comes first,' said Charles. Let's get it over, he thought glumly.

'That'll be Labour. They start on October 3rd and then go on all

193

week. You'll find they don't have as many cocktail parties as the Tories but there'll be a fair amount of ale flowing, so mind how you go.' The HORC consulted some sheets of paper.

'We'll have the usual team from Westminster, Roly Fox and Conrad and Peter Hardiman-Scott. Quentin will be going along as their principal aide, and you'll be the leg-man – mostly rounding up people for interviews and sitting through the conference debates if the others are busy. But you should get something on the air occasionally if there are some extra interviews or there's an unexpected punch-up when the others aren't there. It's all good experience, Charles. You'll enjoy it.'

'It sounds splendid,' said Charles enthusiastically. The HORC's last words were not said to console him, they were more of a command, and he knew better than to protest. But actually he thought it sounded pretty awful.

'Tell Facilities you're going and they'll allocate your hotel room and let you have all your tickets and passes. You'll need dozens of them. You'd better drive up: you'll need the car there for chasing round all the hotels where the delegates are staying. Don't forget your Midget, of course – and what else, Charles?'

'Spare batteries,' said Charles automatically. The HORC chuckled.

'For once it doesn't matter. The engineers up there will have plenty. But it'd be a pity to lose the habit, so take some anyway. You won't need to worry about typewriters and paper and all the office equipment. Prudence will look after all that.'

'Prudence? Is she going?' Suddenly Scarborough seemed bathed in sunshine.

'The reporters' secretary generally goes to these conferences. Somebody has to make sure you've got enough paper-clips and you don't get lost among the hospitality suites. Prudence has been to a couple before. She'll look after you.'

'I'm sure she will.' He did not have to force the enthusiasm now, and the HORC looked at him a little sharply, then tossed in another suggestion.

'Isn't Norfolk on the way to Scarborough? You might like to drop in on your old haunts on the way.'

Charles switched his thoughts from Prudence to Toftham, and from Toftham to Rebecca. He began to wonder if Uncle Bob was tempting him with the best of both worlds, and was waiting to see how he reacted.

'It's not exactly on the way to Yorkshire, but that's not a bad idea.' Obviously, like most Londoners, Bob Corby's knowledge of East Anglia's whereabouts was rather sketchy. It was north of London, so it must be on the way to the North of England. Charles did not bother to explain that in fact Norfolk was not on the way to anywhere. 'I could call in and see my old editor. We haven't been in touch since I left.'

'Good thinking.' The HORC paused for a moment, then seemed to make up his mind. 'I tell you what. You can give Prudence a lift with all that office gear. She can't cart it all up on the train. I expect she'd enjoy seeing a bit of Norfolk on the way.'

'Ah,' said Charles. Prudence in Norfolk?

'I'll be up in Scarborough ahead of you. I'll look forward to hearing how you've got on.' The HORC shot his cuffs again. 'Have a good journey. And be careful – driving, I mean.'

'Of course,' said Charles, and left the office, his mind in a whirl. Was this a Machiavellian plan by the HORC to involve him in an encounter between Prudence and Rebecca, or had he got so used to Mr Juby's devious approach that he assumed everyone else must manipulate people in this way? But how would the HORC know about Rebecca anyway? Was he just testing him out with Prudence, to see if he would behave himself?

He put the thoughts about Bob Corby's motives aside, and considered his own situation. Giving Prudence a lift to Scarborough was a delightful prospect; but taking her to Toftham might have its problems. It would have to be handled with discretion.

He met Quentin in the reporters' corridor and told him what had happened, omitting the Rebecca complication. 'Lucky old you,' said Quentin. 'I took Pru to one of the conferences last year – most enjoyable. But don't forget, dear boy, the P.P.P. still has its eye on you, even in darkest Norfolk.'

'I'll bear it in mind,' said Charles, and indeed he could quite believe it. During his spells at Alexandra Palace and Westminster he had only visited Egton House occasionally, but whenever he dropped into Pru's office, within a few minutes one of the other reporters would wander in with some minor query. He hoped the P.P.P. had been as vigilant with Dickie . . .

'I'll be waiting for you in Scarborough to hear all about it,' Quentin warned.

'You too, eh? Anyone would think I was the Norfolk Rapist.' Charles shook his head sadly. 'You needn't worry while we're in Toftham anyway. The whole town will act as chaperone.' And he went off to find Prudence.

She was sitting in her office making out a list of stationery for the conference. As he came in she swept back her long blonde hair with both hands and gave him her usual dazzling smile. 'I gather you're giving me a lift to Scarborough, Charles, and we're going to see a bit of Norfolk on the way. It sounds lovely.' The HORC had lost no time in confirming the arrangements.

'There won't be a chance to see much, I'm afraid. It's quite a big detour off the A1. But I'd like to show you some of the countryside around Toftham, and Toftham itself is a nice little town. You'll love Mr Juby. If I can prise him out of the farmers' bar.'

As he mentioned the familiar names he felt a little pang of nostalgia. This would be his first visit to Toftham since he came to London. He had sometimes wondered if he might be sent there on an assignment, but not much happened in Toftham to attract the attention of the finest news-gathering organisation in the world; the nuclear scare which had brought Quentin Milton to Marford Heath had not been repeated.

'Why will you have to lure him out?' asked Prudence. 'I don't mind going in for a drink. I quite like beer, if that's all they've got.'

'It's not quite as primitive as that; they do have other drinks besides beer,' said Charles a little reprovingly. Then he had second thoughts. 'On the other hand, I suppose you could say it's primitive in another sense. You see, they don't serve ladies in the farmers' bar.' He smiled at her apologetically. 'As Mr Juby would say, it's still a bit "foodal". They haven't moved on too far since the men expected the womenfolk to stay at home and do the scrubbing. A lot of them still do.'

'But you're very fond of Norfolk, I know. And I'd love to see it. I'm looking forward to it very much.' She sounded as if she really meant it, and Charles felt a warm glow of anticipation, which not even the thought of a chance meeting between Prudence and Rebecca could affect. But anyway, the possibility seemed very remote.

'We'll be travelling up on the Sunday, so Toftham will be pretty dead, I'm afraid. There's no point in hanging about there, once we've seen Mr Juby. There'll be nobody else much about.' And Rebecca ought to be safely tucked away in Remingham. 'So that'll give us more time for a drive round. They'll have finished most of the harvesting, so you won't see much in the fields except sugar beet, but you get a special sort of light at this time of year. If the weather's right, it all looks marvellous, just like one of Crome's paintings.'

She sat listening quietly, smiling a little, her eyes fixed on him, while he talked on about the rolling fields and the vast skies and the salt marshes that ran down to the sea. He was in full spate when the door opened and Quentin Milton wandered in.

'My typewriter ribbon seems to be expiring, Pru. Have we got

196

another one in the magic cupboard?' He smiled serenely at Charles as he went over to the cupboard, and Charles stopped talking, and shrugged, and left. The Prudence Protection Patrol was still on duty.

They met outside Egton House at eight o'clock on the Sunday morning, Charles in his Morris Minor with a small suitcase and the Midget – plus spare batteries – and Prudence in a taxi with three cases and assorted smaller bags which filled up the rest of his boot and spilled over on to the back seat. They fetched the boxes of stationery from the office and packed them into what space was left, with the front seats pushed as far forward as they would go. This meant that Charles's knees were almost jammed against the dashboard, but it also meant that Prudence's knees were much in evidence too, providing quite a distraction for the driver. Even when she kicked off her high heels to make more room for her legs, the knees were still in close-up.

She wriggled into as comfortable a position as possible, and gave Charles one of her dazzling smiles. 'With all this luggage we only need some white ribbon on the bonnet and a couple of cans tied to the boot, and we could be going off on our honeymoon.'

Charles had a quick vision of a Scarborough hotel, bedrooms not too far apart, late-night excursions down the corridor – and Quentin Milton standing guard outside her door.

'With all the stationery we've got, we'd spend most of our time writing letters home,' he replied, just as lightly, and they headed off up Portland Place.

It was a clear, crisp October morning, just the sort of day he had hoped for, and as he drove up through Cambridgeshire and Suffolk he told Prudence his plans. 'If the car behaves itself we'll be in Norfolk before ten, and I thought we might drive past Toftham and get up to the North Norfolk coast for a quick blow on the beach, then we'll be back in Toftham in time for a snack lunch, and a chat with Mr Juby. If we get away fairly swiftly we should get to Scarborough in good time for dinner.'

'It sounds lovely.' She glanced down at her high-heeled shoes. 'I'm not sure about the quick blow on the beach, but I'd love to see it anyway.'

The Morris Minor rose gamely to the challenge and they crossed the Norfolk border at Brandon on schedule. As they drove into High Norfolk he pointed out where the ploughing had already started after harvest, how the sugar beet was filling out ready for lifting, why in some of the fields patches of maize and clumps of kale had been left to provide cover for the pheasants, how some land was good for cereals and some for dairy farming, and some – very little – was good for nothing at all. He had not realised he had learnt so much about it until he started to explain it, and once he got going he was too enthusiastic to notice that Prudence was no longer bothering to say 'Really?' or 'Goodness!' or even to nod. When he pulled up on the hill above Branham Staithe and turned to show her his favourite view of the salt marshes, he discovered that she was fast asleep.

He switched off the engine and she woke with a start. 'I'm sorry. Where are we? Is this Toftham?'

'Not yet.' He waved his hand towards the marshes. 'I thought you might like to see this view. It gives you a real idea of what the North Norfolk coast is like.'

She peered sleepily through the windscreen. 'I can't actually see very much.'

'You'll see better if we stand on the verge,' he said. 'Let's get out.'

It was a mistake.

The North Norfolk coast can vary during the seasons from majestic beauty to bleak desolation, but one factor remains fairly constant at all times of the year, the north wind that blows in off the sea. In summer it can be quite balmy, in winter it is bitter. In early October it can be one or the other. And on this particular Sunday morning it was the other, a biting wind straight from the Arctic which blew Prudence's long hair almost horizontally behind her, and swirled her skirt up round her thighs. She had put on her high heels before getting out and now she teetered dangerously on them, hanging on to the car door for support, in imminent danger of being blown off her feet.

Charles hurried round the car to support her. He had forgotten how powerful the wind could be on this exposed hill above the sea. As he reached her she let go of the car door and clung to him instead, with one arm round his waist, the other trying to control the wild swirling of her skirt.

'Sorry about this. They call it the lazy wind.' He was very conscious of her arm around him, and his bogus Norfolk accent was even less convincing than usual. 'Thass too lazy to go round yew, that go straight through yew.'

'Yes, I'm afraid it does,' said Prudence. Her skirt was still out of control, and her blonde hair had become hopelessly tangled, some of it blowing into her face, some into Charles's. She looked quite entrancing.

198

'To hell with the P.P.P.,' thought Charles defiantly, and put his arm round her waist too.

'Look down there, isn't it splendid? You can see the sun on the breakers out beyond the beach there, and I'm sure those are geese down on the marshes, and a little way along there's Branham Staithe, that was so badly damaged in the floods . . .' He had started talking to take her mind off the chill wind, but now he found himself carried away by it again, this vast sweep of coastline that he had grown to love during his seven years in Norfolk, and which he now realised he had missed so much.

'Charles, I don't want to interrupt, but it really is very, very cold.' She had retrieved her arm from his waist, and he hastily withdrew his. 'Do you think we can get back in the car now? I'm absolutely perished.' Indeed her fingers looked numb and her teeth were almost chattering.

'Oh dear.' He apologised profusely, and kept on apologising as he helped her into the car. 'That was stupid of me. I got used to the wind up here, but you do need to be dressed properly for it. I should have warned you. But I hope you liked the view, anyway.'

'Very nice,' said Prudence. 'Very . . . basic.'

They did not talk much as he drove her back to Toftham, though she tried to make polite remarks about the villages they drove through, perhaps sensing that she had disappointed him with her reaction at the coast. In Tittlesham, for example, she thought that the unremarkable facade of The Hero, a pub which Charles had never liked, was 'full of character', and Mrs Boggis's Post Office Stores, which had its usual window display of cardboard cartons and egg-boxes, was 'quaint'. It was not how he would have described them, but he appreciated she was only trying to please, so he just nodded, and made all speed for Toftham. He had not realised how much he was looking forward to seeing it again.

The market-place was deserted. There was not even the cluster of youths who sometimes gathered outside the Fleece or sat on the steps of the Regal Cinema. As he pulled up in the centre of the square he glanced across at the Journal office. The ground floor window had its customary quota of wedding pictures and club dinners, the photos curling slightly at the corners. Above it the window of his old office was empty, and above that the curtains in Mr Juby's window were firmly drawn. The Journal, like the rest of the town, was at rest.

Prudence pulled on her high heels and wound down the window cautiously to test the air. The square was better protected from the wind than the hill above Branham Staithe, and she found when she got out that she could stand unaided. She smiled tentatively at Charles.

'This is Toftham?' she asked.

'Yes,' he said. 'This is Toftham.'

She looked around her at the jumble of Georgian and Victorian frontages, the crumbling stucco of the Regal Cinema, the mock-Tudor beams of the Red Lion and nearby the battered flint walls of the old Bull's Head. She looked up at the AA sign with its solitary star, swinging over the doorway of the Dog and Partridge, and at the blank windows of the Council offices and Harry Hurn's deserted salon. Then she looked down at the cobbles, which were causing problems for her high heels.

'Very nice,' she said.

Charles pointed at the Journal office. 'That's where I used to work. I was in that office on the first floor for seven years, man and boy. And the one above it is Mr Juby's; goodness knows how long *he's* been there. Nearly as long as those photographs in the front office. I bet they haven't been changed since I left.' He walked over and peered through the window, with Prudence walking gingerly behind, trying not to slip on the cobbles. 'Yes, there's old Herbert Eke and Aggie on their golden wedding day. That was last year sometime. They could easily be dead by now.'

Prudence looked over his shoulder at the photograph, Herbert in his best suit and high stiff collar, Aggie in a plain black dress and shawl, both of them staring fixedly at the camera.

'Very nice,' said Prudence.

'Hang on, this is a new one.' Charles stared at the wedding photograph in astonishment. 'Well I'm damned, it's Anthea from the front office. She didn't waste much time after I left.' He remembered the longing stares, the devotion, the tears. But the Anthea in the photograph looked much plumper than the angular figure he remembered, and a little light dawned. 'Maybe she had to rush the wedding a bit. He looks a nice enough chap; I hope she'll be all right.' He hoped too that she had not rushed into anything because of his departure; he still seemed destined to feel guilty over Anthea. But she looked very happy.

Prudence nudged him gently. 'Aren't we getting a little late?' She indicated the Council office clock.

'Don't worry about that clock. It's never been right since I came here.' Charles looked at his watch. 'It's an hour fast at the moment.

200

They can't have changed it since Summer Time started. We're all right at the moment. But let's find Mr Juby.'

He led the way across the square to the Dog and Partridge, Prudence still hobbling carefully over the cobbles. 'I don't think they do full-scale meals, but I'm sure Maggie can rustle up some sandwiches.'

'Sandwiches?' He was ahead of her and did not see her face, but he heard the note of surprise and turned round. She smiled quickly. 'Very nice.'

They went into the faded front lounge of the Dog and Partridge with its deserted reception desk. Charles could never remember seeing anyone behind it, but it was handy for the corn merchants to lean on while they discussed prices on market day. There was the same seedy armchair beside it, where Mr Futter the junk dealer relaxed between the auction on market day mornings and his first pint. 'You stay here, Pru, and I'll get Mr Juby.'

She sat carefully in the sagging armchair as he pushed open the door of the farmers' bar, his heart beating almost as violently as it did before his television debut; this time not with apprehension but in anticipation.

As always on a Sunday lunch-time the farmers' bar was comfortably full. There was one group standing by the big open fireplace, another watching a game of cribbage in the far corner, a line of broad backsides perched on the stools along the bar. The smell of tobacco and stale beer and well-worn serge, mixed with a faint whiff of the farmyard, took him right back to his first meeting with Mr Juby, when he arrived off the Norwich bus after his train journey from London, miserable and bewildered, and convinced he had reached the edge of the civilised world. Now he felt he was returning to a much more civilised world than the one he had been working in for the past year, and returning in some sort of minor triumph, the almost-local boy who had made good.

'It's the boy Charlie!' Maggie had spotted him from behind the bar and was waving to him over the row of heads. 'Thought you were down in Lunnon, making your fortune!'

Some of the men at the bar turned round, and the group by the fire looked across at him. The other group round the cribbage game did not stir. He recognised some of the faces, and there were a few almost imperceptible nods, and here and there a hand or just a finger was raised in greeting. As the triumphant homecoming of a local hero it hardly set the pulses racing. But it was not the undemonstrative reception that surprised Charles; he was well aware that Norfolkmen were not over-effusive. He was looking at the empty stool at the end of the bar.

'How y'goin', boy? All right, then?' Fred Knock, former scavenging contractor to Launford Rural District Council and once a major force in local politics, now retired, called him over to the bar. Charles had bought a motor-cycle from him, a handsome machine but so redolent with the odours of his calling that for some weeks he had to park it well down-wind.

Maggie was already drawing a pint for him. 'It's the usual, Charlie?' He wondered momentarily how she would react if he asked for a gin and tonic, but the moment passed, and he thanked her and took up the glass.

'So what you bin up to, boy?' Fred Knock was looking at him solemnly. 'Hent seen you about for a month or two. You bin on harliday?'

'I left to join the BBC,' said Charles, somewhat irritated. 'I'm a radio and television reporter. Don't you remember?'

Mr Knock chuckled into his beer. 'That I do, boy, that I do. Don't take on so. We can't have you fancy BBC folk comin' the old squit too much, now can we?' He took a couple of sips, while Charles quietly kicked himself. He should not have forgotten the Norfolk sense of humour.

Mr Knock emerged from his glass again. 'Hent seen you much on the box yet, Charlie. When are you goin' to interview that Macmillan, then? Time you had a mardle with him about these barley prices. He don't seem to know narthin' about barley, not so's you'd notice.'

Charles savoured the rich Norfolk accent that he had not heard since he went to London. He also savoured the question. 'I shan't be seeing Macmillan, but I'll be seeing Gaitskell this week, and Wedgwood Benn, and Frank Cousins, and all that lot.' He paused for greater effect. 'I'm on my way to the Labour Party Conference in Scarborough.'

'Thass a funny way to get there, then,' observed Mr Knock, quite unimpressed. 'Dew you got lost, boy?' Then he relented. 'Well, you mind you have a word with 'em about the barley prices. They need to sort that out if they want my vote, you tell 'em that, boy.'

'I'll tell them,' promised Charles. Then he remembered the empty stool. 'Where's Mr Juby? He's always here at this time on a Sunday.'

Fred Knock shook his head. 'Not for a week or two, he hent. He was took poorly sitting on that stool a week or two back. He say he were all right, but he never finished his special, so we knew he must be sickenin' for somethin'. Maggie here sent for the doctor and they took him off to the Narfuk and Narridge, and he bin there ever since. Thass his innards, they say. They don't reckon he's too good.'

202

Charles was shaken. He could not visualise Mr Juby as a sick man, let alone as a patient in the Norfolk and Norwich Hospital. His health had seemed to thrive on his diet of rum and old ale, the specials he drank every lunch-time and evening; he had never known him even catch a cold. But if he had failed to finish his special, it must be serious.

'Do you know what ward he's in? I'll drop him a line.'

Mr Knock shrugged. 'Thass no need to worry about the ward. You just send it to Mr Juby, that'll find him, boy.'

Charles nodded. 'I'm sure you're right.' By now Mr Juby would doubtless have made his mark. But Mr Knock was looking over his shoulder.

'Now here's a rum 'un. Who's this young mawther, Charlie? Is she with you?'

Charles looked round. So did the group by the fireplace, and the cribbage players, and the line of drinkers at the bar. In the doorway Prudence smiled round at them uncertainly, then spotted Charles and gave him a little wave.

'I'm sorry to butt in,' she said, 'but I really am awfully hungry.'

Charles hurried across to her. 'I'm so sorry. I was just finding out about Mr Juby. He's not here, I'm afraid, he's in hospital. I'll organise some sandwiches out in the front lounge.'

'Hold you hard, boy.' Fred Knock had followed him. 'If the young leddy wants a sandwich there hent no reason she shouldn't have it here. Thass a dull old place to sit in out there, and that hent been dusted for a week or two, I know.'

'But I thought women weren't allowed in the farmers' bar,' said Charles, amazed at this sudden liberalism.

'There's women, Charlie boy, and there's women.' Fred Knock bowed to Prudence with a certain old-world gallantry, then looked across to Maggie. 'If the gal Maggie says thass all right, then thass all right.'

Maggie waved cheerfully. 'That's all right, Fred. She can have Mr Juby's stool; he won't be sitting there for a day or two.'

Charles watched, bewildered, as Fred Knock ushered Prudence to the stool at the end of the bar. So far as he was concerned it had always been Mr Juby's personal property; he had not appreciated the sort of impact that Prudence could make on the male population, even in Toftham. As she perched herself on it, her high heels hooked around the legs and elegant elbow resting on the bar, she looked as if she had been spirited straight out of one of the wine bars near Broadcasting House, and back a couple of centuries into the farmers' bar. It was a meeting of two different worlds; he was not sure that he approved of the combination.

Mr Knock returned to his own stool and started chatting to his neighbour. Old world gallantry did not apparently extend to buying her a drink. Everyone else in the room, taking their cue from the senior club member, returned to their conversations or their cards, and Charles was left in isolation with Prudence at the end of the bar. The message was clear. He was no longer part of the Toftham scene, just a visiting Londoner who once used to work in the town, accompanied by an attractive companion who also had no part in their lives. It was a long time since he had felt an outsider in Toftham, and the feeling was not pleasant.

'What sandwiches would you and the leddy like, then? Ham, chicken, beef, egg, cheese?' Maggie was beaming cheerfully at them, and Charles shook off his gloom. She at least had not changed. 'Don't you worry about this lot,' she said, reading his thoughts. 'They wouldn't stir themselves too much, not if Nelson himself come back to Norfolk and walk through that door. They'd probably just ask him why he'd been playing around with that Lady Hamilton, and hent he ashamed of himself. Now, what would you like?'

They ate their sandwiches quickly, for the most part in an uncomfortable silence. When Prudence did attempt to say anything, if only to praise the quality of the cheese, heads turned and other conversations ceased. Charles rather wished they had braved the discomfort and dust of the front lounge, where at least they could have chatted in peace. As soon as she had finished her last mouthful he was off his stool.

'Time to be going, then.' He helped her off Mr Juby's stool, and again all conversation stopped. 'Thank you, Maggie. That was great.'

'You come by any time,' said Maggie. 'And bring the young leddy too.'

I wonder if I will, thought Charles. I wonder.

'Fare y'well t'gether.' Fred Knock nodded to them both, but did not get down from his stool. 'Mind how y'go, boy, and dew you tell that Gairtsk'll about the barley prices. You give him a blast, boy; we'll be watching for you on the box.'

'I'll do my best, Mr Knock.' He might as well leave that illusion with him. Then he looked round at the rest of the occupants of the farmers' bar. 'Good day, all.'

Again there were the almost imperceptible nods, here and there a hand raised in farewell. Then, like Mr Knock, they all turned back to what they were doing. His departure was as unspectacular as his arrival.

Prudence went off in search of the ladies' room, though he was not sure such a facility existed, and he wandered outside and stood on the steps of the Dog and Partridge, surveying the square. There were a few cars about now, one or two people strolling past the closed shops, a cluster of youths on the steps of the Regal. There had never been anything to do in Toftham market-place on a Sunday afternoon, but people wandered about there anyway, much as their forebears had done, because there was nothing much to do anywhere else in Toftham either. Charles had done it often enough himself, swopping little bits of gossip and occasionally picking up a useful story. Now, as he stood outside the Dog and Partridge waiting for Prudence, it all looked a little aimless, and he realised with a certain sadness, that he was viewing it as a stranger.

'Is there anyone else you want to see while we're here?' She was standing beside him, long hair freshly brushed, new lipstick applied, the swirling skirt now immaculate above the elegant high heels.

Was there anyone else? For a moment his mind turned to a girl with dark hair and freckles and deep blue eyes. Remingham was only a few miles away, and at this time on a Sunday she would probably be at home having lunch, or riding nearby. Then he looked again at the elegant figure beside him, who had stepped into Toftham out of a different world, and was waiting to be taken back to it.

'No,' he said. 'There's no one else I want to see.'

He led the way to the car and helped her into it. Before he got in himself he paused and looked again around the market-place, and then at the silent offices of the *Toftham and Wettleford Journal*.

'Maybe there'll be another time,' he murmured quietly to himself.

Then they left for Scarborough.

FIFTEEN

The lounge-foyer of the Crown Hotel was packed with politicians and journalists when Charles struggled through the door, laden with cases and boxes of stationery, his Midget slung hazardously over his shoulder. Prudence followed him with a couple of small bags, still looking immaculate in spite of the long car journey. But in the doorway the sudden draught caught her skirt, and not for the first time that day it swirled dramatically upwards.

Charles, in front of her, did not notice, and even if he had he would not have been too excited. Norfolk's lazy wind had done the same job much more effectively. But for the crowd in the foyer the sight was impressive as well as unexpected, and the new arrivals walked to the reception desk to the accompaniment of appreciative murmurs and nudges. There was also one whistle, a practised and piercing effort from a stout man sprawled on a sofa by the desk. He had a pork-pie hat on the back of his head, cigarette ash on his lapels, and a glass in his hand.

'What-ho, mate,' said Bill Groyne of the *Sunday Herald*. 'How's the Norfolk dumpling, then? You've come on a bit since that time the Yanks cocked things up. Been on the telly and all.' He glanced at Prudence, who had rearranged her skirt and was now at the reception desk. 'Nice bit o' cracklin' you picked up, by the look of it. Don't let her stand around in that doorway too much. She'll give some of these old blokes a heart attack!' The familiar guffaw resounded round the foyer.

'I didn't know you did political reporting,' said Charles, wondering how he could escape. The last thing he wanted, in these surroundings, was to be labelled an associate of Bill Groyne.

'I'm not here for the politics, mate, I'm just here in case they misbehave themselves. It's amazing what goes on at these conferences after the receptions and the hospitality parties. Round about midnight you'll find those bedroom corridors upstairs are like Piccadilly Circus. You never know when you're going to find an MP wandering about without his trousers. And I tell yer . . .' – he leaned forward and wagged his finger at Charles – 'I keep an eye on you BBC chaps as well. You're all fair game to me, mate, even the new ones. So watch it.' He glanced again at Prudence and winked heavily.

'You're not going to believe this, but she's my secretary.' Charles tried not to sound too pompous, but that is the way it came out. Bill Groyne snorted. 'Of course she is. They always are.' He was still guffawing as Charles joined Prudence at the desk.

'Friend of yours?' she asked innocently, watching the man in the pork-pie hat making his way to the bar.

'Hardly,' said Charles. He signed the register and collected his key. 'He's from the *Sunday Herald*.'

She nodded. 'I should have known.' And they headed for their rooms.

The ladies in Facilities may have foreseen the presence of Bill Groyne, or it may have been standard BBC practice, but they had allocated Prudence a room on the first floor while Charles, with the other BBC men, was two floors higher. He had a quick clean-up, unpacked his case, checked that the Midget had survived the car journey, and went back downstairs, hoping that Groyne had found someone else to irritate. He was, in fact, in the centre of a noisy group at the bar, none of whom Charles recognised from his spell at Westminster. Presumably they were there on the same sort of mission as the *Sunday Herald* man.

'This way, Charles. What'll you have? I'd suggest a beer at this stage. Save the hard stuff until later.' Bob Corby was seated in an armchair with a pile of files and folders on the coffee table in front of him. Quentin Milton was in the armchair next to him, and another man was seated opposite.

'Pull up another chair, Charles. Henry, this is Charles Benson, the newest member of our team. Charles, this is Henry Clegg from the Labour Party's Press Office. You two have something in common, I think. Aren't you from Norfolk too, Henry?'

'That's right, from Swaffham.' Henry rose from his armchair, and Charles could not resist the temptation as they shook hands.

'From Swarf'm? Hent that where they du three days' thraarshin' for narthin'?'

Henry laughed. 'Well, hent that suffin!' His accent was a lot more genuine than Charles's. 'I don't think you'd get away with that in Swaffham. Where do you really come from? It's not Norfolk.'

Charles explained, and when he mentioned the *Toftham & Wettleford Journal* Henry's eyes lit up. 'You must have worked with Mr Juby. How is the old devil?'

'Not too good at the moment.' Charles remembered he must write to the hospital as soon as he had a moment. Since he had arrived in

Scarborough Mr Juby had receded into the background. 'But he was in fine fettle all the time I was there. Just about ran the town, in a discreet sort of way.'

'Don't I know it,' said Henry ruefully. 'Our group on Birmingham Corporation had great plans for making Toftham an overspill town, but they ran into all sorts of unlikely problems. I rather guessed Mr Juby was behind it. No wonder it all fell through.'

'Gentlemen, could you save your rural reminiscences until a little later, please?' The HORC was sorting out the papers in front of him. 'Let's just get tonight's coverage sorted out first.'

'Tonight's?' Charles had been looking forward to a few drinks and a leisurely dinner. 'Surely the conference doesn't start until tomorrow.'

Henry Clegg chuckled into his glass and Quentin raised his eyes to the ceiling. The HORC merely shook his head sadly.

'I'm not talking about the actual conference. The real debates are going on right now, upstairs here and over at the Royal and the other conference hotels. That's where they're planning how to sort out the votes tomorrow and the rest of the week. Anything we can find out tonight, London can use on the early bulletins tomorrow morning. With any luck we'll be able to tell them precisely who's going to vote for what, before the chairman's even called the first speaker.'

Quentin lowered his eyes from the ceiling. 'It's the smoke-filled rooms routine, dear boy. The Party's national executive tucked away in one, the trade union boys in another, the Left-wingers plotting away down one corridor, the Welsh MPs having a moan somewhere else. And those scraping noises you can hear through the walls are the knives being sharpened. Isn't that right, Henry?'

The press officer gave a shrug. 'We have our problems, but I'm sure Hugh can take care of himself. He survived all that row over Clause Four last year, and I think he'll survive again. It's the sign of a healthy, democratic party, you know, all these different opinions being aired so thoroughly. We don't stage-manage our conference like the Tories and turn it into a rally for the Party faithful.'

'It's certainly a lot livelier doing it your way,' Quentin admitted. 'It's just that all that blood looks so messy on the carpets.'

'Right, that'll do. Stop needling Henry. He's got enough to worry about with his own people.' Bob Corby sat up and shot his cuffs. 'Now here's what's happening. Roly and Conrad and Peter Scott are keeping an eye on the activities over at the Royal – that's where most of the meetings seem to be at the moment. So Quentin, you stay here in the foyer and keep an eye open for any of the Shadow Cabinet. George

Brown is certain to drop in for a drink sooner or later, and Tony Greenwood would be a useful chap to have a word with. There's talk that he'll stand against Gaitskell if it all goes wrong for him this week; and Harold Wilson'll have something to say about that, if he finds himself in a three-cornered fight, so watch out for him too. Pity old Nye isn't still around to tell the Left Wing what to do.'

He turned to Charles, who was listening to all this in something of a daze. He had not expected to be in the middle of things so soon. But he wasn't. 'It's door stepping for you, Charles, outside the Cousins camp. I'll show you where they're meeting, then you'll just have to hang about until they come out. It could be hours, I'm afraid, but that's the only way we can be sure of catching them. Frank's not likely to say anything himself, but some of the others may have had a few beers too many. I assume you're up-to-date with the unilateral disarmament story?'

'Yes indeed.' Charles knew that Gaitskell was against unilateral nuclear disarmament, and the Left Wing and most of the unions were for it, headed by the general secretary of the Transport and General Workers, Frank Cousins. But that was about the sum of his knowledge. It was not a subject he found deeply engrossing.

Henry Clegg may have detected a slight uncertainty. 'I can fill you in with any details from the official Party viewpoint. Frank's lot won't be breaking up for quite a while yet. We could have a bite and a beer while I brief you, and then you can tell me how Norfolk's looking these days. I gather you've just been back there.'

Charles accepted gratefully, and the HORC rounded off the meeting. 'We'll assemble here again at around eleven o'clock tonight, in case you've gleaned anything for the midnight bulletin. Then if you've got anything on tape for the breakfast programme we'll go over to the caravan and send it down. The engineers will be on duty for most of the night. So Charles, don't forget to take your Midget to that Cousins meeting. And what else?'

Charles sighed. 'Spare batteries?'

'Can't be too careful,' said the HORC.

Over a beer and a sandwich, Henry explained the background to the disarmament debate for Charles, and admitted off the record that the voting would be touch and go. There was to be one vote on the executive's official defence statement, as backed by Hugh Gaitskell as party leader, and another vote on a resolution calling for unilateral disarmament. If Gaitskell was defeated on both, it could be more disastrous for him than the row over Clause Four of the party's constitution the previous year, when he had cast doubt on its famous reference to 'common ownership of the means of production, distribution and exchange'.

'When he suggested that Clause Four was part of Labour's out-of-date image he brought half the Party down on his head,' Henry explained. ' "Betraying the spirit of Socialism" and all that stuff. But that was only part of the story. They were the same people who were against him on defence and various other policy matters, where they took the traditional, doctrinaire view and he just tried to be realistic. So they've switched the attack this year and there's just a chance that they'll pull it off.'

'How does Gaitskell cope at a conference?' asked Charles. 'I've heard him speak in the House and he's pretty heavy going.'

Henry smiled. 'I expect you remember what Nye Bevan called him: "a desiccated calculating machine". But there's passion there too. If he finds himself with his back to the wall, he'll hit out all right. Don't worry, you'll get your quotes.' He called for more beer. 'Now, that's enough politics over dinner, such as it is. Tell me about Norfolk; is the sugar beet looking good this year? And are they still complaining about the barley prices?'

Later that evening Charles found himself ensconced in the entrance hall of a small hotel further along the cliff road. With him were a score of newspapermen, keeping the barman at full stretch. Somewhere upstairs, in one of Quentin's smoke-filled rooms, the unions were planning their tactics for the disarmament debate.

Ten o'clock came and went. Ten-thirty. Eleven o'clock. He phoned the Crown Hotel and Bob Corby came from the foyer to talk to him.

'They haven't come out yet – no sign of them breaking up before the early hours.' He was hoping for a reprieve, but none came. 'Then hang on till they do. There's always the overseas bulletins; they go out all night.'

Charles left the phone, cursing quietly, and rejoined the waiting news-men, who had been getting noisier and merrier as the evening progressed. He was sorely tempted to have a pint, but he remembered how a slurred syllable could show up so treacherously on the air, and he miserably sipped his half pint of ginger-beer shandy.

'What-ho, mate.' His gloom suddenly deepened; Bill Groyne had arrived. 'I wondered where you'd got to. Couldn't you find her room then? Or maybe she's kicked you out.' Charles waited for the guffaw, and shuddered when it came.

Just before midnight there was a sudden stir among the news-men. Charles could not see any reason for it, but they started drifting towards the foot of the stairs. There had been false alarms before during the evening, and he took his time gathering up his Midget and plugging in the microphone. So he was at the back of the crowd, still adjusting the controls, when a familiar burly figure appeared at the top of the stairs, and behind him a weary-looking group of grey-faced men in rumpled suits. Frank Cousins led them briskly down the steps into the surging cluster of reporters. Into them, and straight through them.

'Any comment, Mr Cousins?' they all shouted, and Charles shouted too, though he was nowhere near him. But the union leader strode straight out of the hotel, and his companions followed him out, ignoring the pleadings of the news-men.

The last one down the stairs was a thickset figure with very large fists, who moved a little slower than the rest and found himself cut off from them by the seething throng of news-men. Charles actually managed to get in front of him, and he waved his microphone under his nose. 'Can you tell us what's happened?' he cried.

The thickset man with the large fists had had a long, hard evening. The microphone in his face must have been the last straw.

'If you don't get out of my way,' he said, slowly and clearly, 'I'll smash your f***ing face in.'

Charles got out of his way.

Back at the Crown Hotel Bob Corby and Quentin Milton were still sitting in the foyer. So were several other journalists, their duties over, and the atmosphere was distinctly relaxed. Charles slumped down beside the HORC and told him that Mr Cousins and his colleagues had declined to talk.

'Have a drink,' said the HORC. He did not sound at all surprised. 'It was only a long shot anyway.'

Charles thought of his tedious vigil and was about to speak, but Quentin thoughtfully interrupted. 'Did you get anything at all, dear boy? There's always a chance someone might use it, even if it's just a "No comment".'

'Now you mention it,' said Charles, 'yes I did.'

Bob Corby sat up. 'Why didn't you say so? Let's hear it.'

Charles settled himself comfortably, adjusted the controls of the Midget to full volume, and switched it on. All conversation stopped as the voice of the thickset man with the large fists blasted across the room.

It was the hit of the evening.

The Spa Grand Hall at Scarborough, normally occupied by Max Jaffa

211

and his Orchestra, had been draped with banners and slogans for the Fifty-ninth Annual Conference of the Labour Party, but its faded elegance still looked more suited to gentle violin music and discreet applause than the bellowed speeches and raucous barracking that had filled it for much of the week. From the Press tables below the platform Charles had listened with increasing disenchantment each day to the long arguments over composite motions and the angry speeches from the floor which had grown so much angrier this morning as the disarmament debate progressed. But even he was affected by the tension when the time had come for the votes, and he had seen Henry Clegg's shrug of disappointment and resignation as first the national executive statement was rejected, then the motion for unilateral disarmament was passed. And now the Leader of the Party was rising to speak again.

In the front seats near Charles's table was the delegation from the Transport and General Workers' Union. Frank Cousins was looking as impassive as ever, but his companions were jubilant. They're going to give the poor chap a rough ride, thought Charles, as he looked up at the pale-faced figure with the crinkly grey hair and the beaky nose, who was gathering himself to address the hall. Beside Hugh Gaitskell the Party's general secretary, Morgan Phillips, looked grim and slightly apprehensive, as if the same thought had occurred to him. Next to Charles at the Press table, Bob Corby and the rest of the BBC contingent, with the engineer who was recording the proceedings, waited with everyone else for what might well turn out to be a resignation announcement.

The speech started quietly, but soon began to build up. The frail figure began to gesture with one hand, then with both. The pale cheeks started to colour, the grey hair became a little dishevelled, and Hugh Gaitskell reached the climax of his message of defiance to the delegates who had rejected him.

'I shall fight, and fight, and fight again to save the Party that I love!'

Half the hall rose and cheered wildly. Even some of those who had voted against him were applauding. Charles glanced across at Henry Clegg again, and now he too was clapping and cheering. But the Cousins delegation was sitting in silence, along with most of the other trade union groups, and Charles noticed that the cluster of Welsh MPs, normally so vociferous, were showing little sign of enthusiasm. Gaitskell had turned defeat into a sort of victory, but he had yet to win the war.

The Press tables were in a state of high excitement. Reporters were gathering up their notes and heading for telephones, cameramen were struggling with each other beneath the platform to get more shots as the Leader made his way off it. Bob Corby and the Parliamentary team had already left for the caravan studio parked outside the hall, where the HORC would select the recorded excerpts from the speech and the others would write their pieces for the programmes they were serving. Charles found himself almost alone as the routine proceedings of the conference were resumed. Then he noticed that Henry Clegg was beckoning him to the door beside the platform where Gaitskell had disappeared.

'If you want to talk to Hugh before he does his set interviews for all your colleagues, I think I can tell you where to catch him.'

'You mean I doorstep him?' Charles tried to sound grateful, but he was remembering the scrum outside the union meeting on his first night.

Henry smiled understandingly. 'Not exactly. We're taking him out the back way so he'll miss all that. He hates it normally. But if you happen to be around on your own he might talk for a couple of minutes. He'll still have quite a head of steam up after that effort; it'll probably have run out by the time he gets to the studios, and he'll be the old desiccated calculating machine again. If you can catch him first and ask him, perhaps, does he really think he can hold the Party together, he might come over in the same way he did up there. It could help us both.'

He took Charles into the maze of corridors behind the platform and pointed out the door they would be using. 'You've got a few minutes yet. Just time to get your tape recorder from the Press table.'

'Thanks, Henry.' It sounded quite inadequate. 'Thanks very much indeed.'

Henry grinned and patted his shoulder. 'Thass all right, boy. We Narfulk folk, we got to shew these furriners we hent so daft, wunt yew say?'

Charles grinned back. 'That I would, marster. That I would.'

He hastened back to the Press table for his Midget and Henry disappeared along the corridors. A few minutes later they met again at the door which Henry had indicated, and this time Henry was with Morgan Phillips and a little group of Party officials. Hugh Gaitskell was in the midst of them. Charles switched on the recorder, took a deep breath, and intercepted them.

'Excuse me, gentlemen. Mr Gaitskell, I'm from the BBC. Have you time for a quick word?'

'Not really,' said the pale-faced man with the crinkly hair and the beaky nose. One of the officials tried to brush Charles aside.

'I just wondered if you really think you can hold the Party together?'

Gaitskell stopped, and turned to him. 'Yes, I do,' he said sharply. 'I'll tell you why.'

And he told him why, with the same forcefulness that he had displayed on the platform. Henry had been right; he had not yet gone off the boil. Charles just stood there and listened, praying with all the devotion he could muster that the Midget was working.

'Thank you, sir.' The little group swept out of the door, and Henry just had time to give him a wink as he went by. Hastily Charles wound back the tape, sent up another silent prayer, and replayed it. The familiar voice came out, clear and crisp, the level just right. He breathed again.

In the caravan studio outside the hall Bob Corby was still listening to the recording of the speech and marking which clips he wanted, when Charles hurried in.

'What have you got there?' The HORC was still engrossed with the speech. 'Not another trade unionist telling you where you can stuff your microphone?'

'Not exactly,' said Charles, and played him the tape.

The HORC listened in silence, quite expressionless, until the final 'Thank you, sir.' Charles waited for the congratulations.

'How did you get it?' asked the HORC. Charles told him, and waited again.

'I see.' There was a pause. The HORC seemed to be searching for the right words. When they came, the words were not what Charles expected. 'I'm sure you mean well, Charles, but we work as a team, you know, and we already have an interview lined up with Gaitskell for Roland Fox. An in-depth interview by an expert, not just one question and a thank you. Now if Gaitskell decides to say he's already done an interview for the BBC, and he doesn't want to do a second one, then that's something of a disaster, wouldn't you say?'

The thought had never crossed Charles's mind, but he realised the implications now. 'But at least we've got this one before anyone else. And he sounds much livelier than he usually does. It could catch an earlier bulletin.'

'It could,' agreed the HORC. 'But we already have these clips from his speech for the earlier bulletins. They're quite dramatic enough to stand on their own.'

Charles tried one last ploy. It was a desperate one. 'I thought we

214

were supposed to be the finest news-gathering organisation in the world. You're always saying so. I was just trying to gather it faster than anyone else. I'm sorry.'

For a moment he thought Bob Corby was going to explode. But suddenly there was a chuckle from the door of the caravan and Quentin Milton stepped in. 'Touché, Bob. He's got you there. I shouldn't worry about Roly's interview. They've got more sense than to miss the chance of a full-length heavyweight interview on *Radio Newsreel* tonight. This one's a bonus. I think Charles has done rather well.'

The HORC said nothing for a moment, and Charles thought he was merely going to divert his wrath to Quentin. Then he waved to him to hand over the tape. 'I suppose Quentin's right. If they do raise any objections Roly will talk them round. And Henry Clegg will presumably back him up. I'll send this tape down the line to London with the clips from the speech. They can decide what they want to do with it.'

His voice sharpened again. 'But in future, Charles, just let me know what the devil you're getting up to. If the Queen offers you a personal audience to tell you the story of her life, I'd appreciate a quick word beforehand.'

Charles nodded silently. But the HORC was consulting a list on the table beside him. 'Meanwhile the Tribune Group are holding a press conference, which is where you should have been ten minutes ago, instead of doorstepping Party leaders. I doubt we'll want anything from it, but you'd better be there, just in case. Now, Quentin, how did you get on with Frank Cousins's lot?'

Thus dismissed, Charles left them discussing the unions' reaction to Gaitskell's speech and wandered back into the conference hall, in search of the Tribune Group. He was not sure whether to be elated or depressed. As he passed a little group of delegates he recognised the rich tones of one of the best-known Welsh MPs.

'Beautiful speech from Hugh, but he won't win my votes with it. I told him last time we met at Transport House: "Hugh", I said, "if you want to lead half the Party, you lead it, but I'm not going to make it easier for you". If he stays as Leader, we'll never win the next election, I promise you that.'

Charles sighed as he walked on. If George Thomas was typical of Gaitskell's critics in the Party his speech had achieved nothing, in spite of all the effort he had put into it. He felt a certain fellow-feeling for the Leader of half the Labour Party.

215

In the lounge-foyer of the Crown Hotel they were celebrating the final night of the Labour Party conference. There were still some intrigues afoot in the smoke-filled rooms, but most of the delegates were attending farewell parties, and those journalists who had failed to obtain invitations were gathered at the Crown, the day's copy despatched and no homework to do for the morrow. The HORC had switched from beer to gin, a sign that work was over, and Charles had followed suit. The senior Westminster men were dining with some of the national executive, so there were just the three of them, Bob Corby, Quentin and Charles, in the group of armchairs that had become recognised as the BBC contingent's unofficial headquarters. Plus Prudence.

Charles had seen very little of Prudence during the week. He had spent most of his days in the conference hall, and most of his evenings attending press briefings or hanging about in entrance halls. Prudence had established herself in the little room that acted as the reporters' office, answering phones, passing on messages, logging the recordings, locating interviewees. She also compiled the usage report, the list of items which had actually been broadcast during the week, and this evening she had brought copies with her and handed them out.

'Not a bad strike rate,' said Bob Corby as he glanced through it. 'Roly and Conrad have got the most on the air, of course, then Peter Scott, but you chaps have done your share.'

Charles looked through his copy. His own name seemed to appear very rarely – with the impressive exception of one day, the day of Gaitskell's speech. His snatched two minutes with the Party Leader had been used on all the early overseas bulletins and some of the later ones, until it had been ousted by Roland Fox's interview for *Radio Newsreel*.

'Of course they've missed out your most spectacular item,' commented Quentin, deep in his armchair. 'That quote from the trade union chap ought to have run and run.'

The HORC smiled. 'I'm saving it for the Christmas party. But you've done well for your first conference, Charles. At the next one we'll find a bit more for you. In a few years' time you'll be doing the main interviews with the top brass instead of having to doorstep them.'

Charles nodded and sipped his gin and tonic. He did not dare say so, but the prospect of party conferences stretching away into the years ahead did not enthrall him. As he thought about it, he realised, with something of a jolt, that he would just as soon be reporting Launford Rural District Council. It might not make such an impact on the nation's affairs, but he did know all its members and officers, the subjects they dealt with had a direct impact on places and people he was familiar with, and if there was the equivalent of a smoke-filled room, then he and Mr Juby would know what went on inside it, without hanging about for hours in hotel lobbies. As for Gaitskell's dramatic speech, he had once heard Fred Knock attack a decision of Lord Remingham and the housing committee with just as much vehemence, and in a Norfolk accent too.

'Another drink, Charles?' asked the HORC. 'I think you've earned it.'

He got up. 'No thanks. I've just remembered, I should have sent a note to my old editor; he was in hospital when we called at Toftham. I should have written to him before. At least I can still make sure it has a Scarborough postmark.'

Bob and Quentin nodded goodbye and Prudence gave him her customary dazzling smile. 'Give him my best wishes too, Charles. I'm sorry we missed him. And do come back afterwards. I've hardly seen you since we got here.'

'I will,' he said, though there didn't seem much point. His vision of late-night assignations in bedroom corridors had long since faded. 'But I think I'll get a breath of fresh air first.'

He went out of the hotel and headed for one of the paths that wound down the cliff to the promenade below. Half-way down there was a seat overlooking the sea, and he sat down on it, his head still a little hazy from the unaccustomed gin. If it had been his usual tipple at the Dog and Partridge he would have felt much better.

The seat faced south rather than straight out to sea, and it occurred to him as he sat there that about a hundred miles in that direction, out there in the darkness, lay the North Norfolk coast. He visualised the cliffs at Hunstanton with their strange stripes of white chalk and red sandstone, and the great sweep of sand and salt marshes between Holme and Holkham beach; the little inlets at Blakeney and Morston and Branham Staithe crowded with sailing boats, the old windmill at Cley with the cattle grazing on the water meadows beneath it, the pond on the coast road at Salthouse where motorists stopped to feed the ducks and geese, the beach at Sheringham where Mr Dumble hired out his deckchairs and windbreaks . . .

'Mind if I join you?'

Henry Clegg had come down the cliff path and was standing beside him.

217

'Of course not.' Henry sat down, and the pair of them sat silently for a while, staring into the darkness to the south.

'I used to know that coast pretty well,' said Henry unexpectedly. They must have been sharing the same thoughts. 'That's where I started with the Labour Party. I used to go canvassing for dear old Edwin Gooch in North Norfolk, and after the 1951 election he asked me to go down to London with him as a researcher. When he was elected chairman of the Party five years later I got to know some of the staff at Party headquarters, and they asked me to join the Press office. I haven't been back since.'

'Do you miss it?' asked Charles.

Henry smiled in the darkness. 'I wouldn't come and sit on this bench every evening during the conference if I didn't miss it. When I saw you tonight I guessed that's why you were here too.'

He paused. 'I suppose one gets a bit sentimental at this time of night after a few drinks, but at the moment, if somebody offered me a reasonable job in Norfolk, I'd go back tomorrow. But that's not very likely, I'm afraid. There aren't too many jobs for Labour Party Press officers in East Anglia.' He dropped back into his native accent. 'That hent just the thrarshin' they do for narthin', boy, the Labour Party don't pay narthin' there neither.'

'Well, hent that suffin!' said Charles, and they both laughed.

'I tell you what, though,' said Henry after a pause. 'I'll go back one day, you know. People generally do. Norfolk gets a strange grip on you after you've lived there for a while. You can move away even for twenty or thirty years, but it'll draw you back in the end.'

'Mr Juby said the same thing,' Charles agreed. Then the mention of Mr Juby reminded him again that he still had a note to write, and reluctantly he got up from the bench. Henry rose too, and they stood for a moment, still looking southwards towards the invisible Norfolk coast.

'I've got a feeling,' said Henry, 'you'll be back there before I am. I've got too involved in this lunatic world of politicians and unions and radicals and moderates, and "you scratch my back or I'll stab yours". I suppose it's really quite fun once you're in the middle of it. But if you can find me a job when you do go back, and you catch me at the right moment, I'll be back there with you – and thass for sure, boy.'

Charles shook his head. 'I can't see myself going back for a long while yet, if I go back at all. There's a lot more things I've got to do, even if it's only to prove I can do them. And this job can be quite fun, just like yours. I might get hooked on it too.'

'We'll see.' Henry started off up the path. 'Come on, just time for a

218

night-cap before they close the bar. That's if the BBC hasn't drunk it dry.'

The BBC, it seemed, had gone to bed. The little group of armchairs was deserted, and only a handful remained at the bar. Most people seemed to be planning an early departure next morning. Henry just managed to order the drinks before the shutter came down.

'What-ho, mate.' Bill Groyne emerged from the little group of drinkers, and Charles groaned silently. 'You've only just missed her; she went upstairs with your friend Quentin about ten minutes ago. Maybe she got tired of waiting for you.'

'Do stop talking such rubbish,' he said wearily. 'You know you're making something out of nothing.' But he did wonder why Quentin had used the stairs with Prudence instead of taking a lift. It was a long climb to the third floor.

'That's my job, old son. You got it in one.' Groyne nudged him so violently that he spilt his drink. 'And I tell you what, mate, I do it rather well.'

'I'm sure you do. Sorry I can't help.' He had had enough. He finished his drink and turned to Henry. 'I'll leave you with Mr Groyne here. You may be able to supply him with some titbits about George Brown dating Barbara Castle.' Then, hastily, as the *Sunday Herald* man started taking out his notebook. 'That was a joke, for God's sake. Goodnight all.'

He went to the lift, and in case Bill Groyne really was good at his job and was watching the indicator, he took it to the third floor. Then he walked down two flights and strolled along the corridor to Prudence's room. Making sure there was no one else in sight, and feeling guiltily that he was sinking one notch lower than the awful Groyne, he put an ear to the door. He could hear quite clearly the elegant, unmistakeable voice of Quentin Milton.

'Sod it,' said Charles. And went to bed.

SIXTEEN

Charles was finishing off a script about an exhibition of old posters for *The Eyewitness*, one of the more obscure BBC programmes serviced by reporters with nothing better to do, when Prudence put her head round the door and said the HORC wanted to see him.

'Right,' said Charles, studying the exhibition catalogue closely in order to avoid the dazzling smile. He had been trying to avoid it ever since that last night in Scarborough; he did not want to be conquered by it again.

'Is anything wrong?' she asked, and he had to look up. The smile had gone, there was just a rather hurt look which demolished him just as effectively.

'Of course not,' he assured her. 'It's this Willette drawing for advertising a Parisian striptease show in 1894. Couldn't take my eyes off it.'

She nodded and left. One day, he thought, he must ask her why Quentin had been in her bedroom, but he was not sure he wanted to know the answer.

He returned briefly to his script to round off the paragraph about the Willette drawing. 'Even in those days poster artists loved a pretty girl, and the fewer clothes she wore the better. One room at the gallery is full of buxom young women, one on a theatre poster in the black stockings and swirling skirts of the Gaiety Girls, another clad more elegantly to advertise a French aperitif. Whether it is a new design for a gas lamp or the National Skating Palace in Regent Street, some-where there's always a smiling, sparkling-eyed, totally enchanting girl.'

He stared at what he had written. Good Lord, he thought, I'm getting obsessed. That's Pru I am writing about. He tore up the page, closed the catalogue, and went to see the HORC.

'What are you doing at the moment?' demanded Bob Corby as soon as he went in.

'I'm writing a piece about an absolutely riveting display of dogeared, faded, largely indecipherable old posters.' He tried not to sound too disenchanted, but it was his third exhibition in a couple of weeks; he seemed to have picked up where Dickie Johnson had left off, several months before.

The HORC grunted. 'That sounds like *The Eyewitness*. You can forget about that.' The cuffs were duly shot. 'You've been waiting for the big one since I moved you into the Fire Brigade, Charles, and this is it.'

The Fire Brigade, as the HORC liked to call it, was the pool of radio reporters on stand by for emergency assignments, anywhere in the world. That was the theory. In practice the 'fires' which Charles had dealt with so far ranged from a dinner at the Mansion House, where his biggest problem was selecting the right knife and fork, to the live coverage of a Head of State arriving at London Airport, where he could see so little that his commentary consisted of 'Here he comes now . . .' followed almost immediately by '. . . and there he goes.' There had also been two award ceremonies, the Royal Horticultural Society's autumn flower show, and of the course the exhibitions. They hardly rated as major conflagrations; any cub reporter could have doused the lot.

'Splendid,' said Charles. 'Where's it to be?' At one time he would have expected a revolution in South America, or at the very least a major train crash in the Alps. Now, knowing Bob Corby's tendency to over-dramatise, he doubted if 'the big one' would be much bigger than the routine jobs he had done before.

'How's your Arabic?' The question brought him up with a jerk.

'Arabic? Not too hot, I'm afraid.' It was actually non-existent.

'I didn't think it would be. Never mind. How's your French?'

Charles was getting more interested. This might be bigger than a poster exhibition after all. 'It's not too bad,' he said, not entirely truthfully. He had not spoken French since he left school. 'Quite enough to get by with, I'm sure.'

'We'll see.' The HORC, he suspected, was not deceived. 'Luckily most people speak English these days anyway. If you get stuck, you can always shout a bit louder. Right, Charles, this is it.' Charles waited for the shooting of the cuffs again, and the HORC duly obliged. Then it came. 'You're going to Tunisia.'

'Tunisia? That's splendid.' Charles paused. 'Er, why?'

'You've not been following events in Tunisia, then?' Bob Corby looked severe for a moment, then relented. 'Well, I suppose there's not much to be spotted on the surface. Luckily our man there has got his ear to the ground. With any luck you could be in on the start of a rather nasty little war.'

Charles tried to think of the right reaction. If he said 'Splendid'

221

again, he doubted he could make it sound convincing. He decided on a cautious, 'I see'.

The HORC did not take much notice anyway. He was just getting into his stride. 'You'll remember that Tunisia got its independence from France four years ago, and then the monarchy was abolished and Bourguiba took over as president?' He paused, and Charles nodded knowledgeably. Bourguiba?

'Well, the place still hasn't really settled down. France left troops there until a couple of years ago, then it agreed to withdraw them all except for the naval base at Bizerte. The French are quite determined to hang on to that, and Bourguiba is quite determined they should go. Now it looks as though it's coming to the crunch, according to our man out there, Freddie Matthews. Actually Freddie isn't *our* man, he works primarily for the overseas services at Bush House; he just keeps us advised. And if things really start happening, then he'll have his hands full coping with his Bush House commitments; he'll have a problem covering for our domestic services too. So that's why we're sending you.'

Charles just sat there. For once the HORC had not overdone the build-up; this really was the big one.

'There's a particular reason why we're interested in all this.' The HORC leaned forward confidentially. 'Normally if the French and the locals have a punch-up we'd just take what Bush House could pass on to us; there's nothing new about that. But the Queen Mother is due to make a State Visit to Tunisia early in the New Year. If they do start fighting out there, then obviously the visit will have to be cancelled. On the other hand, it would be much trickier if they kept it simmering below the surface until she arrived, then they went at each other while she was there. So should she go, or shouldn't she? You'll need to assess all that and do a few think-pieces as well as reporting what's actually going on. Do you think you can handle it?'

Charles was not at all sure he could, but it would have been madness to say so. 'I'll do my best,' he said, as confidently as he could.

'Fine. Freddie will help you out, of course. Speaks Arabic and French, and knows the place inside out – been there for years. Now, all your jabs up-to-date? Passport OK? No problems with your Midget? Right.' The HORC consulted the notes on his desk. 'Then you'll fly out at 09.00 hours tomorrow morning.'

Suddenly, and quite unaccountably, Charles felt physically sick. He had been distinctly apprehensive when Bob Corby talked about 'a nasty little war,' but that was nothing compared with the quite appalling sense of panic that hit him when he mentioned the flight. He had never flown in his life, and somehow, perhaps unconsciously, he had always stopped himself thinking about it. Even when he was put in the Fire Brigade, with its prospects of reporting from overseas, he had blotted out the thought of how he'd get there. Now he was faced with boarding an aeroplane in less than twenty-four hours' time, and he was filled with an unreasoning and quite overwhelming foreboding.

'Are you all right?' The HORC was looking at him curiously.

'Yes, fine.' He forced out of his mind the picture of an aeroplane spiralling down through the clouds, totally out of control. 'What do I do about tickets?' He just managed to stop his voice shaking.

'Facilities will have those for you. They'll tell you where you've been booked a hotel room, and what sort of clothes you need to take. And they'll tell you all about Telexes and Foreign News direct lines, and telegraphic addresses. "Newscasts, London", that's the main thing you need to remember.' The HORC smiled at him. 'You'll get very familiar with that phrase over the years. Incidentally, have you made any plans for Christmas?'

Charles paused before replying. On his last morning in Scarborough, before he drove back alone to London – Prudence was going direct to her home in Dorset for the weekend – he had bought three 'Greetings from Scarborough' postcards. One went to Mr Juby at the Norfolk and Norwich Hospital wishing him well, another had gone to Maggie at the Dog and Partridge urging her to let him know if Mr Juby got worse, and the third he sent to Rebecca in Remingham, saying he was thinking of coming to Toftham for Christmas. None of them had replied.

'No,' he said. 'I have no plans at the moment.'

'Just as well,' said Bob Corby cheerfully. 'Never know how long you may have to stay out there. Good luck.'

The ladies in Facilities had everything ready for him. 'Freddie will be waiting for you at the airport,' said Miss Murchison. 'Do remember me to him. You'll find he's rather a dear.' She smiled reminiscently. 'I used to work at Bush House, a good many years ago, that's how I know him.'

'And how will *I* know him?' asked Charles, still keeping his thoughts well away from the flight itself.

'Oh, you'll know him all right. Just look out for the black Homburg hat.'

Charles blinked. 'A black Homburg hat? In Tunisia?'

'Certainly. Freddie *always* wears a black Homburg.' Then Miss Murchison smiled again, and Charles was sure he detected a certain mischievous twinkle in her eye – a rare phenomenon in Facilities. 'Well, nearly always . . .'

Returning to his own office, laden with spare tapes and batteries, he found Dickie Johnson waiting for him. 'You lucky old devil, Charles. A chance of a real war, then Christmas in Tunis. And all I've got to look forward to is Macmillan making another speech at the Savoy. I had enough of him up at Scarborough.'

Dickie's week in Scarborough with the Conservatives, so Charles had gathered, had been even less rewarding than his own, with not even a 'fight and fight again' speech to enliven it. Since the Party conferences they had resumed their shared existence in the musty little office at Egton House. Charles had tried to detect any growing relationship between Dickie and Prudence, but Dickie only seemed to get a standard share of the dazzling smiles. Maybe Quentin Milton had displaced him.

'Have you done much flying?' he asked Dickie casually, and at just the mention of it, the first time he had allowed himself to think about it since leaving the HORC's office, the vision returned of the plane plummeting out of the sky.

'Just a couple of times, over to Spain and back. Very boring business, trussed up in your seat like a chicken and force-fed with plastic food every hour or so. Let alone all the hanging about at the airports. I can't say I envy you that part of it.'

'It didn't worry you at all, then? I mean, the risk . . .' Charles found himself sweating a little, but Dickie didn't notice.

'There's no great risk, my rustic friend. It's much riskier trying to cross Oxford Street. Unless of course you're thinking of all that awful food. Now that *is* a risk. I had indigestion for days.'

'Yes, of course,' Charles murmured absently. The vision was still with him.

Dickie looked at him more closely. 'If you really are worried, have a few beers before you go on board. Or crack open your duty-free Scotch when nobody's looking, and have a swig of that. Next thing you know, you'll be stepping out into the Tunisian sunshine.'

Charles managed a smile. 'Not necessarily sunshine. Tunis in December has on average only seventeen days' sunshine, with a maximum day temperature of sixty degrees, very similar to October in Britain. If you don't believe me, ask Miss Murchison.'

Prudence came in as he was speaking, and this time there was no sign of the dazzling smile, just a worried frown. 'I hear you're going to Tunisia, Charles. Do be careful, won't you? It sounds as though there's going to be some fighting.'

224

Dickie chipped in before he could reply. 'He's more worried about the aeroplane than the Arabs, Pru. Tell him those pilot chappies must have got the hang of it by now.'

'Are you really bothered about it, Charles?' She was looking at him with some concern – rather more concern than Dickie's flippant remark should have merited.

He smiled a little weakly. 'It's just that I've never done it before. I'm sure I'll be all right once we get going.'

'I hope so.' Again he was surprised at how perturbed she sounded. 'I do hope so.'

He forced the thought of the flight out of his mind again. This was a new Prudence so far as he was concerned, and the chance seemed too good to waste.

'Look here, I haven't had a chance to buy you a drink since that Scarborough trip. We were due to have one on that last night, but you'd gone to bed when I got back.' He paused, but decided not to pursue it. 'Why don't we pop over to the Dover Castle when you're clear?'

Dickie leapt to his feet. 'Yes, why don't we?' Charles turned and glared at him, and to his delight Prudence glared at him too.

'I think he meant just me, Dickie. And yes please, Charles, I'd love to. I'll just get tidied up.'

Dickie called after her as she went out the door. 'Pru, I've got to travel on the Piccadilly Line tonight and I have this terrible phobia about Tube trains . . .'

An hour later, while Dickie sulked in the office, the two of them were sitting in a quiet corner of the Dover Castle. Charles was about to suggest dinner, then perhaps a nightcap at his digs, when she brought up the subject of the flight again.

'If you're really worried about flying, you ought to tell Uncle Bob. He could always send someone else.'

'Don't be ridiculous, Pru. He'd laugh me out of court. I'll be fine, really.' But just the mention of it brought back all the foreboding. And there was that aeroplane again, spinning downwards.

She hesitated. 'It's only that I have a friend who had this sort of feeling about flying. She had it so badly that she couldn't get on the plane.'

He thought he understood what she was driving at. 'Don't tell me there was a bolt of lightning and the plane crashed with everyone on board?' He tried to say it lightly, but his voice was trembling a little.

'Of course it didn't.' Prudence seemed startled. 'That's not what I meant at all.'

'That's a relief. I didn't really think I was psychic.' He tried to smile reassuringly. 'I reckon Dickie's got the right idea. A couple of beers in the departure lounge will soon put me right. I'm sorry I mentioned it.'

'I'm not sorry. I'm very glad you did.' She seemed about to pursue it, but Charles stopped her.

'Let's change the subject, Pru. We never managed to have a decent dinner together in Scarborough. How about having one tonight?'

The dazzling smile returned, but she shook her head. 'I don't think so, Charles. You've got an early start in the morning, and you must have lots of packing to do.'

'You could always come and give me a hand,' he said, with no great hope.

She smiled again. 'You know the rules, Charles. I'm sure Quentin's told you.'

The mention of Quentin at this frustrating moment, and the memory of that final night in Scarborough, were too much for him. 'He's a fine one for rules. Why doesn't he follow them himself?'

'What on earth is that supposed to mean?' She looked genuinely puzzled, and Charles wished he had kept quiet. But it was too late now. 'Didn't he come up to your room on that last night at the hotel?'

'Yes he did.' She stared at him. 'He took me up to my room, then he went to bed.'

'Oh, really?' Charles returned the stare. 'Well, I happened to be passing your door later.' He hoped she wouldn't ask why. 'I heard him talking to you. Very late, inside your bedroom. That's hardly keeping to the rules.'

'You really thought that was Quentin in my bedroom?' Her cheeks were growing pink.

'Of course it was. D'you think I don't recognise his voice by now? The whole damn country can recognise it.' He could hear his voice rising, and one or two people looked round at them.

When she replied she spoke very slowly and quietly. 'It probably was his voice, Charles. It could just as easily have been yours. Or Roland Fox's. or Conrad's, or Peter Scott's.' And now her own voice was rising too. 'I often check through the tapes in my room. I have to time them, and log them, and label the boxes, and all the rest of the little jobs you take for granted, and I don't always get them finished during the day, so I take them back to my room.'

Her cheeks were redder now, and her eyes were blazing. 'I put off doing that lot so I could come down and join you on our last night. You really are the end.'

226

She got up briskly. 'I've got some more work to do. Thanks for the drink.' Then, as he sat there, looking stunned and feeling dreadful, she relented for a moment. 'I hope the flight isn't too awful. I'll be thinking of you. Goodnight.'

The flight was worse than awful for Charles. It was quite appalling. Even after all his apprehension and foreboding he had no idea how appalling it would be. The waiting in the airport lounge was bad enough; every plane that took off made his stomach turn over. When his own flight was called he had to force himself to walk to the departure gate and across the tarmac to the plane.

Half-way up the steps he stopped and clung to the rail, and if it had not been for the press of passengers behind him he would have turned and fled. As it was, the man behind him muttered impatiently and nudged him forwards, and he managed to get inside the door. He saw the rows of seats stretching back down the plane, with the seatbelts neatly crossed on each one. They looked to him like execution chairs, and he stopped again, but this time a stewardess urged him forward up the gangway, and another one ushered him firmly into his seat.

'You've not flown before, sir? I'll help you with the belt.' He sat rigidly as she adjusted it and fastened it round his waist. His expression must have worried her. 'Can I get you a glass of water? I'm afraid I can't serve anything stronger until we're in flight.'

He shook his head, not daring to speak in case it sounded like a sob. This was quite the worst ordeal of his life. And they were not even off the ground.

When they did take off he shut his eyes and thought desperately about anything except flying. He thought about his old office in Toftham with its dusty shelves and battered chairs and the old Remington typewriter on the desk. He thought of the farmers' bar at the Dog and Partridge, and Mr Juby perched on his stool in the corner, drinking his special. He thought of Rebecca at the hunt ball and the freckles on the bare shoulders . . .

'Good morning, ladies and gentlemen. This is your Captain speaking. I'd like to welcome you on board this flight to Tunis. Our flight time will be three hours and thirty minutes, and we shall be flying at 24,000 feet.'

Twenty-four thousand feet. The picture of Rebecca and her freckles faded, and instead he could see the vast expanse of nothingness under

227

his feet, and any moment the plane would be falling and the earth would be rushing up to hit him.

'Drink, sir? Sorry I couldn't bring it earlier.' The stewardess was beside him again, and she still looked a little concerned. He tried to force a smile, and realised it must look more like a ghastly leer. Still not daring to speak, he pointed at the row of miniature brandies on the trolley. She passed him one, and when he kept on pointing she passed him another. Then she offered him a bottle of soda, but he shook his head and took one of the plastic glasses, and poured both brandies into it. When he paid her, she no longer looked concerned, just a little sad. She thinks I'm an alcoholic, thought Charles. He almost wished he was.

He gulped down the brandies, shut his eyes again, and tried to make his mind a blank. It was no good, the image of that long drop beneath him was still too clear. When the trolley came past again he took two more of the brandies.

Gradually they began to have an effect. The image was still there, but it was getting blurred. Then the captain's voice came over the speakers again.

'If you care to look out of the left-hand side of the aircraft you can see the snow on those peaks below us – they look quite dramatic in the sunshine.'

Charles automatically obeyed. He opened his eyes and looked out of the window. The peaks were not just looking dramatic, they looked terrifying, great jagged jaws waiting for the plane to crash down into them. He managed to stop himself crying out, but the sweat ran down his forehead and he had to clutch the arms of his seat to prevent his hands trembling. For God's sake, what was the matter with him? This was worse than his worst nightmare, and worse still, it was really happening.

When the plane eventually landed at Tunis, Charles was so exhausted by his terror, and so awash with brandy, that the stewardess, now showing no sympathy at all, had to help him from his seat and along the gangway. He emerged into the bright sunshine – it must be one of Tunisia's seventeen sunny days – and tottered thankfully down the steps. The relief of being back on the ground was so great that he passed through the entry formalities and the luggage collection and Customs in a happy haze, with only the vaguest idea of what he was doing. Then he reached the arrival lounge and found himself surrounded by Arab taxi-drivers grabbing his arms and shouting in his face, and he remembered where he was and whom he was supposed to be meeting. He looked around desperately among all the flowing Arab headgear in search of a Homburg hat.

'Over here, old boy. This way. Never mind all these chappies, I've got my car outside.'

A large and rubicund man in his fifties, wearing a dark blue city suit with a silver watch-chain across the waistcoat and yes, a Homburg hat, waved above the heads of the taxi-drivers and pushed towards him. He stood there weakly, without the energy to do any pushing himself.

'I'm Freddie Matthews. You're Charles Benson, I assume? Good to see you. Welcome to Tunisia.'

'How d'you do,' Charles mumbled, and swayed a little. Freddie Matthews looked at him more closely. 'Air sickness, was it? Brandy can help sometimes – but not always. I'll get you to your hotel, and you can have a lie-down.'

It was not as simple as air sickness, or even too much brandy, but Charles did not attempt to explain. He allowed Freddie to lead him through the lounge and out into the sunshine again. In the brighter light he could see that Freddie's blue suit was rather dusty, and so was the Homburg hat – in fact they were very nearly as dusty as his once-black shoes. He also noticed for the first time that Freddie was carrying an umbrella, a black one furled rather loosely so that it looked like a gamp in an old-time music-hall sketch, but Freddie bore it non-chalantly on his left arm as he guided Charles with his right.

'Are you expecting rain?' Charles ventured to ask as they reached a small black Citroën which, in terms of dust coverage, made Freddie's suit seem spotless.

'As a matter of fact there is a fair amount of rain at this time of year,' said Freddie calmly, tossing his umbrella into the back of the car and climbing into the driver's seat. 'But the brolly comes in useful as a sunshade too, and it has quite a sharp ferrule if I'm in a hurry.'

He drove Charles to his hotel in the centre of Tunis, helped him book in, advised him to have a nap, and promised to return in the evening to brief him. 'I'll let London know you've arrived, and I'll tell them you're feeling a bit under the weather, so they won't disturb you.'

Charles glanced at him apprehensively when he mentioned being under the weather, and Freddie gave him an avuncular smile. 'Don't worry, I won't mention the medicinal brandy.'

Lying on his bed just before he dozed off, Charles could still not understand what had happened on the plane. It had been more than three hours of enormous tension, interspersed with periods of sheer blind terror. He shivered again at the memory of it, yet his logic told him there was simply no excuse for it. It also told him that he would have to go through the whole ghastly experience again on the flight home, and the way he felt at the moment, he could not possibly face it a second time. Then the exhaustion and the brandy took over, and he passed out.

'You seem to have recovered,' said Freddie, looking at Charles's empty plate, and Charles nodded agreement. 'It was a marvellous meal. Thanks very much.'

'Don't thank me, thank the French.' He brushed some crumbs from his suit; the rest of the dust remained undisturbed. 'They ran this country for seventy-five years, and when they finally departed they left quite a few trained chefs behind them. At some stage you'll have to try the local stuff. The couscous isn't too bad but I should go easy on the lamb stew. You may find the odd sheep's eye floating about in it.' And he chuckled as Charles blanched. 'Don't worry. You may not be here long enough to sample it. I think the Bizerta story is going to fizzle out, so far as you're concerned.'

Charles stared at him in consternation. Had he gone through that appalling flight just to be told the story had fizzled out? 'You mean there's not going to be any fighting after all?'

'What a bloodthirsty young man.' Freddie paused to sip his wine. 'There'll be fighting all right, but not just yet. I've been having a chat this afternoon with Tahar Belkhoja – he's Chef de Cabinet at the Foreign Affairs ministry. I've known him since he was secretary-general of U.G.E.T.'. He saw Charles looking blank, and explained. 'That's the General Union of Tunisian Students, a very activist bunch. He's also married to President Bourguiba's niece, so he knows what's going on. And he tells me the President has clamped down on the hotheads who are wanting to stir up trouble in Bizerta until after the Queen Mother's visit.'

'Why should he want to do that? I thought he liked having a go at the French?'

Freddie poured some more wine. 'He's decided that a State Visit by one of Britain's top Royals is worth a lot more to him in terms of international prestige, and he doesn't want to risk having it cancelled. So he'll get that safely out of the way first, then my bet is that a couple of months later he'll issue an ultimatum to the French to close their naval base, and if they refuse, that's when the trouble will start.'

Charles felt a mixture of disappointment and relief. But overshadowing all that was the thought that he would soon have to get back on an aeroplane.

'Bob Corby won't forgive me if I go back without any sounds of battle on my tapes. Is it worth going up to Bizerta just in case?'

'If you want battle noises,' said Freddie cheerfully, 'I can give you plenty of that. It won't be a real battle, but they do make a hell of a noise.'

'That sounds ideal.' A lot of shooting with nobody actually getting shot was Charles's kind of war. 'Where do I have to go?'

'There's a place called Ghardimaou, about three miles this side of the Algerian border. It's the headquarters of the A.I.N. General Staff.' He saw Charles was looking blank again. 'The Algerian National Liberation Army. Their commander is a chap who calls himself Boumedienne. It's the name of a mountain range near Oran where he used to lead guerrilla raids against the French. He was born Mohamed Ben Braham Boukharouba, but I think he decided Boumedienne sounded a bit more punchy. He's the Chief-of-Staff at Ghardimaou. He's only thirty-three, but he commands a force of about 30,000 men. They have regular training exercises. There's nothing an Arab enjoys more in this part of the world than firing a gun, preferably at a Frenchman, but failing that, just to make a good noise.'

Charles was relieved as well as intrigued. There seemed a chance he could postpone that flight. 'Would this Boumedienne let me see one of the exercises?'

'We'll have to find out.' Freddie emptied the rest of the bottle into their glasses. 'It might suit his book to demonstrate to the French in Algeria what a substantial force he's built up. Or he might want to lie low for the moment, until he's ready to show them personally. But one thing's certain, he won't be too bothered about the Queen Mother's visit; I doubt that the President will include Ghardimaou in her itinerary. If you're interested I'll have a word with Boumedienne's contact in Tunis tomorrow. Meanwhile, here come some more crêpes suzettes.'

The crêpes suzettes came and went, and the brandy came and stayed. At the other end of the hotel restaurant a band played Strauss waltzes; the fans revolved gently overhead. Charles's preoccupation with the horrors of air travel began to fade, and he settled back to enjoy the rigours of being a foreign correspondent. Then Freddie brought it all back again.

'Incidentally, I got through to your office this afternoon. Corby was at some planning meeting, but I had a word with your secretary. She sounds a very pleasant girl.'

'What did you tell her?' Charles asked anxiously.

'I told her you were feeling rather groggy after the flight and I thought you ought to have a few hours' rest. She seemed very keen to know exactly what was wrong. I told her it was air-sickness, but she didn't sound too convinced. She asked if you'd said anything about how you felt when you got on the plane, which seemed a pretty odd thing to ask. But I said you hadn't talked about the flight, you just felt rather rotten. I must say you certainly looked pretty awful when you came off the plane. Does she know something that I don't?'

'No, of course not,' said Charles hastily. 'She's just, well, she does worry about us – all the reporters, I mean. She's very . . . maternal.'

Freddie looked at him sceptically over his brandy. 'From the sound of her voice, "maternal" is not the word I would choose. Sisterly, perhaps. A very close sister.' He waited for a reaction, but Charles decided not to be drawn. Freddie shrugged, and went on. 'Anyway, she said she'd pass the message on. And for the flight back, she said why don't you try tranquillisers; she thought they might make you feel more comfortable. I've never heard of tranquillisers for curing air-sickness, but she was quite insistent. I said I'd tell you, but I wasn't sure we could get them in Tunis without a doctor's prescription. I've never had to bother with them myself. She just said "Do try", in a very, well, sisterly way.'

'Thanks very much, but I'm sure I'll be all right,' said Charles, quite sure that he wouldn't be. 'Let's worry about that when the time comes. Shall we have another brandy?'

So they did, and another one after that. But for the second time that day, Charles found that brandy was not the answer. Even when he finally collapsed on his bed after bidding farewell to Freddie, there was still the thought of the return flight and the image of an aeroplane plummeting out of the sky.

SEVENTEEN

'REQUEST BENSON SCENE-SET BIZERTA UPSUMMING ATMOSPHERE SOONEST STOP ALSO UPDATED MATTHEWS THINKPIECE RE ROYAL VISIT PROSPECTS STOP CIRCUIT BOOKED 1800 HOURS GMT TODAY STOP REGARDS WIGAN NEWSCASTS.'

Charles read the telex that Freddie had brought with him to the hotel. He was feeling much better after a reasonable night's sleep and a good breakfast.

'Is Wigan some sort of joke?' he enquired as he handed it back. He could just about understand the rest.

Freddie raised an eyebrow. 'He'd prefer not to think so. That's Tony Wigan, the foreign news editor. Anyway, it looks as though Boumedienne will have to wait. You'd better get your Midget just in case the Chef de Cabinet has got it all wrong and we find Bizerte has gone up in flames. Then we'll be off.'

It was a sixty-mile drive from Tunis to Bizerta. Charles had expected to be travelling through the desert, but it was a countryside of olive groves and vineyards, and Freddie explained how the Tunisian government had inherited a prosperous agricultural industry from the French which produced a fifth of the country's income. In summer Charles would have seen fields of wheat and barley, very like those he had left behind in Norfolk.

'If we get down to Ghardimaou to visit Boumedienne you'll see some real desert on the way. But Tunisia isn't all sand dunes and camels. I don't suppose the French would have hung on to it for so long if there weren't these fertile plains, and any amount of phosphates underneath them. Probably oil too, if they can find it. Now all they've kept possession of is the naval base at Bizerta, in a nice strategic position between Algeria and Libya. They're not going to give that up without a struggle.'

Freddie went into more detail about the uneasy relations between the Tunisians and the French, so that by the time they reached Bizerta Charles could probably have upsummed the atmosphere without getting out of the car. But they parked near the base and strolled

233

around the adjoining streets, noting the perimeter patrols and the heavy guard on all the gates. They mingled with the locals in some of the pavement cafés and bars, with Freddie doing the talking. He made it very clear that they were British, not French, but the precaution seemed unnecessary. There was obviously no love lost between the Tunisians and their former rulers, but there was also no indication of real trouble brewing.

'It's a lot more subdued than when I was here last week.' Freddie was sipping his coffee as they sat outside a café within sight of the harbour. 'The President's message seems to have filtered down to the grass roots already. I shouldn't say too much about that in your piece, though. We weren't supposed to know there was trouble brewing anyway. How about a general reference to occasional waves of unrest, and leave it at that?'

'Won't that rather kill the story?' asked Charles dubiously.

'I think the President has killed it already.' Freddie put down his cup. 'I'll check with a friend of mine at the police station, just to make sure. You'd better start writing.'

Charles watched the incongruous figure in the dark blue suit and Homburg hat forging a path through the throng of Arabs on the pavement, umbrella at the shoulder-arms position, a British gentleman out for a quiet stroll. Then he stared out at the French warships anchored in the harbour. A year ago, he thought, I would probably have been sitting on the quayside at Branham Staithe, watching the crab-boats unloading. Now I'm in North Africa, at the scene of a potential international trouble-spot and possibly a nasty little war. This is what real journalism is all about. He ought to be feeling excited and terribly sophisticated and worldly-wise. Why did he just feel lonely?

When Freddie returned he had finished writing his upsummer and felt rather pleased with it. He had described the guards at the base and the ships in the harbour, then the crowds in the bars and cafés. He had used the line about 'occasional waves of unrest' then went on to talk of 'an uneasy calm'. He had toyed with 'a powder-keg waiting to explode', then he remembered hearing Ronnie Horton use it, he of the bush hat and the leopard-skin band, in at least a couple of his purple-prose despatches, and decided against it.

Freddie checked through the script for him. When he came to the 'uneasy calm' he pursed his lips. 'My police friend confirms what we've heard. There'll be no trouble until after the Queen Mother's visit, he's quite sure of that. I think just "calm" would do.'

Charles shrugged, and made the alteration. Then he tried out an idea that had occurred to him. 'Suppose I record the piece just here, with the background noise from the café? It should give them some of the atmosphere they were asking for – might make it a bit more interesting.'

'I think not,' said Freddie firmly. 'There's enough background noise on the circuit to London without adding any more. And by the time it's relayed back again on short-wave and picked up on some cheap little radio, the listeners won't be able to understand a word of it. Anyway, if anything else is happening in the world which is more interesting than "No sign of trouble in Bizerta", I expect they'll ditch it anyway.'

Charles looked crestfallen, and Freddie patted his shoulder sympathetically. 'I'm afraid the story's changed since I sent that tip to London. I did tell them the President might hold his people back until after the State Visit, but I think Bob Corby was keen to give you a little overseas experience and this seemed a good excuse. Nobody will blame you because things have quietened down. Whereas they certainly would blame you if you concocted a scare story that doesn't exist.' He picked up his umbrella and prepared to depart. 'The Press can get away with that sort of thing because nobody believes the Press out here anyway, but they do believe the BBC. They think a lot more of it out here than people do back home, by all accounts. So don't forget that anything you send home is going to be heard out here, either direct from Bush House on the overseas service or picked up by the Tunisian Embassy in London and sent back by them to the government here. We have to get things right, Charles, or I'll find myself sitting next to you on the plane back to London.'

The plane back to London . . .

'Can we make a try for Boumedienne when we get back to Tunis?' He was almost pleading.

Freddie nodded cheerfully. 'We'll get a story for you to take back to London somehow.' But that wasn't just what Charles had in mind; a visit to Boumedienne would give him another day or two's respite before that flight home.

Freddie drove straight to the radio station for the circuit to London. The Arab at the desk greeted him like an old friend and took them straight to a studio, and they settled down at the microphone while the engineer started calling up London. Freddie leaned back comfortably in his chair.

'Very helpful lot, these chappies. The Director of the State Radio is an ex-journalist himself, a fellow called Chedli Klibi. Went to France and studied Arabic Literature at the Sorbonne, then wrote for various literary journals until he was made editor of the leading trade union paper out here, round about the time of independence. He's another of Bourguiba's young lions – bound to finish up in the Government in due course. But he knows the problems that journalists face; he's given me some useful tips on occasions.'

'Is there anyone who hasn't?' Charles was not being sarcastic; he was genuinely impressed by the range of Freddie's contacts. Freddie pretended to ponder the question seriously.

'Well, I suppose there's the President. He gets somebody else to leak the information for him . . .'

The engineer signalled to them to put on the headphones, and they heard the crackling line to London. Charles realised why he had not needed any background atmosphere on his tape.

'Hallo Traffic, hallo Traffic,' called Freddie, and a charming female voice replied from Foreign News Traffic.

'Hallo Freddie, nice to hear you again. Do you have Charles with you?'

'Yes, he's here, Margaret. I'll put him on first. Go ahead, Charles.'

Charles went ahead. To his relief he managed to reach the end of his despatch without a stumble. It was the first time he had recorded a piece with a senior correspondent sitting opposite him.

'That was splendid, Charles,' came the charming female voice. 'Very interesting piece. I'm sure they'll be very pleased with it. Shall we call it Despatch Number N.1?'

'Yes, thank you.' Charles was gratified by the praise, but he realised he should have numbered the despatch himself. He only hoped there would be an N.2.

Freddie sent his own piece, an immaculate couple of minutes read from some rough notes in his pocket-book. It was Number N.374, Charles noted, the latest of a long, long line. Again the female voice was most complimentary, and Freddie winked across at Charles as he replied.

'Bless you, Margaret. You always make us feel so much better. It's a pleasure talking to you; it makes the job so much easier.'

'That's sweet of you to say so,' said the charming voice very calmly, 'but that's what *my* job is all about, don't you think? Now Mr Corby would like to have a word with Charles, if he's still there.'

'I'm here,' gulped Charles. What now?

'Charles, how are you?' The familiar voice did not wait for a reply. 'Sounds as if the story's died. Do you think you'd better come home?'

Charles looked questioningly at Freddie and mouthed the word 'Boumedienne'. Freddie nodded firmly.

'Freddie thinks he can get me a visit to the Algerian Liberation Army headquarters in Tunisia. I should be able to get some actuality of battle practice: plenty of shooting and yelling, with any luck. I might even get an interview with the commander, chap called Boumedienne. I don't think he's been done before.'

'Probably because he only speaks French,' said Bob Corby crisply, and Charles's heart sank. He should have checked that with Freddie before mentioning an interview. Across the table Freddie was nodding confirmation.

The HORC's voice came on the line again. 'Never mind the interview, the rest of it sounds a good idea. It'll make the trip more worthwhile.' It'll save your face too for sending me, thought Charles unkindly, but at least he had got a reprieve. The HORC was still talking. 'It'll be no good trying to send actuality over a line like this, though. You'd better bring the tape home with you. Can you do it tomorrow and come home the day after?'

Charles looked at Freddie, who nodded a little dubiously. 'Yes, Freddie thinks so. It'll be a bit of a scramble.'

'Of course it will,' said the HORC. 'That's what it's all about. I'll have you booked onto a flight in two days' time. Make sure you're on it.' Charles could visualise him shooting his cuffs. Then the voice grew gentler; it was Uncle Bob on the line now. 'Prudence tells me you had a rotten flight out. She seems remarkably worried about you. Is there a problem?'

'No, it was only some sort of air-sickness,' lied Charles. He avoided Freddie's eye. 'The flight was probably a bit bumpier than I expected. I'll be fine.'

'She says you ought to take some tranquillisers. Seems to be a bit over the top to me, but she's very insistent. Make sure you don't take too many of them, that's all. I'm not sure the doctor would agree with it anyway.'

'I'll see what I can do,' said Charles vaguely.

'Sorry to butt in,' said the charming voice from Foreign News Traffic, 'but I'm afraid our circuit time is up. Goodbye Freddie, goodbye Charles. Take care.' Then, in a more business-like tone: 'This is BBC London ending the circuit with Tunis at 18.20 hours GMT. Thank you Tunis.'

Freddie thanked the engineer and led the way out of the studio. 'She sounds a nice girl,' he commented.

'You mean Margaret in Traffic?'

'Of course not. Margaret *is* a nice girl, she doesn't just sound

237

like one. I mean your Prudence. She seems very anxious to look after you.'

Charles shrugged. 'Remember what Margaret said? That's what the job is all about, don't you think?'

Freddie shook his head. 'That's rather different. All the girls in Traffic make a point of bolstering morale when they're on the line. It's not too bad here in Tunis, but it can be very depressing, stuck on your own in some far-flung corner of the BBC empire. Those girls are the only link with home, and they try to make it a pleasant one. But your Prudence seems to be performing above and beyond the call of normal secretarial duty.'

'You may be right.' The thought had occurred to Charles too, and he intended to pursue it when he got home. Meanwhile, there was Boumedienne. 'Do you really think you can fix the trip for tomorrow?'

'I think I may.' They had reached Freddie's car now, and he looked at his watch. 'I'll get a message through to Ghardimaou, telling Boumedienne you're only here for another twenty-four hours, so it's his only chance to get the publicity. I'll drop you at the hotel first. His people in Tunis may be a bit wary of strangers. Then I'll let you know how things go.'

Later that evening the phone rang in Charles's room. He had feared the worst as the hours had gone by, but he should have known better. Freddie's contacts had not let him down. 'It's on for tomorrow. A chappie called Mohamed will pick you up. And if you have tranquillisers to take, prepare to take them now – you'll find his driving is a lot more terrifying than any aeroplane. Be ready with your Midget at 6 a.m., and Mohamed will take you to the mountains.'

The car ride to Ghardimaou was not quite as bad as Freddie predicted, but very nearly. Mohamed had a battered old Chevrolet which he drove with enormous abandon, gesticulating fiercely – often with both hands – at anything or anybody which got in his way. Out in the desert the obstacles were limited to the occasional Bedouin and once a stray camel, but when they swept through the villages all manner of vehicles, livestock and local citizenry had to scatter for their lives, and they left behind a confusion of tooting horns, clucking chickens and shaking fists. A flock of sheep did manage to slow Mohamed briefly, but after he had grazed against a couple of them and terrorised the others with his horn, they parted to let him through. As they passed, the shepherd made threatening gestures at them through the window. Then he saw Mohamed's rifle on the back seat, and hastily waved them on.

Charles kept the Midget on his lap, not daring to ease his grip on it in case it was jolted onto the floor or even out of the window. The road surface was reasonably smooth, but whenever there was a pot-hole Mohamed unerringly hit it. In the midst of all the arm-waving and horn-tooting he still managed to smoke a singularly noxious cigar, the fumes of which were almost as disturbing to the stomach as the violent motion of the car. Charles's discomfort on the plane had been more complex than just airsickness, but even straighforward carsickness can be unpleasant enough, and he came hazardously close to losing his breakfast by the time they reached the outskirts of Ghardimaou.

They passed through two check-points manned by armed Algerians before they reached the camp itself, a collection of huts and tents on the outskirts of the town. The flag of the G.P.R.A., the provisional government of the Algerian Republic, fluttered over the largest hut, and Mohamed pulled up outside it. As Charles got out of the car a man in officer's uniform, wearing tinted rimless glasses, came out to meet him.

Charles turned to Mohamed and whispered urgently, '*Ici Boumedienne, n'est-ce pas?*' Mohamed merely looked blank. He had looked blank throughout the journey, ignoring Charles's attempts at schoolboy-French small-talk.

'Welcome, M'sieur Benson. You have made good time.' The English was almost perfect.

'Mohamed doesn't exactly hang about,' agreed Charles, and the young officer smiled gently as they shook hands.

'I am Commandant Djemmal. At least, that is what they call me. We all have *noms de guerre* in this business, I fear. We have families, you understand.'

'Yes of course.' Charles was enjoying the commandant's impeccable English. There might be an interview here after all.

'Colonel Boumedienne gives you his greetings and hopes you enjoy your stay. He does not give interviews himself but he authorises me to speak for him. He is also happy that you should record – how you say? – *l'actualité?*'

'*Oui, l'actualité.*' It sounded much more romantic like that; he hoped the actual actuality would live up to it. 'May we do that first, then perhaps, the interview?'

'By all means.' The commandant ushered him back into the Chevrolet, moved Mohamed's rifle off the back seat and sat down

239

behind him. 'We need to drive over to that rough ground outside the camp. Mohamed knows the way.'

They left the huts and tents behind and headed for a series of ridges covered with boulders and rough scrub. For once Mohamed stayed in second gear and took the road quite slowly, as it deteriorated into a rough track.

'May I suggest,' said the commandant from the back seat, 'that you start recording now. You may have, at any moment, *l'actualité*.'

Not quite understanding why, Charles plugged the microphone into the Midget and set the tape going. The quiet voice came from the back seat again. 'You could perhaps start to describe the scene?'

Charles looked around. They were approaching the first ridge, but the whole area seemed deserted. He looked over his shoulder and the commandant nodded encouragingly. Charles nodded back, pressed the 'Record' button on the Midget, and began.

'This is Charles Benson in Tunisia with Despatch N.2. Going ahead in five seconds.' So there was an N.2 after all, he thought. Good old Freddie.

'I'm at the headquarters of the Algerian National Liberation Army based just across the Tunisian border at Ghardimaou, and we are driving towards the area where Colonel Boumedienne's guerrillas are in training. With me is Commandant Djemmal, who is on his military staff. We are just approaching a ridge and entering a small defile. At this stage there is no sign of any activity . . . Aaaah!'

The cry was quite involuntary. Out of nowhere, so it seemed, a group of armed figures appeared in front of the car, forcing it to halt. More emerged from the rocks and scrub on the ridge at each side of the car and ran down towards it. As they ran they fired their rifles and let out ferocious shrieks and yells, then they clustered round the car, banging the doors and bonnet with the butts of their rifles, and shouting at Charles through the windows.

'*C'est l'actualité, n'est-ce pas?*' murmured Commandant Djemmal softly in the back seat. Charles nodded vigorously and pulled himself together. The tape was still running.

'As you may have gathered, our car has just been caught in a mock ambush.' He tried to eliminate the slight shake in his voice before continuing. 'As you may also have gathered, we were given no warning – but of course that is what guerrilla training is all about. The firing, I'm glad to say, was only into the air, but it could just as easily have been the real thing.' He turned to the back seat. 'Now, Commandant Djemmal, tell me about the men you have here and the training you give them.'

240

Commandant Djemmal told him, graphically and with great fluency, while the noise outside gradually died away and the men made their way back up the ridge. He told him also how the revolt had grown since the first uprising against the French in 1954, how a provisional government was established in Cairo four years later, how hopes were now rising that the French might agree to negotiations. And when Charles asked him to talk about his personal part in the uprising, he told him he was only a child of twelve when he heard of the massacre at Serif in 1945, when the French police opened fire on a mass gathering of Algerians and hundreds were killed. The uprising had been planned from that day on, but his own family lived in Morocco, and he first became involved in the Moroccan section of the Algerian Moslem Students' Union. When the revolt started he was a teacher in Rabat. He joined the group of guerrillas led by Boumedienne and had stayed on his staff and fought alongside him ever since. He was still only twenty-seven.

Charles sat listening to it all, quite fascinated. He had interviewed politicians and academics back home about the situation in Algeria, but this was his first encounter with someone personally involved, who had given up a teaching career to become a guerrilla fighter, and a highly successful one at that. Djemmal told his story without histrionics but with a convincing sincerity. Boumedienne could not have done it better.

He recorded more of *l'acutalité* during the day, sounds of marching feet and shouted orders and guns being fired on the range, but nothing came up to the tape of the ambush. He was rather embarrassed by the strangled cry he had given when the guerrillas appeared, and the initial shake in his voice was very noticeable, but there was nothing he could do about that on the Midget. Maybe the engineers could make some sort of adjustment when he got it home.

By mid-afternoon he decided he had recorded enough. He bade farewell to Commandant Djemmal outside the headquarters hut, and as he did so a lean figure in colonel's uniform came out, the face gaunt and hollow-cheeked, the eyes green and piercing. Colonel Boumedienne nodded to them briefly, and strode away.

'You may not have interviewed him, but at least you have seen him,' said Djemmal quietly, as they watched him go. 'One day you may wish to tell your grandchildren how you first saw the future President of Algeria. *Au 'voir*, M'sieur Benson.'

Charles shook his hand. '*Au 'voir*? You think we shall meet again?'

Djemmal smiled. 'If you continue along the path you are treading,

241

and I continue along mine, then assuredly you will be reporting the independence celebrations in Algiers – and I shall be there too. So: *au 'voir.'*

Mohamed drove back to Tunis rather faster, if anything, than he had driven out, but the bumping and the swaying no longer bothered Charles; even the cigar was tolerable. The tape on his Midget was compensation enough for all the discomfort. Indeed he was in quite a happy daze when he climbed out of the old Chevrolet outside the hotel, and turned to thank Mohamed. Mohamed held out his hand and without thinking he shook it cheerfully. He did not need to know Arabic to understand his reaction.

'Pardon,' he murmured, and handed over what notes he had. He was rewarded with the only English words his driver knew. He had learned them, no doubt, from Freddie Matthews.

'There's a good chap,' said Mohamed.

'I managed to get these from an old Arab doctor in the souk. He swears they're harmless and they'll "soothe the brain". That's the nearest phrase the Arabs have for tranquilliser.'

They were in Freddie's car on the way to the airport. Charles took the little box of pills and thanked him weakly. He had had a sleepless night, in spite of dosing himself liberally with brandy after dinner.

'I expect my regular French quack would have produced something a bit better, but he's away on holiday at the moment and his locum seemed to think I was some sort of drug addict. Quite extraordinary.'

Charles had to agree. Freddie was not everybody's image of a junkie. But an overwhelming sense of foreboding was with him again, and he did not attempt to answer.

'Are you sure you're not sickening for something? You look awful.'

He tried to reassure Freddie, but his voice sounded shaky. 'I just didn't sleep very well. I'm sure these pills will do the trick.'

Freddie frowned warningly. 'For goodness sake don't go eating them like Smarties. God knows what's in them. Just take one if you start to feel too rotten, and see what happens.'

He escorted Charles to the check-in desk, then into the departure lounge. Even in his keyed-up state Charles noticed that all the airport officials seemed to know Freddie; they were waved on past the queues. While they waited, to take his mind off the flight, he asked Freddie if he knew Commandant Djemmal. Naturally Freddie did.

'Very personable chappie. His real name's Cherif Belkacem. His family came from Tlemcen in Algeria originally, before they moved to Morocco. Boumedienne thinks very highly of him, I gather.'

'He talks as if they've nearly won the war already. He reckons he'll meet me in Algiers on Independence Day.'

Freddie nodded. 'If Boumedienne plays his cards right he'll finish up as President and your friend Djemmal will be there with him. But it'll take a couple of years yet before the French pull out, and I should think it'll be a couple of years after that before Boumedienne and his colleagues sort out who's finally going to be boss. There's Ben Khedda and the old guard in Cairo, and that chappie who's in prison, Ben Bella, who'll have the younger men behind him. But of course Boumedienne has got the Army. It'll be an interesting contest.'

Freddie kept up a flow of further information about Algerian politics, to such an extent that Charles guessed he was trying to keep his mind occupied – a sort of verbal 'soothing of the brain' – and he was grateful for it. But when his flight was called the familiar wave of apprehension swept over him again.

Freddie handed Charles his bag. 'Come on, there's a good chap. Time to be off.' He gently propelled him towards the departure door. Charles felt as if a kindly priest was leading him to the scaffold.

'Would you like me to come into the plane with you and get you properly settled?' asked Freddie quietly. 'It'll be no problem; I know the chap on the gate.'

Charles realised he must have an idea of what was wrong. He desperately pulled himself together. 'No, I'll manage. But thank you all the same.' He grasped Freddie's hand and shook it warmly. 'I'm most grateful to you for all your help on that Bizerta trip, and fixing up the visit to Boumedienne, and all the background stuff you've fed me, and, oh, everything.'

Freddie smiled cheerfully. 'All part of the service, old chappie. Remember Margaret's *bon mot*? "That's what the job is all about, don't you think?" '

He turned, and Charles watched the large man in the dusty blue suit and the dustier Homburg hat head back through the lounge, shake hands with the official on the passport desk, and disappear through the doors. Then he gritted his teeth and headed for the departure gate. He was concentrating so intensely on getting there that he did not notice the blue suit and the Homburg re-appear in the lounge.

'Poor devil,' said Freddie Matthews, as he watched Charles's slow progress to the gate, and out on to the tarmac. Then he drove rapidly back into Tunis and booked a call to London.

Charles had reached the steps to the plane when the smell of jet fuel hit him, and the apprehension turned to panic. It was worse than when he boarded the flight from London, because now he knew what lay ahead. But again he forced himself up the steps and into the plane, and even managed to fasten his own seat-belt before the roar of the engines just before take-off started him sweating again. He took out the box of pills and gulped one down, and then another. He longed for them to work before the plane took off, but they seemed to have no effect at all.

As the plane climbed steeply and he glimpsed the airport buildings receding below he was back in the nightmare again. Then he heard the noise beneath him of the undercarriage being retracted, a terribly final sort of noise, and there was the vast void underneath his feet and the Tunisian coastline thousands of feet below. Would they hit the land when they fell, or drop into the sea. . . ?

'Can I get you anything, sir?'

He looked up at the stewardess and for a moment was tempted to start on the brandy again. But he still had to give the pills a chance. He asked for a glass of water, and while he waited for it he sat rigidly in his seat, eyes shut, hands clenched together, heart thumping, the sweat soaking his shirt. As soon as she brought it he took two more pills out of the box, swallowed them quickly and washed them down with the water. As he did so the plane swayed slightly in a patch of turbulence and he very nearly shouted in terror. But he was feeling a little dizzy now, a little light-headed. Maybe the 'soothing of the brain' had begun. He shut his eyes and tried to picture Toftham again, and the Norfolk countryside, but somehow the images seemed to be distorted.

'Have you finished with your glass, sir?'

The stewardess was leaning over him. But this was a very strange stewardess, a woman with staring eyes and a long beaky nose and an enormous mouth. He gazed at her in horror. The ears were enormous too, and her hair actually seemed to be growing longer as he looked. My God, I'm hallucinating, he thought. Those damn pills . . . Then he mercifully passed out.

The plane was approaching the runway at Heathrow when he eventually came round. The stewardess, after consulting her colleagues and checking that his breathing was normal, had made him comfortable and decided to leave him until they landed. When he opened his eyes he had no idea at first where he was, then the noise of the plane's engines registered, and he looked at the rows of seats, and the little windows, and the lights and switches over his head, and as realisation came back, so did the terror. He only had to bear it for a few minutes, as the plane touched down and taxied to the airport building, but it was more than enough. I'll soon be out, I'll soon be out, he kept telling himself.

When the plane came to a halt and he stood up, he found the pills were still having an effect. The rows of seats seemed to move in on him from each side of the gangway, so he had to force his way through the narrowing gap between them with the stewardess helping him along. The steps out of the aircraft seemed to stretch away below him like the side of a mountain, but the other passengers hurried him down, and with his mind still in a blur he found himself inside the building.

He had his passport checked by a man whose hands seemed the size of balloons, and without bothering to collect his luggage he blundered through the Customs Hall and out into the crowded arrival area. As he stood there, swaying and blinking, he heard a familiar voice calling his name.

'Here we are, Charles. This way.'

Was this the tablets again, 'soothing the brain'? No, it was definitely Prudence's voice, and he recognised the vague outlines of two figures hurrying towards him.

'Hallo, Pru,' he mumbled. 'Hallo, Uncle Bob. Greetings from Tunis.' And he collapsed into Bob Corby's arms.

EIGHTEEN

Quentin Milton came into Charles's office, leaned across the desk and shook his hand. 'That was splendid stuff, dear boy. I really thought when those guns started firing it was a genuine ambush. That yell you gave – terrific!'

'Thanks very much,' said Charles. His head was still throbbing, but the potion the BBC doctor had given him when he was brought back from the airport had ensured him a good night's sleep, and now the previous day's plane journey from Tunisia seemed only a ghastly dream.

'Competition, eh?' Ronnie Horton was in the doorway, for once without his bush hat. 'Can't have two of us dicing with death, old sport. I'll have to get you transferred to the obituaries desk.'

Many a true word, thought Charles, but he waved back cheerily. 'Sorry there was no actual blood. Those chaps were hopeless shots.'

The congratulations had been coming in all morning. His recording of the mock ambush, and the interview with Commandant Djemmal, had been broadcast on *Radio Newsreel* on the domestic and overseas services. A memo had already arrived from Tony Wigan, the foreign news editor: 'N.2 was great radio. Congratulations.' Even his old mentor on South-East Region News, Ben Gunn, had taken the trouble to telephone. 'Glad I started you on the right road, young Charles. Make sure you whack up the expenses in Tunis. They can't turn 'em down after a piece like that. Your Djemmal character must have cost you a few dinars.'

It was all highly gratifying, and Charles was doing his best to enjoy it, but after all the congratulations and the badinage he knew there were two people he had to talk to, and with them the conversation would be very different. One of them telephoned as he was talking to Quentin.

'How are you feeling this morning, Charles?' He tried to detect from the tone of voice whether this was the genial Uncle Bob talking, or the business-like HORC, but it gave nothing away.

'Much better, thank you.'

'Then why not step along to see me, if you can spare a moment. And

246

incidentally, well done with that ambush piece. It's made all the Reels, and Foreign News are delighted with it. Well worth the trip. Now please come over.'

As he hung up, Charles's heart sank. The feeling was nothing like the apprehension he had felt when the HORC told him he would be flying out to Tunisia, but it was unpleasant enough. This would really be 'the big one'.

'What now, my rustic friend?' Dickie Johnson, at the other desk, had been the first to congratulate him and had watched all the callers come and go. 'Are you being summoned for a personal commendation from the Director-General?'

'Not exactly,' said Charles. 'I think Ronnie Horton was probably nearer the mark.' And he left Dickie to puzzle it out.

The HORC was studying a document on his desk when he came it. It looked like one of the BBC's official medical reports. He waved him to a chair.

'You're looking quite human again. Amazing what a night's sleep will do.'

'I'm much better,' Charles paused. 'I'm sorry I made such a fool of myself at the airport.'

'Never mind about that. I'm glad Freddie Matthews guessed what was wrong and gave us a ring. But we'd have probably met you anyway. Prudence was in quite a state about you.'

Charles was deeply embarrassed that she had witnessed his collapse. 'I do wish she hadn't insisted on getting involved in all this.'

'You're very lucky she did.' And now it was definitely the HORC speaking. 'She had the sense to realise what the trouble was before any of us. Apparently a great friend of hers suffered from the same problem. Couldn't even get on a plane, let alone fly in it. I gather from this report it must have taken a fair amount of guts to go through with both those flights. But we can't let you do it again. We have something of a difficulty here, Charles.'

'Yes, I know,' he said miserably. He had already worked it out for himself, with all the implications.

'Prudence recognised the symptoms, and I gather she did her best to let Freddie know. But it wasn't too clever to let you have those tablets without being sure what they were.'

'He was just trying to help me through it,' said Charles quickly. 'It was my fault I took too many of them.'

'Well, that's all history. The question is, what can we do about the future?' The HORC started to shoot his cuffs, then stopped in mid-jerk, and picked up the medical report. 'I'm afraid the doctor calls it a pathological fear of flying. It's the same sort of thing as claustrophobia, but a lot worse. And like claustrophobia, they haven't found a complete answer to it yet. He sets it all down here. You could try approved tranquillisers, instead of those knock-out drops you got in Tunis, but they'd still reduce you to half-speed, and that's no way to arrive on an assignment with a deadline to meet. Then he says there have been experiments to cure it by hypnosis, but that's very much in its early stages, and he's not at all enthusiastic about it. He mentions some other treatments, longshots by the sound of them. Some may work and some may not, but all of them take a long time. So you'll appreciate, Charles old son, we have a problem.' The voice had become softer; it was Uncle Bob talking now.

'I know what you're driving at,' said Charles. 'There's not much point being a reporter in the finest news-gathering organisation in the world if I can't get on a bloody aeroplane.' He had not meant to swear about it, but it just came out.

Uncle Bob seemed about to reprimand him, then smiled and shook his head. 'It's not quite as bad as that. I could take you out of the Fire Brigade and limit you to home-based stories, but I can understand that you might find that a bit frustrating, and anyway I'm not sure the admin people would create an extra post for a reporter with that restriction. You could specialise, of course. I could suggest you are permanently posted to Westminster?' He saw Charles's expression and smiled again. 'Well, perhaps that's not your cup of tea. So what else is there?'

He looked through some notes on his desk. Charles just sat, waiting, his thoughts in a turmoil.

'We could move you into the news-room, of course. Or you could even try news-reading. You might find yourself a television star, a household name.' Uncle Bob looked up enquiringly. Charles's expression did not change.

'I'm sorry, Charles, but those seem to be the main possibilities. You could always apply for attachments to other departments, of course, but most of the interesting ones need people who can travel freely, even if it's only in emergencies. And if you're a real news-man, I doubt you'd be happy outside News Division.'

Bob Corby put aside the papers and leaned back in his chair. 'There's no need to make a hasty decision. The BBC takes its time over this sort of thing, and it'll do its best for you, whatever you decide.' He smiled again. 'They don't call it Auntie BBC for nothing.'

'I'm very grateful.' He had guessed these would be the sort of options open to him, but the prospect was no pleasanter, now it had been put into words.

'You're due for some leave. Why not take yourself off home for a fortnight over Christmas? Give yourself time to think things out. Then we'll get it all sorted out in the New Year.'

'Home?' repeated Charles without enthusiasm, thinking of his parents in Wembley Park. He would no doubt be visiting them over Christmas, but he had no desire to spend a fortnight with them, and he suspected they would feel the same way.

'Yes, home.' Bob Corby waved his arms expansively. 'Back to Norfolk for Christmas. It must be marvellous to spend Christmas in the country: carols by candlelight, holly berries in the hedges, sleighbells in the snow – great stuff.'

Charles smiled for the first time since he had entered the HORC's office. 'Either those pictures on the Christmas cards have been getting to you, or you've been reading too much Dickens. It'll probably be all mud and slush, and a howling gale off the North Sea.' He got up, then hesitated. 'Still, I might give it a try.'

Bob Corby stood up too, and held out his hand. 'Good man. You've done well, Charles. This isn't the end of the world, you know; it may be the start of a new one. Let me know what you decide when you get back.' And he ushered him out.

Charles could not face returning to his office. Instead he walked round to the Dover Castle, and from its phone box he telephoned Broadcasting House and asked to speak to the reporters' secretary.

'This is reporters. Can I help you?'

Just the sound of the voice made him feel a little better. 'Yes, you can actually. Very much so. It's Charles, Pru, I've just seen Uncle Bob. I expect you know what we've been talking about. I'm over at the Dover Castle now. Can we meet during your lunch-hour?'

There was a pause before she replied. 'Not at the Dover Castle, Charles, everybody congregates there. Shall we meet by the lake in Regent's Park? It'll only take me a few minutes to walk up Portland Place.'

'Fine.' He thought fast. 'Let's say one o'clock. I'll bring some sandwiches and something to drink. It's not the most lavish way of saying thank you, but it's a start.'

'You don't need to say thank you,' said Prudence softly. 'But I'll be there anyway.' And as an afterthought: 'Cheese and pickle sandwiches would be nice.'

They sat on a bench by the boating lake with the empty bandstand behind them. It was a crisp, dry December day and there was still some white frost on the grass, but it was not cold enough for the lake to freeze and the ducks were splashing about cheerfully. Several of them were out on the grass in front of them, waiting for any remains from the cheese and pickle sandwiches. Prudence was wrapped snugly in a short furry coat over her red skirt. She wore high leather boots and her hair was tucked inside a fur-lined hood. She looked quite enchanting.

'I thought we might celebrate,' said Charles, and produced a half-bottle of brandy from his overcoat pocket. 'I got some of the local stuff in the duty-free at Tunis. We may as well make the most of it.'

'It doesn't look like local stuff,' said Prudence. She was looking at the label on the bottle of French cognac he had bought at the off-licence in Great Portland Street.

'They drink this all the time over there. Ex-French colony – old habits die hard.' He had been in no state to think about duty-free drinks at Tunis airport, but he was not going to admit it. On the other hand he didn't want her to think he had bought it specially.

From his other pocket he produced two BBC cardboard cups, discreetly acquired from the canteen, and poured some brandy into them. He tried to think of a toast, but nothing seemed appropriate, so he just murmured. 'Thanks, Pru'. She smiled at him, the familiar dazzling smile, and they both sipped their brandy. Then they emptied the remnants of the sandwiches on to the grass and sat silently watching as the ducks scrambled round their feet for each crumb. It was Charles who first brought up the subject of the flight.

'I hadn't realised you knew all about this phobia thing. I should have paid more attention.'

She kept her eyes on the ducks. 'I did try to tell you, but it was no good trying to stop you. You had to find out for yourself. But I knew how awful it was going to be. I was amazed you managed to get on board at all.'

'As it turns out, I needn't have bothered,' he said rather bitterly. 'They won't be sending me abroad again.'

'I should hope not,' she said hotly. 'You mustn't go through all that again. But it wasn't a waste of time. You got that marvellous report from the Algerian camp. You've shown you can do it.'

'All right, so I've done it.' He turned towards her, and she faced him too. It was probably the chilliness in the air, but his eyes felt moist. 'So what do I do now, Pru?'

She took his hand. 'I don't know, Charles. That's for you to decide. But I think you must be clear about all the facts before you make up your mind. Not just the facts that Uncle Bob talked about. There's something else as well.'

She looked away from him again and waved off one of the ducks that was trying to peck at her shoe. Charles stared at the ducks too, and waited.

'It's difficult to say, but I think I must, because you may be making some sort of assumption and that may influence you in what you decide.' She stopped again, and he poured some more brandy into the cardboard cups. He thought they might need it. 'You've been very sweet, and I enjoyed that run up to Scarborough and meeting your friends in Norfolk, and I was really worried about you and that awful business with the flying. But that's all, Charles. That's really all.'

Charles nodded, and drank his brandy, and poured himself some more. He added a little to her cup as well. But he stayed silent.

'I thought I ought to say so because, well, you might have started thinking there was more to it, and that might have made you decide to stay here doing a job which you don't really want to do.'

He put down his cup on the grass, and he took her cup and put that down too, and then he put his arms round her and kissed her very firmly on the mouth. She kissed him back, but it was not a passionate kiss, nor a lingering one. He remembered Freddie's description; it was sisterly.

'I think I knew that,' he said, as he let her go. He picked up the cups again. 'If I do stay on, I'll do it because I want to stay with the BBC, even if I'm never going to be another Ronnie Horton. I don't think I'm quite up to wearing a bush hat anyway. Can you imagine how I'd look?'

She could, and so could he, and they both laughed together, then they sipped more brandy.

'What's more,' he said, a little thickly, 'I rather suspect that you wouldn't be too keen on moving from this great metropolis into the foodal society of deepest Norfolk – even if such a magnificent opportunity arose.'

'Well, I liked Norfolk, but it is . . .' She hesitated, and he waved his cup at her cheerfully.

'I know. Basic. It's definitely basic.'

They both laughed again, and the ducks gathered round and watched them curiously as he replenished the cups and tucked his arm in hers, and they silently sipped their brandy. He tried for a moment to imagine they were back in the empty Norfolk countryside, but the grass around them was littered with sweet wrappers and crisp packets, and there was the steady roar of the traffic in Marylebone Road.

Then Prudence turned to him, and looked at him carefully, and took an envelope from the pocket of her coat. 'I think this is probably the right moment,' she said, 'to give you this.'

He giggled rather stupidly. 'If it's your resignation, then I don't accept it. Tear it up.'

'I don't think you'd want me to tear this up,' she said quietly. 'It's from Norfolk. It came this morning, after you'd gone off to see Uncle Bob.'

He took it quickly, expecting to see Rebecca's writing, but the name and address had been written in careful rounded letters, almost like a child's. 'I wasn't sure if it was good news or bad news, but either way I thought you'd had enough to think about this morning,' she explained.

He took out the letter and turned quickly to the signature. 'I expect it's going to be bad news,' he said. The letter was signed, 'Maggie'.

Prudence sat silently beside him while he read it, and she heard his little sigh of relief. 'Not as bad as you thought?'

He shook his head. 'Not quite. It's about my old editor, Mr Juby. You remember he was in hospital when we called at the Dog and Partridge. He got over that, but now he's gone back in again. Maggie says – ' and he smiled in spite of himself – 'Maggie says he hent too clever'.

'I'm sorry.' She squeezed his hand. 'You ought to go and see him.'

Charles put the letter in his pocket, and noticed the empty cups. He poured a little brandy into hers, and the rest of the bottle into his.

'I was going anyway,' he said, and raised the cup. 'Happy Christmas, Pru. And as one of your bosses, you may take the rest of the day off.'

'I think perhaps I will,' said Prudence calmly. 'Uncle Bob knows I was meeting you. He said under the circumstances, I needn't come back this afternoon.'

Charles held her by the waist and stared, rather blearily, into the clear blue eyes. 'You are aware, I am sure, that I am deeply, irrevocably, overwhelmingly in love with you, Prudence.'

He was rewarded with the dazzling smile. 'Yes, I'm sure, Charles. But I think you'll survive.' She raised her cup to him. 'Have a very happy Christmas. In Norfolk.'

She kissed him on the cheek, gave him the empty cup and walked off, not too unsteadily, around the lake. Charles watched her go, slumped on the bench, the two cardboard cups and the empty bottle on his lap. He sat so motionless that the adventurous duck which had attacked Prudence's shoe gently pecked at his ankle.

He stared down at it for a moment, then stirred himself, leaned forward, and looked the duck in the eye.

'Well now, marster,' he said solemnly. 'Hent that a rum owld du?'

There was the familiar wind from the north-east and a hint of snow in the air when Charles drove into Toftham market-place, two days before Christmas. He had come direct from his parents' home in Wembley Park, after a dutiful and unexciting visit. They had got used to him being on duty in Norfolk over the Christmas period, and it would have upset their regular programme of church-going and bridge-playing if he had descended on them for any length of time. Twenty-four hours had been just about right. So he had set off after breakfast in the office Morris Minor – 'Technically you're on call, so you need to be mobile', Uncle Bob had assured him – and he arrived just as the Council office clock was striking one – its current method of indicating twelve noon.

The square was packed with cars and the pavements were packed with people. George Perkins's shop window was festooned with turkeys, and Harry Hurn had replaced the haircream and toothbrush advertisements in the window of his hairdressing salon with the rather battered Nativity scene which he retrieved from his attic each year. The gloomy yellow-painted sheep which dangled over the entrance of the Golden Fleece had been draped with ribbons, and even the front window of the Journal office contained a greeting in cardboard cut-out lettering: 'A Happy Xmas to All Our Readers'.

Charles drove carefully through the crowds spilling on to the roadway, recognising a face or two here and there, until he reached the Dog and Partridge, then instead of parking outside he took the car round the back, past the sign which said 'Residents Only'. For the first time in his long patronage of the farmers' bar he had actually booked a room in the hotel.

When he entered the foyer there was nobody behind the desk. There never was. But he found a note on it, and a key. 'Mr Benson. Room 3, top of stairs and turn left. Any queries, see Maggie in bar. C. Bundock, Prop.' And as an afterthought: 'Welcome to Toftham'.

Room 3 was quite sizeable, with a big double bed, a dark mahogany wardrobe and chest of drawers, and two hard chairs, companions of the one he used to occupy at the Rotary Club lunches along the corridor. It

253

also had a large window overlooking the market-place, just above the swinging AA sign with its solitary star. The view was an exact reversal of the one he used to have from his office at the Journal, and he could see straight across the square to his old office window and Mr Juby's above it. Neither showed any sign of life.

He put his bag on the bed and used the bathroom which Rotarians shared with the residents on lunch days. He peeped in their meeting room and the chairs were ranged in their familiar pattern round the tables. He remembered where he sat listening to Mr Pollitt telling his interminable holiday anecdotes while the other Rotarians slumbered peacefully around him. It seemed like the day before yesterday.

Back in his room he took out Maggie's letter and read it again. He had replied immediately, saying he would be coming to Toftham for Christmas and asking her to book him a room. There had been no word from her since; no doubt if the news was bad she was waiting to tell him herself. He looked across the square again at Mr Juby's office window; the curtains were drawn right across it. It was high time he went to see Maggie.

There was still nobody about in the corridor, or on the stairs, or in the foyer. The whole hotel seemed to have been abandoned, leaving him as the final guest. 'Please turn off the lights before leaving,' he thought to himself gloomily. Then he opened the door of the farmers' bar.

There was complete silence for a second, and for a wild moment he thought the entire clientele of the Dog and Partridge had been turned into stone. Then the silent figures in front of him burst into life, and swooped on him with the most blood-curdling cries. Hands seized him and dragged him across the room, and he was literally picked up and planted down, quite heavily, on one of the stools at the bar. All around him tankards and bottles were being banged on tables, and one of his assailants, whom he recognised dazedly as Freddie Pendleton, the practical-joking undertaker, was actually waving a shotgun over his head. Then the banging died away, the yells and howls dissolved into laughter, Freddie put down the shotgun and slapped him on the back, and from the stool behind him there came the familiar chuckle which he had never really expected to hear again.

'Well now, Charlie boy,' said Mr Juby. 'Thass a *real* ambush, wouldn't you say? Better'n those furriners could dream up, thass for sure.'

He was looking thinner, and his cheeks were paler, and his hand shook just a little as he held it out to Charles, but the old gleam was in his eye, the pipe was going strong, and a half-empty glass of his special was on the bar.

'I thought you were in hospital!' Charles grasped his hand and shook it quite violently. 'What are you doing here?'

'So I were for a spell, but those doctors don't know narthin. I soon told those duzzy fules, they hent keeping me in hospital over Christmas, and they say I can come home, du I don't du narthin stoopid. As if I would, then.' Mr Juby beamed at his special, then turned back to Charles. 'Mind you, du you keep pumping my arm like that, boy, I might ha' to go back again with a dislocairted shoulder.'

Charles apologised and released his hand, and Mr Juby immediately made use of it to pick up his glass. A pint appeared in front of Charles too.

'Welcome back,' said Maggie, smiling at him from behind the bar as she put it down. 'The old devil seems to have got the better of 'em again. He really was poorly a few days back when I wrote to you, but he's tough as an old goose, is Mr Juby. He come back yesterday, but he told me not to tell you. He thought it'd be a surprise.'

'So it is,' Charles agreed. He turned back to Mr Juby. 'Quite the nicest surprise this Christmas. Did you organise this little reception as well?'

Mr Juby shook his head. 'That was Freddie did that. He thought that was a rare good broadcast you did with those Ay-rabs, but he dint want you to think that only the Ay-rabs can put on that sort o' squit. So when Maggie says you were due this lunch-time he kept an eye out for you. He saw you go upstairs and they've been waitin' for you ever since. What you bin doin' up there, boy – stealin' the sheets?'

Charles grinned. 'Just planning my next campaign against the Ay-rabs.' Then he remembered there would be no more campaigns, and the smile faded.

'Well, you shew those Lunnon folk that we hent so daft up here, and no mistake. You done well, boy.' And Mr Juby raised his special in salute.

'They did seem quite pleased,' Charles admitted. He couldn't tell Mr Juby the whole story, not yet anyway. He changed the subject.

'So how's the Journal been getting on while you've been away? Have they sent someone out from Norwich?'

Mr Juby nodded gloomily. 'There's one or two of 'em come out during the week, and the young lad from Wettleford comes over and does what he can, but thass a poor old muddle these days. They say they'll wait to see how I git on before they do anything permanent, but

255

o' course they hent going to wait for ever.' The eyes had lost their gleam now, and the cheeks seemed to shrink a little. 'I tell you, Charlie boy, I couldn't even climb up those stairs to the office these days, or if I did I'd have to sit there getting my breath back till it were time to come back down again. That hent a good situation to be in, and I don't see it getting better.'

Charles tried to cheer him up, but he realised Mr Juby was not exaggerating. Even before his illness he had had to take his time with those stairs. 'You could always move down to my old office, or even down to the ground floor. It can't be compulsory for the editor to have the second floor office.'

'Don't talk stoopid, boy.' Some of the old fire came back. 'I've worked in that office ever since my father died, and everyone in Toftham knows it. They see me having to work downstairs, they'd say poor old bugger, he's past it now, he can't even git upstairs to his own office.' He turned back gloomily to his special. 'There'd be no respect left, boy. I hent having that.'

Charles nodded. He could quite understand. 'You're right, Mr Juby. That was stupid of me.'

Mr Juby settled back on the stool and supped his special. The little outburst seemed to have done him good.

'Anyway, I told those folk in Narridge I was happy to go, du they find somebody to take over who can do the job right. I told them that before they took me off to hospital this last time. And thass a funny thing, Charlie boy, but just a couple o' days ago they come and see me, and they bring some fruit and flowers and all that sort o' squit, and we have a chat about this and that, then very casual-like they say, "If young Charles Benson comes up to Norfolk this Christmas and you happen to see him, then give him our best regards." And I say, "Well now, I do hear he's stayin' at the Dog and Partridge over Christmas." And they say, "Well, hent that handy," they say, "we might catch him there and give him our regards personal-like".'

Charles was about to interrupt, but Mr Juby had not finished. 'Then they ask me what time might be best to telephone you, so I tell 'em if they try about two o'clock, say, then more'n likely you'd just be finishing your lunch in the farmers' bar. And they say, "Excellent, Mr Juby", they say, "we'll try and do that". And off they go.' Mr Juby puffed his pipe and studied his glass very closely. 'Now hent that a lot o' trouble to go to, Charlie boy, just to wish you a merry Christmas?'

'That it is.' The phrase came out automatically. He looked Mr Juby in the eye. 'I can't think why they should bother.' And he couldn't. So far as the people in the Norwich office knew, he had successfully embarked on a BBC career, and he had just pulled off something of a scoop in Tunisia. They had no reason to think he might abandon it so early.

'Ah,' said Mr Juby. 'No more can I. I thought maybe they'd heard something that hent quite reached me yet.' He looked at Charles quizzically. 'But thass hardly likely, now is it?'

Again Charles looked him in the eye. 'Whatever it is, they haven't heard it from me. I've no idea what they're up to.'

'In that case,' said Mr Juby, 'let's not waste any more time on it. Thass your round, Charlie boy. I'll have another special.'

It was exactly two o'clock when Maggie told Charles there was a call for him in the back office. By then it had not only been Charles's round, but Mr Juby's return round, and a round from Freddie Pendleton, and then Fred Knock had appeared and that meant another round from him. So for a moment the significance of the phone call did not register with Charles, and he asked who it was. The name, said Maggie, was Downing, and he was phoning from Norwich.

He remembered then about Norwich, and Mr Juby's hospital visitors, and their enquiries after his welfare. He also remembered Jim Downing. He was the personnel director of Anglian Press who had given him his first job on the *Toftham and Wettleford Journal*.

In the back office, with the door shut to keep out the sounds of continuing celebration in the bar, he took a couple of deep breaths in an effort to clear his head, then picked up the phone. 'Benson here.'

'Ah, Charles. Glad I've caught you. I trust you're well?' The voice was a little fruitier than he remembered it, but it was certainly Jim Downing.

'I'm fine, thanks. I've just been having lunch with Mr Juby.'

'Ah, Mr Juby.' The tone was slightly patronising, and it reminded him of what Downing had said at that first interview. 'Old Juby likes to think he's still Lord of the Manor out at Toftham, but he's not likely to argue if I recommend you.' The personnel director had reckoned that Mr Juby was a back number all those years before; he had not known him very well.

'You'll know why I'm calling, then?'

'As I understand it,' said Charles, 'you wish to give me your best regards.'

'Quite so.' There was a pause. 'But it's a little more than that. The chairman particularly asked me to contact you. If you can spare the time, he'd very much like to see you.'

257

This time it was Charles who paused. 'You mean, so that he can give me *his* best regards?'

Downing gave a rather forced laugh. 'I'm sure that's part of it. But I'd better leave it to him to explain. He wondered if you could have lunch with him tomorrow at the Castle Hotel here in Norwich. Say one o'clock?'

Lunch with the chairman of Anglian Press? At the Castle Hotel? Not even Mr Juby had ever achieved that. He still had no idea what it could be about, but at least he'd get a decent lunch. The Castle was one of the top hotels in Norwich.

'I'd be delighted. One o'clock, Castle Hotel.' The effects of the prolonged lunch with Mr Juby suddenly overtook him. 'Decorations will be worn?'

'I think not,' said Jim Downing, a little coldly. 'Goodbye, Charles. Happy Christmas.'

'Not even *Christmas* decorations?' insisted Charles. Fortunately, the line was dead.

Back in the farmers' bar Mr Juby looked at him enquiringly as he ordered another round. 'Best regards, was it?'

'Best regards,' Charles confirmed. Then he added casually: 'Plus lunch with the chairman tomorrow.'

Mr Juby nodded solemnly. 'Then tea with the Lord Lieutenant, no doubt, followed by a quiet evening at Sandringham.'

'It's true. Lunch with the chairman, one o'clock, Castle Hotel. Decorations will not be worn.'

Mr Juby looked at him again. 'If you're serious, Charlie boy, thass a very rum owld do.' He was obviously greatly puzzled.

Charles beamed happily into his glass. 'That's exactly what I told the duck.' Mr Juby stared at him. 'In Regent's Park,' he explained. Mr Juby gave up, and returned to the lunch invitation.

'The chairman hent got any part in giving out jobs. I must ha' got it wrong.' He shook his head. 'I reckoned I knew the ways of Norfolk folk. I must be getting past it, like that blathering idiot Downing always said.'

'It's quite simple,' said Charles airily. 'He must want me to get him a job at the BBC. I'll tell him I can put in a word for him with the head of the Appointments Board.'

As he said it, some hazy memory stirred. The chairman of the Appointments Board was Sir Greville Taylor; but why should that be significant? Then it came back to him: the overspill plan, and his test piece for the Board, and Sir Greville's wife following it up on

258

the County Council. And she was a Gurlay, one of the Norfolk Gurlays . . .

'Mr Juby,' said Charles thoughtfully, 'remind me. What's the name of the chairman of Anglian Press?'

'Blast, boy, thass too many beers you been drinking, if you've forgotten that.' Mr Juby drained his special. 'Thass Gurlay, o' course, George Gurlay. His family owns the company. How could you forget that, boy?'

'How could I indeed?' Even in his fuddled state, the pieces were falling into place. 'You're right, Mr Juby. How could I forget that . . .'

NINETEEN

Charles was preparing to drive into Norwich for his lunch appointment with George Gurlay when C. Bundock, Prop., tapped on his bedroom door at the Dog and Partridge and said there was a phone call for him in the back office.

So that's that, thought Charles. Jim Downing was just having his little Christmas joke. How he's going to tell me it's all off. And he walked with great care down the stairs, trying not to jar himself as he landed on each step. Lunch with Mr Juby and the other regulars in the farmers' bar had continued well into the afternoon, without any actual food being consumed. When Mr Juby eventually climbed off his stool and took his departure – 'and give my best regards to the chairman, Charlie boy' – he got a couple of cheese rolls from Maggie and took them up to his bedroom, but he collapsed on his bed with the rolls still sitting untouched on the chest of drawers, and slept heavily until mid-evening. He was woken by the sound of revellers in the market-place below, but he could not face the thought of joining them. Instead he ate his cheese rolls, changed into pyjamas, and went back to sleep. It was only now, in mid-morning, that he was beginning to recover.

C. Bundock, Prop., showed him rather grudgingly into the back office. He was a newcomer to the town who had only been Prop. for a few months, and he knew nothing of Charles's connection with it. He had appeared in the bar at one stage and suggested it was closing time, but Charles had assured him that as a resident he was merely entertaining his guests. Maggie had cheerfully confirmed it and C. Bundock had reluctantly withdrawn, but he had obviously labelled Charles as a troublemaker and this use of his office phone was just one more exasperation.

'Don't be too long. I'm doing my accounts,' he warned.

The desk had nothing on it except a copy of the *Toftham and Wettleford Journal*, and Charles was tempted to congratulate him on doing his accounts by mental arithmetic, but he nodded solemnly instead, and C. Bundock withdrew.

Charles picked up the phone. 'Hello again, Jim. Don't tell me the chairman's caught mumps?'

The caller sounded amused, if a little bewildered. 'Not that I know of, Charles, but if he has, then I can probably do something for him.'

'Dr Bateman?' Hearing Rebecca's father on the phone took him quite unawares. After getting no response to his postcard from Scarborough, saying he might be in Norfolk for Christmas, he had not written again. He assumed she would be away, or perhaps she just wasn't bothered.

'Yes, it's me, Charles. I heard from Freddie Pendleton this morning that you were staying at the Dog and Partridge. He came out to collect a certificate for one of his clients. I gather you stepped straight into an ambush in the farmers' bar.'

Charles grinned to himself. News did not take long to travel out to Remingham. 'It was quite a party – I'm just recovering. I hope you're well, doctor, and the family.' he paused. 'Are you all at home?'

'Well, Beccy's not here just at the moment.'

'Oh,' said Charles, and tried not to sound too disappointed, but even that single syllable must have conveyed how he felt, because Dr Bateman added quickly: 'She's only out riding. She'll be back later on. That's why this seemed a good moment to phone you. She wasn't here when Freddie came round so she probably won't know you're in town yet.'

'Not unless she gets it from the horse's mouth.' Charles was suddenly feeling a lot better.

'He's not been talking much lately,' said Dr Bateman calmly, then finished what he was saying. 'We thought it might be a nice surprise for her if you came out to dinner this evening. We'd planned on having a quiet meal, then on to the midnight service across the road. You'd be very welcome to join us. And we could put you up for the night if you didn't want to drive back to Toftham.'

'That sounds absolutely splendid.' And indeed it did. Then a doubt came into his mind. 'Are you sure Beccy will think so? She didn't answer my card.'

'She's not a very good letter writer – you should know that.' Charles did know it, but the way the doctor said it did not entirely convince him.

'Was that the only reason?'

'You'll have to ask Beccy,' said the doctor briskly. 'She's quite able to speak for herself. But never mind that. It would be too bad if you spent Christmas in Norfolk and didn't come to see us. What time shall we expect you?'

The question reminded Charles of his appointment in Norwich. Lunch with the chairman in the Castle Hotel was hardly likely to be as prolonged as lunch with Mr Juby in the farmers' bar, and the after-effects were not likely to be so exhausting. He arranged to be at the Batemans by half past seven.

'Incidentally,' said Dr Bateman before they rang off. 'That piece you did in Algeria was first-class stuff. You must be making quite an impression up there at the BBC.'

'I suppose you could say that,' said Charles. 'See you tonight.'

As he put down the phone C. Bundock, Prop., appeared in the doorway. He had manifestly been listening. 'You'll still have to pay for your room,' he snapped.

As Charles drove to Norwich his thoughts were divided between his visit to the Batemans that evening and his more imminent encounter with the chairman of Anglian Press. Both occasions, he was sure, were going to influence the decision he had to make before his next meeting with the HORC, when he got back to London. But in which direction? He was still pondering when he parked his car on Castle Meadow, under the shadow of the old Norman keep, and entered the elegant portals of the Castle Hotel.

He had never been inside before, but he knew this was where the directors of the Norwich Union entertained their guests, and the founding families of Barclays Bank regularly wined and dined. The two groups, of course, were largely the same people. As a junior reporter he would only have gone there to deliver a message or perhaps a copy of the paper. It was therefore with some relish that he approached the head waiter at the entrance to the restaurant and advised him that Mr Gurlay was expecting him for lunch.

'Certainly, sir.' The head waiter continued to look at him enquiringly. 'And which Mr Gurlay would that be?'

He should have realised that the restaurant was probably full of Gurlays, and all of them were expecting guests. 'The chairman of Anglian Press,' he explained.

'Ah, Mr George. Of course. Please follow me.'

Charles followed him, trying to look nonchalant but managing to bump into a table or two, and tripping over an occasional foot. He was now feeling very nervous indeed.

'Mr George, sir, your guest.'

The man who rose to greet him seemed strangely familiar, though he knew he had never met him before. As they shook hands and exchanged the usual civilities it suddenly came to him, and he couldn't help blurting it out.

'Forgive my saying so, Mr Gurlay, but you remind me tremendously

262

of Lord Remingham, over in my corner of Norfolk. I used to see him regularly at council meetings.'

'Hardly surprising, Mr Benson. He's my cousin.' George Gurlay ushered him to sit down, and passed him the menu. 'As a matter of fact, it was through him I first heard of your existence, soon after you joined the *Toftham Journal*. You wrote a piece about how some council houses had been allocated to people who came to work on his estate from outside the area. They seemed to be jumping the queue. I gather you spotted something in the council minutes and put two and two together. He wasn't too pleased at the time, as I recall; he reckoned you had added them up and made five. Still, it showed you can think things out.'

Charles remembered the story very well. It had been his first experience of what Mr Juby called the foodal society, though he thought of it himself as the Norfolk network. He should have remembered that Lord Remingham had complained to his cousin, the chairman of Anglian Press.

'Now what do you fancy for lunch, Mr Benson? I can recommend the pheasant, it came from my own estate. Most of our bag comes to the Castle. But of course, choose whatever you wish.'

Charles was half-way through his pheasant when George Gurlay got down to business. 'I've asked you to lunch because of the rather unusual circumstances you are in at the moment, Mr Benson. I felt that at this stage the information I have should not go beyond the two of us.'

Charles nodded. 'I imagine the information you have was conveyed to you via Sir Greville Taylor and your sister, Lady Taylor?'

The chairman smiled. He too seemed unsurprised. 'As I said before, you have shown you can think things out.'

'I had a good teacher,' said Charles. 'For thinking things out, there's nobody to beat Mr Juby.'

'Yes, he's a very shrewd man.' George Gurlay looked at Charles questioningly. 'Has he thought this one out yet, do you think?'

'Not yet, but I'm sure he will. His contacts are on a different level from yours, Mr Gurlay, but with respect I think he's just as shrewd as you are at finding out what's going on. You've got him baffled at the moment, but he'll work it out in due time.'

The chairman nodded. 'So he doesn't know yet about your problem over flying? Greville felt I should know about it, so that if you applied to come back to Norfolk I'd know it wasn't because you'd flunked out on your BBC job. On the contrary, he tells me you've done very well. He's sure that if they hadn't had to ground you, so to speak, you'd have become a first-class correspondent. It's a great shame.'

Charles nodded, but said nothing. There was nothing to say.

'Well, I'm sure you've worked out the rest of the story, so I won't prolong it any further. I'd like you to take over from Mr Juby at the Toftham office. I think he'd like you to as well. I haven't left this to Downing because you may not want him to know the background; it's up to you whether you tell everyone about this flying problem you have, or just say you've had an offer you can't refuse. I can assure you the offer will be worth it. You can even say you couldn't bear to stay away from Norfolk, but I think that might be a little difficult for some people to swallow.'

Mr Gurlay leaned back and sipped his wine, and Charles finished off the last slice of pheasant. He had guessed this was coming, but he still wasn't sure it was what he wanted, or whether he could live with it. Some people would always believe he had failed at the BBC: either he had been discarded, or he had given up. As well as that, having sampled life in Bob Corby's Fire Brigade, could he settle back into the life of a rural journalist?

'I can understand your dilemma.' The chairman put down his wine. 'Just bear in mind that running a paper like the *Toftham Journal* is very different from merely reporting for it. There'll be a lot to learn, but if we're lucky, Mr Juby will still be around to teach you. And if you want to, there'll be the opportunity to move upward in the company. We have a thriving daily paper here in Norwich, as well as the evening one, and we have plans to extend and develop. There'll be plenty of room for promotion for staff with local knowledge and national experience. But I wouldn't be surprised if you found the Toftham job kept you quite fully occupied for some time to come. That's if you decide to take it.'

'I'd like to think about it, naturally, but I'm most grateful to you.' Charles paused. 'When shall I let you know?'

'Don't let *me* know,' said Mr Gurlay firmly. 'I'm out of the picture from now on. Just tell Downing as soon as possible. I'll give you his home number: ring him tonight or tomorrow if you like. The sooner we get things moving, the better.'

'But it's Christmas,' said Charles. 'That's not a very good time to disturb him, surely?'

The chairman of Anglian Press raised an eyebrow. 'The BBC isn't the only news organisation that's on duty over Christmas, young man. We have people on call too, you know, even out here in the sticks. And in this case, it's Downing. You needn't go into detail, just tell him if you want the job, and say I approve.'

The words had a familiar ring, and Charles remembered what Jim Downing had said about Mr Juby. 'He's not likely to argue if I recommend you.' Anglian Press may have moved on with the years, but it still worked the same way in some respects.

'If you've no more questions, forgive me if I leave you. Do have some dessert and coffee if you're not in a hurry. I have to get back to the office.' George Gurlay smiled as he got up, noticing Charles's surprise. 'I know that business lunches are supposed to go on all afternoon, but they very rarely do. There's far too much work to catch up with. It's probably not quite the same in Toftham.'

Charles rose too. 'That's true, sir. They have been known to last quite a time.'

The chairman shook his hand briskly. 'Good luck, young man. I'm sure you'll think carefully before you decide. If you can't make up your mind, you can always consult Mr Juby. He'll probably know all about it anyway by the time you get back to Toftham.'

Charles stayed at the table, ordered a coffee, and sat sipping it while he brooded over George Gurlay's offer. He had made it all sound so tempting, but then he was a shrewd businessman who knew what he wanted, and whom he wanted, and was skilled at getting his way. There was another question in his mind which had not been mentioned in their conversation, and he would not know the answer to that until the evening.

Someone came up behind him and tapped him on the shoulder. 'I thought I recognised you. It's Benson, isn't it?' The speaker was strikingly similar to his host.

'Yes, it is. How d'you do, Lord Remingham.'

'Saw you talking to cousin George. Are you thinking of coming back to Toftham, then?'

Charles shrugged. 'Just thinking of it at this stage. Nothing's settled.'

'Well, if you do decide to, then get a move on, there's a good chap. The paper's been going to pot since old Juby's been ill. If I see him, I'll tell him so. Good day to you, Benson.'

Charles smiled ruefully to himself as Lord Remingham walked away. George Gurlay had been right. Mr Juby would probably know all about their meeting by the time he got back to Toftham.

He made slow progress out of Norwich in the queues of early home-

265

goers; not everyone, it seemed, had as much work to do on Christmas Eve as the chairman of Anglian Press. By the time he got back to Toftham the final preparations were being made for the carol service in the market-place. The area around the big Christmas tree in the centre of the square had been cleared of parked cars, and an enclosure was being roped off for the band and the local VIPs. Council workmen were checking the wires that linked the coloured lights on the tree with the Council offices, and the offices themselves had been decorated with bunting and holly.

It all reminded him of the Christmas Eve he had spent on duty in Toftham eight years before, when he had stood inside that enclosure alongside the councillors and magistrates and next to the very pretty daughter of Commander Bludgen, the Clerk to Launford Rural District Council. They had been out a couple of times together after that, but it hadn't come to anything, and later she had married a young district surveyor. What was her name? Mandy? Cindy? Melanie? The events of that Christmas Eve had all been overshadowed by what had happened later that night, when he had been invited to the Batemans' home in Remingham. That was when Beccy announced her engagement to the student from Newcastle and his world had collapsed around him.

Dr Bateman's comment on the phone a few hours earlier came back to him: 'You'll have to ask Beccy why she didn't write.' Was history going to repeat itself tonight?

He parked the car behind the Dog and Partridge and wandered out into the square. It was the first time he had strolled through the market-place since he had arrived, and from the number of cheerful greetings and congratulations that he received, he wished he had done so before. A great many people seemed to have heard his report from the guerrilla camp, and his prestige had apparently soared.

'You hent been shot yet, then?' called George Perkins from his butcher's shop, behind a much depleted pile of turkeys. Then Harry Hurn saw him go past his window and left his customer in the chair half-way through a trim while he came out and shook his hand. 'Thass a bit different dealing with those Ay-rabs than coming to council meetings, eh?' And Charles shook his head and grinned. 'Oh, I don't know . . .'

A plump woman pushing a pram, with two youngsters clinging to her coat, stopped beside him and grabbed his arm. 'It's young Charlie, then, back from the wars!' And with the children still hanging on to her, Big Nellie seized him round the waist and planted a warm, moist kiss on his cheek. He beamed at her and kissed her back. 'You're looking

266

marvellous, Nellie.' He looked at the baby in the pram. 'And you seem to have been busy too. Isn't that a new one since I left?'

She nodded cheerfully. 'They come fairly reg'lar. I hent got the hang of that family planning squit.'

He leaned over the pram and remembered the Norfolk style of greeting for very small babies. 'Hallo, my man,' he said.

Big Nellie giggled. 'That hent a boy, thass a girl, you great fule.'

'Of course it is,' said Charles, and tried again. 'Hallo, my 'ooman.' And Nellie smiled approvingly. 'Thass better, then. You hent forgotten everything you lunt here.'

He smiled back. 'No, Nellie, I haven't forgotten. It's just like coming home.'

She looked at him, quite puzzled. 'Don't talk daft, Charlie. This *is* home. And we're right glad to see you back.' She adjusted the children's grip on her coat, then took hold of the pram. 'I must get this little mawther home. Du you have a good Christmas, my man.'

He waved her farewell as she set off at a brisk pace, using the pram to force a passage along the crowded pavement, with the two children hanging on behind. 'That I will, Nellie,' he called after her. 'It's good to be back.' And at that moment, it was. But for how long?'

He was still asking himself that question as he washed and changed and packed his bag for the overnight stay at Remingham. Through the window he could see the Salvation Army band assembling by the tree and one or two of the dignitaries already taking their places inside the enclosure. George Flatt, the Council Clerk, was checking the seating arrangements, and as he watched Len Cloppett arrived, but this was a transformed Len Cloppett in a smart blue suit and white shirt, with the chairman's chain of office round his neck. The Labour group must have gained control of the council for the first time in the town's history. Would they try to revive the overspill plan again, Charles wondered. This time there wouldn't be a Mr Juby to organise the behind-the-scenes campaign against it. What line should his successor take?

He glanced down at the pavement and saw Mr Juby making his way slowly towards the door below him. He was walking with a stick, on doctor's orders, but he was using it mostly to clear a path in front of him or to wave at acquaintances across the square. He looked up and saw Charles at the window, and waved the stick at him too, before disappearing inside the door. Charles gave him a few moments to reach the farmers' bar and get settled on his stool, then went down to join him.

As he went in Mr Juby was already sipping a special, and a pint of bitter was waiting for him on the bar. 'Sit you down, boy. You've had a rare busy day, I'd say.'

Charles agreed, and drank a little of the beer, remembering he must go easy at this stage, with the evening at the Batemans ahead.

'Big Nellie seemed pleased to see you,' said Mr Juby casually. 'I reckon thass time she try some o' those contrysepshun pills before she lose count o' those kids.'

Charles nodded wryly. Apparently Mr Juby was not only aware of their encounter in the market-place but even knew the gist of their conversation. But it did not surprise him; the square was an easy location for Mr Juby to monitor. It would be interesting to see if his network extended as far as the restaurant of the Castle Hotel.

He did not have to wait long to find out. 'So how did you get on with the gentry, then? I hear his Lordship out at Remingham had a word with you.'

Charles grinned. 'I suppose that was his chauffeur told you? Or that awful butler at the hall?'

'As a matter of fact that weren't either,' said Mr Juby calmly. 'There's a niece o' mine works at the Hall these days. She heard his Lordship mention my name on the telephone so she thought she'd keep an ear on what he say.' He paused to inspect his pipe before filling it. 'Seems I was right, then. They're trying to get you back here to Toftham. They must want you suffin powerful if old George Gurlay has to ask you hisself. Thass Downing's job, not the chairman's.'

'It's all rather complicated,' said Charles. The network, it seemed, had failed at last. Mr Juby still didn't know why the chairman was involved.

'That hent as complicated as all that, boy.' Mr Juby finished filling his pipe and smiled at him blandly before he lit it. 'It's something to do with that brother-in-law of his, I reckon. That one that took you on at the BBC.'

'You know about him?' Now Charles was really impressed. He had never mentioned that Sir Greville Taylor was chairman of the BBC Appointments Board.

Mr Juby made sure his pipe was drawing well before replying. 'I thought that was a rum do last year, Gurlay's sister on the County Council knowing so much about the overspill plan for Toftham and all the meetings we had, even the unofficial ones. Then I remember you said you done a piece about it for your interview up at the BBC, and I knew her husband worked somewhere in Lunnon, so I ask around a bit to find out what he does, and blast if he hent the man did the interview. So thass how she must ha' known all about it; hent that right?'

He did not wait for Charles to confirm it. He was in full flow now. 'That was a fair time ago, o' course, and I forgot all about it till you came up with all that squit yesterday about getting Gurlay an interview at the BBC, then you ask me what his name is when you ought to know full well, and that set me thinking again. That brother-in-law in London must have told him something about you, Charlie, to make him think you'd come back to Toftham, otherwise they'd be daft to try and get you back so quick, with you doin' so well an' all.'

Mr Juby turned to him and pointed his pipe at him in the familiar gesture. which had made him feel like an errant schoolboy during his early days at the Journal. 'What's happened up there in Lunnon, boy? Ha' you made a duzzy fule o' yourself, and you hent told me? If they're sacking you, I shan't think none the wuss o' you for that. They don't know narthin about narthin, those Lunnon folk. But you ought to tell me why, boy, thass all.' His Norfolk accent had thickened, as it always did when he became worked up. Charles paused for a moment before replying.

'No, they haven't given me the sack, Mr Juby, there's no question of that. I think they'd be happy for me to stay on if I want to, but it's up to me to decide. You'd better judge for yourself.'

Mr Juby puffed his pipe quietly as Charles told him what had happened. He did not mention the final meeting in the park with Prudence, but he told him everything else, ending with the options that Bob Corby had put before him. Mr Juby only interrupted once, when he was trying to describe the ordeal that he went through on the flight.

'No need to explain that, boy. My Uncle Josiah, brave as a lion he was, he could deal with a bad-tempered stallion or a charging bull, but one day some fule shut the door on him when he was cleaning out a cupboard, and he screamed and shruck like a mad thing, and when they let him out he was blatherin' like a baby. That trouble you had, thass the same sort o' thing, I reckon. You don't need to say no more about that.'

Charles ended the story with the lunch at the Castle Hotel, when George Gurlay had explained that he was handling the matter himself so that Downing need not know the full story. Mr Juby nodded approvingly. 'There's suffin to be said for the gentry – they know how to do things right. That Downing, he's just a load o' squit.'

He had finished his special, and Charles ordered another. He still had plenty left in his own glass. 'So I have two decisions to make,' he said. 'Do I take the job, and if so, do I tell people what's happened in London? Mr Gurlay said if I couldn't make up my mind, I ought to ask you. So what do you think?'

'George Gurlay said that?' Mr Juby chuckled. 'No wonder he's chairman of the company. He hent no fule, and thass a fact.' He fell silent and studied his special for a few moments, then turned back to Charles.

'I can answer the second question at any rate. If you come back then o' course you tell people what's happened. In a place like Toftham, boy, that won't take 'em five minutes to find out for thesselves, so why make a mystery of it? There's narthin you need be ashamed of about not wanting to fly. I know what most people in these parts would say.' He thickened his accent again, and this time it was on purpose. 'Thass on'y a duzzy fule what'd want to go flyin' in an airyplane in the fust place. That hent natch'rul, boy!'

Charles laughed, and Mr Juby chuckled too. Then he grew serious again. 'So that's settled, boy. But as for coming back, thass for you to say, not me. I can't judge that from where I sit, 'cos I never did much else but look after the Journal, nor ever wanted to. But you've seen more of the world in this past year, and you may think different. There's plenty else to do out there that don't need any riding in aeroplanes. You might want to look round a bit more before you come back. And those other jobs at the BBC, they don't sound too bad to me, but then I'm no judge of that. You've got to sort that out for yourself, Charlie boy; I hent going to say either way.'

Charles nodded thoughtfully. He had not really expected anything else. 'I'm very grateful anyway, Mr Juby. It's been a help just talking about it.' He looked at his watch and finished his beer. 'There's one other person I'd like to have a chat with, then I'll think it through on my own. I must be off.'

'Thass quite right, boy, off you go.' Mr Juby waved his pipe cheerfully. 'She's a sensible girl, that Beccy, she'll see you right.' And he chuckled again at Charles's look of surprise. 'This landlord here, Bundock, he do like to listen in when folk use his telephone, don't he? I hope he's not charging you for your room tonight.'

'You must know that he is, Mr Juby. You wouldn't have missed that.' Charles grinned and made for the door.

'Merry Christmas, Charlie boy,' Mr Juby called after him, and he turned and waved. 'It could be, Mr Juby. I'll let you know.' Then he paused, and corrected himself. 'On second thoughts, you're sure to know anyway. A merry Christmas to you too.'

The snow which had been threatening for the past two days was just starting to fall as he drove out of Toftham and along the familiar road to Remingham. When he arrived at the gates of the Old Rectory, the parish church across the road was floodlit, just as it had been eight years before. This was Lord Remingham's annual gesture to the village at Christmas. But the Old Rectory, which had been hung with coloured lights for Rebecca's engagement party, now had only one light on outside the front door. He was relieved to see there were no cars in the drive; Dr Bateman had said he was the only guest, but visitors were inclined to drop in on Christmas Eve, and the more people who were there, the less chance he would have to see Rebecca on her own.

It was Rebecca who opened the door. For a moment both of them hesitated, then Charles stepped inside and kissed her gently. She did not draw away, but the kiss she gave him back seemed a little perfunctory. The idea of surprising her, it seemed, was not an unqualified success.

'Hallo Charles, it's you. It's nice to see you again. Come through.' And before he could say any more she led him down the hall and into the sitting-room. Her parents greeted him, and they all sat for some time chatting about his activities in London, and how busy Dr Bateman's practice had become, and the increasing amount of work that Rebecca was doing at the hospital, and how crowded Toftham was over Christmas, and wasn't it nice to see Mr Juby out and about again. And every few minutes Charles caught Rebecca's eye and wondered how long it would be before he could talk to her.

'Well now, it's time I saw to the supper,' said Mrs Bateman at last. 'I'll need a hand out there, dear, if you don't mind.' To Charles's relief she was looking at her husband, not Rebecca, and it was obvious the summons was not unexpected because the doctor rose without protest and followed her out of the room.

He waited until they had left the room, shutting the door behind them. 'Alone at last!' he cried melodramatically, and flung out his arms. It seemed as good a way as any to open the conversation.

She smiled, but made no other response, and he subsided onto the sofa. 'I'm sorry I've been away so long again. We keep having to spend so much time getting to know each other, after all these gaps.'

'Well, you haven't been away *all* the time,' she said, a little coolly. 'Didn't you come back to Toftham, somewhere around the beginning of October?'

'Yes I did.' He might have known she would hear about it. 'I'm sorry there wasn't time to come and see you – I was only passing through.'

271

'You were on your way to Scarborough, I gather.' He waited for the rest of it, and out it came. 'And you had some company with you.'

'Ah,' said Charles. 'So that's what it's all about.' He felt enormously relieved. If there had been a repetition of that other Christmas Eve, with its memory of Rebecca standing in this room with her arm around the stranger from Newcastle, he could not have coped with it. But this . . .

He explained who Prudence was, and why he had taken her to Scarborough. When she still seemed sceptical he told her about the Prudence Protection Patrol, and about his mistake over Quentin's voice in her hotel bedroom. Then, inevitably, he had to tell her about his ordeal on the flights and the part that Prudence played in helping him. He tried to make light of what it had been like, but it was at this stage that Rebecca crossed over from her chair to the sofa and sat down beside him.

Then he told her about the talk with Bob Corby and the alternatives he had been given, and finally he told her about his meeting in the park with Prudence, and what she had said to him – though not entirely what he had said to her – and the way they had parted.

By this time his arm was round her as they sat side by side on the sofa, and she was silent for a while after he finished. Then she looked up at him and said quietly, 'She sounds a very nice girl.'

'She *is* a very nice girl,' he said. 'I seem to be able to find them.' And this time when he kissed her the response was not at all perfunctory.

'I'm sorry I didn't seem too pleased to see you when you arrived,' she said eventually. 'I assumed this was just going to be another hallo-and-goodbye, and you'd be back up to London after Christmas for another twelve months or so. I didn't really want to get involved again if it was just for a couple of days. And there was this gorgeous girl they kept talking about in Toftham . . .'

He kissed her again, and it was quite a few moments before she continued. 'So are you going to stay on at the BBC after all this, or is there any chance . . .' She sat up as the thought struck her. 'What about the Journal? Poor Mr Juby can't really manage any more. Have you thought of that at all?'

'As a matter of fact,' said Charles, 'I have.'

'So what are you going to do about it?' she asked eagerly. She was holding both his hands very tightly, and her eyes were shining. Charles looked at her for a long moment, then the decision was made.

'I know exactly what I'm going to do about it.' He let go her hands and got up from the sofa. 'If your father doesn't mind, I'd like to make a very quick phone call to Norwich.'

'To Anglian Press?' she asked. 'But it's Christmas Eve.'

He had the answer all ready, direct from George Gurlay. 'The BBC may be the finest news-gathering organisation in the world, young lady, but they're not the only ones who have people on duty over Christmas.'

When the four of them walked across the lane to the church for the midnight service, Dr Bateman and his wife in front, Charles and Rebecca arm-in-arm behind them, the snow had been falling for some time and everywhere was covered in white. The floodlights picked out the snow on the battlements of the tower and the tall sloping roof of the nave, and there were rows of candles burning in the high windows with holly draped along the sills. The bells were pealing and the sound of the organ came through the west door. The light in the porch shone on the snowflakes as they drifted down onto the churchyard. They stopped in the lane for a moment to take it all in.

Charles had told his story again, much more briefly, over supper, and this time he added on the meeting with George Gurlay at the Castle Hotel. And that was not the end of it. He had told them what he said to Jim Downing on the phone. That was when Rebecca had got up and hugged him, and so had Mrs Bateman, and the doctor produced a bottle of champagne that one of his patients had given him, and they drank to George Gurlay, and to the *Toftham Journal*, and finally, at Charles's suggestion, to the BBC. Dr Bateman had even made a speech, a very brief one. 'Welcome home to Norfolk,' he said.

So the four of them were in a pleasant glow as they stood in the snow-covered lane looking at the picture-postcard scene in front of them. Mrs Bateman glanced over her shoulder and smiled. 'Doesn't it look marvellous, Charles? There can't be anything quite like this in London.'

He nodded and smiled back. 'Yes, it looks as though Bob Corby got it right after all. He generally did, really. Just like Mr Juby.'

He looked round at the little village, the flint walls and pantiled roofs, the fine old church and the Remingham Arms just beyond it, the lane winding off to lose itself in the rolling fields of the silent Norfolk countryside, and above him the vast sweep of sky.

'And I think,' said Charles Benson, though only to himself, 'I think I've got it right too . . .'

EPILOGUE

It was six months later: June, 1961. Charles was working late in his second-floor office overlooking the market-place, finishing off his article for the 'Waysider' column in the Journal. He had spent much of the day following up a quiet word from Mr Juby, about Lord Remingham trying to evict one of his retired farm workers, Luke Winters, from his tied cottage because Luke planned to remarry, this time to a young girl in the village.

'He tell old Luke, if you marry someone your own age then thass all right, but you hent goin' to bring a young mawther into that cottage, he say. You do that and I'll have you out, he say.' And Mr Juby had snorted. 'What right has his Lordship to tell the old chap what age his wife has to be? If that hent foodalism, boy, then I don't know what is.'

So Charles had been out to see Luke Winters on the Remingham estate, and Luke confirmed Mr Juby's story. It sounded like feudalism to be sure, but he had been caught out before in his early days on the Journal when he only heard one side of an argument, and he had been to see Lord Remingham's estate manager as well.

'That sounds pretty heartless the way you put it,' the manager had agreed, 'but the fact is that old Luke has been living rent-free in that cottage ever since he retired five years ago. His Lordship is quite prepared to let him stay there till he dies. He treats all his retired workers like that, and their widows for that matter. But if Luke marries this young woman he fancies, and he dies in a few years' time, she'll say she ought to be allowed to stay on in the cottage as his widow. That could be another thirty years or more, Mr Benson, and if his Lordship tries to evict her, then no doubt folk like you will be along to say what a terrible heartless fellow he is. So that's why he told Luke: if you marry someone your own age then he's no objection, but if you marry this young woman you'll have to go. Doesn't that seem reasonable?'

Charles had to confess that it did. It was not Lord Remingham at fault as much as the whole tied cottage system, and he had been trying to say so in his article. It should be the start of quite a lively campaign.

He finished the final paragraph and typed 'Waysider' underneath it. I'll have to do something about 'Waysider', he thought. It was appropriate enough when Mr Juby was writing complimentary paragraphs about the excellents results of the Poppy Day collections, or even when he was gently chiding the church council over the untidiness of the graveyard, but if the column was now going to be used for serious comment and campaigning, it would need a less folksy *nom de plume*. 'Observer' perhaps, or 'Watchdog', or 'Cerberus'.

No, not Cerberus. The *Toftham Journal*'s readers were not too deep into Greek mythology; they would probably confuse Cerberus with a brand of salt. 'Watchdog' would be better – and it had the same initial as the old name and about the same length, which might ease the change. He started to cross out 'Waysider', then decided against it. All in good time, he thought, all in good time . . .

The clock on the council offices struck eight, and Charles jumped to his feet. He had arranged to meet Beccy at eight o'clock to have a look at an old cottage on the outskirts of the town. It was advertised at a thousand pounds, 'requiring modernisation', which meant it had no mains water, probably an old-fashioned copper to do the washing, and a bucket in the shed down the garden. Beccy had been much more interested in a semi-detached bungalow on a new estate at £1650, but to Charles it looked far too reminiscent of Wembley Park, and he needed to convince her that the quite handsome payment the BBC had given him when he resigned, helped by improvement grants and a four-and-a-half per cent loan from the building society would be much better spent on the cottage.

He was pulling on his jacket when he remembered that the council office clock was still an hour fast, and he took it off again. That was something else that needed sorting out, he thought. It was ridiculous for the principal clock in Toftham to be permanently wrong. On the other hand, everybody in Toftham knew it was wrong, and automatically subtracted an hour. If he persuaded the council to put it right, the whole town could be thrown into confusion.

He hastily switched on the little portable radio on the desk, the only new item of equipment he had added to Mr Juby's office when he took it over. He had not yet shaken off the habit of listening to *Radio Newsreel* whenever he could, even though the familiar voices sometimes caused him a pang of nostalgia.

It came on just as the 'Imperial Echoes' signature tune was being faded out, and he hummed it cheerfully to himself. It was an old friend. Then the announcer introduced the first item.

'Fighting broke out today in the Tunisian port of Bizerta involving some of the French forces manning the naval base which France has maintained there since Tunisia gained its independence five years ago. We have just received this report from Richard Johnson in Bizerta.'

Charles got up and walked to the window as Dickie's voice came over the crackling line from Tunisia.

'There has been trouble building up here in Bizerta since before Christmas last year, but I understand that President Bourguiba was anxious that nothing should happen to prevent the State Visit of Queen Elizabeth the Queen Mother two months ago. That took place without incident, and now he has sent a demand to the French government that all naval personnel should be evacuated from Bizerta forthwith. This has been the signal for several outbreaks of violence around the base. I myself saw a group of French sailors attacked by an angry crowd near the main entrance, and Tunisian troops and police were making no effort to restrain them. Indeed a number of them were joining in. Shots were fired, and I saw several injured on both sides.'

As Dickie's voice continued behind him Charles stared down into the market-place, slumbering peacefully in the evening sunshine. Half a dozen youths were hanging about as usual outside the Golden Fleece, and a couple of old men were sitting on the bench beside the war memorial. Otherwise there were just a few parked cars, including his own new Ford Anglia, dotted about in the square. But he saw nothing of all this. What he saw was a pavement café in Bizerta, overlooking the French warships in the harbour, the crowds of Arabs in the street and the heavy guard of French sailors on the main gate.

'I should be there,' he thought to himself. He found he was saying it out loud. 'I should be there.'

And then he picked up the little radio and shouted at it, above the sound of Dickie's voice. 'I SHOULD BE THERE!'

One or two of the youths outside the Fleece looked up at his window, and Charles stepped back hastily out of sight. He put down the radio, sat behind the desk, and tried to pull himself together. His 'Waysider' article was still in the typewriter, and he made himself concentrate on it. The last sentence looked a little clumsy when he read it through again. If he could re-phrase it more forcefully it might provoke quite a lively reaction from Lord Remingham.

He crossed it out and started re-typing it. On the radio Dickie's report had finished and now Roland Fox was giving the political reaction from Westminster. Charles listened for a moment, but his mind was on the article in front of him. It wasn't just the last sentence; the whole paragraph needed re-writing. But it had the makings of a really controversial piece. He put a fresh sheet of paper in the typewriter, and spoke to the radio once more.

'Fare y'well, marster,' he said quietly.

And switched it off.

HISTORICAL FOOTNOTES

Tunisia
After bitter fighting in Bizerta the United Nations intervened, and in October 1963 the French withdrew their naval forces.

Tahar Belkhoja, Chef de Cabinet at the Foreign Affairs Ministry, became Ambassador to West Africa, and after fluctuating fortunes he was eventually made Minister of the Interior.

Chedli Klibi, Head of the State Radio, became Secretary of State for Cultural Affairs and Information, and a member of the Council of the Republic.

Habib Bourguiba, founder-president of the Republic, remained in office for thirty years.

Algeria
Independence was proclaimed on July 3rd, 1962.

Houari Boumedienne became Commander of the Army and Minister of National Defence, then First Deputy Premier. In June 1965 he deposed Ben Bella in a bloodless coup and became President.

Cherif Belkacem, 'Commandant Djemmal', became Minister of National Guidance soon after independence. He was one of the main planners of the coup which ousted Ben Bella, and President Boumedienne gave him various posts before according him special status as Minister without Portfolio.

The Labour Party in Britain
After the 1960 Scarborough Conference Tony Greenwood resigned from the Shadow Cabinet and said he would stand for the leadership against Hugh Gaitskell. He withdrew when Harold Wilson announced that he would stand too. Most Welsh MPs rallied behind Wilson but the vote was Gaitskell 166, Wilson 81. Gaitskell was still party leader when he died suddenly in January 1963.

It all seems a long time ago . . .